FIRE BENEATH THE ICE

Once the check-in was complete, Ken lifted his bride and carried her to the elevator. Once inside, he took liberty with Omunique's moist mouth. She moaned and whispered terms of endearment against his gently probing lips. He carried her out of the elevator and over the threshold of the already-open door of their suite. Before standing her on her feet, he kissed her deeply.

"Mrs. Maxwell, this is our new home for the next several days. I'm at your disposal from now until forever. What is your pleasure, Princess Maxwell?"

She purred. "Do you have to ask? I thought you knew my every whim, Mr. Maxwell."

"Say no more, sweetheart. I can read the script in those lovely eyes of yours. Oh, boy, when you look at me like that, I have a hard time containing myself."

He lifted Omunique and carried her into the bedroom, where he set her on the edge of the bed. Kneeling down in front of her, Ken lifted her foot and removed one shoe and then the other. Bringing the soles of her feet level with his mouth, he kissed the bottom of the right foot and then the left one. In one gentle motion, he pushed her pink dress up around her waist. He peeled the hosiery off her legs slowly and ran kisses up and down their nudity. With eyes closed, Omunique did her very best to survive the heated seduction.

FIRE BENEATH
THE ICE

Linda Hudson-Smith

BET Publications, LLC
http://www.bet.com

ARABESQUE BOOKS are published by

BET Publications, LLC
c/o BET BOOKS
One BET Plaza
1900 W Place NE
Washington, DC 20018-1211

All Kensington Titles, Imprints, and Distributed Lines are available at special quantity discounts for bulk purchases for sales promotions, premiums, fund-raising, and educational or institutional use. Special book excerpts or customized printings can also be created to fit specific needs. For details, write or phone the office of the Kensington special sales manager: Kensington Publishing Corp., 850 Third Avenue, New York, NY 10022, attn: Special Sales Department, Phone: 1-800-221-2647.

First Printing: November 2001
10 9 8 7 6 5 4 3 2 1

Printed in the United States of America

This book is dedicated to my adorable grandson, Scott Brian Smith II. You are our very special "ups" baby. You have soared into all our hearts on angel's wings. You fill the days of our lives with infinite pleasures. May God bless you and keep you always! I love you deeply!

In memory of my loving father-in-law, Edward Julian Smith. Your beautiful spirit shall forever be with us.

Sunrise: February 14, 1919
Sunset: January 20, 2001

This book is also dedicated to the loving memory of Myron Tyrone Poole, my dearest heart and one of my very best friends. We were inseparable as we grew up, and we shall remain so in the hours of your sunset.

Sunrise: April 15, 1951
Sunset: December 17, 2000

ACKNOWLEDGMENTS

My Father in Heaven—I thank you for such an awesome year of 2000. I thank you for the bounty of blessings that you continue to shower me with. The glory is all yours.

Scott and Arlana—Thank you for giving me such a beautiful grandson. May we always rally together in showing support and love for one another in both our personal and career goals.

Erianna—You are very special to me. A beautiful blossoming flower.

Justified—Thanks for acknowledging me in such a loving way on your music CD, *The Caliway*!

Faron and Joann Roberts of Phenix Information Center— I can't say enough about the way you both have rallied behind me and assisted me in every way possible. You even kept the bookstore open after normal hours for my writing seminars. The radio-show interview with Faron was also an awesome experience. Thank you from the bottom of my heart.

Wallace Allen and Lita Pezant of the *Westside Story* newspaper—You both have been super supporters. Thanks for all the major publicity energy you've generated on my behalf. The numerous articles you've written about my projects and career goals have been spiritually uplifting. Your generosity and continued support are deeply appreciated.

Duane Peters, Vice President for Advocacy and Communications—Thank you for bringing me on board as national spokesperson for the Lupus Foundation of America, for allowing my voice to be heard loud and clear. You have been a great inspiration to me and you *are* making a difference. May God continue to bless you and all your endeavors.

Jenny Allan, *Lupus News* Publications Editor—Thank you for the wonderful feature article that you wrote on my accomplishments in the Spring 2001 *Lupus News* newsletter. It was a glowing piece. Your support means so much to me.

Dr. Lee Brown Rafe—Thank you so much for having me as a special guest on you television talk show *Crossing the Tracks: Celebrating Our Diversity.* It was a very uplifting experience for me.

The crew at the Culver City Kitchen Store—Thank you for assisting me and providing me with access to one of the most detailed Web sites that I've visited to date. I found everything that I needed as well as the answers to all of my decorating and remodeling questions for my novels.

Richard Casey, M.D., Ophthalmologist—Thank you for all your support. I especially appreciate you taking such good care of my optical needs. Healthy eyes are a vital part of my career.

Tanyka Barber, Health Coordinator, NAACP—Thanks for all your assistance in the important mission of bringing about nationwide Lupus awareness. It was an honor to be a part of the health forum at the 2001 NAACP National Convention.

Prologue

Nervousness did its best to overtake world figure skating champion Omunique Philyaw, but she wasn't about to give in to her jitters. This was her first performance ever in the Winter Olympics, and she was there to win a medal. The adrenaline rush actually felt pretty good. She was sky-high and still soaring. While there were no drugs involved, she was addicted to the ice, addicted to Kenneth Maxwell Jr. Just like her love for her fiancé, her love for the ice was incurable.

With her petite ballerinalike figure dressed beautifully in a stunning white sequined costume, she looked virginal. Her smoky gray eyes were bright with astonishment as she did her best to keep her trembling hands from entangling in the thick almond-brown braid she always wore during competitions.

Without the slightest bit of warning the piercing screams of a dying woman giving birth suddenly streaked through her head. The haunting wailing of her heartbroken, grieving father assaulted her ears and brought tears to her eyes. Rasping breathing rang sharply in her ears. A vision of her falling to the floor hard and hitting her head in the restaurant bathroom caused her to shake. The unwelcome flashbacks aroused a fit of panic inside of her.

You've smiled your last smile, popped into her mind.

Even as she desperately tried not to think about it, the

threatening note handed to her at the coastal diner made her insides shiver with fear. Bloody roses appeared embedded in the ice. Her ankle, swollen and mangled, made her wince in pain. Guns raised and aimed right at her heart flashed before her eyes. Marcus Taylor's bleeding body tore at her concentration.

Then a wave of peace unexpectedly engulfed her, bringing her back to the present.

Somehow, she felt her mother and grandmother's spirits blanketing her, calming her. Though she'd never met Ken's mom, she sensed her spiritual presence, too. More than any other spirit, she felt the presence of God. The Father she prayed to every single day of her life.

Soft music played but she could barely hear it for the loud beating of her heart. Pressing her right palm over it, she tried to still the erratic thumping. She looked into the crowd. Ken, Wyman, Max, and Aunt Mamie were out there somewhere, out there waiting to give her their undying love and support; no matter the outcome.

Her coach, Brent Masters, was in place on the sidelines. He believed in her, had unwavering confidence in her. More importantly, she believed in herself, trusted in her skating abilities, trusted and believed in the man she'd come to love.

Softly, gently, the lights came up. Omunique took a few deep breaths.

Out on the ice, before the Salt Lake City, Utah, crowd, she skated to the center, accompanied by cheers and loud applause. Though she couldn't see their faces clearly, there was a sea of people out there. Some attendees were there to cheer her on to victory, and others hoped she wasn't as good as their own competitor. She had news for them. She was every bit as good, if not better; she had already proved herself to be Olympic material.

A true Olympian!

The first instrumental notes to Whitney Houston's "One Moment in Time" inspired her immediately. Ken had chosen this song for her. He'd told her that it was the perfect song for her Olympic debut, the perfect song for someone who'd achieved so much at such a young age. After listening to the words several times, she had agreed wholeheartedly with his choice.

In slow motion she glided over the ice to begin the rousing routine choreographed by Jake Nielson. Without wasting a moment, she went right into a triple Axel, followed by a triple toe loop. The perfect landings brought the crowd to its feet. Spurred on by the frenzied cheers and applause, Omunique went right from an amazing spread eagle into a triple loop. The crowd went crazy. Adrenaline raced through her making her higher than she'd ever been in her life.

Don't breathe too fast. Don't think out loud. Your skates are talking to you. Listen to them. Let them guide you through your routine. There's no tomorrow in this competition. This is it. Right now is all you have. This one moment in time is yours.

"This is your one moment in time . . ."

A sudden burst of astonishing energy lifted her up into the wind. Gracefully, she whirled into a flying camel, followed by a layback spin, and ending with a sit spin. A spiral was accomplished, and then she completed a triple Lutz. A spread eagle led right into a triple loop. Just as the last instrumental chords of the song whispered into the arena, she effected two more triples: another Axel and a Lutz. The gallant metamorphosis that had occurred in Omunique was nothing short of miraculous. She had conquered the flashbacks that had threatened to be her undoing.

Under the constant pressure of her shiny blades, witnessed by the entire audience who now stood on their feet, the silvery ice looked like it had been set ablaze. Set on fire by a petite woman with the heart and courage of a lion.

* * *

Bittersweet tears ran from Omunique's eyes, down her fawn-brown cheeks, over her full, ripe lips as the silver medal was placed around her neck. Inhaling the heady scent of the red roses cradled in her arms, she listened to the Russian National Anthem.

The competition was all over now. She had been edged out of first place by Russian skater Katarina Gorbachev. But that didn't matter. She had given it her all, had given her best performance to date. It was time to move on. The professional circuit awaited her, much to her coach's dismay. Though her decision to go professional displeased Brent Masters, Kenneth Maxwell Jr. was ecstatic. A career in professional skating meant more personal time for them, as he planned to travel with her whenever his schedule permitted.

Inside a Salt Lake City family style restaurant, Omunique and her accompanying party were seated at a large mahogany table toward the back of the large room. A fireplace burned near where they sat. Soft music danced about over their heads.

Brent bristled. "I think those judges should be brought up on charges. The Russian girl made so many mistakes that I lost count. We were cheated outright."

Omunique held up her hand in a halting gesture. "Please don't diminish my win by making charges like that. It's not going to change anything. Do you have any idea how many other skaters were sitting at home watching me perform in the Olympics, wanting so desperately to be in my place? I'm very happy with the outcome. I came to terms with how the judges do and don't do things a long time ago. I came here to do what I did . . . and that was to medal. If they'd given me the bronze, I still would've been happy. You see, I know I'm the best, and I know that I gave the best performance of my life. I don't need to be validated by people that I may never lay eyes on again. I won the whole enchilada because I won it with my heart and my soul. If I accomplish nothing else in this sport I love so much, I've had my *one moment in time*."

Brent leaned across the table and kissed her cheek. "I'm sorry, Nique. I surely didn't mean to lessen the importance of your win. You're right, of course. Now let's get on with the celebration of your extraordinary performance."

With his right arm nestled snugly around his daughter's shoulder, Wyman raised his champagne glass in a toast. "I second that. Max and Mamie, can I get a third and a fourth?"

"Hear, hear," Max and Mamie said in unison.

Kissing her thoroughly, Ken squeezed Omunique's hand. "Extraordinary it was! Girl, you were brilliant out there. What I lost count of was all those triple jumps you scored. And not only that, the fire beneath the ice blazed up into an inferno right before our very eyes."

Brent smiled at Omunique and Ken. "What's next for you two before Omunique goes on the professional circuit?" Although he would remain in her employment as her training coach, he hated to lose her to the pros. He would love to see her take one more shot at the gold.

Ken looked deeply into Omunique's eyes. "At long last, our wedding plans!"

One

With the Olympic competition behind her, Omunique and Ken had just arrived at the lavish airport hotel suite. He'd booked the room for their return home, and they'd gone straight there after claiming their luggage. The nights had been rough when he'd stayed alone, as Omunique had been required to spend her nights in accommodations inside the Olympic Village. It was good to be back home and even better for them to get back to sharing intimate evenings.

Taking both of Omunique's hands, Ken pulled her up from the sofa. "Come on, Omunique. I have something to show you."

Holding her close, he guided her into the bedroom, where he switched on the light. She nearly swooned at his feet. On a corner table, nestled in a silver ice bucket, was a bottle of champagne. There was also a silver candelabra, and a bunch of red roses nested in a heavy crystal vase in the center of the table.

Tenderly, she caught his face between her delicate hands. "I love you, Kenneth Maxwell Jr. I love you," she cried breathlessly. Just like so many times before, the stars in his eyes collided with hers, the universe tilted, leaving him dizzy with longing; a longing that threatened to destroy every ounce of his sanity.

Turning her back to him, she lifted her hair. Without her asking, he unzipped the back of her dress. Slowly, deliberately, he swept kisses up and down her shivering back. When the dress fell to the floor, his hands reached around and tenderly cupped her firm breasts. As he rubbed his thumbs across her hardened nipples, she shuddered. When she turned around to face him, naked passion was aflame in her smoke-colored eyes. His breath caught. Crushing his mouth over hers, he moaned as his tongue was scorched with the fire in her kiss.

The few seconds it took him to strip of out his clothing and garner protection seemed like an eternity. Kneeling down to the floor, drawing her down with him, he wrapped her in the cloak of his fiery passion. In a kneeling position, voraciously, they indulged each other in the pleasures each had to offer. With his hand coiled in the thickness of her hair, he tilted her head back and massaged her neck and ears with the tip of his torched tongue. Moving out of the kneeling position, Ken sat down and drew her down over his swollen manhood. Omunique muffled a scream against his lips as she tossed her head back and wrapped her legs around his waist.

Comfortably lodged in the furnace that housed her eternal flames, they allowed the moist, torrid heat to consume them. Electrifying seismic activity of major magnitudes erupted throughout their bodies, splintering them into trillions of sparklerlike fragments.

Ken lay in the center of the bed with Omunique stretched out alongside him, her hair splashed across his broad chest. Fulfilled beyond description, Omunique smiled at the man who had made an exquisite art form of rocking her world.

She lifted her head up and looked at him. "We never got a chance to drink the champagne."

"Do you want some?"

"No. As usual, I'm already intoxicated just by being with you."

Smiling from ear to ear, he brushed her lips with his

index finger. "I'm happy to hear it. We have a big day ahead of us, and we should try to catch a little sleep."

"We do? What's happening tomorrow, Ken?"

"We're going to apply for our marriage license."

She batted her eyes in disbelief. "Excuse me? Aren't we rushing things a bit? We just got back home less than an hour ago."

"No, I'm not rushing this. Your father has trusted me with you from the very beginning, and I greatly respect Wyman Philyaw, as I respect you. This is our last covert rendezvous. The next time we make love, we'll be husband and wife, sister."

"I don't think so!" To prove her point, she wantonly seduced him, making an ineffective liar out of him. Knowing he was defeated, he surrendered all, without the slightest show of putting up a fight.

With Ken to guide her way, Omunique had grown comfortable with her own sexuality. Unlike in the beginning of their relationship, her shyness had now slipped away and had been replaced with a keen sense of self. A self that had learned how to effectively please her man . . .

After putting Ken through several tumultuous earthquakes, Omunique propped her elbow on his chest. "Now, what were you saying about not making love till when?"

He laughed heartily. "What you did was really unfair, you know. You have literally caught me with my pants down." Her laughter floated past his ear. "Are you happy, love?"

"Ecstatic! But, Ken, maybe we shouldn't rush into marriage. The press will never leave us alone once they sink their teeth into our private affairs."

"Exactly my point. If we're married, they won't be able to continue to try and make a scandal of our relationship. Granted, they'll invent stories there, too, but it won't carry as much weight. What are you really afraid of, Omunique? That possibly our marriage won't work?"

"Nothing of the sort! I just want you to be sure."

"Are you sure, Princess?"

"Yes, Ken, I am. Not only am I sure, I'm positive."

"Then there's nothing to worry about. If I wasn't sure of how I felt about you, you wouldn't have that lovely, very expensive trinket on your finger."

"My father knows all about your plans, doesn't he?"

"We have his blessing, Omunique. I think he's rather relieved over it. He knows we're only human. However, he does want you to have a big wedding. Do you still want that, too, Princess?"

"Yes! I want the marriage I created in my fantasy when I was healing from my ankle injury. I still want that special wedding on the ice." She nestled her head against his chest and once again shared with him her fantasy.

His thoughts carried him away as she wove her magical story. As he listened, he created in his mind quite a fantasy wedding of his own. She ended the story with a deep sigh.

"My father's going to have a hard time giving me away. I've been his all my life. He's probably at home right now contemplating how empty the house will be without me." She sighed again, lifting her head from his chest.

"You'll always be his, Omunique. It's just that now he'll be sharing you with me."

"Do you think we'll be able to keep our marriage a secret, Ken? And what will you do when I'm out of town, when I'm busy training for hours on end?" He looked puzzled.

"A secret? Why would we keep it a secret?"

"Oh, I thought it would be fun to do that for a while. Then we could sue the press when they write some lie about our torrid affair, especially when they see me leaving your house every morning. That brings up another question. Will we be living at your place?"

"My place is too small. We should start scanning the real estate section as soon as possible. Our first house can be our dream house, which will make it our last house." He frowned.

"I hate moving. What do you have in mind for our dream house?" When she didn't respond, he looked down at her. So much for dream houses, he thought in amusement.

Omunique had to be very tired, both physically and mentally. She had worked extremely hard on her quest for Olympic gold. Though the judges hadn't awarded it to her, like so many others had already expressed, he felt that she had indeed placed first. As far as he was concerned, she'd given an elite performance. The gold medal should've been placed around her lovely neck.

Omunique appeared to be in dreamland. From the slight smile on her face it looked as though she was having a sweet dream. Drawing her closer to him, he threw the sheet over her nude body. Resting his chin in her sweetly scented hair, he closed his eyes, happy to have her back in his arms again. Soon, very soon, she would sleep in his arms every single night.

"Morning, Daddy! Did I wake you?"

"Morning, Nique. You didn't wake me up. I'm already dressed. How's my only girl?"

Wyman had spent the better part of the night sitting up in a chair in his bedroom. Earlier, as the hazy sun rose out of the ocean, he'd gasped at its beauty. All he had been able to think of was his daughter. As if she'd felt this thoughts, she was on the phone. Wyman had already showered and dressed in dark slacks and a white knit pullover. He had been brushing his wavy hair when the phone bell had crashed into the silence of the room.

"Making plans for our wedding. But I guess you already knew that, huh?"

"I guess you could say that. Congratulations on firming things up, sweetheart! How do you feel about getting married right away?" He had been delirious with joy when Ken had asked his blessing for marriage. He already knew how much they loved one another, had never seen Omunique happier or more content. He'd always known this day would come, yet he hadn't expected it quite so soon.

Marriage would mean that she would be leaving the nest; a nest she'd rarely flown far away from. When she did have to travel, he'd always been with her. Ice-skating competitions had taken her all over the world, but he'd never missed a single performance.

"It may take a little getting used to, but it feels wonderful, Daddy. Listen, I called to tell you that I won't be home until late this evening, if at all."

"I figured as much. What's going on, Nique?"

"Ken and I are going to run a few personal errands. There's so much stuff to do when planning a wedding. We're also going to look at a few houses. We read the real estate section over breakfast. I'm really excited about us having our own home."

"You sound excited. Are you sure this is what you want, Nique?"

Knowing he wasn't getting any younger, he was relieved that someone so responsible would be caring for his most prized possession, someone who would treat her the way she deserved to be treated. Wyman knew that Ken would love her the way she needed to be loved, not that she would settle for anything else. She loved Ken every bit as much as he loved her. He believed that Ken Maxwell Jr. would make her an excellent spouse, although he wished they would wait just a wee bit longer.

Maybe they would, he considered, though he seriously doubted that. She loved him. He loved her. What was there to wait for? He suddenly realized that no one could have stopped him from marrying Patrice. More than that, no one who knew him would have dared to try.

"Absolutely! I can't think of anything I want more than to marry Ken. I'm very lucky. I have two wonderful men who love me. Daddy, I promise you that you'll never feel left out. I know we'll have to adjust to living apart permanently, but it shouldn't be too difficult. Ken thinks the world of you and he won't want to keep me from you. He's already said as much. Besides, one day we'll need a baby-sitter!"

Wyman was comforted by her sincere words, amused by her sense of humor. Those were some of the fears he hadn't voiced and he knew his daughter had sensed it. "I'm glad to hear that, Nique. I was already feeling a little lonely. I'll be fine now. I'm grateful that Ken's so understanding. We'll talk about the baby-sitting job at a later date. I'm taking Mamie to breakfast. I don't want to be late."

"Oh, really now! That's wonderful. I'll see you tonight, Daddy." Wyman rested the phone receiver in the cradle and started for the front door. Tears splashed from his eyes as he stepped into the crisp morning air.

Ken had thought of everything when he'd planned for them to spend the night at the hotel. Omunique was astonished at how well he had put an entire outfit together for her, right down to the silky soft undergarments and the beige leather pumps. He had excellent taste, which was pretty much the same as her own. Day after day, they were discovering how many things they had in common. Marriage would only serve to enhance all of the wonderful things they truly felt for one another, a marriage made in heaven.

When she came out of the bedroom, she was dressed in the rich creme-colored pants ensemble. The jacket draped across her upper body, tying to one side. The tapered pants were sharply creased at the legs. The entire outfit was a superb fit.

Having felt her immediate presence, Ken looked up when she stepped into the room. His smiling eyes scanned her from head to toe. "Now, you look super in that!" He patted himself on the back. "Not bad for a man who has never shopped for girlish things."

She dropped down into his lap and kissed him tenderly on the mouth. "Not bad at all. I love this outfit. Thank you. It's nice to know that I'll have a shopping partner. Daddy hates to go shopping with me. He says I can never make up my mind."

Ken frowned. "I'm not sure I'm going to like it any better than he did, but I'm willing to give it a try. I'm willing to try anything that will keep you happy."

"You better hold those type of comments in reserve. I've been known to have a lot of crazy whims that I thought would make me happy. At one time, I even thought of trying skydiving." She laughed. "Daddy was so horrified that he threatened to disown me if I dared."

"Oh, boy! One of those, huh? A crazed female daredevil. Your legs are priceless. What made you want to risk them by skydiving?"

"The thrill of it all, Ken, only for the thrill. But that was a very long time ago. A time when this young girl had nothing else to do but train hard and dream about life after a medal-winning performance in the Olympics."

He glanced at his wristwatch. "And you've certainly done all that and more, but speaking of time, it's time for us to get going. We're going to have to fight the morning airport traffic as it is. Did you get a hold of Brent?" He lifted her up and stood her on her feet.

"Yes, but he still isn't too thrilled about me turning pro. He's going to have to understand, though. Brent is as pointed as nails, but I know how to smooth out his sharp ends."

Ken smiled with knowing. "I'll bet you do! I just bet you do." She had certainly smoothed out his rough edges, had also tamed the pantherlike instincts in him. Only this time, he was permanently contented with his beautiful prey.

Ken gathered all their belongings. They left the suite and took the elevator down to the lobby. As they stepped off the elevator, they were met with flashing light bulbs coming from every direction. Suddenly, the once peaceful lobby turned into a three-ring media circus. Reporters were everywhere, shouting intimate questions at the couple. Both appeared to be in a state of shock. Although Omunique was used to flashing bulbs and a heavy media presence in her space, she sensed that there was something eerie about this occasion, especially since they'd already been met at the airport with a huge fanfare. Concerned about what this all meant, she buried her head in Ken's shoulder as he led her through the throng of media.

As her knight in shining armor, he swept his arm around her waist. "It's okay, sweetheart. Just keep walking. I have an idea," he whispered. "Just follow my lead." Ken came to an abrupt halt. "I know that you all have a lot of questions that you want answers to, but for those of you that know me, you already know this isn't the way to get them. There's a reception area down the hall and to the right. If you'll be so kind to go there, we'll give you a brief press conference. We knew we couldn't keep our recent marriage quiet for long. Give us time to check out and then we'll join you there."

Whispers flowed from one reporter to another, as they buzzed like busy bees, making their way to the designated area; happy to be the first to report the marriage of the heir apparent of Maxwell Corporation to his gorgeous Ice Princess, Olympic Silver Medalist, Omunique Philyaw.

Omunique was stunned by Ken's announcement, but she was able to comprehend the method to his temporary insanity. Before she could have another thought, Ken whisked her down the corridor and out a side door. The car was only a few yards away, but he could clearly see that he hadn't been able to outsmart everyone. A formidable opponent had cut off their escape route.

Leaning against the door of Ken's shiny black sports car was none other than Jack Prescott, the most clever, slimiest reporter for the *California Sun*. The large grin on his face was despicable. Jack was a large beefy guy with red-hot cheeks. A long cigar stuck out of his puffy lips. "Well, well, young Maxwell. I seem to have played my hunch right. You've never, ever been so cooperative before, so I knew you had something devious in mind."

Ignoring Jack, Ken disengaged the car's alarm system and opened the trunk to store their bags. Without uttering a word, Ken calmly pushed past Jack and opened the passenger door for Omunique. "I'll take care of this, sweetheart. Don't worry. We'll be out of here in seconds."

Ken walked back to where the reporter stood. "Jack, I'm only going to say this once, so you should listen up. My wife and I are on our way to an important appointment and I don't have time for this now. If you'll kindly remove your wide butt from my car, we'll be on our way. If you should decide not to, then I'll have to move you. With my car." Ken's extreme calm caught Jack off guard. Ken patted the top of his sports car. "She's a powerful piece of machinery, Jack. I don't think you want to mess with her!"

Jack laughed in Ken's face. "You've done some crazy things, Maxwell, but even you aren't that stupid. Trying to run me down with your car could be considered attempted murder!"

Ken raised his eyebrows satanically. "Attempted?" Moving with quick deliberation, Ken got into his car, started the engine, gunning it to show just how powerful it was.

Jack's adrenaline flowed through him like a shooting geyser. From the look on Ken's face, Jack wasn't at all sure that he wouldn't make good on his threat. Yet Jack stood his ground. That is, until the car backed out with such force that Jack was driven to make a snap decision, the only decision, to move out of the way.

Ken waved as he sped off. About the same time the car pulled off, the other reporters descended like acid rain onto the parking lot, but all they could see was the tail end of the sports car as it turned the corner. The bunch of duped reporters were now like a swarm of angry bees, as they gathered around Jack, hoping he'd share his good fortune with them. Jack was too embarrassed to let them know what had really happened so he just walked away. Ken had turned his knees to water, yet Jack had to laugh.

Ken and Omunique were also laughing. She was so proud of the way Ken had defended her honor. "You're a fast thinker, Mr. Maxwell. You leave me breathless."

"Jack's probably a little breathless himself. He's such a slimy character, but I'll admit that he had me worried for a minute. And I can assure you that he's not finished with us. So brace yourself. Tomorrow's *Sun* will be sizzling hot!"

Omunique scowled. "Yes, I'm sure it will be. I was afraid of that. We've managed so far to escape the poisoned pen, but I knew our time was running out. You lied about us being married, Ken. How are we going to handle that?"

"Easy! By the time they learn the truth, if they do, we'll be married. If they print that we're already married, we can sue them for misquoting us."

"But they won't be misquoting."

"Did you tell them we were married, Omunique?"

She looked worried. "No, you know I didn't."

"I sure as hell didn't!"

Amused, she shook her head and laughed. Ken was too much, and she was sure that the press hadn't seen anything yet. He wasn't a man who was easily conquered.

"I'm going to call Max and give him an update on our wedding plans, or should we stop by and see him? Either way, he'll be delighted. He had a pretty good idea that I was going to ask you to get married right away."

"Let's stop by. It'll be fun to see his reaction. Max is going to be a wonderful father-in-law to me, as Daddy will be to you, Ken."

* * *

In the swanky offices of Maxwell Corporation, Max was having his first cup of coffee when his thoughts turned to his son. He looked at his watch, wondering if Ken was going to make it into the office this morning, or if he was otherwise engaged. Max chuckled to himself, knowing that he probably wouldn't see his son for days. And he couldn't be happier over the reason.

Max walked into the reception area and handed the secretary, Thomasina Bridges, a letter he'd drafted. "I need this to go out in the afternoon mail. Can you have it ready by then?"

"Sure thing, Max. By the way, where is Ken this morning? I haven't heard from him."

Max smiled. "You probably won't either. He's probably deeply engaged in making his wedding plans."

Thomasina actually looked grief stricken. "Marriage plans already?"

"You got it, young lady. My young son is still head over heels in love. For the next few days or so, we probably won't see hide nor hair of him."

"Is it the Ice Princess?" Thomasina's inquiry had come with a hint of sarcasm, which Max quickly picked up on.

"Right you are. She may be an Ice Princess, but she's the warmest and friendliest young woman he's ever brought around me. She's a feisty little thing, too. Ken has finally found his equal. Omunique is quite a knockout and it looks like she's knocked him out of the running as the most sought-after bachelor. I'll be proud to have her as a daughter-in-law."

Max was as pleased over the upcoming marriage as Wyman was, but unlike Wyman, he never even considered that he might be left out of their new life. He and Ken were best friends.

Thomasina tried to hide the displeasure she felt by putting on a big smile. "I'll have this letter ready in a jiffy, Max. I'll bring it in for your signature."

"Thanks, Thomasina. I'd like for you to hold all my calls for the next hour. I need to look over some important papers."

"Sure thing, Max." The moment Max strolled off, Thomasina put her head down on the desk and bit back the anguished scream she desired to release.

Ken had long ago set the record straight with Thomasina Bridges. Even though he'd never done or said anything to make her think that he could be remotely interested in her, she had convinced herself that he was. She had somehow tricked herself into thinking that the Ice Princess was just a passing fling and that he would eventually turn to someone with more depth. Someone who would appreciate him and who would make a comfortable home for him. And someday fill that home with his children. Someone just like herself.

He didn't need someone who flew all over the world for competitions, someone who showed off her body in next to nothing. Even though she had once thought he liked his women in tight-fitting clothes, she had changed her image the moment he'd brought it to her attention. How could that type of person be there for him emotionally? When would the Ice Princess find time to meet his needs? Certainly having babies would be out of the question. She wouldn't want to ruin her ballerina figure, not to mention enduring the pain that came with childbirth and motherhood.

No, Omunique Philyaw wasn't the type of woman Kenneth Maxwell Jr. needed or should be saddled with. Off and on since day one, Thomasina had deluded herself with these sorts of thoughts, which was now causing her to become somewhat irrational. She'd constantly run hot and cold about her feelings for Omunique, but she was now sure he'd chosen the wrong woman.

If Ken married Omunique, then Thomasina would simply have to resign her position, she hastily considered. There was a time when she'd thought that Omunique was sweet and friendly, but after she'd put Ken through all those weeks of misery during her ankle injury, she sensed that she'd been wrong about them having a happy life.

But since she really didn't know all the particulars regarding what had happened between them back then, she began to thoughtfully reason it out. Maybe she had come to the wrong conclusion about quitting; yet working closely with the man she so wantonly desired would be very, very hard.

She did need her job. But there were more ways than one to get paid . . .

Startled, Thomasina looked up when the front door to the office suite opened up. Seeing a smiling Omunique and Ken holding each other in a loving embrace caused her even more anguish than she already felt. She groaned.

Concerned that she'd had her head down, Ken walked over to where Thomasina sat amid the fine oak furnishings of the computer center. He briefly touched her hand. "Are you sick?"

"No, I'm just fine. I was just resting my eyes."

Omunique came over and touched Thomasina's forehead. "I hope that's all it was, but at least you don't feel warm. Perhaps you should take a few minutes' break, anyway. I'd be happy to answer the phones for you."

Thomasina shook her head. "Thanks, but I'm okay." Thomasina thought it was enough that Omunique had the man she wanted, but she was sorely mistaken if she thought she could take away her job, too. It would be her own decision whether to leave the company.

Ken took Omunique by the hand. "That was a sweet offer, Nique. Thomasina seems fine now. Let's go find Dad so we can share our plans with him." Ken turned around at the door of Max's office. "By the way, Thomasina, Omunique and I have started our wedding plans." Before she could respond, he and Omunique had already gone into Max's private office. Thomasina was glad Ken hadn't waited for her response because she didn't know what she would've said since she wasn't the least bit thrilled by the so-called good news.

Max had tears in his eyes when he took Omunique in his arms and hugged her. "This is so great, kids! I know you're going to be happy together. I imagine Wyman is feeling the same as I do about you finally settling the plans for your upcoming nuptials."

Omunique scowled. "I think he was a wee bit out of sorts with us getting married so soon, but I'm sure I calmed the brewing storm. We're all that each other has had for such a long time now. It's always been just Dad and me."

"He'll be okay," Ken interjected. "We'll both see to that."

Max embraced his son. "I know you will, son. How about letting this old man take you two young whipper-snappers out to dinner tonight to celebrate? If you agree, I'll call and invite Wyman to join us."

Ken looked to Omunique and she nodded her approval. "Barnabey's?"

Knowing that's where they'd had their second business encounter, which had quickly turned somewhat personal, Max grinned. "Absolutely."

Ken patted Max on the back with affection. "We can get there around seven-thirty."

"Seven-thirty it is," Max repeated.

Two

Kenneth Maxwell Sr. entered Barnabey's restaurant with a stunning-looking woman holding on to his arm. Max's dress attire was impeccable and he looked dashing. Looking to be at least twenty-five years his junior, the curvaceous woman was a stunning class act in an eggshell white silk Dior dress. Her dark brown hair was done up stylishly. Her bronze complexion was flawless, with the exception of a small mole on the right corner of her generous berry-colored mouth. Cinnamon-colored eyes shining brightly, she looked up at Max in adoration.

Max looked around the restaurant for his son. Apparently, Ken and Omunique hadn't made it there yet. He was about to go wait in the bar when he saw Omunique sitting at a table all alone. He leaned down and whispered something to his companion. With her arm tucked under his, they strode toward where Omunique was seated.

It took them quite a while to reach their destination since a couple of people that he knew had stopped Max for a brief chat. Max was disliked by very few. Those people that did condemn him were only jealous of his success. He'd done extremely well for a poor boy from the wrong side of the tracks. Like the rules played by his father before him, and those now played by his own son, dedication and hard work had put the Maxwell men way over the top financially.

Reaching the table, Max bent over and kissed Omunique's cheek, causing her to loudly gasp since she simply hadn't seen him coming.

Max gently touched her cheek. "I didn't mean to startle you, sweetheart. Omunique, you look breathtakingly beautiful, as you always do."

As Omunique looked up, she noticed the woman with Max. He then introduced her to his date, Courtesy Evans. The two women smiled brilliantly at each other, but a strange feeling had suddenly come over Omunique.

"Where's that son of mine?" Max pulled out two chairs, seating himself after Courtesy sat down.

"I have no idea, Max." Omunique was worried by Ken's sudden disappearance since he hadn't said where he was going.

The candlelight was reflecting in Omunique's gray eyes, turning them into brilliant flashes of silver light, yet Max saw fear there. She still hadn't recovered from his sudden appearance. Although there were other people all over the place, she still felt terribly vulnerable when alone. There were times when having been stalked by Marcus Taylor still haunted her. His tragic death had caused a tremendous shock to her system.

Grinning, Max pointed across the room. "There's that handsome devil now. I can't imagine him leaving you alone for a solitary second, especially with so many eligible male hunters in the room." Omunique and Courtesy laughed. As always, Max was as charming as his young son. Even at his age, he still knew exactly what a woman needed and was always quick to deliver.

Ken's smile broadened as he drew closer. He was thrilled to see his dad, but seeing Omunique always did crazy things to his heart. His breath caught as she smiled at him, and he loved how her silver eyes lit up when she looked at him. Before thinking of speaking to the new arrivals, he leaned over and kissed Omunique. The touch of her mouth against his always impaired his power of thought.

"Did you miss me?"

"Utterly." Her quick and honest response caused his pulse to race.

"Dad, I'm glad you finally made it! I was getting worried. Where's Wyman?" Ken spoke to Max, yet his eyes were glued to Omunique as he slid into the chair next to hers.

Max was moved by the sincere show of love his son spilled out over Omunique. "Wyman will be along shortly. He talked about bringing Mamie with him, if she was free."

Max threw Ken an uncomfortable glance. "Son, I want you to meet Courtesy Evans, my date for the evening."

Until now, Ken hadn't even noticed the other woman. Omunique was always the only woman in the room for him. Yet when he looked at Courtesy, a quiet disturbance appeared in his eyes. "Ah, yes, Courtesy Evans." Ken had said her name as if the unusual moniker rang a silent alarm. "I believe we've met before."

Courtesy flashed Ken a fleeting glance of indignation. "If we've met, I don't recall. But in your line of work, I guess everyone starts to look alike."

Maybe so, Ken thought, *but none had a name like Courtesy.* And if he recalled correctly, she was anything but courteous . . . If anyone noticed the slight air of tension between Ken and Courtesy, they didn't comment on it.

Before Ken could finish his thoughts, the band started playing the music to "Every Time I Close My Eyes," a slow song that both he and Omunique loved. He stretched his hand out to her. "One of our favorites by Baby Face."

She rapidly rose to her feet. "So it is. And I'm so glad that you got me and I got you, too."

Ken excused himself and Omunique to the others. "We rarely sit out the songs we love." Smiling, Max watched as Ken and Omunique practically drifted onto the dance floor.

"Max, you seem so distracted. Is everything okay?" Courtesy inquired. Her voice was drowsy with lust, sound-

ing as though she'd just finished making love and was ready
to go to sleep.

Max touched the back of her hand. "Everything is fine,
Courtesy. Just indulging myself in a few fantasies." He
laughed. "As the youngsters would say, that boy of mine
has been totally sprung!" She looked perplexed. "In love,
Courtesy. In love!"

Courtesy allowed her cinnamon-brown gaze to land on
the closely entwined couple. *Ken Maxwell Jr. loves no one,
with the exception of himself,* Courtesy thought with deep
agitation.

With her head nestled onto his chest, Ken expertly guided
Omunique over the dance floor. Tilting her head back, she
studied Ken's handsome features. "What gives with you
and Miss Courtesy Evans?"

Ken was amused by her keen perception. It had ceased
to shock him a long time ago. For someone so young, Omunique was the most perceptive woman he'd ever encoun-
tered. And after all this time, she could still read him like
the bold print on the daily headlines, easily . . .

"You noticed, huh? I hope Dad didn't." Ken looked worried. "I can't believe she's here with him. Our names are
exactly the same, so there's no way she couldn't have known
who he was. And to think she would lie about knowing
me."

Omunique gave him an impatient look. "Who is she?
More to the point—who is she to you? That's precisely what
I want to know."

"Just someone I knew a long, long time ago."

"Knew in what capacity, Ken?"

"You're not going to let this drop, are you? I guess you
deserve to know. I took her out a couple of times, but it
didn't take me long to decide that we had nothing in common. In fact, nothing was there for me, period."

"A couple? How many is a couple? And if there was nothing, why more than just once?"

He was growing impatient with her line of questioning, yet he knew he would've reacted the very same way had the tables been turned. "Listen, Omunique, it was only twice. We didn't even finish the second date. I walked out on her and I never returned any of her later phone calls. The woman is a leech, a gold digger. I have every intention of warning my father about her. After that, it's on him. He's a grown man."

Omunique wanted to know why he walked out on her, but she didn't dare ask. She had sensed his growing irritation. "Do you want to leave, Ken? It might get awkward for you. I know that Max hasn't really dated all that much since your mother passed away. I would understand."

His expression softened at her sensitivity toward him. "No, sweetheart. I'll be just fine. I *want* Max to find someone that he can spend the rest of his days with. But Courtesy Evans is not that person. Max dating doesn't bother me at all. In this instance, it's who he's taking out."

Her gentle laughter soothed him. "In that case, I guess we'll have to endure her throughout dinner. After all, this is our celebration. I wouldn't dare be rude to Max, but I got a strange feeling about his date even before you said you knew her." She smiled impishly. "Besides, I'd like to keep my eye on Courtesy Evans."

While shaking his head, he gently scolded Omunique with his eyes. "You'd better go freshen your face. You've got cream all over it! We wouldn't want Miss Evans to know what you're up to, now would we?"

Ken waited by the ladies' room door for Omunique, wanting to see everyone who entered after her. With his formidable presence standing guard, he felt that no one would dare to accost her ever again. He had no intention of letting anyone get near Omunique like Taylor had. Making sure that his enforcer was there, he patted the bulge under his arm. Under his suit jacket was a concealed shoulder holster that housed a nine-millimeter. Kenneth Maxwell Jr. had become a licensed packer since Marcus Taylor had turned Omunique's life upside down.

As soon as she reappeared, he took possession of her lips. Willingly, she gave them up to him. By the time they arrived back at the table, Wyman and Mamie had joined the group.

Wyman immediately stood up. "Hello, kids!"

Omunique kissed her father and then she kissed Mamie. A twinkle of hope appeared in her gray eyes. "Aunt Mamie, you look splendid!" Mamie's dusky brown skin glowed with motherly pride. Her eyes, the color of fine bourbon, sparkled. Her new, stylish black dress was backless, a daring change for someone who was fifty-five. Mamie had always been a conservative dresser.

"Thank you, Nique. You're looking splendid, as well. I do love you in green!" Mamie then looked up at Ken Jr. who stood over her chair. "It's always nice to see my favorite nephew-to-be. Kenneth, are you still taking good care of my child?"

Ken bent over and kissed her cheek. "Knowing I'd have you to contend with, Aunt Mamie, you bet I am." Mamie brightly smiled her approval, glad that Omunique had found love with him.

"This is like a family affair," Courtesy remarked rather waspishly. "I wonder who's going to show up next." She would have a hard time charming Max with the heir apparent to the Maxwell fortune hanging around. To see the look on Ken's face was the only reason she'd come on the date.

Ken looked down his nose at her. "This *is* a family, a family that has each other's back."

Ignoring Ken's pointed, terse response, she sniffed and turned her attention back to Max. "Max, darling, would you mind ordering me a dry white wine."

Max smiled. "Not at all."

Sincere congratulations were given to the happy couple during the dinner hour. Throughout the rest of the evening Wyman and Max entertained the group with a bunch of nonsense, yet everybody enjoyed their tall, whimsical yarns, which Omunique thought to be outright lies. A cocktail waitress kept their glasses full and she loved the hefty tips being shelled out by the three extremely handsome men. Their generosity toward her was exceptional.

When Max asked Omunique to dance, Wyman pulled a reluctant Mamie out of her seat, leaving Ken alone with Courtesy. Omunique anxiously glanced back at Ken as Max led her onto the dance floor. To reassure her, Ken winked at his future wife.

Lifting the champagne flute to her ripe, berry-red lips, Courtesy coolly looked Ken over. "Aren't you going to ask me to dance, Mr. Maxwell?"

He gave her a look that would burn acid. "Are birds wingless? Besides, we've never met."

Her widely spaced cinnamon eyes grew larger and then narrowed to thin slits of turmoil. "I can see that you're still arrogant as hell! You're nothing like your charming father." She had purposely baited him. But she hadn't considered one thing; he wasn't biting.

When he stood and reached for her hand, she looked dumbfounded, unable to believe that he was actually going to dance with her. As she arose from her seat, her heavy perfume insulted his sense of smell. The scent smelled like a wreath of cheap funeral flowers.

After guiding her onto the dance floor, Ken walked straight toward Max and tapped him on the shoulder. He then placed Courtesy's hand in Max's. Ken reached for Omunique. "I'll take over from here. And, Dad, while you're dancing with Courtesy, please explain to her that birds have wings. Perhaps she was absent during nature classes."

Max had no idea what Ken was referring to, but he didn't like his rudeness. Without further comment, Max brought

Courtesy into his arms. He didn't ask her what his son was talking about and she didn't offer any explanation. It was so unlike Ken to be rude to anyone. He knew how arrogant his son could become, but not without just cause. Max's antenna went up immediately, warning him to beware of his seemingly charming companion.

Encircling Omunique in his arms, Ken kissed her as though she'd been absent for months. "I love you," he whispered.

"I love you, too." She recalled a time when she was uncomfortable with his confession, a time when she believed that he'd run out on her if he'd known her true feelings for him. There was a time when she'd thought he would simply disappear from her life. The chase would be over and she'd become just another trapped prey. Prey that would be left bleeding and dying in a steel trap that she wouldn't know how to extricate herself from.

She looked back at him. "What happened when you were alone with Courtesy?" When she'd seen Ken leading Courtesy to the dance floor, she had nearly raged inside with jealousy.

He ran his thumb across her left cheekbone and then rested his palm on the left side of her face. His other arm still tightly encircled her waist. His muscular thighs pressed against her petite body. "Something tells me I shouldn't have told you about Courtesy. You're going to drive yourself insane over it." He tilted her chin. "The woman meant nothing, means nothing. After I talk with my father, there'll be nothing between them. Will you trust me on this one?" She always trusted him. If she didn't, she couldn't love him the way she did; consummately . . .

Once everyone was back at the table, the conversations flowed in every direction, never suffering for lack of an interesting topic. However, Max was somewhat distracted. The exchange between Courtesy and his son still worried him. Max himself had been suspicious of Courtesy's motives when he'd met her at the health spa where he worked out five days a week. At that time, he'd contributed it more to their age difference than to anything else. She was the one who'd asked him out first. He'd get to the bottom of this matter with his son later. Tonight was for celebrating.

Ken and Wyman were engrossed in a quiet private conversation. Omunique often felt left out when those two put their heads together, yet she was happy they'd grown so close. She had often wondered if Wyman would have preferred to have had a son, but if he had, he'd never given her any reason to believe he'd wanted anything but what he had in her: a healthy, beautiful daughter.

Ken pushed his chair back. Standing, he reached for Omunique's hand. "Folks, its been a great evening, but we have to run. Omunique and I have early morning appointments." He kissed Mamie's cheek. "Take care of these guys for us. They can get out of hand if left to their own devices for too long."

Mamie laughed. "As you stated earlier, I got their backs."

Omunique kissed Mamie and the other two men in her life before moving away with Ken. As if it was an afterthought, she turned to Max's date. "It was interesting meeting you, Courtesy."

"Same here. Take care of yourself. I'm sure we'll be seeing each other in the future."

On what Ken thought to be a sour note, he steered Omunique away from the table. "Not if I have anything to do with it. If Max is as smart as I know he is, he'll leave that one alone."

Settling into her old routine was much easier than Omunique would've guessed. She and Ken were now busier than ever with their prospective careers. Each of their days was hectic, allowing them only late evenings to spend time together. Making wedding plans kept her moving in fast circles. They'd received numerous invitations from friends wanting to celebrate their upcoming marriage, which left them with barely enough time for each other. But it deeply saddened her that no one had offered to throw her a bridal shower, not even Mamie.

Omunique and Ken were inside his condo seated at the kitchen table. They'd just finished having breakfast. She perused the newspaper while Ken read over a new contract. Looking like a trapped doe caught in the bright headlights of a fast-moving vehicle, Omunique bit down on her lip hard enough to draw blood. She flung the paper in Ken's direction. "Look at this garbage! How do they get away with writing this type of trash? This is the poisoned pen's finest hour. I can't believe this libelous article is in the *Sun.*"

Ken set his cup down before looking up. He then took a few minutes to read the headlines. "Oh, no!" Jack Prescott immediately came to mind. Ken had no doubt that the story was Jack's idea of sweet revenge, but there wasn't anything sweet about the lies that Jack had written. The tears in Omunique's eyes twisted the knife deeply imbedded in his gut.

Ken got up and settled himself in the chair beside her. He took her hand. "I'm sorry, Omunique. You know this is the result of the little confrontation I had with Prescott at the hotel. I really thought we had gotten away with it when days had passed without him writing something scathing."

After brushing her tears away with his lips, he kissed the tip of her nose. "It's all a pack of lies. And I've given Jack more credit than he obviously deserves. He must've been really ticked off at me to make such a serious blunder. Jack usually covers his deceptions a whole lot better than this. These are outright lies. I'm sorry I lied about us being married. That's how this all got started. If you were pregnant when we got engaged, you'd be close to a delivery date by now—and you certainly wouldn't be training as hard as you do. But Jack wouldn't think about that."

Omunique started to sob. She stopped suddenly, sucking in a deep breath. "No, I won't allow this to hurt me or you. I'm going to take Jack Prescott and his rag-sheet style story on. Next, just to cover his muddy tracks, he'll be saying that I aborted this so-called pregnancy. He's going to wish that he didn't know how to spell my name, let alone use it for slander. I'm going to strangle him with his own shoe-laces. This was once a very reputable paper, for goodness sake."

A burst of laughter escaped from Ken. Then he quickly apologized. He realized this wasn't the time for humor. "I would hate to be in Jack's cheap shoes. I believe you're capable of strangling him with his own laces. Sounds like he's in serious trouble with you, but we're not going to allow anybody or anything to place another wedge between us. We've been through enough."

"You're right about that, Ken. I knew we were going to take a few direct hits from the press sooner or later, but I never expected them to throw a punch this hard. However, we're going to put Superglue on all those wagging tongues. Oh, my goodness, if Daddy has gotten wind of this, there may be nothing left of Jack Prescott for us to get at. He won't tolerate this at all. We'd better call him and try to get him to cool his jets. I certainly don't want my father to land in jail."

"Yeah, I hadn't thought about what Wyman would think. I'm sure he's busy drawing up war plans, that is, if he hasn't already charged into battle. Max won't take this too kindly, either. He doesn't care one bit for Prescott, anyway." Ken's eyes clouded with serious thought. "Maybe we should just leave it alone for now, Omunique. We don't want to make things worse by riling Prescott further. Max and Wyman are both very levelheaded men, and it's possible that they might not have seen it yet. Let's take a shower and then go for a walk on the beach."

"That sounds nice, but I think I'd like to go to the ice

arena. A good workout will help me get rid of all the tension. Do you mind?"

He nibbled at her lower lip. "I mind, but I won't object. I can think of a few other intriguing ways to ease your tension."

A deep smile danced across her lips. "I like the sound of that. Ease my tension, sweetheart!"

Needing nothing more to encourage him, Ken trailed hot kisses up and down her neck, making her squeal with pleasure. Completely putting the workout session out of her mind, she willingly succumbed to his thrilling caresses.

Instead of a shower, Omunique and Ken indulged themselves in a hot tub of scented bubbles. While their troubles were temporarily lifted into the rising steam, Omunique enjoyed every touch and caress that Ken lavished on her body.

More than an hour later, feeling happy and completely satisfied, Ken and Omunique began to dress for what promised to be another busy day. Earlier, Ken had taken a moment out to call Frank Green, his best friend, and tell him about the article; then he'd called his attorney with questions about filing suit. The phone rang as Ken was buttoning Omunique's blouse. He loved to help her dress and undress. She thought it was one of the most sensuous of the many sweet things that he did for her.

"It's Marion." He handed her the phone. "I'll pick up the other extension."

"Hi, Marion. How are you?" Omunique asked.

Seated at the kitchen table in her swanky townhouse, lavishly designed by her own clever hands, Marion, the raven-haired beauty who was Frank Green's fiancée, had just finished reading the morning's headlines. "I was fine until I read this horrible newspaper article. I couldn't believe my eyes. How can they say these sorts of things? I had laid the paper aside, only to pick it up again a few seconds later. I'm totally baffled."

"I'm sorry you had to read that garbage. But none of

it's true. It seems like a lot of people are going to be baffled by what was said to have been a marriage. A lot of speculation will circulate, yet none of it will include the simplicity of it all. The fact being, we simply love each other and want to spend the rest of our lives staying in love," Ken told Marion.

"I'm glad that there wasn't a photograph of you two to accompany the headlines. But what I don't understand is the part about you two actually being married. Did you guys elope?"

"Of course not. Ken's somewhat responsible for that particular lie." Omunique went on to explain to Marion what had happened at the hotel.

"How chivalrous of you, my dear brother. So like you to be Nique's hero every step of the way, but it looks like things may have backfired. This feature story has every seedy thing that those rag newspapers love to feature, but I can't believe the *Sun* is indulging in rag news. This is hardly Ken's first time as a star in a messy feature story, but none of those stories were true either."

Hearing Frank's key turning in the lock, Marion turned to face the kitchen door, waiting for him to appear. "It sounds like Frank's here. Before doing anything else, he always looks for me when he comes over, unless he's in a rush to use the bathroom. Even then he shouts for me to make his presence known."

Right on cue, Frank yelled, "Marion, where are you? I smell coffee, so you must be in the kitchen." He followed the scent of fresh brew. "Ah, there you are. How's it going, honey?"

"I'm talking to Omunique and Ken." As soon as he was seated, she shoved the newspaper under his nose. "You're in for the shock of your life. Read these headlines and weep. I'm holding a shoulder in reserve for you to cry on." Frank only smiled when he read the headlines, which seemed to suggest that this wasn't at all news to him.

Marion frowned. "Did you know about this? You don't seem surprised."

Folding the paper, he laid it aside. "Ken called me before I left the house. He's outraged by these headlines, but he and Omunique weren't all that surprised. They'd expected something scathing about them to appear long before now, but they had no idea it would be a story of this magnitude . . . and all lies, to boot. He's thinking of filing a lawsuit, but I told him to just beat the living crap out of Prescott and be done with it. A lawsuit is only going to make things messier."

"Marion, have you forgotten we're still on the phone?" Ken asked.

"I'm sorry. Frank just came and I was filling him in, but he seems to already know everything."

"We talked a short time ago. After talking to the lawyer, we're considering taking Frank's advice. It makes sense," Ken explained.

"You're going to go and get yourself into a physical altercation with a reporter? That doesn't sound like good advice even if the man I love is the one that gave it to you. It's ludicrous."

"No, Marion," Omunique interjected. "We're just thinking of dropping the matter to keep from adding more fuel to the fire. The lawyer is going to talk with the newspaper owner about filing suit because he thinks they might just want to settle out of court."

"All the damages we're seeking is the forfeiture of Prescott's press credentials," Ken interjected. "If he gets away with this one, he'll think he's been licensed to go out and murder the reputations of others. You guys go ahead and enjoy each other. Omunique and I have tons of things to do today. We'll catch you guys later."

"Okay. See you two at dinner tomorrow night. Love you both," Marion sang out.

Ken brought Omunique into his arms. "Ready to tackle that cold, mean world out there?"

She kissed his chin. "Without a doubt. But if one reporter comes near me, I'm going to deck them hard, male or female." She went into a karate stance, causing Ken to howl. "Like James Brown said long before we were born, I may not know karate, but I know *crazy.*"

"World, you better look out this morning. Omunique is going to kick butt first and ask questions later. Since I'm a black belt in karate—and my brand of crazy can come on without a moment's notice, they'd better stay out of my way, too."

Omunique gave Ken one long, passionate kiss. "This is why we're so good together. Let's take our usual morning's romantic stroll on the beach now. We have so many happy days ahead of us that we can't think of letting one slimy character make us lose sight of our dreams."

He kissed the tip of her nose. "Our dreams carved in ice."

Three

At the front door of Marion's townhouse, conscious of her looks, Omunique smoothed her clothes. The black-and-gold crochet dress she wore on her petite figure was fashioned with intricate open work detail. Black and gold leather sling-back pumps complemented her attire nicely. Freshly washed, her hair hung down loose and free. In her ears she wore large gold hoops. The only other jewelry she wore was her watch and the magnificent engagement ring Ken had chosen.

As she entered the foyer, Omunique was totally surprised when Marion suddenly slapped a blindfold on her. She then guided her into the beautifully appointed living room of her large four-bedroom townhouse. All the female guests were seated around the room looking on in eager anticipation of Omunique's response to her surprise wedding shower.

Omunique thought she and Ken were having dinner with Marion and Frank. Just before they'd left the condo, Frank had called and told Ken that he was having a problem with his car. Then he'd asked Ken to drop off Omunique at Marion's before picking him up. He'd said that Marion needed to talk to Omunique about something personal that had to do with the wedding. And she wanted to do it before they all got together over dinner. Marion had been planning the shower for weeks now; it looked as if it would be all that she'd hoped for.

Laughing, Marion spun Omunique around a couple of times, making her a little dizzy. The majority of the guests were Marion's friends; most were unknown to Omunique—and vice versa. But when Marion told her friends who the surprise shower was for, everyone that followed her skating career acted like Omunique was one of their dearest and oldest friends. The type of friendships Omunique had dreamed of having, but had had no spare time to develop.

Each of Marion's friends became intrigued with the idea of personally meeting the extremely talented African-American Olympic silver medal winner, Omunique Philyaw. Sara Davies was more than happy to be a part of the festivities. Marion had also invited Thomasina Bridges, but she'd declined, citing no special reason for doing so. Omunique's loving Aunt Mamie and Amanda Steele, Ken's godmother, had also been invited to the party. Mamie had helped Marion with every aspect of the catering. It took her a while, but Mamie eventually talked Marion into letting her do most of the preparations. The only thing Marion wouldn't agree to have her do was the cake. That she wanted to special order.

"One, two, three, four, five," Marion started counting, zipping off the blindfold when she got to ten. It took a few moments for Omunique's eyes to refocus and readjust to the light. As everyone shouted "surprise," shocked beyond belief, Omunique's hands went up to her face. Instant tears came to her eyes. No friend had ever done anything so wonderful for her, simply because she hadn't ever had this type of friendship with anyone, not before she'd met the loving, generous Marion Washington. A true friend; another dream come true.

Marion handed Omunique some Kleenex tissues. "I knew you were going to need these." Marion embraced her best bud's fiancée with genuine affection. "Congratulations. I know that you and Ken are going to be very happy together. You two are *so* in love. May God bless your union."

After everyone clapped and cheered, Marion took Omunique around and introduced her to her friends.

Omunique dabbed at her watery eyes. "Thank you, Marion! This is the best surprise I've ever had in my entire life. Thank all of you." She then spotted Mamie who was seated with her best friend, Teresa Banks. Amanda sat alongside them. "Oh, look who's here. I'm so happy to see all of you." Omunique hugged all three women, embracing Mamie the longest.

With her mouth wide open, as if something had just dawned on her, she turned back to Marion. "I thought the four of us were having dinner here. Frank's not having car trouble, is he? Did Ken know about this? You guys really fooled me. I didn't get suspicious of anything, or think anything out of the ordinary until you covered my eyes with that blasted blindfold."

Marion laughed. "No car trouble—and Ken doesn't know a thing. In fact, Frank's throwing him a bachelor party at his place. My fiancé and I came up with the idea together. This way, Ken wouldn't have to be home alone waiting for you during your party. And when he had his, you wouldn't have to sit at home and wait for him. Great plan, huh?"

With her eyes tearing up anew, Omunique embraced Marion again. "The greatest!"

Marion clapped her hands. "Okay, let's get this party started. Put your hands up in the air if you're ready to bust loose from your weary souls." All hands swayed back and forth. "Let's eat first. Then, girlfriends, we're going to give Omunique a night to remember . . ."

As Omunique was the guest of honor, Marion had her sit down on the sofa so that she could be served. "I know everything you can eat and everything that you shy away from. Just sit tight and relax. I got it all under control." Marion kissed the top of Omunique's head before leaving.

Marion got away before Omunique could tell her that she wasn't in the mood for eating healthy tonight, not at her own wedding shower. Still in awe of what was happening, Omunique took a minute to catch her breath and look around at the decorations.

Lavender-and-white crepe paper wedding bells were hung all about the room. Streamers in the same color scheme were twisted into diamond shapes and strung along the top of doorways. Lavender and white helium balloons hung from the ceiling. Two of the lavender balloons had names penned on them in white letters, her own and Ken's. That made her smile. But what made her smile even brighter was the life-size cardboard cutouts of her and Ken.

In the center of the room, situated on an easel, a picturesque board caught Omunique's eye. In all the excitement she'd missed it, but she didn't know how . . . since it was filled with pictures of her. As she drew closer to the display, she saw that there were pictures of her at all different ages, many poses of her on the ice, as well as an array of photos with her and Ken. Her love-struck eyes brightened the room as she gazed at Ken's favorite picture of the two of them.

Leaning on the front bumper of his black sports car, he held her intimately as she leaned back into him, her head nestled beneath his chin. With both of his arms wrapped around her, his hands, clasped together in front of him, rested on the flat of her abdomen. The next picture was Ken's very favorite one of her. The one of her dressed in a very revealing leotard, the pose that could thaw the ice she stood on. It was the first picture he'd ever seen of her, the one that had been sent in with her bio. His second favorite choice was one of her with the two colorful cockatoo birds.

Omunique took her seat when Marion showed up with a plate full of goodies for her to eat.

"Here's all the uncooked veggies you love, along with your favorite low-calorie dressing for dipping. Just the way you like them, the grilled chicken wings are marinated with teriyaki sauce. We used fat-free salad dressing in mixing the deviled eggs. And you'll just have to deal with the pasta salad or pass on it 'cause I don't know what's in it."

Omunique held up her hand. "Thanks for being so thoughtful, but I'm not trying to pass up a single delicious food item this evening. I'm going to eat everything you prepared, Marion. It looks so good and I'm hungry. As of right now, my special diet is on hold."

"I'd love to take the credit for all this wonderful, great-looking food, but this is Aunt Mamie's grand buffet of delightfulness. She insisted."

Omunique grinned. "Sounds about right. I should've known. She rarely takes no for an answer. Since Aunt Mamie cooked everything, she knows just how to fix dishes that won't entirely destroy my dietary regimen. Low on fat and calories but divine to the taste buds."

"Aunt Mamie fixed everything but the cake, but she wanted to bake that, too. I had already ordered it and paid the deposit when she first asked me about catering the party herself. She is a regal lady, a real gem. The old girl can work with some pots and pans, too. I'm surprised some hungry man hasn't snapped her up by now. I'm not going to name any names, but some big, handsome guy that we call Wyman Philyaw does come to mind."

Nique laughed as she leaned forward to whisper in Marion's ear. "I've been trying to get those two together since forever. It doesn't look like it's going to happen, at least no time soon."

"Well, we're going to have to see about that later. But right now, we're going to get this party going. Taking Omunique by the hand, Marion led her to the chair she'd placed in the center of the room. "We're going to get a few other preliminaries out of the way before we get to the main event: opening the gifts."

Marion passed out postcards with two different poses of Omunique, one in her fancy skating costume, the other in Maxwell athletic wear. She held one up in the air for everyone to see. "Omunique, there's not one person in this room who doesn't want your autograph, myself included. Would you please sign these now to keep us from forgetting to do it later?"

"I'd be honored. But where did you get these? I've never seen them before."

Marion winked. "Amazing things can happen when someone is engaged to the groom's best friend. Actually, Frank told Ken I'd like to have a picture of you. When Ken showed him all the proofs from the photo shoot you did when you guys first met, Frank chose this one. I chose the photo from the bio; Ken's favorite. Especially for this wonderful occasion, I then took them to a printing place and had them do the postcards. Luckily, neither photo was copyrighted."

By writing the name of each person on the cards, Omunique's task was made much easier and was completed much faster. However, Omunique called out each person's name so that she could see who the autograph was for, as well as learn the names of the guests she didn't know. With the autographing session over, Marion asked those who knew Omunique to say a few words.

"Since I'm the host, I'm going to go first. I met Omunique a little over a year ago, when Ken brought her to our house for dinner. Our dear friend talked about this woman to Frank and me like she was more precious than gold. Just a short time after meeting her, when he told us he was in love, I must admit to getting a little worried about the brother. It was too late; he was gone on her.

"As you all know, Frank and Ken accuse me of being the mother hen over them. Well, it's true. These two were my guys—had been so for many years—and I wasn't too eager to share their attention with someone else. I also wanted to make darn sure that this woman Ken was going on and on about was worthy of the great guy that Ken is. Frank and I definitely knew of her because we followed her career, but that didn't tell us anything about her true character.

"After being in her company for only a short time, I must say that I understood exactly why Ken had fallen so deeply in love with her, so quickly. She was beautiful inside and out, fresh, and so lively. As she talked about how she began skating, her world travels—and how she'd won umpteen competitions, I was surprised to learn how humble she was. But what impressed me the most were the personal things I learned about her later.

"Ken had told us that she had the courage and heart of a lion. Then I found out for myself. It came at the time when she'd given up the one thing she loved most in this world, Kenneth Maxwell Jr., because she thought that giving him up might save his life. She is truly a courageous woman in her heart and soul. Omunique, I'm honored to call you friend." Marion warmly embraced Omunique as everyone clapped while trying to keep from crying.

Amanda Steele spoke after Marion, in which she gave a very compelling story of her brief history with her godson's fiancée. Sara could barely get her comments out because she couldn't keep her emotions under control, especially when she talked about what a great source of comfort and encouragement Omunique had been to her when a serious injury ended her skating career.

Mamie was the last to speak about Omunique. With deep emotion and heartfelt love, Mamie spoke about the little baby girl's christening that she'd attended in her mother's place, because Patrice had gone unto the presence of the Lord. There wasn't a dry eye in the room after she finished singing her goddaughter's praises. So overwhelmed by it all, Omunique nearly went through an entire box of tissues; no one had ever done anything like this for her before.

With the speaking forum over, Marion moved to the center of the room. "Listen up, everybody. It's Electric Slide time, but we're gonna do it to the Harlem Shuffle, the remake of the oldie by Mick Jagger . . . and now that one's an oldie. For sure, older than all of us in this room."

Amanda Steele cleared her throat. "I think a few of us in here were around during the time of the *first* oldie. What do you think, Mamie and Teresa?" Both ladies nodded in agreement. "Think we should get out there and show them how to do the Harlem Shuffle while these youngsters *work* the Electric Slide?" The young women all laughed at Amanda's hip choice of words.

"In my opinion, the two dances are one and the same," Mamie offered. "Come on, Teresa, let's get up and get on the dance floor. This is what will keep us young, at least, at heart."

Marion first moved the easel out of the center of the room. And then she took up the throw rugs covering the shiny hardwood floors. With one flick of the remote control Marion held in her hand, the funky beat of the Harlem Shuffle came blasting into the cavernous room.

After the group of women formed several lines, moving bodies swayed as fast moving feet kept in tune with the soulful music. Omunique didn't know how to do either of the dances but she was a quick study. Within just a short time, after a few blundering missteps, she had easily learned all the moves to the popular line dance. Her ability to rapidly learn new choreographed routines was one of the reasons her choreographer loved to work with her. The same song was replayed three times before everyone became too tired to move another muscle.

Everyone was back in their seats, with something to drink in hand, when Marion and a few of her girlfriends began to bring the shower gifts in for Omunique to open. Marion announced that this was a *personal* shower, which meant that all the gifts were personal items for the bride.

* * *

A good solid hour had passed by the time Omunique finished opening all the beautiful gifts. Everyone had brought very sexy lingerie or lounging attire; most of it purchased from Victoria's Secret, at Marion's suggestion.

The largest and most surprising gift of all came from Mamie and Amanda who'd gone in together on it. Though it wasn't lingerie, it was definitely personal. A satin bedding collection: sheets, pillowcases, shams, a reversible comforter in gold and black, and a bed skirt. The one side, done in gold-spun silk, was trimmed in black satin binding, and the black side was edged in gold.

Omunique stood up. "Thank you all so much for making this occasion so very special for me. For those of you that I didn't know before, I'm happy that I met each and every one of you. This shower has been a wonderful surprise. These beautiful gifts are magnificent, not to mention sexy, some even risqué. The latter are sure to become Ken's favorites."

Turning to Marion, she brought her into her embrace. "Thank you from the bottom of my heart. I'm so delighted to have you as a friend." Omunique smiled brightly. "Now, speaking of our men who just happen to be best friends, exactly what do you think is going on at that bachelor party Frank is throwing for my fiancé? Nothing too risqué, I hope."

Marion could only shrug. "Your guess is as good as mine. But when Frank asked my opinion on hiring a stripper . . . well, let's say that he won't forget my response any time soon. I think he was just pushing my buttons. If so, they were pushed hard enough for him to receive a colorful commentary from yours truly." Everyone laughed heartily at her comical remarks.

The bachelor party at Frank's house was in the process of winding down. Plenty of good food had been served along with good wine and imported beer. No hard liquor had been made available for the party. Although none of Frank and Ken's friends were heavy drinkers, Frank wanted to ensure that the party didn't get out of his control.

Despite the absence of a stripper, the guys hadn't been completely banished to an evening without sexy topics and even a sensuous vision or two. One of the guys had brought along videos, one of a swimsuit competition that featured sexy women modeling the skimpiest in swimwear. The second video was of busty women wearing very revealing lingerie and loungewear, nothing close to what Omunique considered risqué. These exotic items were way over the top, way beyond definition. Even the sexually stimulating attire at Frederick's of Hollywood placed a distant second to the intimate apparel worn in the video.

Ken had watched both videos but nothing aroused his sexual appetite the way Omunique did. Most of the evening was spent with him thinking about getting back to her. He was as surprised as she was over the celebration, but the most delightful surprise for him was reuniting with an old friend of his and Frank's from high school and college, Brandon Blair.

Frank had run into Brandon at the Beach City marketplace a little over a week ago. Knowing Ken would be thrilled to see their old buddy, he had invited him to the surprise bachelor party. Brandon was also engaged to a superstar, rhythm and blues singer, Hillary Houston.

To heckle Ken the movie *Best Man* had been shown, but Ken was totally undeterred by the story line. His best friend and best man, none other than Frank Green, would never even entertain libidinous thoughts about his fiancée let alone act upon them. Ken and Omunique had seen the movie before and they both loved it.

It was after midnight and everyone was moving toward the door when Ken asked to have everyone's attention. As the room grew silent, he moved to a position where he could see all the guests. "The only thing I can say is thanks, guys. This has been a great night for me. A surprise bachelor party isn't something I would've expected from Frank, not the Frank I know and love dearly. Throwing me a computer-game party or a stock-and-bond presentation sounds more like him. Knowing that Marion is doing the same for Omunique, I'm sure they put their two heads together on this one. Thank you again."

Frank stepped up next to Ken. "He's right about Marion helping me to pull this together. As he's already stated, I'm no good at these sorts of things. But I need to say a few things before we shut this party down. Not to embarrass Ken, but I have to tell you a short story. It's a must for me.

"Many of you know that my grandparents raised me after my parents got on drugs and destroyed their lives." Tears welled up in Frank's eyes. "My grandmother died in my first year of college, and my grandfather died a year later. After burying them, there was no money left to help pay my tuition. I was going to drop out of school altogether. I wasn't making enough money at my part-time gig to carry the full load. My grandparents' pensions had been instrumental in sustaining me up to that point, which had completely stopped when they died. What this man here did for me can never be repaid." Frank's voice broke.

"Without my knowledge, Ken immediately went to his father with my dilemma. Before it's impossible for me to go on, I'm going to finish this up in a hurry. Kenneth Maxwell Sr., Ken's biological father, a surrogate father to me, paid my tuition. Up until I landed my first good-paying job, Max saw to it that I had everything I needed. Both Max and Ken were always there for me, as they still are up to this very day. I love you, brother."

Somewhat emotional, Ken hugged Frank in the way most men do. The sincerity in the hard poundings to each other's backs was in no doubt. "This man here *is* a brother to me, and I love him like one. We've been close friends since high school and we've always had each other's backs. My getting married will in no way interfere with the lifelong bond we've created. On a less emotional note, I'm hoping to see all of you at my wedding. Frank's been a little upset because I'm beating him to the altar, but he's been engaged a lot longer than I have. So what does that tell you? It tells me somebody's dragging big feet. Anyone care to take a guess at who?" Everyone laughed.

Ken looked at his watch. "I know all of you that have wives or girlfriends should've checked in on the home front long before now, if you haven't already done so. For me, I have to pick Omunique up at Marion's . . .and I'll be the first to admit that I'm extremely eager to do so. We have a little private celebrating of our own to do."

"They're all over at Marion's. So I say we all go over there and crash the party. They might have a male stripper up in there . . . even though my lady threatened me within an inch of my life if I dared to hire one for Ken's party." Ken frowned. "Don't look like that, brother. We know you got private plans for yourself and that lovely fiancée of yours. We understand. And we also know how to party without you . . ."

Clad in silk pajamas, Omunique was already in bed when Ken slid in beside her. He looked over at her before turning out the light. She was asleep. This would be the last night they'd spend together before their wedding. Omunique had a lot on her plate with all the wedding plans that had yet to be executed. He decided not to awaken her. She needed to be well rested in order to keep up the hectic pace that had her running here and there. It wouldn't be much longer before they were married. And he couldn't wait for them to sleep together every single night and to awaken together every morning. Due to her professional obligations, and sometimes his, they wouldn't be together every morning and night, but it wouldn't be like that forever.

While most of their leisure time was spent together, she still resided at her father's house in Hermosa Beach. Since Wyman had moved back into his home permanently, out of respect for her father, Omunique only stayed overnight at Ken's place when Wyman was out of town on business, as he was now.

Even though he'd had every intention of running in to get her from her surprise party and running right out, they were coerced by the others into staying a couple of hours more. That's why Omunique was dead tired. Though she'd been in an exuberant mood over the surprise shower, Ken realized they hadn't done much talking on the way back to the condo from Marion's. He asked her if she'd had a good time and she'd asked him the same. That had been the extent of their conversation about the two parties. Omunique had dozed off and on during the short ride to Venice. Once inside the condo, she'd headed straight for the bedroom.

Cuddling up behind her, he stroked her hair. For bringing him the greatest love, the only love of his life, as he closed his eyes, he sent out a silent prayer of thanks.

The vapors coming from the ice were especially cold this morning. Dressed in black stretch pants and a black knit sweater, Omunique went back to the bench and put a hooded sweater on top of the other and zipped up the front. She had come to the arena to rehearse a special routine she'd had Jake choreograph for her. Her performance would include two songs: "The Sun Will Shine Again" and "Hero."

In a continuous flow of soft twists and turns Omunique began to execute her special routine. Careful not to put too much strain on her feet, she singled a lot of her jumps rather than taking unnecessary risks with the double and triple jumps. Moving with her usual elegance and grace, Omunique stayed in perfect time with the music as she whirled into a spiral. As always, the swaying movements of her hands dramatically told the story of the lyrics of the song.

After working her very special program for ninety minutes straight, Omunique left the ice and sat down on the bench to remove her skates. Her eyes misted as she looked around the arena, the place that she worked out in since she was a small child, the same place where she was to be married. This was the very last practice session before her wedding day, the very last performance ever for her as a single woman.

The next time she graced this arena with her presence she'd be Mrs. Kenneth Maxwell Jr.

Four

The magical fairy-tale setting looked as though it belonged to another space and time. In designing the arena setting, the decorators had followed Omunique's specifications to the letter, just the way she had imagined it. Satisfied with the majestic outcome, she smiled her approval.

Pink and white mums, satin bows, and dainty streamers were tied around the ends of the bench-style seating. A shimmering white castle was imperiously stationed on the center of the ice. A picturesque white drawbridge covered with English ivy led up to the castle's mock arched entryway. Soft pink rosebuds and white baby's breath covered the arch. A pink velvet kneeling bench was positioned inside a white gazebo. The sparkling snowlike runner ran from one entrance to the ice and all the way to the castle door. Snow banks of cotton glimmering with silver glitter strategically placed around the castle and drawbridge represented a winter wonderland.

An altar laden with pink and white roses faced the bench. Silver candelabras were delicately placed at each end of the altar and another one in the center. Hung from the rafters of the arena were pink and white balloons and several more streamers. The ice arena was simply breathtaking. Laced with all its quixotic fantasy and magical grandeur it was more than any bride could ever hope for on her wedding day.

As Ken paced the floor in the men's locker room, Kenneth Maxwell Sr. recalled being just as nervous on his wedding day. Noticing the same kind of apprehension happening with his son and namesake, he chuckled inwardly, stroking his neatly trimmed snowy-white beard. Max and Ken's best man, Frank, smiled knowingly. Each of the three men stood over six feet, Ken Jr. being the tallest. Max not only looked just as physically fit as his younger counterparts, he was.

His autumn-gold eyes lighting up his dark caramel complexion, Max ran a hand through his shocking snowy-white curls. "Why don't you give the floor a break, son? You don't have too much longer to wait."

"I know, Dad." Ken wiped the thin line of sweat from his caramel-brown face, only a lighter shade of brown than that of his father. "I'm just anxious to get this over with."

Frank's burgundy eyes gazed at Ken with concern. "You're not having second thoughts, are you, man?"

Possessing the same autumn-gold coloring as his father, Ken's eyes flared with brightness. "No, no, that's not it. I'm anxious about getting away with my bride. We'll just have a few weeks before she has to report to the professional training camp. Not once have I had any doubts about marrying her. She's the only woman for me. Like I said before, I see all my dreams in the reflections of her silver eyes. I'm ready for those dreams to become our reality!"

Max affectionately patted Ken on the back. "I'm glad to hear that her beautiful eyes are still reflecting your dreams. I'm really happy for you both. Omunique is a lovely person and her brilliant energy always amazes me. I'm proud to call her daughter. You have made an excellent choice for a bride!"

"Tell me about it, Dad! We have been down some tough roads, but we're about to take a walk down a path that will be filled with love, champagne, and roses. It's a day that I've long awaited. Dad, Frank, this is without doubt the happiest day of my life. I only wish Mom were here to celebrate my wedding day. I know she would've loved Omunique as much as you both obviously do." Talking about his mother made Ken emotional.

Tears misted in Max's eyes. "Yes, son, she would've loved your bride. They're a lot alike, in many ways. In the absence of her own mother, Julia would've stepped in and helped Omunique pull off the wedding of the century. I'm glad she had her Aunt Mamie to assist her with all the plans."

Frank grinned. "Don't leave out Miss Marion Washington. That fiancée of mine acted like this was our wedding she helped to plan. The girl has damn near become psychotic over this day. She wanted everything to be perfect for Omunique."

Ken looked over at Frank and smiled. "I know. Omunique appreciates all that she's done, too. They've become very close over the past months."

"Close as some sisters, Ken. With all of us being only children, it's been easy for us to become like brothers and sisters to one another. We've never had any siblings to bond with in that way. It's a great feeling. It's hard to believe we haven't known Omunique as long as you, Marion, and I have known each other. We've been friends since high school and Marion came into our lives in college. But it seems like we've always been together as best friends with Omunique."

Ken snapped his fingers. "Speaking of old friends, I'm sure glad you ran into Brandon Blair. When I saw him at the bachelor party, I nearly flipped. I haven't seen Blair for several months now." Ken took a minute to reminisce about all the good times they'd had in high school.

"Off and on through the years, Brandon and I have managed to stay in contact by phone. The last time I saw him he was half crazed over breaking it off with Hillary Houston. We really talked a lot when his best buddy, Aaron

Samms, was on his honeymoon. It seems that Aaron married Hillary's best friend. That old stuff that happened with the girl back in high school seems to have carried over into Brandon's adult relationships, which really affected his love affair with Hillary. Both Omunique and I are thrilled that Hillary offered to sing at our wedding when she heard that we hadn't found a soloist yet. She definitely has the voice of a angel."

"I can't wait to hear that girl sing live! Marion and I love her voice. Boy, that was a hoot of a time back in high school. A girl trading a jock for a scholar wasn't the most popular thing to have happen to you. I think it was more about the ribbing Blair took from us guys than anything to do with the girl. We were pretty rough on him."

"Rough doesn't begin to describe it. All you jocks on the football team ran him into the ground with it. I felt sorry for him. At any rate, he's worked through all that old stuff and he's a highly successful architect. He and Hillary are getting married soon."

Max chuckled. "You two are talking about something that happened a lifetime ago. Don't you both think that you need to concentrate on the present? A grand wedding is about to take place, your wedding, son. And, Frank, yours is not too far off. I bet Omunique's not thinking about yesteryears, not when she's about to ride off into the sunset with her Prince Charming."

Marion tried her best to comfort Omunique, but she was inconsolable. Wanting her mother there for her wedding in the worst way, Omunique had given in to a bout of near hysteria. Tissues were strewn all over the locker room and her nose and eyes were red and puffy from crying. Marion hadn't yet been able to apply Omunique's make-up because of all the tears.

Dressed only in a slip, Mamie stepped forward and

brought Omunique's head to her full breasts. "Sweet darling, don't do this to yourself. Patrice is here in spirit, just as she's been with you all your life. You have a handsome prince of a groom out there waiting for you to become his princess bride. Neither Patrice nor Ken would want to see you this anguished. Don't you want to get married today and begin a new life with Ken?"

Omunique lifted her head, fresh tears brimming in her eyes. "Oh, I'm being so selfish. It's just that. . . . I don't know. It does seem silly of me to carry on this way. But doesn't every girl want her mother on a day like today? I can't stop myself from wishing she were here to hold me the way you just did, to tell me all the secrets a woman should know on her wedding night, to assure me that she'll be there for me no matter what the future brings. I simply want my mother." Omunique's lower lip trembled violently as she fought the waves of emotions overtaking her all over again.

Marion dragged gentle fingers through her short raven-black hair. Possessing a beautiful sienna complexion, she stood over average in height and had a model-slender figure. "Of course you do. Let me get your dad. Do you think that might help?"

Omunique hiccuped on a jagged sob. "Would you mind? I do need to see him. He's played both parental roles to me, and I can't even imagine getting through this day without him."

Marion hugged Omunique. "I'll get him. Slip into your robe so I can do your make-up right after you see your dad." Marion rushed off to find Wyman before Omunique could thank her.

"Aunt Mamie, I'm sorry for acting so childish. You've been just like a mother to me and I'm so happy to have you to turn to. Please don't think I'm not grateful to you."

Smiling with her beautiful bourbon-brown eyes, Mamie took Omunique's hand in her dusky-brown one. At fifty-

five, she still had a firm, shapely figure. Over a year ago
she'd had her silver hair rinsed a deep chocolate brown.
Because of all the compliments she'd kept the stunning
color.

"This is understandable, Nique. It's your wedding day."
A firm knock came on the door. "That's probably your dad.
I'm going to slip into the adjoining room to finish dressing.
It'll be okay, love. Wyman's here to make it better. Like
always, he'll kiss all the boo-boos away."

Not yet dressed in his wedding attire, Wyman Philyaw
looked concerned as he made his way into the locker room.
"Honey, what's going on in here? Marion says you're terribly upset. Oh, look at your eyes. You've nearly cried them
out." With his tall, large, but well-proportioned frame
dwarfing her, he gathered his petite daughter against his
broad chest. Holding her slightly away from him, his wal-
nut-brown eyes drank in his daughter. Even with red puffy
eyes he thought she was extremely beautiful. "Tell your
dear old dad what's going on with his only child, his best
girl."

Omunique sniffed and then blew her nose. "It seems that
I'm missing Mom today more than ever. I want her here
with me but I know that's not possible. Aunt Mamie reminded me that Mom is here in spirit. I know I'm being
silly, but I've missed out on so much by not having a mother
around. My heart aches so badly for her tender touch."

"Mamie's right, you know. But so are you. I can't change
what you've missed, but I would move mountains if I
thought I could make that all up to you. Patrice would love
to be here today. She often talked of us having a daughter
to spoil. She used to say that our baby girl was going to
have a wedding day like no other. Though, she didn't know
for sure that you were a girl, she somehow felt that she
carried one. Your mother would love Ken just as I do. She
would say that he is perfect for you and that no mother and
father could ask for a finer son-in-law. If your mother was

here, what would you say to her, what questions would you ask of her?"

"First I would tell her how much I love and need her. She would know how I felt about her every time I saw her. We would go shopping, and then stop at one of our favorite places for lunch. I'd make her my own personal advisor. She'd teach me her beauty secrets and perhaps share an intimate confidence or two and I'd teach her all the latest dance steps. We'd do the movies once every two weeks and have a mother and daughter phone chat for a few minutes everyday. We'd sit in her kitchen and have tea while she taught me how to bake bread and cook delicious meals. If I lived alone, I'd like to have her come over for a mother and daughter pajama party once every few months. We'd giggle and then cry while she told me about how you and her fell in love at first sight. And she'd read me some of those love letters and fantasy stories she'd write to you . . . and those that you'd write to her. Then we'd cry and laugh some more. As well as mother and daughter, we'd be best friends, with our relationship boundaries clear.

"Then I'd ask her how did she have her husband come to love her so consummately? What did she do to make his love for her remain and be faithful to her far beyond her death? What does a woman do to keep her man happy and satisfied in and out of the bedroom?" Omunique laughed gently when Wyman looked embarrassed by her comment. "How did she keep her husband coming home to her after work every evening, night after night, month after month . . . and year after year? Those are just a few of the things I'd say to her. There are so many more things that I say to her every time I talk to her when I'm feeling her absence. The problem is, she never answers me."

Tears ran down Wyman's cheeks as he crushed his daughter against him. "Oh, Nique, I know it hurts, honey. In answer to your questions, your mother would tell you that her husband loved her so consummately because she loved and respected herself and would settle for nothing less from him than his very best. He remained faithful to her after death because he knew he'd never find another Patrice, that he'd never love that deeply again . . . and that he'd always make unfair comparisons. She would tell you that she was very creative in and out of the bedroom. That she never ceased to amaze and delight her husband with little surprise packages of baked goodies, love notes plastered everywhere, and a few other delectable things that her husband dare not discuss with their daughter.

"Her husband couldn't wait to get home to her, night after night, year after year because he never knew what to expect from her, but he knew whatever it was, it would be so good. Patrice was always a mystery in the making, one that he never fully solved simply because she wrote the script that way. In fact, he hated to go to sleep at night for fear he'd miss her too much, miss out on some delicious moment that she'd carefully planned for him. The relaxing bubble baths, hot oil massages, poetry and novel readings, carpet brunches, and romantic movies in front of the fireplace on lazy, rainy, or perfect-weather evenings are what had him breaking the speed limits to get home.

"You're going to *live* the answers to these questions, daughter, because you have found the same kind of husband in Ken that your mother had in hers. With all that said, are you ready for me to give you away? I imagine Ken is getting pretty fidgety right about now. Max has probably had to give him a tranquilizer of some sort."

Omunique's laughter filled the room, bringing her father untold joy. "I'm ready. But I better not go out there in this state of dress. Ken would think he was marrying a crazy exhibitionist of some sort."

Wyman hugged her tightly. "Ken Maxwell Jr. knows exactly who and what he's marrying . . . and I'm sure he can't wait to have the minister pronounce you two husband and wife." He kissed her softly on the lips. "I'll be eagerly waiting to walk my favorite girl down the aisle. See you in a few minutes, Nique."

"Love you, Daddy!"

He turned back for one last look at his beautiful daughter, the daughter who was about to become the center of another man's world, just as she'd been the center of his. "I love you, too!"

The stunningly beautiful Hillary Houston began to sing the words to Mariah Carey's "Hero," Ken and Omunique's favorite song. As the organist played the music softly, Ken, Max, and Frank exited the locker room. Frank looked more nervous than Ken. Remembering Ken's once confirmed bachelor status, he couldn't believe that Ken and Omunique were beating him and Marion to the altar. Max and Frank were dressed in dove-gray tuxedos accentuated by rose-pink bow ties and cummerbunds. Ken's tuxedo was a lighter shade of gray, accented by a deeper pink. Each man had a pink rose in his lapel.

As Hillary soulfully, emotionally crooned another of Omunique and Ken's favorite songs, the men took their places to the right of the flower-covered altar. Ken stood as erect as any proud soldier would. His eyes glowing with sentiment, he looked around at the seats already filled with numerous guests. Glad to see his friend, Ken nodded as he caught Brandon's eye. Practically everyone had tears in their eyes as Hillary finished her emotionally charged performance.

Max and Frank looked to Ken as the organist sweetly strummed the bridal march. Simultaneously the three men turned and watched as Mamie floated down the aisle dressed in a blush-pink silk dress. She carried a bouquet of pink and white orchids. Smiling brightly, she took her place to the left of the altar.

Omunique's skating peers and close friends, Sara Davies,

escorted by Omunique's practice partner, Ian Swanson; Marion Washington, escorted by Roy Baer, another old friend of both Ken and Frank; and Phyllis, a Philyaw neighbor escorted by her husband Raymond, wore the same dress as Mamie in rose-pink.

A young black minister entered from a side door. A videographer stood in the wings to record the ceremony in its entirety. Everyone waited with bated breath for the lovely bride to appear.

Looking much calmer and certainly more poised, United States Olympian Omunique Philyaw finally made her grand entry. Marion had applied the bride's make-up with close to near perfection, having paid careful attention to her puffy, reddened eyes.

Proudly, smiling widely, Wyman escorted his beautiful daughter down the long aisle strewn with pink and white rose petals. He looked handsome in a dove-gray tuxedo, an oyster-white shirt, and the same rose-pink accessories as the other men. Tall and stately, Wyman was a picture of health. The broad smile on his face spoke of a rapturous, overflowing with love occasion. On his arm was his greatest accomplishment in life, his greatest treasure, his daughter.

Omunique mirrored royalty in an ivory chapel-length antique-satin gown boasting a delicate sweetheart neckline. The bodice was sprinkled with dainty white seed pearls; the sleeves, long and puffed at the shoulders, were covered with delicate white satin bows and seed pearls. Her satin slippers were designed with the same seed pearls and satin bows. Burnt-almond hair cascaded down over her shoulders. A delicate tiara inlaid with dainty pearls circled the crown of her head.

As the bride reached the altar, Ken's eyes shone like brilliant flecks of gold. He marveled at her exquisite fragility, thunderstruck by the inexpressible beauty of the young woman who was his bride-to-be.

"Who gives this woman away?" the minister asked.

Visible tears ran down Wyman's cheeks. "As her father, I do." Gently, without hesitation, he placed his daughter's delicate hand in Ken's. Wyman then kissed his fingertips and pressed them onto Omunique's lips in a fleeting moment of deep emotion.

Max had to bite back his rising emotions. He'd never seen a more beautiful couple, and he couldn't help but wish that Julia Maxwell was there to experience their son's wedding ceremony. Ken and his mother had doted on each other. Just as Max and his loving wife had adored each other.

Ken stared into Omunique's beautiful gray eyes. "My darling, Omunique, I promise to value your love, to honor your independence, to respect your right to choose and decide what's best for you, to protect you, heart, body, and soul, to cherish your companionship, and to be there to meet your every need, your every desire. In good times and bad, I will remain steadfastly by your side. These things I pledge to you from the depths of my heart." Conquering his desire to kiss her right then and there didn't come without extreme difficulty.

Omunique took hold of both Ken's hands. "My dearest, Kenneth, I promise to love you, to cherish your love for me, to honor your dignity, to never challenge your manhood, to offer you shelter in the storms of life, to protect you in the heat of battles, to never leave your side in sickness and in health. All these things I pledge to you from within the heart of my soul."

Tears came for them at the soft exchange of their heartspoken vows they'd both written. Gently taking Omunique's hand, Ken guided her to the kneeling bench, where they lowered themselves to their knees. His heavy voice booming over the loudspeakers, the minister prayed fervently over the loving union taking place.

"By the powers vested in me by God and the state of

California, I now pronounce you husband and wife. Kenneth Maxwell Jr., you may kiss your lovely bride."

Ken wasted no time in sealing their vows with a staggering kiss; a kiss that swept Omunique completely off her feet. Loud cheers and applause followed. Hand-in-hand, they walked to the altar. Each taking a candle from its holder, they lit them from another candle and touched their lighted candles to an unlit one. The candle lighting service was symbolic of their lives being joined together as one, in an unbreakable bond.

Pride showed on the face of the minister. "I present to all for the very first time, Mr. and Mrs. Kenneth Maxwell Jr." He kissed Omunique and shook Ken's hand. "Congratulations!"

Simultaneous with the loud clapping and cheering coming from the guests, the arena lights dimmed, bathing the fairy-tale setting in a glowing, angeliclike softness. A snowflake quietness immediately settled over the entire arena.

As Ken led Omunique from the altar, ice-skaters attired in shimmering skating gear glided onto the ice from every entryway in the building. The skaters held hands and formed a massive circle around the newlyweds.

Two male skaters escorted Omunique to a bench, where they sat her down. After taking off her satin slippers, they laced up her ice skates. Every guest in the house was shocked as two female skaters did the same for Ken. As far as everyone knew, Ken couldn't skate. Omunique was sure that he couldn't, yet he didn't appear to protest his inability to do so.

A bit shaky on his feet, he slowly skated over to Omunique and offered her his hand. The cheers and applause echoed throughout the arena. "May I have this dance, Mrs. Maxwell?" As he grinned from ear to ear, incredulity blazed in her smoky eyes. Taking his hand, she followed him onto the ice, without the least bit of reluctance. How she loved the sound of her newly acquired name.

Singing her platinum single "Destiny," Hillary Houston's voice sweetly gravitated from the speakers as the couple flowed together. Ken was extremely careful of his every step knowing that any false moves could possibly send him sprawling across the ice. Barely moving atop the freshly laid surface, they swayed to the music. Looking deeply into one another's eyes, completely mesmerized by the love for each other shining so brilliantly, this magical moment was so much more than either of them could've ever dared to hope for.

While engaging her in yet another staggering kiss, Ken could feel the world at his fingertips. Omunique was his forever. "You haven't told me what you think about my skating talent, Mrs. Maxwell." His whisper came softly as his lips made contact with her ears.

Just another one of his hundreds of smiles got trapped in her heart, filling it with an overpowering joy. "You did this all for me, didn't you? This is the best wedding present a girl could ever ask for. Thank you for being you, Kenneth Maxwell Jr.!"

His suggestive smile taunted. "The best wedding present is yet to come. That one will be presented when I have you all alone. If I have to say so myself, those few lessons I took seem to be paying off. The rapturous look in your silver eyes tells me it was all worth it. Maybe we could team up as pair skaters." He couldn't help laughing at his own silly remark.

She laughed heartily. "Not on your life, but thanks for the offer. And thanks for making this the happiest day of my life. I love you, Kenneth Maxwell Jr.!"

"I love you, Omunique Philyaw-Maxwell! Now we better get off this ice before I turn our wedding into a fiasco. I've done what I came here to do; to marry you and show you just how big a fool I'm willing to make out of myself for you."

They were still laughing when the same four skaters ap-

peared and escorted them from the ice. Much to the dismay
of her new husband, the two male skaters whisked Omunique away. After nearly carrying her to the locker room,
the two skaters waited outside while she changed clothes.
The time had come for her to give her new husband his
wedding present . . .

Flanked by the same two males, the stunning black Ice
Princess reappeared in a matter of minutes. She wore a
costume fashioned after the wedding gown she'd worn earlier. The skating attire only covered the upper portion of
her thighs. A short billowing train flowed from the low-cut
back. A wreath of white orchids surrounded her head.

Illuminating her delicate features, the dazzling spotlight
came to rest on her ballerina figure. Skating to the spiritually uplifting gospel tune, "The Sun Will Shine Again,"
recorded by Patti La Belle and Wintley Phipps, Omunique
began her performance with an amazing pirouette.

As her own sweet and troubled memories of the last year
lit up her mind, she felt an urgent need to valiantly express
each and every emotion she felt. The gentle, provocative
swaying motions of her hands hypnotized. Twisting and
turning in every direction, she skated on the turned-in edges
of her blades, floating around the outer rims of the ice.
Taking off from the back inside edge of one foot, she made
a perfect landing on the back outside edge of the opposite
foot. Ken was positively dazzled by the woman he now
called wife.

Crossing one foot over the other, she turned the corners
like a speeding projectile. In a series of jumps and spins
she touched the tips of her skates, landing smoothly, gracefully. To bring her touching performance to a riveting finale,
she raised her leg high up behind her and spun around
slowly. Drawing the ice blade of the extended leg level with
her head, she gripped the blade and slowly rotated herself

on the axis of one skate. Bowing gracefully in her trade-mark show of humility, she waited for the other skaters to join her. The roaring applause of their guests sent the tears fleeing from her smoky eyes as she began to skate to "Hero."

As the lights came up, she caught the kisses Ken blew toward her. Joining in with her comrades for one final performance, she threw her head back in laughter when she heard the song her friends had chosen to skate to. Barry White's soulfully sultry voice crooning "Practice What You Preach" practically echoed the voice of the sultry baritone she was now married to. She couldn't wait for the lessons he was going to teach . . .

Skating over to Ken, she kissed him deeply and returned to the ice. Since she hadn't been able to practice the routine along with everyone else, she took center stage doing her own thing, whatever came to mind. Abandoning their carefully rehearsed routine, the other skaters joined her in a delightful, flirtatious performance.

The large arena had been cut down the middle, separated by a partition. The grand reception was now in full swing. Hand in hand, Ken and Omunique walked into the exquisitely decorated room of the large reception hall. Placed in the center of a flower-decorated table was a huge ice sculpture carved in figures of a princess and a prince exchanging gold rings. Crystal vases of pink and white roses graced the other lacy-linen draped tables.

As the happy couple moved further into the room, Max stepped forward and smothered Omunique in his arms, kissing her face and hair. He then drew his son into the circle. "It is my prayer that you two will always be as one. No problem will ever be too big to solve when you let the Master be the head of your household. Always talk to each other even when you don't feel like talking. I love you and wish you every joy and success that life has to offer."

Seeing that Max was finished with his speech, Wyman opened his arms to Omunique. As she flew into his embrace, he held her, squeezing her tightly. Tears floated in his eyes. "My darling daughter, I don't know what my life is going to be like without you around the house, yet I know I'm so very happy for you. I'll always be here. I love you, my one and only daughter."

"Oh, Daddy," she cried, "I love you, too. I'll always love you. I love you so very much!"

Smiling with fatherly pride, Wyman turned to Ken. While giving him a huge bear hug, he patted him hard on the back. "Son, I'm counting on you. I am entrusting you with my most valuable and cherished treasure. I expect you to handle her with extreme care. She's precious and oh, so fragile. I know that you will be good to her, Ken."

"I will, Dad. You have my unbreakable word." Wyman's tears spilled over at Ken's sentiment. Ken put his arms around his father-in-law and hugged him. "We're all one big, happy family now. Omunique and I hope you two have spouses by the time we get back from our honeymoon." Ken's teasing remarks made Wyman and Max laugh.

The dancing commenced and both fathers danced with the bride before Ken had his chance to whirl Omunique over the floor in their second dance as husband and wife.

Beautifully dressed in a pink two-piece crepe suit, Omunique, readied for travel, joined up with Ken. Dressed in a dark sports coat, dress slacks, and a pink silk shirt, he looked as handsome as ever. Eager to get on with the honeymoon, they waited patiently as the group of seemingly neverending well-wishers continued to congratulate them.

Mamie, Frank, and Marion had their private moment with the newlyweds, voicing their love and joy for each. Ian and

Sara were busy keeping the press at bay but took time out to wish their dear friends a happy life together.

Omunique embraced Hillary with warmth. "You did a fantastic job with the songs! Thank you so much for offering to perform for us on our wedding day. You were wonderful and an absolute lifesaver. I hope we can get together when we return from our honeymoon."

Hillary squeezed Omunique with affection. "Congratulations to you and Ken! I felt honored to be a part of the ceremony. I'm glad Brandon and Ken got together again. I'm sure they'll keep in closer contact." Hillary turned to Brandon and smiled. "I'm sure they won't deprive you and me the chance of getting to know one another." Brandon smiled back at the woman he cherished.

Brandon gently embraced Omunique. "You can be certain of that. Ken and I will not be losing contact again. Congratulations to both of you!" Ken and Brandon embraced like long, lost friends, promising to stay in touch.

Omunique's coach, Brent Masters, Bruce Smith, her agent; Lamar Lyons, her attorney; and Jim Schmidt, another coach were all there to wish the couple well. Andy Tarpley, arena maintenance, and Claretha, his wife, and Teresa Banks, Mamie Gordon's best friend, were also in attendance. Thomasina Bridges, the secretary for Maxwell Corporation, and Jake Neilson, Omunique's choreographer, hadn't attended the wedding but were present at the reception, along with Dr. Wise, Omunique's sports physician. He hadn't attended the wedding, either. Ken's godparents, Ralph and Amanda Steele, wouldn't have missed the wedding and reception for the world.

Sara caught the tossed bridal bouquet and Frank ended up with the borrowed blue garter.

Ken hugged Omunique. "Good luck to those who caught the garter and the bouquet, but I made the luckiest catch of all. Omunique Philyaw, my very own Ice Princess!" Unable to contain his joy, he kissed his wife passionately on the mouth.

Once the photographer was through with his latest flurry of photos, the couple was followed outside by the entire wedding party. Before disappearing inside the waiting limousine, a cache of brightly colored butterflies was released into the air. Ken and Omunique couldn't believe their eyes. Marion and Frank had arranged for the butterflies as a special gift to the newlyweds.

The entire group stood in front of the arena as Omunique and Ken disappeared inside the white stretch limousine. The windows were heavily tinted denying Wyman and Max a last glimpse of their only children's happy faces, children who were now adults, children who had entered into the sanctity of marriage. A marriage that would hopefully last forever . . .

The white stretch pulled away from the curb and entered the nearby freeway ramp. Ecstatic, Omunique couldn't get enough of the potent kisses her new husband smothered her with.

Eyes wide with wonder, she gasped for breath. "Can you believe we're actually married?"

"Legally, yes, but I've been soulfully married to you since the first night you gave yourself to me. Omunique, if you hadn't agreed to marry me, I would've never been able to forgive myself."

Sadness touched her eyes. Perplexed by his comments, she ran her fingers through his hair. "Forgive yourself for what, Ken?"

"For taking your innocence so carelessly, for risking your precious life and your career. After each time we made love, I swore I'd never let it happen again. But I did, again and again. When you touch me, my thoughts are paralyzed by your tenderness. Every second that I went without making a commitment to you, I cheated you. Now that I've made it right, know this, I don't believe in divorce, as I've told you before. The commitment I just made to you is for life."

Posturing in disbelief, she leaned back to take a good look at Ken. "This should be the happiest day of our lives, yet you're sounding anything but happy. Did you only marry me to make an honorable woman of me?"

He sighed. "I guess I brought that on myself. I married you because I love you, because I can't and don't want to have a life devoid of your presence. Now kiss me so I can stop rambling on like a silly fool."

Her expression was smug. "You're no fool, Mr. Maxwell. You married me! Had you let me get away, I might consider you a darn fool. But you're a very wise young man."

"And you're a very wise young woman, Mrs. Maxwell. Ah, Mrs. Maxwell. How I love the sound of that!" She loved it, too, especially the smile it brought to his eyes and lips when he rolled out her new name.

Five

Looking extremely happy with one another, Ken and Omunique boarded a private plane bound for the continent of Asia. While Maxwell Corporation often leased out a private plane for overseas business trips, this time, Max and Wyman had gone in together to pay the honeymoon expenses, and Max had personally handpicked the crew. A crew that both he and Ken knew very well and had flown with on numerous occasions.

Once he'd made sure that Omunique was comfortably seated, Ken went up to the cockpit to talk to the two black pilots, Captain Jasper McKnight and his copilot, Kendall Beverly. McKnight was one good looking, fair-skinned man in his late thirties. Beverly was very handsome in a rugged kind of way. He had a dark, smoky complexion.

After a few minutes of animated conversation, Ken returned to his wife, disappointed at finding her asleep. It had been a long day and they'd had very little sleep over the past week. Picking up a magazine, Ken sat across from Omunique, careful not to disturb her. When the aircraft took off, she wasn't even aware of it. Although he busied himself leafing through the gazette, his thoughts were on his new bride. Lowering the publication, he glanced over at her sleeping figure, mesmerized by her gentle beauty. Their lives were one now. She was his to take care of from this day forward. He knew his strength could carry the extra weight, gladly so.

Never dreaming that he would ever be married, he marveled at how quickly she'd unwittingly altered his single status. A happy confirmed bachelor was now a deeply satisfied married man. Gently, he touched the band of solid gold encircling his finger. Just like the solid band of gold, their marriage would be strong, precious, and unbroken. Their life would be complete, happy, forever after . . .

Slowly, Omunique opened her eyes. Looking around for Ken, she spotted him stretched out in the seat across the aisle. She smiled. "Hi, husband."

He'd barely heard her softly spoken greeting, but he'd read her lips. "Hi, wife. I see that you flaked on me. That's okay since you're going to get very little sleep in the next couple of weeks. I intend to ravish you."

She giggled at the seductive implications. "That's if I don't seduce you first." She rubbed her arms. "I'm cold. I need your warmth," she whispered across the aisle. That was all he needed to hear, coupled with the vulnerable look on her face. Before she could bat an eye, he was holding her against his body, brushing her lips with a tenderness that nearly brought tears to her eyes.

Many hours after crossing the International Dateline, the Gulfstream V touched down safely on the runway of the Narita Airport, Tokyo, Japan, and taxied to the facility's private terminal. The couple was lost somewhere in the clouds when Kendall Beverly walked up quietly.

He cleared his throat. "Excuse me, but you two have a limousine waiting." Then and only then did the Maxwells realize that they were no longer alone.

"This is one overseas trip that certainly seemed quick." Ken had a huge smile on his face. "I could've sworn we were still flying."

Kendall laughed. "You were, my man. You were." Reaching over Ken, Kendall briefly placed his hand on Omunique's. "Hello, Mrs. Maxwell. I'm Kendall Beverly, the copilot. It's nice to finally meet you. I'm sorry I was so busy with instrument checks when you first boarded. Congratulations on your marriage and your Olympic medal winning performance! I hope you and Ken will be very happy."

Omunique liked the quiet strength of Kendall Beverly. She also liked the sincerity she saw in his deeply set ebony eyes. "Its nice to meet you, too, Kendall. Thank you. I'd be honored if you would refer to me as Omunique or simply Nique. Whichever you prefer."

"That's very generous of you, Omunique. I hope your new husband won't mind." Kendall flashed a strong white smile at Ken.

"No, her new husband won't mind. And if he did, it wouldn't matter. Omunique Philyaw-Maxwell has always been her own woman." Admiring her personable ways, her husband kissed her gently. "Come on, Omunique, lets get to our hotel. Our time meter is rapidly ticking away."

Kendall helped Ken to gather up their belongings and assisted in getting them out to the limousine. Jasper McKnight waited at the door of the plane. He, too, congratulated Omunique, letting her know how happy he was for them. Jasper also stated that he thought she'd won the gold. Smiling sweetly, she thanked him for his kind remarks. Though a lot of people had expressed the same sentiment, she didn't allow it to become an issue . . . nor did she encourage further dialogue.

After Ken and the pilots briefly went over the travel schedules again, customs formalities were realized, and then farewells were said. Omunique and Ken slid into the car and the limousine driver sped toward their hotel located in Tokyo's fascinating *Shinjuku* district, the city's center of business, shopping, and entertainment. That's where they'd spend the first several nights of their honeymoon. Several other exotic Japanese cities would play host to the Maxwells before their return to the United States.

The small but highly polished Park Hyatt Hotel awaited its newest arrivals. The honeymoon suite had been available when Ken's travel agent had called for reservations. Wanting no interruptions whatsoever, Ken had advised only Max and Wyman of where they'd be staying.

Once the check-in was complete, Ken lifted his bride and carried her to the elevator. The English-speaking Japanese bellhop trailed behind. Seeing how cozy the newlyweds were, the hotel attendant decided to use the service elevator, hoping to be out of the way before the couple arrived at the suite.

Inside the elevator, Ken took liberty with Omunique's moist mouth. She moaned and whispered terms of endearment against his gently probing lips. He carried her out of the elevator and over the threshold of the already open door of their suite. Before standing her on her feet, he kissed her deeply.

"Mrs. Maxwell, this is our new home for the next several days. I'm at your disposal from now until forever. What is your pleasure, Princess Maxwell?"

She purred, "Do you have to ask? I thought you knew my every whim, Mr. Maxwell."

"Say no more, sweetheart. I can read the script in those lovely eyes of yours. Oh, boy, when you look at me like that, I have a hard time containing myself."

"Hush-up, Ken," she softly commanded. "My libido is going crazy . . . and selfcontainment is the last thing I want you to exercise." He laughed, sealing his lips with a zipperlike gesture.

He lifted Omunique and carried her into the bedroom, where he set her on the edge of the bed. They were so caught up in the heat of passion that they barely noticed the luxurious surroundings. The spacious suite had an exotic flair, done in highly lacquered dark and light bamboo woods, and rich, bright colors, and intricate designs representative of the Asian culture. Beautiful Japanese figurines graced the mantel over the fireplace and several wonderful works of Far East art graced the walls.

Kneeling down in front of her, Ken lifted her foot and removed one shoe and then the other. Bringing the soles of her feet level with his mouth, he kissed the bottom of the right foot and then the left one. In one gentle motion, he pushed her pink dress up around her waist. He peeled the hosiery off her legs slowly and ran kisses up and down their nudity. With eyes closed, Omunique did her very best to survive the heated seduction.

His lips searched and discovered her weakest spots, making her gasp with pleasure. Her small hands wrestled with the buttons on his silk shirt. As she buried her lips in the thick mass of curly chest hair, he reached around to her back unzipping the dress and slipping it over her head. Carelessly, he tossed it aside. The only article she wore under the dress was a pair of white silk bikinis. Her nude upper body afforded him easy access to her luscious, creamy breasts. Immediately, he drew one into his mouth, biting gently down on the nipple. She screamed out from the shards of pleasure rippling through her. The wonderful sensations made her cry out for more.

He possessed her mouth with all the fire and desire within him. "I love you so much."

"Love me, Ken," she softly encouraged. "Love me the way that only you can. I'm your wife now. Withhold no good thing from me!" His heart thundered like a runaway freight train. Her seductive words excited him even more as he swept away the last vestiges of their clothing.

His fingers slid inside of her, causing her to writhe without control. Her fingers tenderly took the pulse of his wildly throbbing manhood. Feeling the satin beneath them, Ken reached out and moved the spread to one side. He then placed his wife in the center of the ivory softness.

Drawing him down next to her, she stroked him passionately. As he traced her navel with his tongue, she entangled her fingers in his satiny curls, tugging gently, causing thrilling sensations to ripple through his scalp. Knowing they had all night and the rest of their lives, he slowly burned his way into her soul. She was crying softly now, begging him to put her out of her misery; the misery of wanting him so bad that it hurt . . .

Like a sleek panther, he crouched over her, entering her with a titillating, snail-like pace, which nearly drove her insane. Arching her back, lifting her lower body, she raised up to meet the full length of him. Dazed with passion, she welcomed him to her very private, warm home, a warm home that was exclusively his.

She clawed at his back as he smoothly glided in and out of her secluded abode. Withdrawing, reentering, time and time again, he teased her until she could stand it not a second longer. Holding him prisoner with the power of her athletically built legs, she moved under him with a fiery passion that made him scream out her name, sweetly, passionately. He loved the fury she unleashed under him, matching her impassioned fury with his own frenzied strokes. The spirited rhythms of her gyrating body were exotic, exquisite, nothing less than flesh tingling.

Unable to hold back her release, she exploded into a trembling fireball, crying out his name in a strangled voice. He exploded along with her, savoring the thrilling flood of sensations coursing through him like a raging river spilling over its banks. Burying his face in her thick mane of hair, he whispered his undying love for her.

The marriage had been deliciously consummated . . .

The early morning found the Maxwells stretched out across the bed, planning the activities for the day. Omunique wore a special gift from Ken, a white pure-silk gown and

Kimono-style robe that had been handmade. While Omunique slept, he'd gone down to the lobby and secretly purchased it in the hotel's gift shop before it had closed the
previous evening.

Omunique couldn't make up her mind which attraction
she wanted to see first. She wasn't sure if she wanted to
go to distant Mount Fuji or spend the day scanning the
fabulous *Shinjuku* department stores. Ken was more interested in visiting one of the lovely Japanese gardens, but he
wanted Omunique to make the first choice. He'd promised
to go shopping with her before they'd gotten married, but
he wasn't too keen on it at the moment.

Omunique laid down the colorful brochure she was holding. "You know, I think we should just take the days as
they come. The reason I wanted to come here was to experience the real flavor of this mysterious country. I was
so little when Dad brought me here that I hardly remember
anything, only what he's told me. Can we just venture out
and see where it takes us? We're on our honeymoon and I
want to concentrate mainly on us. I'm plain tired of rigor-
ous schedules, plans, and difficult decision-making proc-
esses. I have to return to that world soon enough as it is."

"I think that's the best idea yet. We've already ordered
room service. As soon as we eat, we can get dressed. We're
right in the heart of some of the most exciting action Tokyo
has to offer. Covering a fraction of what the *Shinjuku* district has to offer will be one huge adventure in itself."

The sudden but not unexpected knock on the door had
Ken looking around for his robe since he was totally nude.
"I knew they were coming, but not this quickly." Omunique
laughed as he jumped up from the bed and scrambled to
make himself presentable.

In a matter of seconds, Ken had signed the service bill.
The waiter then placed the dishes on the lovely set table.
Ken and Omunique washed their hands before seating
themselves.

Now, seated across from one another, Omunique bowed her head as Ken passed the blessing. Not quite ready to try out the local cuisine, they'd ordered a traditional American breakfast consisting of scrambled eggs, toast, cold cereal and a variety of fresh fruits.

Already sectioned for her, Omunique scooped out a chunk of ruby-red grapefruit, wondering if the fruit was an import. Much to her surprise, the grapefruit was much sweeter than she'd anticipated. After taking out another juicy chunk, she held the spoon up to Ken's mouth. "This is so sweet and juicy."

He took a moment to savor the taste. "You're right. It's sweet, but not nearly as sweet as the taste of you."

He still had the ability to make her blush. "Want another taste of me to make an accurate comparison?" Her eyes flirted openly with him, offering him yet another challenge.

Before she could take another breath, he was kneeling before her, to in fact taste the sweetness of the woman he couldn't get enough of. With breakfast forgotten, Ken carried his wife back to bed, ravishing her as he'd earlier promised.

The late afternoon found the Maxwells in the midst of the hustle and bustle of picturesque *Shinjuku's* busy shopping district. The click-clock of old traditional Japanese *geta,* thong style foot apparel, could still be heard on the busy streets of modern times. Intent on hearing more clearly, Omunique stopped to listen to the rhythmic striking of the *geta* against the cement.

"Can you hear that, Ken?"

"Hear what?"

"The clicking noises made by the old-style wooden shoes still worn by many of the Japanese people. They have such a rhyming beat to them. Listen closely. Do you hear it now?"

"I can hear it—and I now see what you mean." Looking down at the feet of those passing by, he got a glimpse of the sandal style shoe. "There goes a pair, and another," he pointed out to his wife who wore a wondrous expression.

"Daddy was right about the spiritual feel of this country. I feel sort of a beckoning to my soul here in this spot. It's a very peaceful feeling."

"When you're at peace, I feel at peace." He moved toward the small Japanese restaurant to peruse the menu displayed in the window, written in both English and Japanese. "Are you ready for a bite of lunch?"

She came up beside him and looked at the menu. "I'm hungry, but I'd like to experience something Dad told me that I found intriguing. He told me about purchasing a *bento,* which is a boxed lunch, from the basement of one of the department stores. We can then take it to one of the nearby parks or gardens to eat it. Just another tradition-steeped idea according to Dad."

"Sounds okay to me. There's a pretty big department right store across the street. Let me take a good look at the Japanese translation pronunciation guide while we make our way over there. I probably won't get it right, but I hope to stay somewhere in the ballpark."

She touched her husband's hand. "English is a required second language for the Japanese people, with the exception of possibly some of the much older generations. I'm sure you'll be understood. After we eat, I'd like to check out the shopping lanes at the Nakamise Arcade. I want to take this city at a slow and easy pace. Our schedules are going to return to hectic all too soon."

Seated on a park bench under a large tree, Omunique yawned. "I could use a good nap right about now. The noodles and meat dumplings were good, but I'll be ready for something a lot more filling than that come dinnertime. Eat and sleep is about all we've really done since we arrived."

Ken raised an eyebrow. "I know for a fact that's not *all* we've done. But I guess our lovemaking does speak to appetite, a voracious one, no less. We've practically devoured each other since we set foot in the hotel suite. Our hormones are definitely out of control."

"Doesn't sound like too bad of a thing to me. We *are* on our honeymoon, you know."

He gave her a knowing look. "Yeah, but we'd better be a little more careful since we decided to wait at least a year or so before considering having our first child. Though I know you're on oral contraceptives, I haven't used protection since we got married. I've also noticed that we've been more spontaneous because of it. I can't tell you how I hated to stop and fumble around with putting those damn condoms on, but that was something we couldn't think of ignoring. To give us a little more insurance, since the pill isn't foolproof, either, I should probably continue to use them."

"Maybe we should just let things happen naturally." She gave Ken a thoughtful glance. "Preplanning a family is fine, but I love making love to you without worrying whether I might get pregnant. I did a lot of that before, especially with my career at stake. Our lovemaking seems more natural now and I like it much better that way. I'm totally relaxed when we come together intimately. I don't want that to change. I'm more turned on without the worry."

Though he smiled at her last comment, Ken looked somewhat puzzled. "Are you saying that you won't mind it if you should happen to get pregnant right away?"

Omunique grinned. "Are you saying that you would?"

He smiled wryly. "I think we should discuss this matter in a more private setting. There are people all over this park."

"Sounds like you have a little more in mind than just a discussion. Am I right?"

His eyes openly seduced her. "All this talk about us getting pregnant, which comes as a result of making passionate love, has me a bit worked up over here. Do you want to feel what I'm talking about? I've also got the visual thing going in spades . . ."

She threw her head back in laughter. "I don't have to do that to know what you're saying since I can see it. If you stand up right now, you're going to really embarrass yourself. Your soldier is already standing at attention. It may start saluting in front of all these people if you don't get a grip on those visuals. Take a few deep breaths, honey." Her loud laughter rode into the wind, causing those sitting nearby to take a covert look in their direction.

Ken laughed, too. "You mesmerize me." He kissed her hard on the mouth. "But we'd better get going on our sightseeing expedition. We have a lot of territory yet to cover."

"Okay, if you insist, but I'd rather just lie here and watch these fascinating people. I'm surprised at the near-even mixture of those wearing western clothing and the traditional garb. But it seems to be mostly the elders wearing the native style of dress."

After helping Omunique up from the carpet of grass, the couple strolled across the street and joined the lively throng of local shoppers and foreign tourists. Rows and rows of colorful goods were all laid out in many different styles of bins and on hanging racks. Omunique loved the feel of the raw silk beneath her fingers. When she couldn't make up her mind which patterns she liked best, she ended up purchasing several bolts of fabric in an array of prints and solids. Aunt Mamie was an excellent seamstress and Omunique knew she'd be happy to fashion her a few articles of clothing out of the rich fabrics she'd chosen.

Omunique pointed out a group of leather backpacking young children wearing plaid uniforms and yellow hats. The boys wore black backpacks and the girls wore red. "I guess the U.S. schools are not the only ones that believe in the uniform. It certainly keeps things simple."

"You can say that again. With so many American kids being killed over wearing apparel, especially in the inner cities, I think it's a wise choice."

The better part of their day was spent shopping and discovering the everyday life and the numerous rituals of the Japanese people. Tokyo appeared to be an industrious city of happy, hardworking people. More excitement went on in *Shinjuku* than any other place, which was known as the engine of Tokyo. While visiting there, Ken and Omunique learned that Shinjuku Gyoen Park, boasting French, English, and Japanese gardens, was one of the most delightful places to visit during cherry blossom time.

With 15,000 pachinko parlors, a pinball machine–like game, those numbers easily made Tokyo one of the largest gambling cities in the world. Before ending the shopping spree, Omunique was in possession of several exquisite Japanese silk fans, which she hoped to display throughout their new home once one was purchased. The arrival of evening found the newlyweds back in the hotel soaking in a hot-springs bath known simply as *onsen*.

Seated on the sofa, Ken tossed his arm around Omunique's shoulders. "We've had a full day and an even busier evening."

She looked over at the bed. "Can't wait to go to sleep. That hot springs bath was so relaxing. I don't know how we've managed to stay awake."

"Sitting here talking about all the colorful sights of Tokyo's nightlife is probably what did the trick. You want some tea before calling it a night?"

"That sounds like a must-do ritual. The tea is certainly nothing like what we drink at home. It's also a lot stronger than what we're used to."

Ken nodded. "For sure. Go ahead and get ready for bed. I'll place a call to room service. Do you want something to snack on?"

"I think I saw vegetarian egg rolls on the menu. As small as they are, I could eat a few of those."

"One dozen egg rolls and a pot of hot tea coming right up."

"One more request," she called out from the bathroom.

"What's that?"

"Another night of sensuous lovemaking between the bride and groom."

He grinned. "That's a sure thing."

Omunique's apparent change of heart in regards to having a child had come as surprise to Ken when she'd brought it up earlier. She seemed happy as a lark for them to start a family right away, but not so long ago she'd made an impressive case for waiting a year or two. He had to agree with her about their lovemaking. It was more relaxed and less rushed, but the fulfillment had always been right up there in the midst of heaven. Even now, as he thought about loving her, he could almost hear the angels singing with joy. Wasn't it too early for them to hope for a family? Perhaps it was. Omunique needed to experience the pro circuit before she settled down into motherhood with all its never-ending responsibilities. He certainly didn't want her to come to resent her decision, or him, a short time into pregnancy. He'd bring the subject up again later, but now wasn't the right time. When Omunique made a decision it was hard to sway her otherwise.

She nudged him playfully. "Where are you? Usually it's me that's out to lunch. You seem to have a lot on your mind. Anything wrong?"

As if it were magnetized, his hand was drawn to her breast. "Just one of those visual things again. I was just thinking about our lovemaking. When you nudged me, I was getting ready to make love to you under the Santa

Monica Pier, on a blanket, lying beneath the brilliant stars." His hand closed around her breast, squeezing gently. "I'm ready to turn that visual into something more tangible. Come here and satisfy my cravings for your delicious body. Let's make love."

She began to remove his robe. "How about in the shower? Let's reenact that scene in *Stella,* the one where Taye Diggs redefines erotica."

He silenced her with a drugging kiss. "I'm feeling you."

The remaining days and nights of Omunique and Ken's honeymoon led them to one fascinating attraction after another: Mt. Fuji, Hakone, Mashima, Kyoto, Osaka, and several other main attractions. The numerous Japanese destinations were reached by using the local bullet trains and buses. A couple of destinations were reached by air and a limousine was also used on a few of the sightseeing excursions.

After traveling along the scenic road to Mishima, the couple boarded the bullet train bound for Kyoto. Ancient Kyoto was the imperial capital of Japan for over a thousand years. Surrounded by scenic hills to the west, north and east, the city reigned from 794 to 1868 as the cultural and artistic center of the nation and was also known for its more than 1,600 Buddhist temples and 270 Shinto shrines.

High on top of beautiful Mt. Fuji, Ken and Omunique found that beautiful views and photo opportunities were practically endless. A cruise of Lake Hakone was followed by a cable car ride up Mt. Komaga, where panoramic views were also breathtaking.

The late afternoon found them settled in a quaint hotel in Osaka, where they later paid a visit to the city's landmark, the majestic Osaka Castle. Here in Osaka, they also enjoyed a night of engaging entertainment in a Kabuki theater.

On the fourteenth day of their honeymoon, Omunique and Ken bid farewell to the rich cultures of Japan and later boarded the private jet that would take them back to the United States.

Six

The grass felt cool beneath Omunique's bare feet as she scrunched her toes into the ground, loving the feel of the earth. The large tree she and Ken sat under provided adequate shade for their outdoor luncheon. The sun was still high, even though the air was cool and brisk.

Ken poured two cups of hot chocolate from the thermos. "Can you believe that the building of our dream house has come so far in just a short span of time? Do you still like the lot we've chosen?"

Omunique's eyes widened. "Like it? I love it. I can't believe we've been able to sit here time after time and watch our very own house being built. As for your friend, Brandon, he really seems to know what he's doing as an architect. You seem to know him so well, but I've never heard you mention him until the night of our surprise parties."

"I've known Blair since high school, but sometimes it gets hard to keep up with your old friends. Until the night of the bachelor party at Frank's place, I hadn't seen Brandon in several months. I knew that he had turned out to be a great architect. It seems like he came back into my life at the right time, especially with us deciding to custom build. In just a few weeks, we'll be calling this very spot home. And we owe all the rapid progress in building to Brandon."

"Yes, the man who's engaged to superstar Hillary Houston."

"I have both of her music CDs. He said that she'd probably feel honored to sing at our wedding, after he learned we hadn't gotten anyone yet. Want to go to one of her future concerts?"

"Is it even possible to get tickets? I hear the girl's always a sellout."

Ken grinned. "They're going to invite us to the upcoming L.A. performance as special guests. Blair says they've been engaged over a year now. They plan to marry this summer."

"Wow! That's super. Maybe we'll even get an invitation to their wedding."

"Now that he and I are back in close contact, I'm sure we will. I guess I should warn you that a rapper is the opening act for the L.A. concert. He calls himself Justified."

"Justified! I like his style. I have his CD *The Caliway*. Why did you think you had to warn me? Why a *warning* of all things?"

"You're the last person that I ever thought would listen to rap. Besides, I've never heard you play it in all the time we've been together. It looks like we'll always be learning new things about one another. Rap is often an unsavory style of music. The cursing and disrespect to women and all is what bothers me the most. But I guess there are some respectful rappers."

"That bothers me, too. When I heard one of Justified's cuts on the radio, I really liked it. But I didn't learn he was a rapper until after the song played. This particular song was a love duet. I saw that he was really versatile, so I went out and bought the CD to see what else he had to offer. There's a mixture of stuff on there. He even has a gospel rap called *Late Night Talks*. Now I love that one. While there is some cursing on the album, it's nothing like some of the extremely vulgar stuff I've heard. I'd love to see him in concert. He has to be good if he's opening for a megastar like Hillary. He also has a great video for his song entitled "Rock With You," which is just another piece that showcases his versatility. I may have Jake choreograph a skating routine using some of his songs. I need to show that I can be versatile, too, especially with so many special events that come up in the professional arena. I think it would go over big with the younger audiences. Sometimes you have to look past the cursing in rap to really get the messages being conveyed. This young brother has written some really deep lyrics."

"It would also be a very bold move on your part. I haven't seen one single skater use rap in their routine. I kind of like the idea. You'll have to let me listen to this CD when we get home so I can see what you're raving about."

"You're on." Omunique rested her hand on her outstretched legs. "It's so peaceful way up here on top of this hill. I'm so glad that we decided to build here in Rancho Palos Verdes. We're still close enough to Los Angeles and less than a two-hour drive to Lake Arrowhead, where I'll do most of my professional training. I'm also hoping that we don't have to cut down all these beautiful trees. It'll be nice to have them as part of the landscape."

"It's three acres of practically nothing but forest, Omunique. Some more of these trees will have to go, but we'll make good use of them. For sure, they'll come in handy as firewood."

He saw that she still didn't look too happy regarding cutting down the trees. "Come here and let me hold you. Our future is coming together so nicely. I want to share this very touching moment with you wrapped up tightly in my arms."

Omunique scooted across the blanket and nestled her head against his shoulder. His arms tightened around her waist as his lips met with hers.

"This is so nice." She looked up into his eyes. "Do you think we'll always be as happy as we are right now?"

"Even happier, if I have my way. You're the red and gold

bows on the total package that I've been putting together and wrapping up for years. We'll be happy because we respect each other first as human beings, as professionals. Most importantly, we respect each other as man and woman, husband and wife. I can't see that ever changing. We've had some bad miscommunications in the past, but I believe we now have those tackled. The separations are going to be the hardest when you're on tour. You in one city and me in another aren't soothing thoughts, but we'll overcome that, as well. The Olympics seem so long ago."

"Not that long ago, my love. Once we realize our dream of owning and operating an ice arena—that will keep me closer to home for a long while. I've come up with so many ideas for the arena that's it's hard to wait for it to happen. Hopefully the endorsements will start to pour in, at least one or two megadeals. You have great ideas, too. That's why we're so good together."

"Hmm, those words have a familiar ring to them."

She nodded. "Yeah, I remember you telling me that not long after we started dating."

Passion blazed in his eyes. This happened every time he looked at her, every time he thought of her, especially when they were apart. He loved making love to her, anywhere and everywhere. Their souls had a way of connecting. In fact, every fiber of their being connected whether making love or not. She had matured in the physical sense—in many delectable ways.

"I know that look, Ken. You're making me hot. But I hear that the sex drive between married couples dwindles after the first five years. What do you think?"

"I don't, since we have eighteen hundred and twenty-five days of lovemaking before we have to decide one way or the other. Multiply that number by three times a day and we won't have time to think about it. I don't see it happening. We have so much more going for us than just a physical relationship. That's what I was talking about and that's why my eyes flare with passion every time I think of you, of us." He never had a problem expressing himself to her.

"I get those same feelings. When I'm skating to a romantic piece of music, I think of you, of making love to you, of you making love to me. Do you remember the first time we actually made love?" She closed her eyes to capture the image of the most wonderful night of her life.

"Every minute detail. Though you tried to be blasé about it, I know you were scared to death of us coming together in such an intimate way." He rubbed her arms. "I'll never forget the look on your face when I first asked you to help me put the condom on that time."

She blushed hotly. "Don't remind me of that. I felt so embarrassed. I couldn't imagine anyone ever being that intimate with another, but I do have to admit that I enjoyed it tremendously. Boy, you had me smoking in my hot silk that night."

His eyes flared even brighter with unfettered passion. "I want to make love to you right here and now. Right here under this tree."

She batted her eyelashes. "Well, there's no one up here on this hill but us chickens. But it is a little chilly. However, you do pack the hottest heat in that magnificent body of yours."

"We've got an extra blanket in the car. How's that for being prepared for the unexpected, which you and I always seem to find ourselves in the midst of? I'll be right back."

"Hurry, Ken. The fire in my desire is increasing. Please hurry up, Ken."

Laughing, he jumped up and ran toward the Jeep. Quickly, he returned with the blanket and covered them both up. Beneath the covers, they stripped the lower half of their anatomies, taking time out for arousing foreplay. Ken's eager mouth found her erect nipples and he gave special attention to each one. As his tongue trailed a moist path from her breasts down to her thighs, the sudden crunching of tires atop the gravel brought them both up into a sitting position with a start. Immediately protective of her partial nudity, he pulled the blanket up high under her neck and held her close to him.

Ken looked perplexed. "What's that truck doing way up here? This is private property." He took a closer look at the vehicle. "Oh, it's from BDB Architectural."

"On a Sunday? I hope it's not Hillary and Brandon. They're going to think we're crazy."

Ken burst into a gale of laugher. "No, they'll just think that we're crazy in love."

"The truck is leaving," she whispered.

"And so are we. Let's get off this planet if only for a little while." Ken pressed Omunique's back down onto the blanket to continue the aborted journey to worlds unknown.

Stretched out beneath the old oak tree, Omunique and Ken had fallen asleep for a short time. Fully dressed now, they packed away the leftovers and folded the blanket.

Inside the Jeep Ken leaned across the console and kissed his wife on the forehead. "If Brandon was in that truck, I'm going to hear about our little hilltop rendezvous." He chuckled. "Yeah, he'll rib me but good on this one."

"Who cares? We're married. By the way, we need to get some milk before we go home. We have Aunt Mamie's chocolate fudge cake to try and polish off before she comes around with another delicious dessert."

"Only my favorite dessert, cake and milk. That is, outside of you."

She rolled her eyes at him. "Glad you amended that, Mr. Maxwell."

Each day of watching their house being built was an awesome experience for Omunique and Ken. While they only stayed a short time during each visit, they went there every weekend to see what progress had been achieved. Ken was thrilled to have Brandon Blair overseeing the entire project. On this particular project, Brandon even supervised those jobs he normally farmed out to other firms, because of the large volume of business his own firm received.

The Maxwell condo was cluttered with numerous decorating books. Omunique shook her head as she looked around at all the mess they'd made. Material swatches, wood samples, shutter styles, different types of moldings, ceiling and lighting fixtures, ideas for use on blocked glass, ceramic and marble tile selections, kitchen and bathroom counters, and dozens of color charts for selecting shades of paints and enamels had nearly buried the living room.

Seated on the sofa next to Ken, Omunique turned the page on one of the sample books. "Wow, I didn't realize there were so many choices in interior decorating samples, materials, and colors. How are we going to make all these decisions? This is a lot to take on."

"Don't worry, we'll get it done. We have Brandon and Marion to guide us through all this stuff we don't know beans about. Brandon says to select our choices and he'll explain what we've chosen and advise us on other choices if he thinks there's a better alternative. Don't worry too much about prices, Nique, since this will probably be our first and last home. Besides, you can spend some of those megabucks you're getting from the Maxwell Corporation endorsement," he joked, making her laugh. "Brandon says he purchases a lot of his materials from a great place called The Kitchen Store, and that we can walk in and visually check out various displays of kitchens and take at look at a variety of decorating materials."

"Where's this place located?"

"Culver City. That's just a hop, skip, and a jump away."

"I guess we can also look at Home Depot and places like that."

"Yeah, we could, but I'd like to go on Brandon's recommendations when it actually comes to the purchases. Brandon's a valued customer at The Kitchen Store, which helps him secure the best deals around, according to him. Most of these brochures came from there."

"I love the way these new-style shutters can be easily opened and closed. What about us ordering them in antique white?"

"Antique white is always a nice complement to any color scheme." Ken grinned at how easily she'd made her first choice. "That was painless, now wasn't it?"

"Yeah, it was. I guess once I get into it, it won't seem so difficult. From looking at all these detailed brochures, I can actually visualize what they'll look like in our house." She giggled. "I'm getting excited all over again. This might be a lot of fun for us. But I certainly felt intimidated on the first look at so many items to choose from."

"It's going to be great fun. Do we want shutters in all the rooms, Nique?"

"Just the bedrooms and the rooms we'll use for offices and relaxation; like the family room and the den. As I think about it, I really wouldn't mind having them on all the windows that are low and within easy reach. I don't see the point in having them on the windows that no one can reach without a ladder."

Ken couldn't keep from laughing. "Windows that no one can reach, or those *you* can't reach, Mrs. Maxwell?"

"Whatever, man! We *do* have some windows that are way up high. Windows that not even *you* and your six-feet-plus can reach, so there."

"Okay, don't go getting all bent out of shape. Just teasing. And this is just the beginning of a long process. We won't need to cover the higher windows since they're designed to bring in an abundance of natural sunlight."

"Exactly. And I'm not bent out of shape. I know you were only having fun at my expense." She leaned over and kissed him. "I enjoy doing this with you. With that said,

I'm still not sure if we want to go with the traditional drapery in the formal areas. What do you think?"

"That's your department, Nique. Drapes are a lot of trouble, especially when it comes to taking them down and sending them out for cleaning . . . and then putting them back up. We have to take our busy schedules into consideration when it comes to maintaining our house. Low maintenance items work for me. You could possibly order some fancier shutters and window dressings that will allow you to eliminate the drapes."

Smiling devilishly, Omunique raised an eyebrow. "That was sure a lot of input for it being *my* so-called department. Great input, though. I'll look through some of the window dressing brochures to see what else we can do in place of drapes. Thin sheers may be a good option, but that still requires putting up and taking down to clean. We should go for decors that we won't easily tire of. I don't see us redecorating for at least five to ten years."

"What about wallpaper for some of the rooms, Nique?"

After picking up the wallpaper selections, she opened the book and quickly thumbed through it. She pointed to one sample. "What about this marble effect? Or this nice linen-look for the bathrooms?"

"With four and one-half baths we can go half-and-half, Nique. I'd like to do the solid wallpaper in marble and linen and use bold borders. I can see just borders in the kitchen, too. It might make a nice contrast for white semigloss walls."

"As long as they're colorful, Ken. I like a really bright kitchen. It picks up my mood when cooking, especially after I burn something." They both laughed. "I like lavenders and deep purples but I think I'd get tired of that in a hurry."

"I like simple black and white with a sunny yellow to brighten things. We can order black appliances and black and white ceramic tile, or even Corian counters, which is a lot more expensive but it's darn good stuff. Something like a salt and peppered Corian may be a lot less dramatic than ceramic tile. Visualizing black and white checkerboard tiles has me rethinking my choice. But I guess we don't have to go for the checkerboard effect."

She kissed his cheek. "Black and white is a nice decorating touch, but I don't think so for the kitchen. White and a soft yellow might be good. What do you think?"

"Sounds good, especially if we splash another softer color around with it. Perhaps a soft blue, pale lavender, or even a peach color might work. All this talk about kitchens is making me hungry. What about taking a break and having a piece of that chocolate cake? The milk we just bought should be pretty cold by now."

"Okay, in just a second. I think your idea about the borders is a good one. We could do the yellow and white and use some of the colors you mentioned for the borders."

"You got my vote. Now let's wash up and hit the kitchen."

After placing a huge chunk of cake in front of Ken, Omunique joined him at the table. The doorbell rang before she had a chance to get settled in. Not expecting anyone, they looked at one another with puzzled expressions.

Omunique shrugged her shoulders. "I'll get it. I know you can't wait another minute to delve into that piece of chocolate cake. Your expression said it all when the doorbell rang."

He grinned. "You're just too good at reading my expressions. I'm going to have to find a way to fake you out."

"Just don't end up faking yourself out in the process, Mr. Maxwell. The truth is that you read me just as well as I do you."

The doorbell pealed again and she took off running, leaving her husband looking somewhat amazed. Astonished at the fact that they had grown to know each other so very well.

Much to Omunique's surprise, not to mention utter shock, Aunt Mamie stood on the other side of the door. What actually shocked her was that she was with Max instead of Wyman.

Mamie saw Omunique's shocked expression and wondered if they'd interrupted a golden moment. She had totally misinterpreted her godchild's look. "Hey, did we come at a bad time?"

Omunique had a hard time finding her voice . . . and she had to clear her throat to do so. "No, no . . . not at all. We were just sitting down to enjoy a piece of that cake you brought us."

Max stepped inside after Mamie. Taking his daughter-in-law in his arms, he kissed and hugged her with deep affection. "Where's your hero?"

"In the kitchen. Come join us, Aunt Mamie and Daddy-Max."

Max loved the endearing name Omunique had dubbed him with. Since she simply called Wyman daddy, she had explained to Max that she didn't like to use the term father. It wasn't endearing enough, so she'd asked if he'd mind if she just called him Daddy-Max. He'd had no objections whatsoever to it. She made it sound like a very loving term of endearment.

Ken's shocked expression was more obvious than Omunique's had been. Seeing his father with Mamie was certainly a welcome change from Courtesy Evans, but he couldn't help worrying about what Wyman might think. While he knew there wasn't exactly a romantic liaison between the two, he somehow thought that something wonderful might happen between them in the future. For that matter, Omunique had been hoping the same thing for some time.

The two elder comrades sat down at the table while Omunique hurried about the business of cutting them a piece of cake and pouring two more glasses of cold milk. Once her tasks were completed, she joined everyone else at the table.

Ken eyed Mamie and Max with a mixture of curiosity and humor. "So, what brings you two out here to our little beach condo this evening?"

Mamie smiled sweetly. "Mr. Maxwell just happened to call to see if I was busy. He wanted to see you two and he thought I might like to come along, as well. I wasn't busy so I accepted his invitation. But Omunique's expression at the door had me worried. I thought we might've interrupted an intimate moment. We must remember to call first from now on."

Ken grinned. "Our moments together are always intimate, but we just happened to be in the process of getting ready to devour some of this sumptuous dessert you baked for us. We were visiting our lot earlier and then we stopped by the store and got some milk on our way home."

Max's eyes affectionately encompassed Omunique and his son. "You two love visiting the building site, don't you?" Smiling, they both nodded in agreement. "I imagine it's a wonderful thing to watch your first house being built from the ground up. How's it coming?"

"Everything is going great and the builders are actually ahead of schedule," Ken offered. "I think it's because my old friend, Brandon Blair, is overseeing the building of our house as if it were his own. I feel really blessed to have hooked up with him again. He's a brilliant architect."

Omunique could barely contain her excitement as she told their guests about how the house had taken on so much shape in such a short time. She was also excited as she told them about the possibility of her and Ken going to one of Hillary's upcoming concerts.

Max shook his head. "I don't know how you two find so much time to do all these exciting things. When I was starting out as young executive, I couldn't seem to find enough hours in the day to do all the things I wanted to.

Julia spent many nights at home alone in the beginning of our marriage." Max's eyes saddened for a brief moment. "But I'm glad that it didn't stay that way for very long. I'm so happy that we got to spend so much quality time in the last years before her untimely death. Had I known I was going to lose Julia so soon, I would've never worked all those long hours. Having Julia with me played second to nothing in my life. Kids, please continue to make the most of each second you have together. I don't mean to put a damper on your fresh love, but just remember that no one knows what tomorrow will bring."

Mamie put her arms around Max's shoulder in a comforting way, in the way a friend would do. "I agree wholeheartedly with Max. Live each day as though there's no tomorrow." The widowed Mamie had never remarried, but she hadn't yet ruled out the possibility.

Ken reached across the table and hugged Max. "We promise not to forget." He then kissed his wife gently, as if to seal the promise he'd just made on her behalf.

No sooner than everyone began to eat the cake, the doorbell rang again. Ken stayed Omunique with a gentle hand to the right side of her shoulder when she started to get up to answer it. "I'll get it, sweetheart."

Omunique looked puzzled. "I wonder who that could be. We're getting the company today. This is so nice to have you all drop by like this. Aunt Mamie, the cake is divine."

"I second that," Max chimed in. Mamie smiled her thanks before giving a verbal one.

Ken had Wyman right behind him when he returned to the kitchen. Because they only had four chairs to the table set, Ken pulled up a stool from the breakfast bar. Though he tried to hide being stunned, Wyman's expression at seeing Max and Mamie seated at the kitchen table was the most priceless one yet.

"Well, look who's here." Wyman hugged Mamie and shook hands with Max. "It seems like we all had the same bright idea. I was reluctant to come up because I just called and didn't get an answer." Laughing, Omunique and Ken exchanged knowing glances.

"We admit to turning the phone ringers off early this morning." Ken didn't need to go into anymore detail than that since everyone appeared to know why the phone bells had been turned off in the first place. "Looks like we forgot to turn them back on."

Omunique blushed heavily. "Hey, you guys, remember that we're still newlyweds. Ken stole a do not disturb sign from one of the hotels in Japan. So if you ever see it on the front door, you'll know not to knock because we won't be answering." The elder three laughed at Omunique's blushing face, recognizing the flushing color of love often worn by a new bride.

"My son, a thief?" Max joked. "I thought I taught you better than that, Ken."

Ken shook his head. "At those hotel prices, not to mention the unbelievably uneven rate of money exchange from dollars to yen, I paid for that sign a few times over. I should've taken a few towels and those plush white guest robes. I feel like we paid for those a couple of times, too." He grinned. "But I guess I shouldn't be too proud of myself. It *was* stealing."

"At least it was only worthless paper." Wyman eyed the cake wistfully. "What about a slice of that chocolate delight for your other dear old dad. Mamie, you must have baked it, because I know Omunique is not that far along in the cooking classes Ken's been giving her."

Omunique shot her father a haughty look. "For your information, Aunt Mamie is the one that's going to teach me how to bake cakes like she does. Ken can do some baking, but nothing like this is going to come out of our kitchen."

"Ever," Ken interjected. "Aunt Mamie might teach you how to bake, but it will never taste like this. This divine piece of chocolate moistness can't ever be duplicated. This has Aunt Mamie's personal signature written all over it."

"Thank you, kids, for the compliments. But I think you're both right about what you've each said. People surely can be taught to cook and bake, but rarely does it come out as good as the teacher's products. It's not that I'd withhold any sort of recipe or cooking technique information from you, I've just been at it a lot longer. We develop our own special methods. As good as my baking is it can never compare with my mother's wonderful cooking skills."

Omunique kissed Wyman softly on the mouth as she placed the cake plate in front of him. "How was my mother at baking?"

Wyman closed his eyes expressively. "She was a wonderful cook, but not as good as my mother or hers. Mamie knows what she's talking about." Wyman turned to Ken. "How *are* the cooking lessons coming that you've been giving your wife?"

Ken laughed heartily, stopping abruptly when he saw the *I-dare-you-to-tell* look in his wife's beautiful gray eyes. "It's been going okay." Unable to help himself, Ken busted up with laughter. That made everyone more than just a little curious about what had been going on in their very modern kitchen.

"Come on," Max urged, "give us the skinny on the classes. We promise not to laugh."

Omunique sucked her teeth loud enough for everyone to hear it. "I'll tell you myself so that he doesn't over exaggerate, which he has a tendency to do. Especially when it's at my expense. I've burned everything that I cooked on the first try. And I do mean everything. On the fried foods, I let the grease get too hot. Or I set the oven up too high on the roasted foods. I thought that the meat would cook in half the time if I did so. I always left it up after Ken initially told me what temperature to turn it down to, after the higher temp sealed in the natural juices. Okay, everyone can laugh now. But I think I should warn you, you're all invited to dinner Sunday after next, when I get back from training camp. So I wouldn't laugh too hard since I'm the one doing all the cooking."

"Fabulous!" Clapping her palms together like the mother's character in the movie *Nutty Professor*, she gave everyone a sarcastically sweet smile. They did their best not to laugh too loud or for too long. However, no one could keep from laughing, period. Not even Omunique could keep her own laughter at bay.

Ken stood up and pulled Omunique out of her chair and into his arms. "You're so brave, my lovely heroine." He rained kisses all over her face. "Even I wouldn't have told them all that. That was quite a bit of information. Now that you've told them all the bad stuff, tell them how that second omelet of yours came out." Smiling at each other, they sat back down.

Enthusiastically, she clapped her hands again, beaming with excitement. "It was absolutely too die for! So fluffy and so full of cheese and fresh veggies was my great omelet that Ken mentioned how it simply melted in his mouth. And I did it all by myself. In fact, Kenneth Maxwell Jr. wasn't even in the kitchen with me. Hah! How do you like that one? He ate every single bite. Said he couldn't wait for me to fix him another one."

Omunique's smile was smug. "Now, there, you have all the skinny on Nique and the adventures of cooking class." Laughter filled the room at the dramatic way Omunique flung her arms about as she finished giving her side of things.

"Bravo!" Wyman cheered.

After about two hours of more lively conversation, that included many delightful stories from everyone, Max glanced as his watch as he got to his feet. Tension seemed to fill the air at his unexpected move. Ken and Omunique exchanged uneasy glances.

"As much fun as this has been, I've got to get going. Early morning meeting." He turned to Mamie. "Ready, my dear."

Smiling, Mamie also got to her feet. "As ready as you are, Max. It has been fun. You two young people are treasures, and it's such a delight to be in your presence. May you always be this happy and this in love with one another. You two old fogies keep things interesting, as well," she said to Wyman and Max. They both laughed at the unattractive name she'd called them.

Wyman watched closely as Max helped Mamie into her lightweight jacket. He had to admit to himself that this was very awkward for him. Max was doing the very thing for Mamie that he'd always done. Was there something romantic going on between the two of them? He couldn't help wondering. He thought he and Mamie shared all their newsworthy stuff about their personal lives. Obviously, there were a few things she hadn't bothered to share with him.

Wyman's thinking had gotten the best of him. It actually made him begin to feel a little threatened. "Mamie, if you're not ready to go yet, I can drop you off at home a little later."

Tensions mounted again as another exchange of wary glances passed between husband and wife. The question made them nervous as they awaited Mamie's answer.

Mamie smiled adoringly at Wyman. "Not to bother, Wyman. I'm ready to go. Max and I have a lot to discuss on the ride home, don't we?" She winked her eye at Max in a playful manner." All eyebrows were raised at that little flirtatious gesture.

"Yes, we do. Quite a lot to discuss, I must say."

Before deciding it was time to go, Wyman stayed another half an hour or so. Omunique knew he'd just been biding time. He seemed distracted ever since Mamie and Max had left together. Both Omunique and Ken could tell that he wasn't quite himself. At the door, after giving Wyman his farewell hug, Ken left his wife to have a few moments alone with her father.

Omunique eyed Wyman anxiously. "Are you all right, Daddy?"

He pulled his daughter close to him. "I'm fine, sweetheart. Just been doing some thinking about a few things in my personal life."

Omunique frowned. "Anything to do with seeing Daddy-Max and Aunt Mamie together? Were you upset by it?"

He feigned surprise. "What in heaven's name would make you think that? I don't see anything wrong with them being together. Do you?"

"Oh, of course not. I admit that I was a little surprised to see them show up here together since that's never happened before. But I certainly don't think there's anything wrong with it."

"Good! Neither do I. Now let me get out of here so you can tend to that new husband of yours. I'm not too old to remember how the first months of marriage can be."

Then why don't I quite believe you about Aunt Mamie, Daddy? Omunique asked him in silence. *You may not know it, but I think you're beginning to question your true feelings for your deceased wife's best friend, my godmother.*

As Wyman wrapped his arms around her in a bear hug, Omunique basked in his warm affection. "Okay, big guy, you drive safely. Don't forget that you're invited to Sunday dinner week after next. It won't be the same without you. I'll call you and discuss the menu with you after I return home. I may need a few professional pointers from my very capable chef of a dad."

"Anytime, sweetheart. Good night!" Wyman leaned his head back inside the doorway and kissed his daughter's forehead before finally taking his leave.

* * *

Ken was eagerly awaiting his wife when she popped into the bedroom. "Was that the strangest visit we've ever had from those three, or what? I wonder what's going on with my dad and Aunt Mamie. Did you get the impression that Wyman was a bit uneasy about seeing them together? He seemed so discombobulated right after they left."

She plopped down on the bed and snuggled up against Ken. "Dad denies it."

Ken looked amazed. "You mean you had the nerve to ask him about it?"

"Are you trying to tell me you're not going to ask Daddy-Max the same thing?"

He grinned. "You got me there. I can't wait until tomorrow to talk to Dad at work."

"Kind of a sticky situation, huh? I think Dad's starting to assess his real feelings for Aunt Mamie." She looked worried. "Oh, my, that would be horrible if both of them were to fall in love with her. That would be too doggone rich."

"I hadn't thought that far about it. That would be some kick in the pants for all of them."

Omunique grinned. "Aunt Mamie must be on cloud nine about now. I know she had to recognize how Dad was vying for her attention when he asked about taking her home. I can't imagine having two men pining away for me at the same time. That must be a great feeling."

Ken shot her a discomforting look. "Don't you think you're taking this thing a bit far? As for you having two men, you can lose that thought, sister. The only man for you is me."

"You sure about that?" Her eyes twinkled with mischief.

He looked at her incredulously. "What are you trying to start up in here, World War III? We're just barely married . . . and you're talking about how nice it would be to have another man yearning for you. Girl, you're losing it, but you better get it back quick and in a hurry . . . before I lose it."

She fell into laughter. "Sounds like you're jealous. That can't be. Not you, iron man."

"I got your iron man. Get over here and let me make you my love slave. When I get through with you, you wouldn't *dare* another man to look at you, let alone lust after you."

"Ooh, baby, make me your slave girl." She stretched out fully in the bed and tossed her hands high over her head in a show of surrender. "Okay, lover, let me experience what erotic techniques you're going to use to keep me from becoming a runaway wife. Take me to private school, my wonderful master. Your love slave eagerly awaits her first lesson."

"Oh, girl, this is going to be some education. And what I'm going to teach you won't be called the 'miseducation' of Omunique Philyaw-Maxwell. That you can be sure of . . ."

She raised up to capture his lips. "Lauryn Hill, eat your heart out!"

Hours later, well after midnight, while taking a steaming hot shower, Ken and Omunique had lathered one another from head to toe with lavender-scented body wash and had taken delight in scrubbing each other squeaky clean. After drying one another off, they both donned matching forest-green terrycloth robes and went into the kitchen. Famished after all the wild lovemaking, they took inventory of the refrigerated foods to see what could be used to make a quick late-night snack. Each of them did their best not to dwell on her leaving town.

Ken picked up a package of Kraft cheese slices and showed it to Omunique. "What about grilled cheese sand-wiches?"

Omunique smacked her lips together. "That's a winner."

"Do you remember how I taught you to make them?"

"Of course I do. I'll just get a skillet."

He swatted her on the behind. "Are you sure you know what you're doing? I'm too hungry to withstand any cooking mishaps tonight, dear wife. I'm ravenous after all that love slave mastering you had me doing in the bedroom and in the shower."

Sucking her teeth, she rolled her eyes at him. "Cut the crap. If you don't think I can handle it, then do it your darn self."

Losing his nose in her neck, he pulled her back into him. "Slow your roll, girl. I have faith in your newly acquired abilities. But I have an idea. Why don't you try that George Foreman grill we got as a wedding present since we haven't used it yet?"

"I don't know. You didn't teach me on that."

"It's just a little different concept of cooking. The preparation steps are the same."

"Okay, go get it. I was reading the direction pamphlet the other day. You have to heat it up a few minutes before each use. You also need to wipe it off first since it's never been used."

While Ken rattled around in the kitchen closet for the grill, Omunique pulled from the refrigerator a loaf of wheat bread, butter, and cheese.

"Okay, here goes. First, I put two slices of cheese between two slices of bread. Then I generously butter the bread on one side. Next I spread butter on the other side once it's on the grill. When one side of the bread gets nice and toast-brown, I turn it over. You see, I do remember all the steps, Ken."

She stuck her tongue out at him as he came up beside her. Taking full advantage of what seemed like an invitation to him, he brought her tongue into his mouth, kissing her until she managed to squirm out of his grasp.

As he fumbled under her robe, she swatted away his next amorous advance. "Chil'," she said in her best Caribbean accent, "you best go away from here, boy, and let me do my thing. Don't you know that you should never, ever mess with a woman who has a sharp knife in her hand, mon?"

He couldn't help thinking how adorable she was. This woman had it all: stunning looks, a quick wit, indelible charm, unbelievable intelligence, a dynamic sense of humor, and a body that might tempt a man to sell his soul to the devil in exchange for just one night in bed with her. And she was all his. "Thank you, heavenly father, thank you a thousand times."

"What are you going on about? You're supposed to be getting the grill ready."

"Just thanking the Lord for bringing us together. Girl, you just don't know how blessed I feel to have you in my life. Doubly blessed to have you as my wife." He nuzzled her neck.

Titling her head back, she smiled softly. "I feel just as blessed." She kissed him full on the mouth. "Now let's cook and eat before I commit a heinous crime up in here."

He laughed at her comment as he checked the grill for warmth. "It's ready. Go do your thang, Olympian girl."

Omunique made the most perfect grilled cheese sandwiches. Proud of herself, she patted herself on the back. After devouring the snack, they shuffled off to bed for a good night's rest.

As it was both their morning and nightly rituals, Ken read a few passages from the Bible, though they also took turns reading from an inspiration book of passages. After turning off the light, they snuggled up close in bed to enjoy their last night together before Omunique hit the road. Each was eager to see what joys the darkness of night would bring to their love nest.

Seven

Missing Ken like crazy, but glad that training camp was almost over, Omunique listened to all the various instructions being given by one of many professional coaches. This was different from amateur competition, a lot different. Professional skaters had a lot more to be concerned with than just competitions.

Everyone had to be in sync during many of the tour performances; a major obstacle for even the most seasoned skater. It was hard enough to skate with a single partner, but many routines called for several skaters to perform together. However, there would also be numerous single skating routines for her to participate in. Oftentimes, the only time a group of skaters performed together was during the grand finale—and perhaps one or two routines in the middle of a performance. Even then, it was a tough assignment.

While there were also numerous competitions against other professional teams, especially teams from other countries, the routines wouldn't be as demanding as in amateur events. The special events and charity performances were also going to be a lot of fun, as well as less critical. Still, a figure skater had to be on top of his or her game to be competitive enough to stay in the pros. From what she'd already witnessed, this particular group was inundated with very savvy skaters, some of the best in the business, Olympic gold medal winners.

Meeting new people on the circuit was always fun and the opportunity to see older acquaintances was usually a blast. When she learned that Ian had turned pro, she was happier than just plain happy. He'd kept it from her as a surprise. Seeing him in the lineup, she realized his going pro was indeed a well-kept secret. Sara, who had a hard time containing any good news, hadn't whispered so much as a single hint to her. She hoped that she and Ian would get a chance to skate together on the routines that called for pair skaters.

Omunique stretched her limbs as she prepared to get involved in a strenuous workout session. As her left leg nearly buckled, she winced in pain. Aware that she had grown a little rusty during her off time, she decided not to push herself too hard or too fast, at least not until she got used to the practice routines.

Smiling, Ian came over to where she carefully paced her warm-up exercises. "Hey, Nique, how's things going for you?"

Wrinkling her nose, she smiled back at him. "I'm a little tight in my calves, but I realize I haven't skated much since the Olympics. I've gone to the local arena to let off steam a few times, but nothing compared to what strenuous paces I'm used to putting myself through."

He grinned. "That's what married life will do for you! How *is* your marriage going?"

A bright beam of light appeared in her eyes. "Oh, Ian, Ken is everything I could've ever hoped for. He's a very considerate man, but that's just a small part of all his wonderful attributes. For a woman who's never had a personal relationship with any man, I certainly love the heck out of being married. Ken has even taught me how to cook a lot of dishes. He's very patient with me through so many of the things that I haven't been exposed to."

"Sounds like you landed a great catch."

"I certainly did. How are things with you and Sara?"

He took his turn to smile brightly. "Sara's amazing. I can't figure out why it took me so long to notice her as a very attractive woman. I always felt kind of sorry for her after her career-ending injury, but she's the last person anyone needs to pity. I'm really gone on her, but I had no idea she'd had a crush on me for such a long time. I've even encouraged her to skate with me a couple of times during practice. Of course she can't do all the things she did before her injury, but she can still skate for pleasure. She's really glad I talked her into it."

"That's great, Ian. I'm happy for both of you. How are you liking the pros so far?"

"It's all good. I just knew that I wasn't getting any younger . . . and since I've failed at making the Olympic team during the last two trials, I decided to go pro. I surely thought that you'd stay in amateur competition and try once more for the gold. You absolutely skated your heart out. And I still can't figure out how the judges decided that the Russian girl bested you. You were on the very top of your game during your Olympic performance."

"Like I've been telling everyone who has commented to me on the event, I know that I did my very best. I know that I won the competition. You know as well as I do that the judges always do whatever they darn well please, whenever they want to. I'm a champion in my heart, Ian. I gave it all I had. There was nothing else that I could've given to that particular performance. On that glorious day, I poured out everything that I had within me . . . until I had nothing more left."

"That's a great attitude you have, Nique. But I still would like to see you in the Olympics one more time. They wouldn't be able to deny you the second time around."

"There's no guarantee that it would happen. Believe me, I'm just so happy that I won a medal at all. Like you, I'm not getting any younger. I also have other dreams to fulfill.

When I get my own arena, I'll have attained the most important of my lofty goals."

"Have any major endorsements come your way yet?"

"Outside the Maxwell Corporation endorsement, I only have one other major deal on the table. A soft drink company. Bruce says there have been a few rumbles from some other large companies, but no one has rumbled loud enough for him to enter into negotiations. If it's meant to be, it will happen . . . and I hope that it does. Running my own arena won't happen without lots of money."

Santana's "Maria, Maria" came soaring like an eagle through the arena's overhead speakers. The funky Latin music caused Omunique's hips and hands to stir and sway to the beat. "I love that song. Jake has been working on choreographing a routine for me to skate to Latin music. Want to go around on the ice with me a few times? This song is certainly making me want to burn up the ice. Ken loves it, too."

Ian held out his hand to her. "Sure. Let's do it, Nique."

They had never rehearsed together to the beat of the Latin song, but it appeared that they had. Ian softly called out different skating commands and she fell right into place with each one. She liked the fact that she'd be able to skate to all kinds of music in the pros. She smiled when she thought of her father telling her that she and Ian should team up as pair skaters. She had to admit to herself that they were really good together. Though she would be involved in routines with many other skaters, she still loved the singles' skate the best.

Like two combined whirlwinds, they gave the ice beneath their skates a good pounding. Omunique was as confident as ever as she spun into a flying camel. It felt good having the hardened surface at her beckon call. Now that she had split from Ian, to effect a triple toe loop, the fire inside of her took her emotions right to the top. This is what she loved to do. All that she'd once lived for. That is, until Ken and his unrivaled love had come into her life.

After effecting several extremely hard skating techniques, Omunique and Ian quickly fell back into formation. Once again, they skated together in perfect harmony. When the song was finished, they retired to one of the metal benches to remove their skates.

She smiled at him as she unlaced her skates. "What I'm going to like best about the pros is that we'll learn the routines and then the team will be able to rehearse them together a couple of days before the event. The pro schedule can get pretty rigid at times, but for the most part it doesn't seem like it's going to be too bad. Ken tells me to just think of the type of homecomings that I'm going to receive from him. He says that that alone should make it all worthwhile."

Ian grinned. "You newlyweds! I'm sure it's nice to have someone to come home to at the end of the work day for both you and Ken . . . and at the end of a tour for you."

"Awfully nice. For me to have had to stay in the Olympic Village was hard on us, but it was all worth it. The ability to concentrate on what I had to do was the most important thing at that crucial time in my life. That Ken understood perfectly is what was so nice about it all."

"I second that. In this business, you do have to have an understanding mate."

"Have you and Sara reached the stage yet? You know, where you begin to think about or perhaps even discuss marriage?"

Ian shook his head. "Not at all. In no way am I ready for that yet. The road trips can be rough on a marriage. How do you and Ken plan to combat the numerous road trips?"

"We've pretty much worked things out. Ken is going to go on the road with me as his work schedule permits, but we know there are times when we'll have to be apart. We've even talked about him becoming my manager. Besides, I don't know how long I'm going to be on the professional circuit." She giggled. "As for having children, we're letting nature take its course. So that means I could get pregnant at any time."

Ian looked stunned. "Pregnant? I thought you wanted to wait several years before having kids. Knowing you, I'm sure you weren't pressured into this decision."

She shook her head. "No way would Ken do that. He was as stunned by my decision as you obviously are. It's just something that I want. I love being with my husband without the worry of what could happen. So I suggested that we stop using protection altogether."

Ian's face turned beet-red. He and Omunique were very good friends, but they'd never had this intimate of a conversation before. "Wow, maybe that's more information than I needed," he joked. "I'm really surprised at how much you've matured since your marriage. I can't remember us ever having a conversation like this. In fact, a couple of months ago it would've embarrassed the hell out of you if I mentioned a word like 'protection.' That is, as it pertains to anything sexual."

Omunique laughed. "Maybe not. I don't know. It probably would've embarrassed me because I didn't know a darn thing about it. Anyway, let's change the subject. Just talking about this has me missing Ken even more."

"Well, you'll be home in a couple of days. With practically a month off before the first major event is scheduled. But long, hard practice sessions are still required of us. Are you still working with Brent Masters?"

"Oh, yeah. Most definitely. He's one of the best coaches in the business. Brent and I have a long history. Like you, he wanted to see me stay in amateur competition for another shot at the gold, as well. I just have to move on to other things. My time has come and gone."

Ian helped Omunique pack away her skating gear before taking care of his own. After promising to get together for another practice session once the group session was over, they went their separate ways. Omunique couldn't wait until the camp came to a close. She missed her husband and was sure that he was missing her just as much. As she thought about the dinner she promised to cook when she got home, she wished she hadn't done so. Just thinking of his heated touch and sweet kisses made her want to have him all to herself, until it was time to hit the road again.

On her way back to the hotel, Omunique thought about all the things she'd like to say to her husband when she called him, wonderful things, sweet things, things that turned him on both physically and emotionally. He knew how to express himself so well to her, but she often stumbled or became embarrassed over the intimate things she wanted to tell him.

First, she was going to take a hot shower and get into some relaxing clothes since she'd opted not to take a shower in the locker room. She was so eager to get to the hotel to call Ken that it had kept her from showering at the arena.

She saw that the red message light on the telephone was flashing when she stepped into the hotel room. Hoping it had been her loving husband, she sat down on the side of the queen-size bed and picked up the phone. She then went through the recorded prompts that would get her into the message center.

Hi, Princess, just wanted to hear your sweet voice. Hope all is well. We'll talk tonight, came the recorded message. *I love you.* Before she could inhale another breath, she hung up the phone and began to dial home. When she thought of taking the steaming hot shower, guaranteed to relax her, she aborted the call. She wanted to be squeaky clean, to smell wonderful, and already be in the bed when she talked to her man. As if she thought he would be able to smell her clean scent right over the phone lines, she rushed into the bathroom and turned on the hot water.

The shower relaxed her instantly. After putting on a pair of pink silk pajamas, she brushed her hair and climbed into bed. Reaching for the phone, she dialed her home number. Sounding half-asleep, Ken answered on the third ring.

"Hi, love, it's me."

"Nique, baby, I've been waiting to hear from you. I think I fell asleep for a short time. Are you back in your hotel room?"

"I've been here long enough to take a shower. I got your message, but I wanted to be totally relaxed when we talked."

"Are you in bed already?"

"Just where I wanted to be when we got the chance to talk. How was your day?"

"The days at Maxwell Corporation are getting busier and busier. I guess that's good for me with you being away. It keeps me busy, but not busy enough to keep me from thinking of you. Getting back to you being in bed, have you eaten anything?"

"Not yet. I may call room service and order a sandwich or something else that's light. I'm really not all that hungry."

"Maybe not, but you still have to keep your strength up. One day soon, you may be eating for two. We are working on a baby, remember?"

Her smile came gently. "Yeah, won't that be something? With Ian and I doing all that talking about sex, I started having the same type of visuals you have so often."

"What? You and Ian talking about sex? That doesn't sound too kosher to me."

"Oh, it wasn't like that. I was just telling him about our decision to let nature take its course. That was the extent of it. I didn't mean to make it sound like our conversation was all that intimate. It wasn't."

"I'm going to have to get used to how you say things, to stop taking them in a negative way. But, sweetheart, don't ever tell your husband that you've been talking about sex with another man, especially when you're spending several nights away from home. That can make a guy go kind of crazy. But it has nothing to do with me not trusting you. I know that I'm the only man for you. At least, on this planet."

She laughed heartily. "You sound a little overconfident to me, Maxwell. Don't ever start taking me or my love for granted. That could be a big mistake."

"Don't worry, I won't. And I'm supposed to be confident about the love my woman has for me. Aren't you confident in my love for you?"

"You know that I am. I just like harassing you every now and then."

He grinned. "I can think of a few ways that you can harass me, but it will get us both all hot and bothered."

"I'm all for finding out."

"We're not going there. I wouldn't be able to stand the pressure of wanting you so bad. I'm already feeling it just thinking about you being in bed. I don't want to go through that kind of physical pain. Besides, you're going to find out in a couple of days exactly what I'm talking about. I got major plans for you when you do get back here."

"Hmm, sounds intriguing. But speaking of plans, have you forgotten that I invited the family over for Sunday dinner?"

Ken groaned. "How can I forget it? I'm only off on Saturday and Sunday, and you don't get home until late Friday night. That only gives us one full day alone, but we're going to make the most of it. Just know that we're not leaving the bedroom except to eat and use the bathroom. As for the dinner party, I don't think it would be too cool of us to cancel out."

"We shouldn't cancel. I don't go back on the road for

several weeks. We'll have plenty of time to catch up on our sexual escapades. Gee, that's all we seem to talk about lately."

"That's not such a bad thing to talk about, Nique. The bad part is that you're not here for us to do anything *but* talk."

"I guess you got a point there. But it won't be much longer now. Have you talked to Dad since you spoke with him the other night?"

"We had lunch today, in fact. I forgot to mention it. We had a great meal and we talked a lot about you, of course. Wyman misses you a lot, too. It seems like you've been gone longer than you actually have. He mentioned our dinner invitation and he's looking forward to us all getting together. However, he is a little concerned about your culinary skills. He made me promise that I'd keep an eye on you while you prepare the meal."

Omunique snorted. "You guys never stop, do you? I'm going to surprise everyone and fix the best meal yet. I haven't forgotten a thing you've taught me. All of you will see. And I hope you're gracious enough to admit that you have egg on your face."

"I'm not the one that's worried about your cooking abilities. I know you can do it. I'm an excellent instructor."

"That you are, Mr. Maxwell, in more ways than one. I've surely loved your special instructions in anatomy. I must say that I've learned quite a lot."

"You've certainly earned high marks in that class, but I may make you repeat it a few times so that you can stay on the honor roll."

"Oh, how white of you. I may not be an experienced instructor like you, but I think I've taught you a lesson or two, as well." She giggled softly. "Even if I didn't know what the heck I was doing at the time."

"That's why it was so special for me. You did just fine. I miss you, sweetheart, more than I can adequately express."

"Wish I could count to a hundred and have you appear. But I'd be counting for a few days for you to get to me here in Denver."

"Count, anyway. With us being so busy, hopefully the time will fly by. I have to say that it doesn't feel like it's going fast for me so far. How's the training going?"

"Good, real good. There's a lot to keep up with. I believe I can do it. In fact, I can do anything with you by my side."

"Ditto, love. You're starting to sound a little drowsy. Are you tired?"

"Very tired. I guess I should cash in my chips. I'll call before you go to work in the morning. I won't be any good if I don't start my day out talking to you."

"I know what you mean. But, Omunique, please eat something before you go to sleep. I don't like it when you don't eat properly. That's not a good habit to get into."

"You're right. I promise to call room service as soon as we hang up. I love you so much, Mr. Maxwell."

"And I love you just as much, Mrs. Maxwell. I'll wait to hear from you. Sleep tight, my love. I'll keep you wrapped up in my dreams. And you do the same for me."

Omunique blew a few kisses into the phone before hanging up. Just as she promised, she called room service and ordered a chicken salad, a slice of sourdough bread, and a pot of hot tea. The moment she hung up the phone it began to ring.

"Hello."

"Sweetheart, it's me. I want you to listen to something. Okay?"

"Okay."

Omunique sat straight up in bed when superstar Monica's remake of Richard Marx's song, "Right Here Waiting" came through the receiver. In a matter of seconds tears ran down her cheeks at the tender words, but all the while she was smiling. Ken was so thoughtful and she loved him deeply for it.

"I'll be right here waiting for you. Good night."

"Good night, Ken. In less than forty-eight hours, I'll be back in your arms."

While nuzzling his nose in the soft folds of her neck, gently, Ken shook Omunique. "Wake up, sweetheart. We have to get the dinner going. Our guests will definitely be on time. You know they can't wait to see how your meal is going to turn out."

She turned over and went right into his arms. "I can't believe our intimate time alone is up already. It seems like I just got home. And pretty soon it'll be time for us to have to share each other with three more people. Can't we lie here just a little longer?"

"We haven't been able to accomplish that feat yet. We always talk about lying in bed for a little longer but we always end up making love. More often than not, I just barely make it to work on time." While kissing her forehead, Ken brushed her hair back from her face.

"We can't help wanting each other so much . . . and we shouldn't have to." She smiled up at him. "It's so good to be home, home in our own bed. I'm sick of hotels. That is, when you're not there to sleep with me. Glamorous it's not."

Placing the palm of his right hand on her flat abdomen, tenderly, he kissed her mouth. "I know. It's not easy for either of us to be apart from the other. But it's not always going to be like that. We have more time together than we do apart. Come on, let's get into the shower."

Since they were both already nude, Ken nudged Omunique across the bed until she reached the very edge. He then got up and stood her on her feet. "The pots and pans are calling you, girl. You got yourself into this, so you've got to get in the kitchen and do your thing."

She moaned. "Don't remind me."

* * *

Ken reached for the can of vegetable cooking oil and handed it to Omunique. "Now that the Cornish hens are seasoned and ready for the rotisserie, spray this all over the prime rib." She did as he had directed and then looked to him for further instructions. "Now cut small slits in the top of the rib roast and insert the thin slivers of garlic cloves you sliced earlier."

"Okay, now what?"

"Take your cracked-pepper-and-seasoning mixture of garlic and spread it all over the meat. Then insert the meat thermometer once that's done."

"Now I place it on this roasting rack. Do I need to put water in the pan?"

"None at all. Have you set the oven?" She shook her head in the negative. "Do you remember what temperature to set it at?"

"Four hundred fifty degrees for the first twenty minutes or so to seal in the juices, and then I turn it down to three hundred fifty so the meat can cook slowly and evenly. Right?"

"Right, sweetheart. You've really been listening. Just make sure that you turn the temperature down this time. Prime cuts of meat need to cook slowly. What would you do if you wanted part of the meat medium and the other side well done?"

"If I wanted to cook it the same through and through to the same doneness, I wouldn't cover it with anything. But in the case of two different desires of doneness, I would cover the top portion of the meat with foil after it seals and browns so that it doesn't cook as fast as the bottom. But since everyone coming to dinner likes medium well, I won't have to use the foil."

She smiled happily. "So that's all there is to it. I thought cooking a roast would take a lot more work than it has. I can't wait until you teach me to cook a rack of lamb."

"All in good time, my love. I first want to teach you how to cook things that aren't too much bother. Then we can move on to the more difficult items."

She clapped her hands with enthusiasm. "I can't wait until I can come into the kitchen and cook divine dishes without you having to coach me. I've learned so many things already. I can now cook eggs several ways, grits, rice, macaroni, and spaghetti, just to name a few of my major accomplishments. Learning to sauté mushrooms has also been a great lesson."

Bringing her to him, he kissed her forehead. "You're getting good at this, kid. I think our very first dinner party is going to be a great big success. One more question. What do you do to make the au jus?"

"I would use the pan drippings and then follow the directions on that little packet of dried au jus mix." She laughed. "I wish I wouldn't feel guilty about ruining a cut of meat. But there are too many starving people in the world for me to do something as wasteful as that."

"What's that supposed to mean?" He frowned.

"I would love to burn it to crispy black and serve it to our guests just for a reaction. I'm sure that Dad, for one, doesn't think I can pull this dinner party off. He'll probably eat before he comes so that he can say he's full in a hurry."

Ken busted up laughing. "That would be funny. But I don't think you want to do that even if you wouldn't feel guilty. I want you to show them how good of a cook you're becoming. And Wyman is not going to eat before he comes. He wants you to succeed as much as I do. You have to give him more credit than that even if he knows I'm not going to let this become a total disaster for you. He knows I love to rescue you. That's what heroes do for their heroines."

"Oh, I do give him credit, for lots of things. But he has no courage where my cooking skills are concerned. He's eaten some of my cooking before, and he did not spare my feelings in the least. If it was bad, and it always was, he told me and commenced throwing it away. I tried to cook him some oatmeal one morning, when I was a teenager, and he actually gagged on it. I used way too much water and I didn't put anything else in it for flavoring. It looked like thin gruel. The first taste sent him running for the trash can to spit it out." They both laughed at that.

Ken hugged his wife. "This evening's meal is going to be quite different. You've come a long way. We still have to get the potatoes ready for baking, but we don't need to put them into the oven until an hour or so before dinner. The macaroni and cheese can be made and we can put it in the oven about thirty minutes ahead. The green beans will be quick and easy." He snapped his fingers. "Dessert? What are we doing for dessert?"

Smiling smugly, she pulled a pink box from the refrigerator and opened the lid. "How's that for a delicious dessert? This whipped cream cake has fresh strawberries in the center of it."

He scowled. "That's cheating, Nique."

"Cheating? How's that?"

"You promised, or should I say threatened, everyone that you were cooking the entire meal. And you *did not* bake that strawberry cake."

She looked anxious. "But I'm not that good at baking yet."

"You can follow directions, can't you?"

"You mean cake out of a box?"

"Can you bake one from scratch yet?"

Remembering her first attempt, one that Ken didn't even know about, brought a heavy scowl to her pretty face. "You know the answer to that. Don't get ridiculous on me. This is serious."

"Look, don't make such a fuss over this. Just whip up a cake from the box and be done with it. This is your evening and I don't want the local bakery getting any of the credit for it."

"Are you suggesting I should make the wine and the sparkling cider, too?"

He popped her on the behind. "Now who's getting ridiculous? Come on, it'll be a piece a cake for you. No pun intended."

She pulled a face. "We have no cake mix. Now what?"

"There are *only* about four or five grocery stores in our community. What type of cake would you like to make?"

"Good question, but I don't know the answer. We just finished a chocolate cake. What about a lemon one?"

"That's good. You can follow the recipe on the box for the pound cake version. I'll buy some instant lemon pudding."

"Why instant pudding?"

"A pound cake recipe usually calls for it. Adding the pudding and extra oil makes it very moist. So is it lemon?"

"Lemon it is. Hurry and get back. You don't want to leave me to my own devices for too long. Strange things have been known to happen in this kitchen when I'm left by myself."

Thinking about the morning she'd tried to boil him eggs when they were dating, he groaned. "Boy, do I know it." She threw the dishtowel at him. "Okay, I'm sorry. That was unfair of me, especially when you're so serious about this whole thing. But lighten up, Princess. It's going to be all good."

She kissed him hard on the mouth. "You're forgiven and thanks for the vote of confidence. Now get to stepping so you can get back here in a hurry. And don't forget what you said about loving to rescue your heroine, my hero."

"I won't forget." A quick kiss to her lips and he was gone.

Pleased with what she'd accomplished so far, she smiled to herself despite all the previous kitchen mishaps. "Yes, it's going to be okay, today, tomorrow, forever. My husband will see to that."

While waiting for Ken to return from the store, she went into the laundry room. He had also been teaching her to wash clothes and she had gotten pretty good at it, but not until after she'd washed a bunch of white clothes with darker ones. Everything had gotten faded, but Ken had understood that, as well. Because she'd always washed her personal items out by hand, and Wyman had done all the other laundry, she hadn't acquired any skills in that area either.

She cringed at thinking about all the things she hadn't known how to do before Ken, as it related to domestic chores . . . and there were still lots of things she still didn't know about being a wife, a good housekeeper, and a cook. She didn't even want to think about what she didn't know about becoming a mother. She could easily write a book entitled *Domestication? Clueless!*

Despite all that she wasn't, she was a professional figure skater, a great one, an accomplished one, an Olympian. Being a champion was something she knew all about. Thinking about the upcoming event schedule made her a little sad because it meant another separation from her husband. But skating was what she did best and she'd now turned from amateur to pro and would earn top dollars for her finely honed skills.

Not a lot of companies had been knocking down her door offering endorsement contracts since she'd won the silver medal, but that wasn't so unusual for African-American Olympians. In fact, her agent had prepared her for the possibility of that.

As she thought about becoming the spokesperson for Maxwell's Athletic Wear, she also gave a minute's thought to the soft drink endorsement package that was on the table, although no concrete deal had been reached yet. Her agent, Bruce Smith, and her attorney, Lamar Lyons, two of the best representatives in the business, were still ironing out the wrinkles with the big boys who controlled the company's purse strings. "Whatever will be, will be. I've got other things to think about right now. Like making this a sensational culinary experience for all my distinguished guests." With excitement setting in on her over her first dinner party, she laughed.

Eight

Omunique was seated at the breakfast bar reading Emily Post's book on etiquette when Ken came in from the store. Not exactly sure of the proper way to position the stemware, the eating utensils, and the napkins, she had gotten into the chapter on how to set a perfect table.

Ken placed the grocery bag on the kitchen table. "Got the cake mix. Even though we hadn't thought about it at the time we talked about baking a cake, I bought some boxed icing. It only has to be mixed with softened butter and a few drops of water. How's the cooking going?"

She looked up at him as he stood over her chair. "It's going great. Can't you smell it?"

Sniffing the air, he glanced down at the book she held. "I love the way it smells, delicious. What are you reading?"

"In trying to get everything just right, I thought I'd check out the etiquette book given to us a wedding present. I'm reading the chapter on setting the perfect table. It has great illustrations to follow. I don't think it's going to be that difficult to follow the diagrams."

Quelling his laughter, Ken came around and sat down on the stool next to his wife. That Omunique didn't even know how to set a dinner table was darn near intriguing. The fact that she wanted to learn everything she could about these sorts of things made him feel proud. Although she was aware that he knew how to set a beautiful table, he decided to let her learn this one all on her own since it was important enough to her to pull out a guide book.

She held the publication out in front of him. "This is one of the pages that shows how everything should look on the table. I'm going to use our Wedgewood china for the first time. This dinner is definitely a special occasion." She put a finger to her temple in a thoughtful gesture. "Maybe I should save the china for the first dinner party in our new home. We have another new set of good dishes that I could use. What do you think?"

He put his hand to the side of her face, drawing her head against his abdomen for a brief moment. "The new china, without a doubt . . . and don't forget about the Waterford crystal. I don't see the point in having all these fancy things and never using them. I want us to use everything we have. People store beautiful things away for years without ever allowing others to see their beauty. Then they die and their valuables often pass on to someone who doesn't appreciate their value in the same way. I don't want us to do that." He grinned. "So, shall I break out the new china and the crystal?"

Smiling, she slid her flattened palm down his thigh. "So you shall. We're going to have to wash everything first. You get the china and I'll get out the crystal. We can also use one of those beautiful table cloth sets that we got. I think a fancy lace one is the look I'm after."

"This is your party, sweetheart. Whatever your heart desires."

With moisture in his eyes, Ken smiled at his wife. "The table is exquisite. Everything looks wonderful. You really did a fantastic job. I'm proud of you."

"Thank you. I'm proud of you, too. You helped me out a lot. The table is something we can both be extremely proud of. Thanks for lending your girl an extra pair of hands."

"You're welcome." He wrinkled his forehead. "Something's wrong here. I'm thinking that there's something important missing from the table. What do you think?"

She looked perplexed. "I don't know what it could be. All the dinnerware, silverware, napkins, and stemware are in place. What else is there?"

"Hold up. I'll be right back."

Omunique was studying the table so hard that she didn't notice Ken come back in the room with a lovely centerpiece of fresh flowers with four candles positioned in the middle.

He tapped her on the shoulder and she turned to him. "Flowers! Oh, you do think of everything. Darn it, I saw a centerpiece in the illustration I was following, but it didn't even register in my brain." She slapped her forehead with an open palm. "I'll get it right one of these days, but I've got a feeling it'll take me longer than most."

After situating the centerpiece in the middle of the table, he brought her into his arms, kissing her softly on the mouth. "Nique, you re coming along just fine. Don't fret. You've created a romantically soft ambience for our guests to enjoy. Someone could easily fall in love in this romantic setting. All I know is that I keep falling deeper and deeper in love with you."

Her eyes misted. "That was so sweet. I feel the same way." She kissed him to show her appreciation of him. "Speaking of falling in love brings a good question to mind. Who's going to fall in love with each other, Dad and Aunt Mamie or Daddy-Max and Aunt Mamie?"

"Ouch! I'm not touching that one, wife. You've created the perfect setting for falling in love, so I guess we'll just have to wait and see which two of them it sets on fire."

"We're so bad. While I've always hoped for Dad and Aunt Mamie to find one another in a romantic way, she couldn't do better for herself with either of our dads. Watching this scenario unfold is going to be very interesting."

"Indeed."

With everything set in place but the guests, Omunique and Ken escaped to the bedroom to change into dinner attire. Omunique owned so many clothes that she wasn't able to bring them all from her Dad's house. She and Ken planned to move the rest of her things when their home was ready for moving in.

She held up a rather daring but sophisticated raspberry-colored spandex dress. "What are your thoughts on this one, dear husband?"

Though he already knew his answer, he studied the fine details of the elegant stretch woven sheath paired with a tonal, silk knit cardigan. He liked the boat-shaped neckline and the discreet back slit. The length was perfect, not too short, and nowhere near too long. "I love it. But I have to admit that I'm going to have as much fun taking it off later as I'll have watching you put it on. Unzipping the back of it might take me a minute or two. But that will give you a chance to get steamed up first."

She laughed. "Why do you always go there?"

He raised an eyebrow. "Why not?"

"Because we're expecting company. You know what that kind of talk does to me."

"Come here, sweetheart. Let me help you calm down a bit."

"No way." She ran for the bathroom, but he caught her as she tried to pass by him.

Twisting his fingers in her hair, he tilted her head back for his lips to take liberty with her soft neck. As his hand slid up under her sweatshirt and cupped her breast, she gyrated against him, burning from his intimate touch. His hand roved over to her other breast and she moaned against his parted lips. To encourage him further, now that he had her so worked up, she slipped her hand down the waistband of his sweatpants, touching him down there until he groaned with desire. After lifting the sweatshirt over her head, his mouth went hungrily from one breast to the other. Her sweatpants were the next to go. As he slid hers off, she busied herself removing his. While each wiggled their feet loose from the elasticized material at the bottom, Ken slowly edged them toward the bed. At his wit's end with wanting to be so deep inside of her, he placed her at the very end of the bed. Holding her tenderly, he entered her with one gentle thrust.

More than ready for him to take her to the deep valleys of ecstasy, she lifted herself up to meet his mild plunges into her moistness. While wrapping her legs around his waist, she wantonly kept up with the gyrating rhythms of his highly sensual movements inside of her. Losing themselves to this blissful moment, their gentle lovemaking quickly grew into something hot and heavy, something neither of them could control. Sweat poured from their bodies, making them hotter and hotter, causing their bodies to sizzle.

Without withdrawing, kissing her all the while, Ken lifted her up and carried her into the shower and turned the water on full blast. The pinprick sensations of the pounding water against their naked flesh heightened their desire for fulfillment. With her back firmly planted against the cool tile, her arms entwined around his neck, she kept her legs wrapped around his waist. No longer in control of their erogenous senses, they brought each other to a galvanizing climax.

When his weakened legs nearly buckled, he sat down on the shower floor, with her still stuck to him like glue. Omunique clung to her husband as she tried to calm her breathing. His lips sought hers in a passionate embrace, taking away what little breath she had left. Hungrily, she kissed him back, not caring that she had to gulp for air between each devouring kiss.

Suddenly, Omunique screeched, "The cake, Ken. We forgot about the cake."

He couldn't help laughing at the panic-stricken look on her face. "I think we have about ten more minutes before it'll be ready to come out the oven."

She looked at him with suspicion. "How do you know that?"

He capped his laughter, but it had already settled in his eyes. "I looked at the clock before we came in the bedroom, so I knew how much time we had left."

"Why would you do that?"

"Because I planned to seduce my wife. I just made myself aware of the time."

She grew huffy. "Are you saying you timed this little rendezvous? That's an insult."

"Let me answer before you consider it an insult. Of course I didn't time it. I was prepared to let the damn cake burn if necessary. But I felt that this was one of those times that we would probably explode within minutes. We've *only* been apart for two weeks, sweetheart, with only one night to try and make up for lost time. You and I both were hotter than hot for one another."

Removing a towel from the metal bar, she held it at both ends and looped it around his neck. "I'm happy that you seduced me." She gave a blushing smile. "I have to admit that I was closely checking the time, too, hoping we had enough for a quickie?"

"Quickie?" He was amazed at her choice of words. "Where'd you get that word? Who've you been hanging out with? I hope it didn't come from Ian."

She smiled smugly. "Actually, it came from Marion. One day she said that she had to hurry home to Frank so they could have a quickie before it was time for him to catch his flight to Sacramento. I'd never heard that before so I asked her what she meant by it. I knew that I'd said something terribly naive when she laughed so hard that she got cramps in her side. I'm sure I turned multishades of red when she answered my sillier-than-silly question."

"Oh, baby, you're so darn cute. You have to be the most adorable woman on the planet when you don't understand something. The befuddled expressions that cross your face are worth millions to me." Taking the towel from her, he began to dry her off "Unless we want it to burn, we need to take care of the cake. Coming with me?"

"We already did that. If we do that again, then the cake will burn for sure."

"My, my, you're starting to talk that talk just like your husband. Keep the spice coming. I love it." She reached for her bathrobe. "Hurry up so we can get back in here and get dressed. We got company coming. We still have to ice your baking project, though, it has to cool first."

Ken was busy tucking his black silk shirt into his gray dress slacks when the doorbell pealed. Unable to find one of her shoes, Omunique was hopping around on one foot in the walk-in closet. She had pinned her hair up in a so-phisticated style, but one thick section of hair just wouldn't cooperate. It kept falling in her face, annoying her to the point of wanting to scream.

"Are you going to get the door, Ken? I can't find my other freaking shoe."

"We're getting the door together."

She rolled her eyes at him. "I just told you my dilemma. Go, before they think we've stood them up. I gotta find my shoe."

His look was matter-of-fact. "Together, Nique, you and me, at the door. We can find your shoe later. No one cares if you walk around barefooted in your own home, especially family."

"No, they're only going to think I'm half-baked." She

kicked the other shoe off as he practically dragged her to the door. Max and Mamie were all smiles when they entered the house. At seeing Mamie and Max together again, Omunique got that same uncomfortable look. At a loss for words, Ken shrugged his shoulders and welcomed them to their home.

Briefly, Ken thought about Courtesy Evans . . . and was so glad Max had decided on his own not to see her again. Ken had told his Dad his minute history with Courtesy after Max told him that she was a bit too much for an old man like himself. But Ken assured him that he wasn't that old. Then he went on to tell him that he'd just unleashed himself from the worst kind of woman, a woman who had single-handedly made an art form out of professional gold digging.

Everyone warmly embraced each other before retiring to the living room. Omunique couldn't stop thinking about Wyman's feelings, wondering why he hadn't gotten there yet. The thought of something happening to him had just barely crossed her mind when the doorbell rang for the second time. She smiled when she saw her Dad come through the door. Kisses and hugs were once again passed around before everyone settled down in the living room.

"Wine for anyone?" Ken asked.

"White zinfandel for me," Mamie responded, smiling.

"You got any merlot back there behind that bar, son?" Max inquired.

"You bet, Dad. What about you, Wyman?"

"I'm going to stick to sparkling cider this evening. Since you know how much both my beautiful daughter and I love it, I'm sure you have some on hand." Ken turned to his wife before filling everyone's order. "What's your pleasure, Nique?"

"Nothing for me, sir." Blushing, she looked down at her bare feet as she bit down on her lower lip. He saw the guilty look in her eyes. Was she actually feeling guilty because they'd made love before the company arrived? He tossed her a heart-stopping, telltale smile—and her cheeks grew flushed. The language between them was far from foreign, because the elders were able to decipher what those blushing looks of hers meant . . . also what Ken's loving smiles said as he poured the drinks. The newlyweds couldn't keep their eyes off one another. It was an intriguing sight to behold.

"Enough of that goggle-eyed stuff, you two. You're making us feel real old, reminding us of what we're missing out on. It looks like you need to feed us so we can let you two fly back to 'kingdom come,' " Max teased.

Omunique gave a look of apology. "No one is going anywhere. You all have lots of cooked crow to eat. And I'm gonna enjoy feeding it to you." Everyone laughed. "Make yourselves at home while we slip out of here and put the food on the table." She threw her hands up in mock disgust. "Oh, dear, I hope I didn't burn all of it too badly." Laughter rang out again as she and Ken retreated to the kitchen.

Omunique's giggles grew louder as she entered the kitchen. She couldn't seem to hold them in. "Do . . . you think . . . they guessed?"

"Guessed at what?"

"What we were doing just before they got here."

"And if they have?"

With a shocked expression, she opened her mouth wide. "I won't be able to look at one of them in the eye for the rest of the evening. I'm so embarrassed."

He pulled her to him. "Everyone out there knows what time it is. They've already been there and done that. Stop feeling guilty about making love to your husband. And if you can't look them in the eye, please don't ever stop looking into mine. Our eyes converse with each other so well." He kissed her deeply. "Let's get this food on the table. I'm sure they're paying more attention to their growling stomachs than they are to us."

"I see your point. But I still have to find my shoe. I feel silly without them."

She watched as Ken removed the roast from the upper oven. Tears filled her eyes. "It's so beautiful, so golden-brown, so perfect looking." She jumped up and down. "I pulled this thing off! Can you believe it?"

His heart became full at her excitement. "You did all of it. And you're certainly entitled to feel so proud. Our guests will be as proud of you as I am." He kissed each of her eyelids.

"Oh, gosh, let's get started. I can't wait to see the look on their faces, especially Dad's. He's going to bust a gut from disbelief."

Ken transferred the roast to a heavy silver platter. Almost in a ceremonial way, Omunique carried the roast into the dining area. Grinning from ear to ear, she placed it on the temporary serving table that Ken had set up to hold all the food. Once the other foods were put into place, hand-in-hand, husband and wife went back to the living room.

Beaming from head to toe, Omunique spread out her hands, turning her palms up. "Dinner is now served!"

Wasting no time, the ravenous family members filed into the dining room. Standing back a slight distance, Omunique quietly observed the reactions from each of her guests. When her father turned around and gave her his most endearing, pride bursting smile, she exploded into joyful laughter. Congratulations came from the others as they sat down to enjoy the meal that Omunique Philyaw-Maxwell had prepared with her own two hands. But she knew that she'd never have gotten through it without the love and encouragement from her extremely devoted mate. Ken had been by her side to guide and direct her through each preparation. Her heart fluttered with a loving, quirky feeling for him as he passed the blessing.

Once everyone was seated, Ken lifted his glass in a toast. "To the newest cook in our house, Chef Maxwell. May our kitchen always be filled with the love that she poured into preparing this feast for us to enjoy." Melodies of concurrence rang out, causing Omunique to clap her hands zealously.

As the food was eaten, Omunique looked around the table with discretion. Though she guessed the outward expressions addressing pleasures of the palate were for her benefit, she thoroughly enjoyed each one. Wyman rolled his eyes back to show his delight in the meal, Max closed his in an expressive manner, and Ken simply licked his lips. Aunt Mamie's deep smile of approval touched Omunique's heart the most. Because Mamie's culinary skills were the absolute best, her approval carried the most weight.

Wyman reached down and took his daughter's hand. "You did us proud, Nique. Everything tastes divine. Now, let me ask you this. How much help did you really get from hubby over there?"

Seeing the downhearted look in his wife's eyes, Ken quickly intercepted the question. "Nothing more than directions came from me, which she followed to the letter. My lovely wife's two hands prepared everything we've eaten thus far. Let there be no mistake about that."

Omunique's eyes brightened at Ken's valiant defense of her. Sensing that he'd hurt her feelings, Wyman hugged his daughter as he apologized profusely.

"It's okay, Daddy. I understand why you'd question my abilities. I told Ken about the oatmeal I made for you when I was a teenager." Wyman pulled a face that made everyone laugh. It also put his daughter at ease.

Omunique got to her feet. "Is everyone ready for dessert?" Positive nods came from around the table. "Be right back." As Ken got to his feet, Omunique shook her head. "You stay seated. I've got it all under control." Smiling, she disappeared into the kitchen.

Wyman looked to Ken. "I'm sorry I hurt her feelings like that. Thanks for rescuing me from my ignorance."

"Doing this for you guys meant a lot to her. I remember someone telling me that she was so very fragile at times. This was one of those times. She wanted this dinner to be perfect."

"And it is," Wyman remarked.

"Even in all her stubbornly independent ways, she's always been overly sensitive. Our Nique is still very young . . . and in some ways very immature. We should try not to forget that when dealing with her. She'll come into her own right in time," Mamie offered.

"Thanks, Mamie. I won't forget what you've said. My daughter has really grown up in the last year, but with still a ways to go. Twenty-two years have come, and are about to be gone, but she'll always be her Daddy's little girl."

Silence took over when Omunique came back into the room carrying cake plates with thick slices of her lemon delight. She made another trip before everyone was served. As she joined the others, she smiled over at her father. But Ken was the only one to notice the devilish glint in her eyes. And he was downright puzzled by it.

Once again, she watched for everyone's reaction after taking the first bite of the dessert. Then her eyes stayed on Wyman as he took his third bite. Coughing and sputtering, he pushed back from the table. What appeared as bubbles came rushing from his mouth, causing Ken to look horrified. He remembered that he *had* left her alone when she mixed the cake, but for only a few moments. Had something happened then? Or was Wyman having a sick spell of some sort?

Unable to hold it in any longer, Omunique unleashed ripples of laughter, making everyone look her way. "I thought you needed your mouth washed out for that undeserved sarcastic comment you made in reference to my cooking skills, so I added a bit of dishwashing liquid to your special piece."

While wiping out the inside of his soapy mouth with a

napkin, Wyman gave her a look fraught with incredulity. A bit of strained tension permeated the air as everyone awaited Wyman's response to the unusual, juvenile punishment that Omunique had leveled against him. Finally, he burst into uncontrollable laughter. When his laughter brought forth a trail of tiny bubbles, everyone else felt free to let go, too. Omunique looked on with a smug but gleeful expression in her twinkling eyes.

With his laughter now under control, Ken looked as his wife and shook his head. "I see that I need to be very careful of what I say and do to you. That was cruel. You're treacherous, woman. I still can't believe you did that."

"Dad knows. He's gotten back at me plenty of times when I've been insensitive. We understand one another perfectly. Don't we, Dad?"

As he moved forward and embraced his daughter, his deep love for her was abundantly clear. "Just remember that payback will occur."

She smiled at him. "That *was* payback. Remember when you hid one of my ice skates, before one of my not so important practice sessions? He'd put it high upon a ledge in the family room. I would've never thought to look up. And even if I had, I couldn't have reached it. I ended up renting skates that day because he didn't show me where it was until after I got home."

Wyman laughed heartily. "That was punishment for often failing to put your things where they belong. We've done a lot of mischievous but harmless things to one another over the years. I'm sure this won't be our last prank to pull. But you can be sure that my next one is going to best this one. Well, I guess I won't be able to say that I've never had my mouth washed out with soap. Nique, you're quite creative. Now that you've had your fun at my expense, your favorite saying, may I please have a soap-free piece of cake?"

The worrisome look on Ken's face caught Omunique's

attention. He'd grown very quiet during her exchange with Wyman. That concerned her. "What's wrong, Ken? You're looking rather strange." All eyes turned on him. Without comment, he got up from the table and headed toward the bedroom. More concerned than before, she followed right behind him.

Inside the closet, he removed her missing shoe from high up on the shelf, where he knew she'd never think to look. Because of her inability to reach very high, she kept all her shoes on the lower shelves. With the shoe behind his back, he emerged from the closet. After seeing what Omunique had done to her dad in retaliation for his off-color cooking comments, he wasn't looking forward to her wrath against him.

She frowned. "What are you doing in there? You know we still have guests."

He brought the shoe forth and handed it to her." I hid it from you when you went in the kitchen to ice the cake." He looked like an errant child awaiting punishment.

Not the least bit amused, she cast a disparaging glance his way. "Hid it where?"

Moving back into the closet, he pointed at the highest shelf "Way up there."

There was no way she could be upset with him, not when he looked so apologetic, so boyishly mischievous. Falling into his arms, she laughed until tears rolled from her eyes.

Still laughing, they rejoined their guests. Ken's punishment was to share with everyone what he'd done. Wyman howled the loudest, marveling at how much he and his son-in-law had in common. For sure, their sense of humor ran along the same lines.

Omunique wagged her finger at both Ken and Wyman. "Let me put you two on notice. From now on, I *will* be looking up when something of mine comes up missing. This thing you all have about making fun of my height has to stop." The sparkling gleam in her smoky eyes belied the tone in her sassy remarks. "Now I need to get Dad's piece of cake."

Alone after a wonderful evening of dining, great conversations, and nonstop fun, Ken and Omunique had curled up on the white rug in front of the fireplace. Their first dinner party had been a success and Omunique couldn't have been more pleased with her accomplishments. Ken was happy that she was so pleased with the way things had turned out.

Looking down at his wife, he saw that she could barely keep her eyes open. He nudged her gently. "Ready to go to bed?"

Yawning, she stretched out both of her arms. "Aren't you forgetting something?"

He shrugged. "What?"

"You talked about having as much fun taking my dress off as you had watching me put it on." A light came on in his eyes. "Now that I see you remember talking the talk, I'm ready to go to bed but not to sleep. I'm eager to see if you can walk the walk, in keeping with your jive talk."

A couple of dozen tea-lights twinkled their soft illumination, bringing forth a dazzling glow into the darkness of their bedroom. As the tiny candles cast shadows on the walls of their intimately entwined figures, their gyrating bodies appeared to dance within the soft glow.

Lying naked beneath her nude husband, as he made sweet, diamond-shattering love to her, Omunique looked up into eyes burning with pure ecstasy. As her fingernails slowly titillated the small of his back, he dove deeper into the wet flesh between her legs. Omunique tightly gripped the bare, tight flesh of his rounded buttocks. As his majestic maleness, now fully lubricated with her natural moisture, thrust deeper and deeper into her heated flesh with such engaging tenderness, she moaned with mindless, gratifying agony. His hands, cupping softly, gently caressing, moved back and forth between the burgeoning fullness of each of her breasts.

The smoothly effected act of Omunique bending her knees, planting her feet alongside him opened her legs even wider for him. Thrusting deeper, he groaned, lamenting at the eternal bliss that came while making love to his wife. Every time the needs of her body matched his stroke for stroke, his body trembled with the thrill of her moving so wildly beneath him.

Their breathing quickened as their hands gripped one another. As the force of the insuppressible climax seemed to spilt the world in two, thundering through them at lightning speed, they became one.

Sweaty, thirsty, and energy depleted, their satiated bodies collapsed against one another. Too tired to even utter a word, they fell asleep locked in one another's arms.

Nine

With his arm planted firmly around her waist, Ken and Omunique took in the beauty of their exquisite interior decorating skills. Their new home looked magnificent. Their minds had created every fine detail down to the hand-carved banisters and wood paneled family room. BDB Architectural Engineering had done a fabulous job in designing and custom building the European castle–style structure. The sparkling running brook beneath the ivy covered bridge served as their mock moat.

Marion had guided Omunique and Ken in choosing some of the finest marbles, ceramics, hardwoods, and other custom enhancements, such as shutters and miniblinds, but all the ideas had been strictly their own. The island-style kitchen was open and airy with sliding glass doors that led out to a lovely sunroom. French doors off the sunroom led out to the pool and patio area.

A two-bedroom guesthouse and an exercise/fitness room, fully equipped with sauna and whirlpool, were also located on the three-acre estate. The massive custom home featured both living and dining formals, a large family room with a fireplace, six bedrooms, each with an adjoining bath. The master suite had a double fireplace that could be enjoyed from both the bedroom and the adjoining sitting room which was equipped with a wet bar and a big screen television. Another set of French doors led out to a terrace off the master suite. Both Omunique and Ken had taken one of the bedrooms for their private offices. The house and its decorations spoke to many different cultures and lifestyles, including African, European, and Oriental themed rooms; just a few of the places Omunique had been blessed to travel to.

Smiling, Ken kissed Omunique's forehead. "I can't believe we're actually finished with everything. It's breathtaking, just like my wife."

"It really is. What's so awesome is that we did it all to our own specifications and satisfaction. May our home always be filled with the wonderment of our love and may God always be the head of our household. I love you for all that you are, Kenneth Maxwell Jr."

Her squeezed her waist. "That's been the key to our success thus far, God and love."

"I remember Daddy telling me that love's ultimate goal is reconciliation. I pray that we will always be able to reconcile our differences. True love dictates it."

Wanting to make love to her right on the spot, he kissed her thoroughly. But they had company coming. In less than two hours their home would be filled with people who'd come to join them in celebration. He hoped it would be the kind of housewarming they'd often dreamed about, sometimes aloud, as they spent hours on end planning their very special dream home.

Playfully, she palmed his perfectly rounded behind. "We have to get dressed."

He grinned mischievously. "Getting undressed is more like what I had in mind."

"Hold all those deliciously erotic thoughts until after the party. Then you can share them with me through the gift of motion."

"How did you know I was thinking erotica?"

"I can feel your thoughts pressing into my thigh. To be more specific, hard-as-granite thoughts." Laughing, she took off running toward the bedroom. Catching up to her just inside the doorway, he brought her to him, kissing her until she gulped for air.

Ken waited until Omunique stepped into the walk-in closet before attempting to present her with the package he'd hidden under their bed. He nudged her from behind. "Trying to decide what to wear?"

"You know me. I really should've gotten that new dress I wanted the other day. It would've been perfect for this occasion. Oh, well, we know that's not the first time I've passed on something that I really wanted, only to wish later that I'd gotten it."

"Are you talking about that little hot black number with the sheer sleeves and bustline?"

She sighed wistfully. "Yep, that's the one. It *was* the cutest, the sexiest."

He brought the box from behind his back. "Maybe you'll like this one just as well."

She shrieked with joy. "You bought me a new dress! I'm sure I'll love it, too" She kissed him gently on the mouth, ripping the paper to shreds at the same time.

"My, you're certainly eager to see what's in that box. Tell me something. Are you excited, or what?"

"Something like that. Oh, my goodness . . . no you didn't! It's the very same dress from Nordstrom." Beaming from head to toe, she held the dress up to her. "It's fabulous."

"Glad you like it."

"I love it. I love you, too. You're always so thoughtful. But I thought of you, too." After disappearing into the closet for a few seconds, she came out with a gift-wrapped box, as well. "I bet you can't guess what's in here."

"Bet you I can."

"No way."

"The black silk banded collar shirt you were admiring the same day we saw the dress."

A hint of mischief appeared in her eyes. "You saw me buy it, didn't you? That's why you pretended you had to go to the bathroom, isn't it?"

"Neither. I just happen to know you. I wanted to purchase the shirt myself, but I didn't want to steal the pleasure of you wanting to surprise me with it later."

With box in hand, she flung her arms around his neck. "Life with you will never be dull, not for a second. And I'm so grateful for that. Please open the box, anyway, even though you already know what's in it."

"Anything for you. The shirt will look good with my new boxed-plaid sport coat. Please tell me I don't have to wear a tie tonight." He pulled a face, making her laugh.

"It won't bother me. Just tell me I don't have to wear any panties."

He looked shocked. "What?"

She laughed enthusiastically. "Just kidding!"

He got a devilish glint in his eyes. "I feel a compromise coming on."

"What sort of compromise?"

"Just don't wear any panties to bed tonight."

"Since I rarely do anyway, that's a given. In fact, I don't plan to wear anything to bed tonight. How's that for compromising?"

"Girl, I'm going to be wishing people out of here early if you keep talking like that."

"That's sounds like a great plan, lover. Now open that box."

Much to Ken's surprise and pleasure, Omunique had purchased the same shirt in several different colors: gray, beige, brown, and dark green.

"I won't need to buy another shirt for months. You really liked this shirt, didn't you?"

"Didn't you?"

"Loved it. Thank you, sweetheart. I'll thank you again each time I wear one. You'll also get a big kiss."

"As if you could manage *not* to kiss me," she quipped with smugness.

"You're right about that. Come on. Let's get that shower."

She made cooing sounds. "Together, no doubt."

The Maxwells didn't have a minute to spare after getting showered and dressed. The doorbell pealed constantly for the next half hour. Everyone loved the doorchimes that played chords of "Hero." Ken had special-ordered the musical chimes for their first home.

Soft jazz from piped-in music coming from the audio-visual salon of their posh home filled the freesia-scented, candlelit rooms. The soothing music was low enough to converse without strain. The hosts gave a short guided tour after all guests were present and accounted for. With the special event being catered by an outside source, from bartenders to several waiters, Omunique and Ken were able to relax and enjoy their guests.

After the waiters filled each glass with champagne, Wyman gathered everyone in one spot and then lifted his glass. "Max and I would like to offer a toast to our children. Max, you go first . . ."

Max smiled warmly. "This is indeed a joyous occasion that we've all gathered here for. As this magnificent place is our children's first home, we give thanks for the bounty of blessings that they've received. While they had to grow up without the benefit of having their mothers around, we Dads did our very best to raise them to be wonderful human beings and responsible adults. Wyman and I are extremely proud of them and their incredible accomplishments. May God continue to bless you and keep you in His tender care, Omunique and Ken. Here's to your new home. May it always be filled with the joy of your love, the warmth of the fire of your passion. One day, may we hear the sweet pattering sounds of our grandchildren's little feet."

Everyone lifted their glasses in a toast before sipping the champagne.

Wyman grinned. "I don't know if I can top that but I have no desire to. Omunique and Ken, you are two of the greatest kids a parent can have. You're both very kind and considerate, great assets. May you find your every desire in each other and in your new home. May you constantly fill these four walls with your sparkling laughter and your tireless dedication to one another. Like Max expressed, may these ceramic and hardwood floors hold up under the little feet that may, one day, scurry across them. God bless you both and your beautiful home."

Smiling broadly, Ken slid his hand into Omunique's. "Omunique and I thank all of you for coming to help us celebrate and to christen our new home in the presence of those we love the most. We want to offer a warm welcome to each of you. May you all find the same kind of warmth and comfort here that you find in your own homes. Make sure to enjoy yourselves since we may not invite you over again for the next six months or so. I'm sure you can all guess why."

Omunique blushed. "He's exaggerating. Four or five months sounds more like it." To everyone's delight, Omunique planted a riveting kiss on her husband's sweet lips.

Once the toasts were all delivered, the neatly dressed waiters snapped into action, passing around platters of delicious-looking finger foods. A variety of cracked crab, jumbo shrimp, and other seafood delicacies were plentiful. Chicken fingers, mozzarella cheese sticks, zucchini, and other lightly fried vegetables were served with creamy ranch dressing and fresh marinara sauce. A large platter filled with an array of fresh vegetables and dips was also passed around. Pickled delights and relishes were just another of many dishes served. Carrot cakes, strawberry cheese tarts, key lime pies, and homemade peach cobblers were the selections for the dessert menu.

While munching on the special dessert treats, everyone gathered in the beautifully appointed family room, where the fireplace dazzled with color and crackled with warmth. Everyone was made comfortable in the home built with all the wonderful ingredients of love.

Though the honeymoon to Japan had been over for months, Ken pulled out all the pictures and videotapes they'd shot during their visit to the Far East. He and Omunique took their guests through a thrilling narration of all the places they had visited and had captured on film. They had brought the guests into the fabulous Oriental room for the show-and-tell.

"This native-costumed, fascinating looking woman agreed to take a picture with Omunique after she practically begged her to. Omunique couldn't believe she was a geisha girl. Also, she could barely believe seeing the hundreds of vending machines that carried everything imaginable, from condoms matching men's blood types, to hot noodles. She really freaked out when she had to use the bathroom at Mt. Fuji, learning that both males and females used the same stalls—stalls without doors." Everyone laughed. "Needless to say that she didn't go to the bathroom until we got back on the train. By then it was a real emergency."

"Despite all that it was a fantastic trip. I loved eating *yakatori,* meat grilled over an open fire on shish kebab–style sticks, but smaller and thinner. I stuffed myself with *gyoza,* a delicious meat-and-vegetable dumpling that can be eaten either fried, or boiled and then lightly grilled. My favorite was *yakisoba,* thin soba noodles sautéed with cabbage, onions, and different luncheon meats. I thank the world traveler sitting over there, my dad, for teaching me how to use chopsticks. I, in turn, taught Ken. We had a blast learning how to use them the right way since I hadn't quite mastered them myself. In the beginning, we dropped more food than we ate."

Omunique eagerly pulled out all the colorful bolts of silk fabric she'd bought in the exciting shopping lanes. "Feel this, Aunt Mamie. Isn't it incredible?"

Mamie smiled. "It *is* that. But is there a particular reason why you're showing me all this expensive fabric?"

Omunique grinned. "I'm sure you can guess. You're only the greatest seamstress. I have several outfits in mind for me, but I want you to first pick out for yourself the fabric you like best." She looked to Marion and over at Amanda Steele. "You get to pick, too. Don't worry that we're leaving anyone out. We have lovely Oriental trinkets this evening for all our guests."

On Omunique's cue, Ken passed out to all the guests a variety of small but magnificent Oriental fans, freshly minted Japanese yen coins, and several more moderately priced Asian treasures. "We would've given these out when we first got home, but after talking about it, Omunique and I decided it would be nice to save it for the housewarming. I think we made a great decision." Everyone clapped in approval of his statement.

Ken once again called everyone's attention to him. "Before we get too far into the evening, I'd like to present a special housewarming gift to my wife. If everyone will follow us outdoors, I'll do the unveiling."

With a flick of a switch, colorful lights softly lit up the vast acreage behind the house. Ken directed his guests to the grounds surrounding the patio. He then pointed to a mound where dozens of rose bushes had been planted in the shape of two hearts intertwined.

"While I had the gardener prepare the ground with the outline for the design, I planted each of these rose bushes with my very own hands. I want my wife to have fresh roses every single day for the rest of her life. It's my desire that blooms will always be present in the two hearts to represent the love that'll forever blossom inside our flesh-and-blood hearts."

Plenty of astonished gasps and animated cheers over the dozens of beautiful bushes came from the guests. But Omunique was by far the most impressed with her husband's gift to her. Unable to keep from kissing him another second, she practically threw herself into his arms.

"You are incomparable! God only knows how much I love you. I feel so blessed. Thank you, darling. That was such a loving gesture. Just when I think you can't possibly outdo yourself, you manage to do it all over again. Isn't he one of the most romantic men in the world?"

Everyone clapped and cheered their positive response. Another kiss from Omunique and then they led their guests back indoors. A few people stayed outside to walk around the lovely grounds. Back inside the house conversations picked up where they'd left off. Everyone joined in to resume the lively party held in honor of the recent newlyweds and their first new home.

Hours later, after a smashingly successful housewarming, Omunique and Ken lay in bed, where Omunique couldn't stop talking to Ken about the evening. She dwelled on the rosebushes for quite a bit of time because she still felt so overwhelmed by his loving gesture.

Nestled into his arms, Omunique looked up at her husband. "Our house is so special, so blessed. We're also blessed to have so many people to love us and care about our future. The gifts were absolutely awesome. The pair of magnificent Waterford crystal flutes are too beautiful to describe. They also match the set of stemware Aunt Mamie gave us for our wedding. She has exquisite taste, not to mention expensive."

"I agree. It was a great party and I know everyone had a good time. Despite the great time I was having all I could think about was being alone with you again. I love it when it's just the two of us. Like now. I love having our family and friends around, but more than anything in the world, I love our private time together. We *are* truly blessed, Nique."

She kissed the tip of his nose. "Definitely blessed." By his comments, she couldn't help wondering if he'd had second thoughts about having kids as soon as possible. Deciding the timing was wrong for her to make any comments, she didn't broach the subject.

Ken engaged his wife in a hungry kiss. Within seconds, their desire for one another came at them with an uncontrollable force. Just as the evening had been, their lovemaking was relaxed yet full of physical and emotional excitement.

Well into the early morning hours, Ken and Omunique found infinite pleasure in being in love, in being married, in being as one.

Awakening to what sounded like sobbing, Ken rolled over and turned on the bedside lamp. Noticing that Omunique wasn't in bed, he sat still and listened intently to find out where the noises had come from. Now there was nothing but silence. He looked toward the adjoining bathroom but the light wasn't on in there. The sobbing sounds came again, only louder this time. He was in no doubt about where they came from now. Immediately, he leapt out of bed and ran downstairs in search of his wife. Curled up on the sofa in the family room, Omunique's sobbing sounded as if her world had suddenly come crashing down on her. Before falling asleep, she'd been so filled with happiness that she could hardly contain it within herself, he recalled.

Furnished with camel-beige sectional seating done in Italian leather, with built-in recliners on each end, the open concept family room was one of their favorite places to relax. Several works of African-American art graced the paneled walls. A fireplace and mantel, with built-in bookshelves housing a forty-plus-inch television screen, loads of candles nestled in unique brass and crystal holders, and the white rug from the condo, added a touch of romance to the comfortable decor. A matching stand-alone recliner, much larger than the ones on the sofa, was Ken's favorite place to sit when he was in the room alone, which mostly occurred when Omunique wasn't at home. Hardwood flooring and solid oak coffee and end tables completed the relaxing decor.

Seating himself on the edge of the sofa, Ken drew her into his arms. For several minutes he said nothing. Finally, lifting her head, he studied her tear stained face with deep concern. "I know there has to be something wrong or you wouldn't be crying. But the question is do you want to tell me about it? Or would you rather be left alone?"

She loved him for his sensitivity. He never tried to force her into revealing anything she didn't want to . . . and he always gave her an easy out. "I wanted to tell you, but you were sleeping so soundly that I would've felt guilty about waking you. That's one of the reasons why I came down here." She wiped her red and swollen eyes with the back of her hand.

"Okay. I'm awake now." His voice was soft as cotton. "I really want to know what's wrong." The distress in her eyes increased his worry. "I'm always here for you."

She twisted her bottom lip with her forefinger and thumb. "I don't think I can cut it in the pros. I may have made a mistake by joining the professional circuit."

"What makes you say that?" She stuck her feet out for him to see. He gasped at their swollen condition. Gently, he wrapped his hand around one of them. While his four fingers massaged the top of her foot, his thumb caressed the bottom. "How long have your feet been like this, Nique? I'm sorry I haven't noticed your discomfort." His hand went to her other foot.

"They started aching a little during the latter part of the

evening, but I didn't think much of it. Normally, when a serious flare-up occurs, the pain is much, much worse than what I felt then. When I got up to go to the bathroom, I knew I was in trouble. I could barely put any weight on them, especially the right one." She choked back a sob. "The condition seems to have worsened as I've grown older. I won't last in the pros if it keeps on getting worse."

He felt bad for what she'd already gone through with her feet, and for what she was going through now. "Maybe the hard training sessions you just finished caused this flare-up. I know how hard you work at your profession, but maybe you need to ease up a bit the next time. Have you soaked them yet?"

She shook her head in the negative. "I was on my way to the weight room to prepare the Jacuzzi with the herbal therapy to soak them in because I didn't want to disturb you by turning on the whirlpool jets in our bathtub. But when I finally reached the bottom step, I just broke down and started crying. The pain was that bad."

He ran his fingers down her thigh. "I don't ever want you to think you can't wake me up, Princess. Especially when you're in this kind of distress. I think we should get dressed and go to the ER." He massaged her shoulders with much tenderness, hoping to bring her emotional relief.

"Let's try the therapy first. If that doesn't reduce the swelling after a couple of hours, I'll take you up on your suggestion." A fat tear squeezed itself from her eye, and he kissed it away.

"Are you sure you want to wait that long?"

Looking crestfallen, she nodded. "A lot of times the therapy treatment is all it takes."

"I'm sure you know what's best. Lie here and rest while I fire up the Jacuzzi. Can I get you anything before I go?" She puckered up her trembling lips. Eagerly, he fulfilled her silent but demonstrative request to be kissed. "Be back shortly. How about something cool to drink? You're going to be up to your neck in hot water in a couple of minutes."

"That sounds nice, but I'll wait and take it into the weight room with me."

"I'll get the drink as soon as I get your herbal bath ready. Everything will be okay."

While waiting for Ken to return, she picked up the Avon catalogue off the end table, remembering that she'd forgotten to call her Avon lady, Esther, to put in this month's order. Omunique loved all the Skin-So-Soft products, especially the soft and sensual bath oil and foam bath. Glad to see that her favorites were on special, she made a mental note to called Esther first thing Monday morning. Needing something to do to try and keep her mind off the throbbing pain, she picked up a pad and pencil to jot down the items she planned to purchase.

Ken came back into the room carrying an extra-large frosted mug filled with ice, cranberry juice, white grape juice, and a splash of 7-Up, having attempted to create at least a variation of his Aunt Amanda's fruit juice concoction. Immediately, she closed the catalogue and set it aside. "Feeling any better?"

"A little. That looks delicious. What's in it?" He gave her a rundown of the ingredients. "Ah, stealing Aunt Amanda's recipe, are you?"

Relieved to see her smiling, he grinned. "I didn't use the exact ingredients 'cause I don't know what they all are, but I'll let you be the judge of how close I came. Ready to get into the Jacuzzi?"

"I think it's time."

As she attempted to get to her feet, he set the mug down on one of the coasters on the coffee table. "Let me help you out."

"Okay, but let me carry the drink so you won't have to come back for it." After lifting her off the sofa, he lowered her just enough for her to pick up the drink.

The trek down the long hallway and out the side door leading into the weight room located at the very back of the house was accomplished rather quickly. After helping her remove the emerald-green silk robe she wore, which left her totally nude, he lifted her up and then lowered her into the steaming, swirling waters. "I'm going to get you a bottle of cold water, also."

He gave her a boyish grin. "I think I need something else to cool me off, too. Seeing your naked flesh always produces desertlike conditions for my body." Appreciating his comment, she smiled up at him. After setting the timer on the tub, he walked to the other side of the room and opened the fullsize refrigerator and grabbed two plastic containers of ice-cold water.

With the Jacuzzi surrounded by steps leading up to a ledge of ceramic tiles wide enough to sit on, Ken positioned himself closest to where he'd situated her in the tub. "Any relief yet?"

"I can feel the treatment starting to work already. I won't mind if you go back to bed. You've been up since the crack of dawn working your fingers to the bone to make things right for our successful housewarming. I'll be okay by myself."

He ruffled her hair. "I'm fine. I'm going to stay in here until the treatment is complete. Close your eyes and relax. I'm going to move over to the sofa. It's getting steamy over here."

Seating himself on the black futon where he could keep a close eye on her and the wall clock, even though he'd set the timer, he picked up one of Omunique's BET magazines, *Heart and Soul.* He opened the African-American women's health publication and flipped through it. His eyes immediately latched onto an article entitled "Women & Arthritis." As he perused the print, he felt as though he'd been led there by divine powers. While reading the article, he began to get a much better understanding of what type of pain his wife suffered.

The article was so interesting that he lost track of time. When the Jacuzzi's buzzer sounded, he was glad he'd had the presence of mind to set it. It was time for her to come out of the tub. So engrossed was he in the article he hadn't checked on her in the last twenty minutes. Seeing that she appeared to have fallen asleep, he set the magazine aside and walked the few steps to the tub.

Gently, he lifted her chin up. "Hey, sleepyhead." She opened her eyes and smiled. "It's time to come out of there." He stepped over to the nearby massage table and picked up a fluffy white bath-sheet-size towel and laid it aside. Removing her from the water, he sat her on the ledge of the tub and began drying her off.

"You're spoiling me, but I do appreciate all the special attention you give to me."

"This is what a man is supposed to do for his woman . . . and vice versa. You take pretty good care of me, too. When it seemed that I had sprained my back while working out in the yard, you were right there to see me through it."

"We were both glad it turned out to be just a lumbar strain, but you were hurting as much as I was earlier. I think the therapy did the trick."

"We can go back to bed. As hard as it'll be for me, I promise to let you go right to sleep."

Ten

The pain was horrific. Forcefully sinking her teeth into her bottom lip, she held back her tears. Omunique wanted to scream for the doctor to take care of her right this minute, but she wasn't the only patient needing immediate treatment. Still, the pain in her feet had nearly become unmanageable. Why had she waited so long to come to the ER? The nurse had already been in to talk with her, but she hadn't seen anyone since. Though the curtains between the two treatment rooms were partially open, she only saw the empty bed in the next cubicle.

Bloodcurdling screams caused her to sit straight up. Scream after scream made her flinch inwardly. The partially open curtain allowed her to see the paramedics transferring a female patient from the ambulance gurney to the hospital bed.

"Help me," the woman screamed. "I'm bleeding to death . . . and my . . . baby is . . . drowning in it. Please save . . . my baby."

In the next instant Omunique saw the snowy-white sheet and blanket turn crimson. Seeing the blood-soaked linens caused nausea to swirl in her stomach, making her feel faint. She actually felt the color draining from her face while her breathing grew shallow. Loud shouts came from every direction of the ER as medical personnel swarmed the area surrounding the bleeding patient.

"We need to transfuse, STAT," shouted an anxious voice. "Do a type and cross-match. Hurry, damn it, we're running out of time, people."

"Oh, my God, we're losing her," another voice shouted. "We have to deliver this baby now. Move it. Get her feet up in the stirrups. Come on, people, we don't want to lose this battle."

"Severe drop in blood pressure! Where's that damn blood? Get the lab on the phone . . ."

Omunique muffled the screams filling her lungs. Is this what had happened to her mother? Did she suffer in agony like the woman on the gurney? Was this woman going to die like her mother had? Unable to hold back her tears, Omunique released them. Forgetting her own excruciating pain, Omunique cried and prayed at the same time for the woman she didn't know from Adam, cried for the baby who might grow up without a mother just as she'd done.

A loud, consistent beeping noise was followed by seconds of silence . . . More shouting out of orders went on for the next fifteen minutes. Dead silence followed . . .

"We've lost the mother," a male voice shouted. "But we can still save her baby."

Only minutes later the seemingly healthy cry of a newborn rang out.

Daring to look over at the woman who now lay so still, Omunique watched in both horror and amazement as the doctor lifted up a blood-covered infant, a baby boy. She instantly thought of how Wyman must have felt when he learned of her mother's death. A painful sob tore from her throat, causing several of the staff members to look in her direction. Without any consideration whatsoever of what Omunique had just witnessed, one of the nurses yanked the curtain shut, cutting her completely off from the painful, sorrowful scene.

But Omunique didn't need to see any more. She'd seen enough. The woman had died fighting to give her child life, the same as her mother had done for her. Filled with an ominous terror, she began to shake all over. She and Ken wanted children . . . and she'd convinced him on their honeymoon that she didn't want them to wait to start a family . . . and that she wanted to start right away. How could she do that now after what she'd just witnessed? How could she do something that might kill her and possibly end up taking the life of their child?

It had grown dreadfully silent. As though her body moved of its own accord, she got up from the gurney. Slowly, she inched her way to the abandoned mother who'd died the same way Patrice Philyaw had died. With tears in her eyes, she reached the bedside. Without a thought to later consequences, she pulled back the sheet covering the woman's face and her once-pregnant body. As though her hand was drawn there, she smoothed back the dead woman's hair. She was still warm but life no longer ebbed within her, yet she'd managed to *give* life. Had she known it was her last, most important contribution to the future of the world?

Omunique's feet practically left the ground when a hand suddenly clamped down on her shoulder. Startled, she turned around, lowering her eyes to the floor when she saw the pretty Hispanic nurse there. Witnessing such a morbid scene had left Omunique terribly shaken.

"You can't be in here, ma'am." The voice was gentle, soothing. "The morgue is already on the way to transport the remains. Let me help you back to your bed."

Deeply sorrowed, Omunique looked into the jet-black eyes of the female attendant. "It didn't seem right that she should be left alone. I wouldn't want to have been left by myself. Doesn't she have family waiting out there?"

Seeing the anguished look in Omunique's eyes, Melinda Sanchez briefly touched her hand to bring her comfort. "There's no family to speak of. According to the records, she was giving up the baby for adoption. The department of social services has already been notified. The baby will probably be placed in foster care until he's adopted. However, all the necessary paperwork has to be in order before anything can occur."

"Oh, how terribly sad for the newborn. My mom died right after she gave birth to me, but I was fortunate enough to have my dad and my paternal grandmother there to care for me. My mother's parents were also deceased when I was born. But this little one will only come to know strangers. My heart bleeds for him."

Melinda helped Omunique back to her cubicle when it looked like she might faint. "Sorry for the long delay. I'll try to get a doctor in here right away. You look totally exhausted. This must've been horrible for you, especially given your own personal history."

"Not as horrible as it might eventually be for the infant."

"The agency will find the baby a good home. Most adopting parents desire a newborn over older children. The little one will be just fine."

"I hope they find an excellent home for the baby boy. He's going to need a lot of love and nurturing. But nothing can ever fill the void of a loving mom. I know that firsthand."

The doctor finally came in to see Omunique. Only a short period of time had passed before he had her on her way, having given her the same old instructions on how to care for her badly swollen feet. Lots of bed rest, a prescription for more analgesics, and hot-water soaks.

Out in the corridor, Omunique pushed the elevator button and waited for the car to come. As she looked down the hallway, she gasped in horror, nearly gagging on her own saliva. The hairs on the back of her neck stood at attention. Seated in a wheelchair was a man that looked exactly like Marcus Taylor. As the wheelchair turned the corner, forgetting the pain in her crippled feet, she ran after it. By the time she got to the end of the corridor, the wheelchair had totally disappeared. With an eerie feeling settling deep inside her stomach, frantically, she looked all around her. The only people she saw milling about in the corridor appeared to her as hospital staff and a few visitors. Scared to death, wondering if she was losing her mind, she walked back toward the elevator that would take her to the upper-level parking garages.

Marcus Taylor was dead, wasn't he? Of course he was dead, she told herself. Though he'd been shot only once in the shoulder by the police, the newspapers had all reported that he'd actually died of another gunshot wound. Omunique shivered with fear as she recalled pushing him out of the way of the torrent of bullets flying his way that terrifying night. Shortly after she'd saved his life, the half-crazed police officer that had stalked her unmercifully had apparently shot himself right in the head with his own service revolver. She was sure that he couldn't have survived that type of serious injury. No way possible . . .

With the ER doctor's instructions in her hand for tending to her swollen feet, Omunique entered the master bedroom. Heading straight for the bathroom, she sat down on the dressing table stool and removed her unlaced sneakers. Still active in her mind, the horrifically sorrowful scenes from the hospital had stayed with her throughout her drive home. What was even more horrifying was that she actually thought she'd seen Marcus Taylor.

Lying across the bed, she engaged in a bit of somber thinking. Life and death, death and life, born to die, die giving birth. It seemed like such a waste. Omunique couldn't help wondering what special circumstances had prompted the mother to decide to give up the baby for adoption. The woman looked to be only in her late twenties. She certainly hadn't been a teenager making what she may have thought of as the best decision for her child. She appeared fully mature, but that didn't necessarily mean that she'd been a responsible adult. Or her life could've been a very hard one, the type of life that she didn't want her child to come to know.

Though she fell asleep within minutes of lying down, Omunique tossed and turned, having gone to sleep weighted down with thoughts of the tragedy she'd witnessed. She had also fallen asleep worried and deathly afraid over the dead officer she couldn't have possibly seen.

Ken called out for Omunique as he came down the carpeted hallway. After unloading his briefcase in his office, located right across the hall from the master suite, he came into the bedroom and immediately lay down next to his wife. His weight on the bed caused her to awaken immediately.

She rubbed her eyes. "Hi, lover."

"Hi, beautiful. How was your day?"

She burst into tears. "Horrendous. This has been an absolutely horrible day."

Concerned, his eyes went straight to her feet. He recalled the episode she had a few nights ago as well her earlier complaints of them hurting before he'd left for work. "I see what you mean. Let's go to the hospital."

"I've already been to the ER, but I don't know why I bother." Her lower lip trembling, she wiped her eyes with the heels of her hands. "The course of treatment never changes. The pain was so unbearable that I thought I'd better have them looked at just in case something out of the ordinary had developed. It was the same-old same-old."

After loosening his tie, he pulled her into his arms. "Ready to soak your feet in a hot tub of water?"

She nodded. "In a minute. I want to lie here with you

for a while. You need to relax a bit since you just got home. How was your day?"

He kissed the tip of her nose. "Busy, as usual. We've got so many new clients to tend to. Nelson Warner up in Washington state has referred a lot of business to us. He really loved the deal I put together for him despite his attempt to get us to lower our bid." Rolling up on his side, he brought her full against him. His lips met with hers in a soothing kiss. "I think we should get you into the tub now. We can relax once that's taken care of."

"Maybe so. Are you hungry?"

"Not really. Since you don't need to be on your feet, I'll order a pizza or something else that can be delivered in."

"That won't be necessary. Aunt Mamie brought over a heap of food: collards, potato salad, and barbecued chicken. We also have enough garden salad left over from last night. It should still be fresh."

"Sounds delicious, but what's the occasion?"

"You're going to have to get used to Aunt Mamie's thoughtful ways, but you should know by now that she doesn't need a special occasion to cook. She just felt like cooking dinner for us. She came over just before I left for the hospital."

"Did you mention where you were going?"

"I didn't want to worry her, but I think she sensed my discomfort. She kept asking if I was okay, saying that I didn't seem like myself."

Omunique thought of telling Ken about the death of the woman that she'd witnessed at the hospital, but something told her not to. He didn't need to hear any more bad news, especially since he'd just gotten home from a long day at the office. As for the Marcus Taylor situation, she wouldn't even allow herself to think about it, let alone address it. As far as she was concerned, her stressed-out mind was beginning to play cruel tricks on her, flashbacks of the worst kind.

Wanting to feel his naked flesh beneath her hands, Omunique completely removed his tie and slowly unbuttoned his shirt. Bending her head, she kissed each of his nipples, circling them with her tongue. Aroused by the hardening of them, she loosened his belt buckle and opened the top of his slacks. As her hands heated up his flesh, he began to disrobe her. With the sudden sight of the dead woman popping into her head, she pushed him away.

"What's wrong, Nique?" He looked puzzled.

"A jolt of pain just shot through my left foot. I better go and do as you've suggested before my feet burst wide open from the swelling. I'm sorry. But I do promise to finish what I got started here." *That is, if I can get these bloody images out of my head.*

"Since we're working on a family, I'll have to hold you to your promise." Leaping off the bed, he ran into the bathroom and turned on the water jets. He then poured a generous amount of Epsom salts under the strong flow.

In the same moment Ken disappeared into the bathroom, Omunique opened the nightstand drawer and popped a birth control pill into her mouth. In the absence of water, she swallowed it dry. She hated that she'd felt compelled to push Ken away—and had now resorted to deception. Her body desired him, but the image of the dead woman, with her blood everywhere, had stymied her sexual appetite. It had made plenty of room for old fears to arise.

On swollen, tender feet, with her husband's help, Omunique made her way into the bathroom. Ken kissed her softly on the mouth. "I'm going to go down and warm up the food. Do you want to eat up here in the bedroom?"

"Sounds nice. Give me twenty minutes or so."

"Take as long as you need, sweetheart. I'm going to slip into some comfortable duds before I head down to the kitchen."

Thinking that she would eventually come to terms with everything, that she'd get back to normal in just a short period of time, she relaxed in the tub, allowing her feet to soak up the healing crystals Ken had put in the water. Everything would be okay with time. It had to be . . .

The dining table in the bedroom would easily accommodate up to four people but was perfect for just the two of them. Situated near the antique-white French doors, the location of the table gave them a splendid vista of the grounds below, as well as an excellent view of the hearts of roses. The outdoor pool and Jacuzzi could also be seen from most areas in the bedroom.

Wrapped only in a bath-sheet tied sarong style, Omunique pulled a chair from the table and sat down. It wasn't quite time for sunset, but dusk was quickly approaching. With a great view of the mountains, they often watched the sun go down from the fully furnished sundeck off their bedroom.

Omunique looked up when Ken came into the room carrying a leather case, which he opened up and removed several plastic vials of soothing lotions and herbal balms. Winston Bailey, her physical therapist, kept them supplied with all the essential healing ointments needed for administering the proper therapies when it wasn't possible for her to seek him out.

Kneeling down in front of her, Ken first went to work on the left foot, massaging it and kneading it tenderly. Omunique closed her eyes, loving the feel of her husband's gentle but firm hands, gifted hands. She relished all the pleasure his hands had brought to the different parts of her anatomy. They'd come to know her body as well as she did. At one time or another, his lips and hands had caressed every minuscule inch of her.

Her mouth opened, and she emitted a soothing moan. "That feels divine, love. Your hands should be packaged but not sold, because I'd never want them to touch anyone but me. Can I have a kiss?" She looked so vulnerable to him, yet so sexy, so very desirable.

"I may not be able to stop at just a kiss. Our kisses have a way of setting uncontrollable fires. Arsonlike infernos."

She stuck her own finger in her mouth, sucking provocatively on the tip. "I know. Why do you think I asked for one?"

He grinned. Removing her finger from her mouth, he placed it in his own, moaning with pleasure. "You're so sweet, but I know other places on you that are even sweeter."

Her nipples hardened as his moist tongue circled the tip of her finger. Using her own wet finger, he drew circles around her erect aureoles. The soft flesh between her thighs pulsated with a powerful need, an urgent longing. Guiding his hands betwixt her legs, she tossed her head back and closed her eyes. While controlling his hand, she took pleasure in moving it over the places burning for his thrill-invoking touch. Moving over to the bed in a few limping movements, she rested back on her elbows and opened her legs to him, wanting him inside her pool of singeing heat. Desperately, she needed him to wipe away the horrible, painful images of earlier in the day.

"Nique, you're pretty hot, baby. Are you ready for me to cool you down?"

"Are you sure you can?" Taunting him, she once again sucked the tip of her finger.

He took his tongue to her ear. "Are you sure you can stand the pressure of my needs?"

To further provoke his desire, she lay on her stomach and parted her legs just enough to make him question his sanity. In one fluid motion, he was on top of her, burying his face against the back of her head. Lifting her hair from her neck, his lips sought out her burning flesh, savoring the sweet taste of her. Rolling on his side, he brought her flush against his full length.

Biting down gently, his teeth teased her lower lip. "Baby,

you're my world. It's rocking from side to side right now."
He guided her hand to his erection. "This is what happens
to me every time I think of you. In the office is especially
hard for me. Many times each day, I find myself wanting
to rush home to you and have you relieve the pain of my
wanting you so badly."

She kissed his mouth. "It's no different for me. Just imag-
ining us making love leaves me breathless with longing. I
can't wait for you to be inside of me. Are you ready for
us to come together?"

"Come together? I hope you mean that literally. But I
think we do a hell of a lot more than just coming together.
TNT explosion is more like it."

"Hush," she gently commanded. "Let's get our explosion
on before I die of sheer sexual need. I'm already on fire
for you. If you keep me waiting, we may need the fire
department."

"Indeed! And I'm ready for us to explode all into one
another, time and time again."

After getting Ken to turn over on his back, Omunique
straddled him, lowering herself down on him, allowing her
burning desire to meet with his. Gently, sweetly, they surrendered themselves to the rhythm of an unfinished song,
to the sweetest of melodies, writing the romantic lyrics of
love as their bodies dictated each erotic, sensuous note.

Lying atop the man she adored, rocking back and forth
with a near feral urgency, Omunique kissed her husband's
eyes and throat. Pleasurable agony coursed through him,
causing him to match the unfettered strokes of her magical
ecstasy.

He looked up into her pleasure-glazed eyes. Slightly embarrassed by what she felt, darn near barbaric carnality, she
closed them. "Open your eyes, baby," he whispered. "I want
to see all that you're feeling. I want to see the fire burning
there in your gray eyes. Oh, you're beautiful, so beautiful,

Nique. Talk to me. Let your eyes tell me what you know I want to hear."

Locking her eyes with his, she licked her lips in a provocative way, allowing her tongue to linger on her lower lip. As always, her low guttural moans excited him. She lifted herself up until withdrawal was practically complete. Slowly, she lowered herself back down, repeating the arousing impact over and over again.

"Tell me, Nique. Tell me now . . ."

Aware that he was ready for release, Omunique told him through her eyes and in the language of her gyrating body all that he desired to hear. The course of their lovemaking rapidly changed from smooth and easy to wild and frantic. As bare, slick skin met with heated flesh, need matching need, desire piled on top of desire welled up to consume them in a firestorm of lustful cravings. While searching and finding every conceivable and implausible pleasure, release came as hot and steamy, tropical-like heat waves, leaving them drenched with perspiration but exhaustively fulfilled. Evaporation seemed to hover over them like an emancipated rain cloud, but they were too weak from pleasurable overindulgence to even care.

The type of riotous, highly emotional orgasms that Ken's hot lovemaking produced for her always left her sobbing uncontrollably against his chest. While her breath heaved with short, quickened gasps, her body vibrated all over as she tried to regain at least a smidgen of control.

"I know," he soothed. "I feel just the same emotions as you. Our lovemaking is almost wicked at times. Try and calm down now."

She lifted her head up and met his gaze. "Calm . . . down!" She gasped for breath. "Damn near . . . impossible. If you can tell me . . . how, I'll be . . . glad to."

This woman sure knew how to stroke his ego without even trying. Seeing her all lathered and heated up, her eyes wild and dazed as she gasped for control did amazing things for him. Knowing his lovemaking had that kind of effect on her had him feeling like the only strutting rooster living in a barn filled with hens. But this cocky rooster only had the *hots* for one chick.

Freshly showered, with both dressed in loose-fitting attire, Omunique and Ken practically devoured the food Ken had warmed and brought upstairs. Sipping on his special blended juice concoction, Omunique looked to be deep in thought. He'd noticed how distracted she'd become. But, as usual, he was willing to wait until she addressed whatever she had on her mind.

As if she'd read his mind, she looked up at him. For a couple of seconds she chewed on her lower lip. "Do you think it's possible that Marcus Taylor may've survived his gunshot wounds? Any possibility at all in that happening?"

Unable to hide how much her question had caught him off guard, his mouth dropped open. He just stared at her for several moments. "I know it hasn't been long enough for you to be completely over the most horrific episode in your life. But is that what you've been thinking about over there? And what has prompted such an odd question?"

"It may not be so odd. I thought for sure that I saw Marcus Taylor at the hospital right after I left the ER. A man in a wheelchair looked just like him. I chased the wheelchair down, but it seemed to disappear into thin air." This statement surprised him more than her first question.

"Sweetheart, I can't imagine Taylor surviving a bullet to the head. Not that it hasn't happened before, but the odds of that are very slim. Besides, we read practically every newspaper and heard every newscast reporting the story of his death. The funeral was private, but that doesn't prove a thing. A lot of families have private services." He thought the whole idea was ludicrous but he didn't want to challenge her on what she thought she'd seen. That might only make her more emotionally upset . . . and possibly cause her to become upset with him.

"I'm sure you're right. I was in so much pain I could've imagined the whole thing." Images of the dead woman came to her and she closed her eyes to ward them off. Not before Ken saw a brief flash of terror in them. That type of look in her eyes made him nervous.

Thinking she still harbored thoughts of Taylor being alive, he decided to let her work through it herself for the time being. Maybe the thoughts would just go away in a short time, like before. While he didn't think there was a remote possibility that he was alive, he had to admit she had him questioning the likelihood of something like that actually occurring.

To take both their minds off of it, he turned on the television to see what movies were on the cable networks. "Anything in particular you want to watch?"

"Guess."

"Figure skating."

Smiling, she nodded. "I can watch it in another room if you want to see something else."

"First, let me see if any of the channels are carrying an event. Then I'll decide if I want to watch something else. If so, I'll go into the audiovisual room. You need to stay off your feet and keep them elevated for the rest of the evening."

Surfing through all the channels, not once but twice, Ken still couldn't find a single skating event on any of the major sports channels or the local networks. "Looks like you're out of luck. But we have plenty of video recorded skating. You want to watch a taped program?"

"I'm going to do just as you suggested. Lie in bed and prop up my feet."

"I think I should get a little work done on the papers I brought home to look over. I'll be in my office for a short while. Do you want anything before I get started?"

"Nothing at all. I need to call Dad. I haven't talked to him today."

"I know you're going to nose around in his personal business. Aunt Mamie showed up with Wyman at the housewarming, so I'd like to know what's up with those three myself."

"I'm sure they'll tell us when they're ready, but a little prompting from me won't hurt."

"Unless he tells you to mind your own business." He started laughing. "I've been meaning to ask you something for a long time now. When you pulled the prank on Wyman for insulting you about cooking, how did you manage to conceal the dish-soap?"

She grinned. "It was easy. Dad usually eats large chunks of cake, so I cut a huge piece in half and stuck it back together with the liquid soap. I had some extra icing left over so I used it for camouflage. Pretty clever, huh?"

"You certainly could say that. What I'm waiting for is his retaliation. I thought it would've come by now." He couldn't help wondering what he had in store for her—and when.

"Dad's been known to wait it out for a long time. The element of surprise is the tactic he uses best. He tries to wait until he's sure I've forgotten all about it. He'll come up with a good one. Count on it. I know it's coming but I'm not looking forward to it."

"Let me help you get into bed before I go." A veiled message for him? he wondered.

"Go ahead and do what you have to do, Ken. I can manage that small feat. The bed is only a few feet away. I don't want to lean on you too much, especially when it's not necessary."

"Okay. See you in little bit. Enjoy your chat with Dad." Bending over the chair, he gave her several quick kisses and one long one before leaving the room." He wanted Omunique to lean on him whether it was necessary or not.

He was sure she already knew that. But he had no problem with it when she decided to assert her own independence.

Ken looked at the red phone buttons to see which line Omunique was on before he punched in the unlit one for use of the other line. Omunique thinking she'd seen Taylor concerned him more than he wanted her to know. After punching in the memory button that stored his godfather's home number, he waited for an answer. Glad that Ralph had answered the call and not his godmother, Ken greeted him and inquired of his health before launching into his concerns. He allowed a few minutes of chitchat to occur and then he got down to business. He stated his concerns clearly, precisely.

"Ken, anything is possible, but I haven't heard a thing about Taylor being alive. Are you sure Omunique hasn't suffered any flashbacks in recent weeks? This is typical of the victim's behavior when that occurs."

"*Victim,* how I hate that word."

"I'm a cop, son. I've been one all my adult life, which is why I came out of retirement. It's what I do, what I am. Please forgive the everyday shoptalk. I know it's not a comforting word in reference to someone you love."

"When I hear that word, I think of someone who didn't survive the perpetrator's crime. By the grace of God Omunique survived . . . and I want to make damn sure there isn't a chance that this lunatic might not be taking a permanent dirt nap, after all. Six feet under isn't deep enough for me, not when I think of what he did to my wife. More so, what he didn't get to finish when he took her on that intended death ride in his van."

"Not something any of us likes to think about, especially Omunique. Has anything unusual been going on with her in the past few days?"

"It's not unusual but her feet are giving her major trouble again."

"Is she on any type of pain killers? Some medications have a tendency to induce psychosis in some people. When that occurs, they often see and hear things that aren't there."

"She did go to the ER. Whether she was given any type of pain medication, I really can't say. I know she takes Motrin and other similar types of analgesics. I'll inventory all our bathroom medicine cabinets. What should I be looking for?"

"Prescriptions that have codeine or even morphine in them. Controlled substances normally have a red warning label on them. They're also federally monitored to circumvent chances of abuse. A small amount of these drugs can have mind-altering effects in people who suffer from drug sensitivities. Check it out and let me know. If you do find something, you need to check with her doctor and get his opinion. We have to assess her state of mind first."

"That isn't something I'd think of doing without alerting her to the fact. She'd throw a hysterical fit if I go behind her back like that. I'll never forget what we went through when Wyman hired a security team against her objections. That was lesson enough for me."

"I've got one very reliable source that I can turn to. He'd never talk to me about highly sensitive matters unless I ask him directly. If there's anything to this, my source will know."

Eleven

Seated on the leather sofa in Max's office, Ken and his father were taking a coffee break. Ken had just finished running down for his father the concerns that he had about Omunique. He had decided not to mention the situation with Taylor until he heard back from his godfather.

"How are her feet doing now?"

"Much better, Dad. But she's afraid that her condition is worsening with age."

Max laughed. "She's only a tender twenty-two. It probably won't get that bad until she's much older, if it does at all."

Ken picked up the mug of coffee. "You have to remember that she's been plagued with this problem all her life. Her first surgery came when she was just a little thing. She's even talked with her agent and attorney about renegotiating her contract. She's now only interested in doing special events and other guest skating appearances. Her situation warrants her to exercise the part of the contractual agreement addressing the problems with her feet. She and Lamar had that clause built in for this very reason. Also, I strongly suspect that Omunique has decided that she doesn't want to be away from home for weeks at a time. That certainly works in my favor. At any rate, she's convinced that she needs to take a short break from event skating."

"Excuse me a moment, son."

Max got up from the sofa and went to the file drawer built into his desk, where he removed a manila file from its folder. He came back to Ken, handed the file to him, and then took his seat. Max closely studied his son's expressions as he perused the contents of the folder.

Amazed at what he'd just read, Ken looked up at Max, a whistle escaping his lips. "Dad, this is fantastic, but far too generous." Scowling, Ken scratched his head. "We may have one big problem: Omunique. She might not accept this from you. This is *her* dream to accomplish."

Max grinned. "She *has* accomplished it. She won the Olympic silver medal, not that I have to tell you that. Listen, son, Wyman is invested in the arena, as well. In fact, we all are. But Omunique's name is the only one that will appear on the deed. We're just silent partners. If she's having doubts about being able to cut it in the pros for medical reasons, I see this proposition as a great alternative. Isn't this also a better option than going to a bank for a loan that will have astronomical interests rates attached to it? Regardless of how many major endorsements she gets, she will need to borrow money to get started in business. The first rule of thumb in starting a business is to use someone else's money; not your own."

"You don't have to convince me about this. I agree with what you and Wyman have done. Knowing my wife, she's not in this for profit or personal gain. She merely wants to introduce minority children and those from low-income families to the world she's lived in. She wants to give them a chance at something new, exciting, and wonderful. But I'm afraid that she's the one you're going to have to convince. Where's the arena site located?"

"We've purchased a huge chunk of land in an old abandoned industrial area of Los Angeles. It's actually between Compton and L.A. Her inner-city dream. Wyman and I tossed this around thoroughly before we purchased the land. This way she can build to her own specifications, just as you two have done with the house. But if she doesn't accept it, Wyman and I came up with a few good other uses for the land. If our daughter decides that she wants to do this alone, though we hope she accepts our proposal, we're going to build, anyway."

"Build what?"

Max stroked the hair on his chin. "I've been thinking of us having our own athletic wear store that consumers can actually come into and purchase our sports gear. So far we've only designed and supplied our gear to professional sports teams, little league teams, different high school and college teams, and so on and so forth. With our own stores, we can get our slice of the pie. Such names as Nike and Reebok have made a killing selling their gear in retail stores."

Ken grinned. "Dad, you and I really do think a lot alike. I've been writing up a proposal to present to you and the board on this very issue. The proposition keeps getting better and better. Who knows? Maybe my wife will love the idea of a family arena."

"Son, Wyman and I have discussed this matter in great detail. We would like for you to present it to Omunique. Or at least feel her out and see what she thinks of the idea."

"That's all well and good, but I think we should all sit down and discuss it together. She's either going to be for it or against it. And she will let you know in no uncertain terms which way the wind is blowing for her. Something tells me that Omunique wants her ice arena—and that she's worried about how to come up with the money. Since she hasn't yet signed a major endorsement, she may go for this deal. We don't like being away from each other. I also see this as a solution to that problem, as well as the problem with her feet."

"If she is in fact worried about the money, Wyman and I can simply become her lenders if she has a problem with accepting our gift."

"What are you doing this evening? Maybe we could get together with her then."

"I'm free, but I don't know about Wyman. And he has to be in on this. I'll give him a call. I'll tap into you as soon as I have something definitive."

"Okay, Dad. I'll check and make sure Omunique doesn't have any plans for this evening, as well. Now, we Maxwell men had better get back to work if we're going to accomplish all of our dreams."

Thomasina was on the phone when Ken passed through the reception area. Before he could reach his office door, he heard her calling out to him. He turned around and walked over to her desk. "What do you need, Thom?"

As if she felt somewhat reluctant to speak, she bit down on her lower lip. "I have a little problem. My car is on *whack* again. Do you think you could give me a ride home this evening?"

This was certainly one question he hadn't expected from her. "I don't know. Max is trying to schedule a meeting for us this evening." He suddenly realized that his answer had not been definite enough. He shouldn't give the impression that she could ever rely on the boss for her transportation problems. "In fact, the more I think about it, I see that it's an impossibility for me to accommodate you. Perhaps you should call a cab. It appears to me that what you need to do is obtain more reliable transportation. Your car seems to break down at least twice a month. Your repair bills must be phenomenal."

Thomasina snorted under her breath. "Thank you. A cab would cost a fortune, but I'm sure I can find another way home."

Her attempt at getting him alone hadn't worked like the charm that she thought it might. However there would be other times, other circumstances that she'd be alone with the boss. They had worked late into the evening in the past. Once the honeymoon phase was over, and with all the new business coming in, she was sure he'd revert back to working overtime. He also had a tendency to stay in the office late when dear wife's profession took her out of town.

Back at his desk Ken thought of Thomasina's request. Had it come as a result of him driving her to the company Christmas party last year? Max asking him to do him a favor of picking her up was one thing, but him giving her rides home suggested something altogether different. He certainly wasn't a taxi service. Besides, he didn't want to encourage her in any way.

They'd already had one sticky situation when he'd confronted her over wearing inappropriate apparel in the office. Though he was sure he'd put her in her place on all fronts then, she had become a little more openly flirtatious with him; even more so since his marriage. Although he wasn't the least bit flattered by it, he hoped that he wouldn't have to address it either.

Max's home was modest with inviting warmth, which fit his personality to a T. He had a penchant for old-world style furnishings. Most of them were eighteenth century heirloom reproductions, done in cherry and other fine dark wood veneers. The rooms actually defined the character of the man: strong, reliable, and of very good quality. In Max's den, barrister bookcases and an eighteenth century escritoire could be seen from the double doors that opened off the living room. Queen Anne tables, which made wonderful accents, completed the period decor.

Over a quiet dinner, which had been catered, the group of five was seated at the mission-style dinning table. Since everyone had finished the main course and had started on coffee and dessert, Max and Wyman were now preparing themselves to present their plans to Omunique. Wyman had brought Mamie along for support. If his daughter happened to rebel against them, Mamie knew exactly how to calm her, and at least get her to listen to the voice of reason.

Wyman thought that he should go first in order to clear what could prove to be a stony path. As he laid the plans out in a cautious but factual way, Omunique listened intently. She paid very close attention to every minute detail of what he had to say. Her heart beat faster and faster with each spoken word. She actually felt the tension coming from the others, but she understood it perfectly. It was no secret that her independent, rebellious nature would surface when she suspected someone of trying to take over her life and to make decisions that she was easily capable of making for herself.

What appeared to be a discomforting frown was present on her face by the time Wyman was finished. Despite the disconcerting look on Omunique's face Max forged ahead in presenting his side of the issues. Just as Wyman had done, he did a marvelous job of stating his case. Both sides had made a compelling case once Max completed his presentation.

Frowning heavily, Omunique looked at Ken. "Do you have something to say, as well?" Ken took the frown as a good indication that she wasn't having any of it.

He threw up a hand. "This is Max and Wyman's show. I'm listening just like you are."

She boldly eyed her husband with suspicion. "Are you saying that you haven't heard this pitch before now?"

"I'm not saying that at all. It was only presented to me earlier today. They thought I should be the one to run it by you, but I thought that we should all sit down together and discuss it as a whole. Regardless to what anyone wants or thinks, the final decision lies solely with you."

She raised an eyebrow. "You don't say! It looks to me like I've been set up real good."

Intently, she eyed every man at the table. The room was quiet enough to hear a cotton-ball drop on the carpet. As she looked over at Mamie's worried expression, Omunique's gray eyes began to shine with a near-blinding brightness. Then came a smile as bright as her eyes. "I think it's a marvelous idea, brilliant, fantastic!"

Audible sounds of gushing breaths of relief came from everyone at the table, but she'd only given them what she knew they'd probably expected from her. She was relatively sure that everyone had decided that she would more than likely blow a gasket.

"And you know what, I've been thinking long and hard of asking if anyone was interested in making the ice arena a joint venture, a family business, so to speak. I would've gone to Ken first because I value his opinion as well as his feedback. Even when it's something I've already made my mind up about." She leaned over and kissed her husband. "Had you worried there for a minute, didn't I?"

Ken grinned. "You had us all worried. Now that we know you're okay with this is there something else you'd like to add?"

"A lot. I especially like the idea of building to our own specifications. If everyone is okay with it, we can use Brandon's firm again. We've seen the results of his gifted skills right in our own home. But listen to these ideas. I think we could have a fabulous boutique inside the arena, one that sells only Maxwell athletic gear." Max and Ken exchanged bewildered glances.

"Since a lot of people will pass through the arena, salespersons, delivery people, etc., I'd like to see Dad set up an insurance agency within the same structure. If this is going to be a family business, we need to include each of the existing businesses. Furthermore, I think Aunt Mamie could have a small café-style eatery since she loves to cook and bake. We could have the regular snack bar items, like potato chips, drinks, hot dogs, and other munchies along with Aunt Mamie's delicious specialty food items. And I would like to try and steal Andy Tarpley away from the Palos Verdes ice arena and have him as chief of our maintenance department. Or perhaps hire him on a part-time basis and let him select a competent staff."

Looks of utter amazement passed between the other four at the table.

Ken looked at his wife with deep admiration. "Wow, you are something else, a woman after my own heart. Since we've heard from everyone else, except for Aunt Mamie, can I take a shot at presenting my ideas?"

"Let's hear them," Max said. The others nodded in agreement.

"What about offering the use of the facility as an official training site to other figure skaters, amateur or pro; even to professional hockey players? It could be used as a place of practice when professional skating tours and events come to Los Angeles. There's nothing like it in the area where we plan to build. Omunique can teach her skating classes as often as she likes. We'll just put a wall up between the two areas. One side of the arena will only cater to pros."

"What a brainchild you are," Omunique enthused. "It would certainly bring in the kind of revenue we'll need to operate an arena on that grand of a scale. Hockey is definitely seasonal, but professional athletes often train in off-season just to stay in shape. The skating lessons can be given all year long. I think we're onto something big here. Look out sports world, the Philyaw and Maxwell families are breathing right down the necks of those who have had a corner on the athletic-wear market for years!" High fives were passed among everyone as loud cheers of approval went out. "When can we see the Los Angeles site that you have in mind?"

"First thing in the morning is okay with me," Max replied.

Omunique looked to Mamie. "You're so quiet over there. What's your take on this? Especially the café idea?"

Mamie shook her head. "Your four minds are nothing

short of brilliant. I'm in absolute awe over here. Your business minds have practically all run the same way. The ideas are different ideas but each has the same purpose in mind, which is to make this venture work. As for the café, do you really have to ask? I'm in. Just let me know what investments are required of me: monetarily and time-wise."

Wyman leaned over and hugged Mamie and then his daughter. "Let the building begin! How's nine-thirty for everyone?"

"A.M.?" Omunique inquired.

"Too early for you, Nique?" Wyman asked.

"I was thinking more of seven-thirty. Early is better for me. I'm already bursting with anticipation. I can hardly wait to see the site."

"Seven-thirty it is," Max chimed in. "Can I get a show of hands on the time?" All hands raised in agreement.

Ken went from bathroom to bathroom in their home checking for prescriptions. When he found nothing more than the analgesics he'd already mentioned to Ralph, he went upstairs where Omunique was getting ready for bed.

Finding his wife in their bedroom retreat, he sat down on the sofa next to her. "I have a question I'd like to ask. When you went to the ER the day you thought you saw Taylor, were any medications prescribed for you? Medications that are considered controlled substances?"

"What kind of question is that?"

"I talked to Uncle Ralph about your seeing Taylor. He asked what type of pills you were taking to rule out the possibility of medication-induced psychosis." The look on her face told him that he hadn't come across the way he'd intended.

"Is he trying to say that I'm seeing things because of the medication I may be on? I don't believe that I'm just seeing things, Ken. I'm darn near positive that the man in the wheelchair was Marcus Taylor. I only know what I saw. I don't know how to explain this." She balled up and unfurled her fists to ease the tension inside of her. "It was more than just seeing him, I felt him. The hairs on the back of my neck stood up that day. Those were my instincts telling me that something was amiss. I'm not psychotic and I'm not on any drugs that would produce that kind of effect. I hope you believe me."

He guided her head to his shoulder. "Of course I believe you. It's just something that we needed to rule out. Uncle Ralph is doing some checking. He'll call me when he finds out something concrete. Do you think you should consult a doctor?"

"Just a doctor or a *psychiatrist?* Do you really believe I'm having psychiatric problems?"

"I don't know what I'm supposed to believe. Flashbacks are a real possibility. You told me that you had serious flashbacks of many horrible times right before your Olympic performance. That wasn't so very long ago, Nique. I just think we need to be sure before we raise a lot of questions that could prove embarrassing to you if Taylor is in fact dead. You've been under a lot of strain over the past year. It won't hurt for you to get yourself checked out."

Beginning to tremble, she buried her face against his chest. Tears swam in her eyes when she looked up at him. "Whatever it takes, Ken. I guess I need to be one hundred percent sure. I'll make an appointment to see a shrink." She licked her lips, as they'd suddenly become dry. "Will you come to the doctor with me?"

Lifting her chin, he kissed her gently on the mouth and then her forehead. "I wouldn't have it any other way. I'm not making any judgments one way or the other. If there are medical reasons for what's going on with you, we need to find it out as soon as possible. If Taylor is still alive, we need to know that, as well. To be honest with you, I'd much rather it be that you've been under too much pressure . . .

which I feel can easily be remedied. As for it being the other choice, I can't even put my feelings into words if it turns out that he's still alive."

She shuddered. "I know what you mean. I'm also scared of that outcome more than the other one. Like you said, being under pressure is something that can be dealt with. His being alive is something that I don't want to *have* to deal with."

Her body was shaking so badly now that Ken brought her closer to him for solace. "This is going to get solved one way or another. Trust me. We're going to get to the bottom of everything. Do you have a doctor in mind that you'd like to see?"

"I'll talk with Dr. Wise and have him do a referral. Skaters go through trauma like everyone else. Actually, Dr. Wise wanted me to get psychological help when I went through the injury to my ankle. I refused it then, which is why I'm not going to make that same mistake twice. I realize now that I could've used someone to talk with while I was healing. But my main focus then was on getting well enough to continue on with my bid for the U.S. Olympic team."

"That was understandable. You'd only trained most of your life for it."

She took his hand. "Ken, I've been through some things that I'm not always able to talk about. My childhood was not a typical one by any stretch of the imagination. It's not that I don't trust you with these deep-seated things that I sometimes struggle with, it just means I haven't yet come to terms with them. I'm glad you came to me with Uncle Ralph's concerns. I feel a lot better about ruling out other possibilities first. Please bear with me in all of this. I do have a tendency to withdraw into myself at times. I constantly try to manage those feelings. It's then that I need the most understanding. Please don't take it personally when that happens."

As she and Ken walked into their bedroom hand-in-hand,

she couldn't help wondering if the hospital event had somehow traumatized her to the point where she might start having flashbacks on a regular basis. Reliving those horrible scenes was a terrible thing to have happen. And she'd had plenty of flashbacks since that day in the ER.

Satisfied with her decision to seek help, she nestled into Ken's arms. Prepared to do whatever was necessary to have things right again, she snuggled in closer to him. As always, his arms made her feel safe. He had become her hero in more ways than one. His strength gave her strength enough to face things instead of running away from them like she wanted to.

Even as she lay in the safety net of his arms her thoughts couldn't be quieted. Her eyes were closed but her mind was wide open. No one really knew how difficult her younger years had been, not even Wyman. She'd internalized a lot of the bad stuff because she hadn't had any friends to share her private hurts with. Kids actually teased her about not having a mother, had even suggested that her mother had abandoned her and her father for another man, that her mother wasn't even dead. Omunique had been accused of telling lies about her mother dying in childbirth because she was too embarrassed that her mother had run out on them.

To share those events with Wyman would've hurt him even more than he was already injured by the loss of his precious wife. To know that his daughter was being victimized by downright cruelty would've turned his emotions inside out. He wouldn't have handled it well.

These were still her very private wounds, wounds that never seemed to heal.

At one time, she'd even wondered if what the kids had said were true. Those types of thoughts added to her burdens and the guilt of questioning what she'd been told. How could she have dared to question her father's integrity? But she had. Omunique found it hard to believe that he

3 QUICK STEPS
TO RECEIVE YOUR "THANK YOU" GIFT
FROM THE EDITOR

Send this card back and you'll receive 4 FREE Arabesque novels! The introductory shipment of 4 Arabesque novels – a $23.96 value – is yours absolutely FREE!

There's no catch. You're under no obligation to buy anything. You'll receive your introductory shipment of 4 Arabesque novels absolutely FREE (plus $1.50 to offset the costs of shipping & handling). And you don't have to make any minimum number of purchases—not even one!

We hope that after receiving your books you'll want to remain an Arabesque subscriber. But the choice is yours to continue or cancel, anytime at all! So why not take us up on our invitation to receive 4 Arabesque Romance Novels, with no risk of any kind. You'll be glad you did!

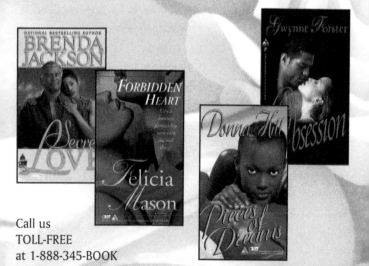

Call us
TOLL-FREE
at 1-888-345-BOOK

THE EDITOR'S "THANK YOU" GIFT INCLUDES:

- 4 books absolutely FREE (plus $1.50 for shipping and handling)
- A FREE newsletter, *Arabesque Romance News*, filled with author interviews, book previews, special offers, and more!
- No risks or obligations. You're free to cancel whenever you wish... with no questions asked.

BOOK CERTIFICATE

Yes! Please send me 4 FREE Arabesque novels (plus $1.50 for shipping & handling). I understand I am under no obligation to purchase any books, as explained on the back of this card.

Name _____

Address _____ Apt. _____

City _____ State _____ Zip _____

Telephone ( ) _____

Signature _____

Offer limited to one per household and not valid to current subscribers. All orders subject to approval. Terms, offer, & price subject to change. Offer valid only in the U.S.

Thank you!

AN111A

Accepting the four introductory books for FREE (plus $1.50 to offset the cost of shipping & handling) places you under no obligation to buy anything. You may keep the books and return the shipping statement marked "cancelled". If you do not cancel, about a month later we will send 4 additional Arabesque novels, and you will be billed the preferred subscriber's price of just $4.00 per title. That's $16.00 for all 4 books for a savings of 33% off the cover price (Plus $1.50 for shipping and handling). You may cancel at any time, but if you choose to continue, every month we'll send you 4 more books, which you may either purchase at the preferred discount price. . . or return to us and cancel your subscription.

THE ARABESQUE ROMANCE CLUB: HERE'S HOW IT WORKS

PLACE
STAMP
HERE

ARABESQUE ROMANCE BOOK CLUB
P.O. Box 5214
Clifton NJ 07015-5214

would've lied to her, but it surely didn't make sense that a bunch of kids would do so. She now knew it was her immature mind that couldn't assimilate so much negative information. No one in their right mind visited a gravesite every week to put flowers there if no one was buried in the plot. Every single Sunday, right after church, she remembered Wyman taking her to the gravesite. Her paternal grandmother had accompanied them when she was alive. After she died, they took flowers to her, too.

Ken immediately felt the tension that her thoughts had brought on. Her body having turned rigid against his was indicative of someone in emotional distress. He looked down at her. Though her eyes were closed, he was sure that she was awake. Instead of engaging her in conversation, or trying to make her talk when she probably didn't feel like it, he tenderly stroked her arms. Omunique had a lot on her mind and he didn't think it all had to do with Taylor. Though, the Lord knew that that was enough to deal with all by itself.

The frightening screams that had come from her during the night had convinced him that she'd really seen Taylor. He was no longer sure about that now. Her agreeing to see a doctor so readily came as a surprise to him, but he couldn't be happier about her decision. The time for that appointment couldn't come soon enough for him. They both needed to get to the bottom of it before closure was even possible.

The first thing the next morning Omunique called the doctor that her sports physician had recommended for her to see. Much to her surprise she was able to get an appointment right away to see psychiatrist Beverly Jackson, due to a last-minute cancellation. More to her surprise was that the appointment would include Ken for only the first half hour of the session. The second part of the appointment was reserved for the one seeking treatment.

According to the receptionist, Dr. Jackson always set her appointments this way when a husband and wife were involved. It gave each party the opportunity to be open and honest without worrying about feelings getting hurt. When Omunique explained that she wasn't seeing a doctor about her marriage, the receptionist said that appointments were set up this way no matter what the problem was.

Nervously rubbing her thighs, Omunique and Ken were seated in a relaxing setting inside Dr. Jackson's comfortably furnished office. Simple but very nice, the office was furnished with wall-to-wall bookcases, a sofa, two extremely comfortable-looking chairs, and lots of green plants. The decor of the room offered a light and airy feel, which was designed with the idea of keeping both doctor and patient mellow during even the tensest sessions.

Looking chic, Omunique was comfortably dressed in beige stretch pants and sweater. She also wore a rich plum-colored blazer over her top. Even though he looked refined in his attire, Ken only wore a simple long-sleeve gray cashmere polo-style sweater and casual dark slacks.

Dr. Jackson, slender, about five-seven in height, looked to be in her late thirties, but she was actually fifty. Possessing a lovely warm-brown complexion, she wore her reddish-brown hair in a short sister-lock style that was actually very becoming on her.

Smiling at the couple with her topaz eyes, she picked up a pen. "Mrs. Philyaw-Maxwell, I first have to say that I'm honored to have you seated here in my office. When I first saw your name on my appointment schedule, the Maxwell part threw me. Then I recalled reading a story in the paper about your wedding. As a nation, we're very proud of you. As an African-American sister, I'm ecstatic over your Olympic performance! You represented us well as a people, having done us proud. Thank you, my sister."

"You're very welcome. And thank you for your warm comments. As I tell everyone, I gave my very best. But all the glory goes to God. I hope my fans understand it now that I've decided to take some time away from skating to deal with some of my personal problems. My agent and lawyer are working on seeing that I take a much needed time-out."

"Well, now that we have that out of the way, I'd like for you two to tell me why you're seeking my expertise. I'm sure it will help explain why you need time off from your career."

Omunique filled the doctor in on all that happened as it related to Taylor, but she didn't mention the hospital situation. Ken took up where Omunique left off, backing up her account and then covering the things she hadn't mentioned.

"Although I read the story in the papers, I must say that this *is* an incredible firsthand account." Dr. Jackson took a few quiet moments to assimilate her thoughts. "Mrs. Maxwell, given your profession and what major feat you've just accomplished, I imagine there had to have been a lot of stress accompanying all the things going on in your life prior to the big event. And someone terrorizing you and holding you hostage had to make your situation even more stressful. But I'd like to know from you—how often do you experience these flashbacks? What time of the day is it? What are you doing when they occur? How long do they last? The answers to these questions will help me better understand what's been happening to you."

Omunique bit down on her lower lip. The reluctance came as a result of knowing that she couldn't reveal everything that had occurred during those times, not with Ken present. "Lately, the flashbacks occur at least once or twice a day, but some don't come in such a dramatic way as others. It has happened in the daytime, but they usually occur late in the evening. As for what I'm doing at the time, I'll have to think about that one. The length of time varies."

"Okay, Mrs. Maxwell, you've given me something to go

on. And I must add, that I think you are right to take some time off. You've been in the pressure cooker for many, many years now. Have you ever been present during any of these times, Mr. Maxwell? If so, what types of things did you observe in your wife's behavior?"

"The only times I've observed anything out of the ordinary is when she wakes up screaming in the middle of the night. Right after the hostage situation, Omunique had nightmares regularly. Then the frequency diminished. When it did happen on occasion it was bad. She sweats profusely, her eyes bulge with terror, and she trembles almost uncontrollably. Getting her calmed down used to take a much longer time than it does now. But it seems that over the past weeks she's beginning to regress. I had a time of it getting her calm a few nights ago."

"Thank you for your input, Mr. Maxwell. I'm sure you both already know that the fact that her personal terrorist may not be dead as initially believed figures greatly into what's been happening. This is not unusual. Flashbacks can occur years later even when several years have elapsed since the last occurrence."

Dr. Jackson looked down at her wristwatch. "Mr. Maxwell, as is my customary rule, I would like to talk with Omunique alone for the next half of the session. This is not intended to shut you out. I do this to give my patients an opportunity to open up to me without reservation. For the very reasons that you've stated here today, being that Omunique's use of drugs has come into question, I need to find out how she's taking that. It has probably unnerved her a bit. I want to hear how she really feels about what some might consider a personal affront without her worrying that feelings may be hurt."

Ken got to his feet. "I understand. She discussed this with me already. We both drove our own cars so that I could go to work after you talked with us together. But let me say this before I go. There *is* no issue of her using drugs.

Omunique has never been accused of using drugs. It was suggested that the medications that she has to take for her feet might possibly be inducing psychosis of some sort. There is no question of impropriety on her part."

"Thank you for adding that to your comments. The suggestion *is* the problem. Just to imply that her medication may be causing the problem might make her feel that someone's doubting what she's saying, what she's experiencing. It could also insinuate that she's using the medications improperly, perhaps taking too much. I don't know the answers right now, but I hope to after Omunique tells me what she's going through."

"I see what you mean. Thanks. It was a pleasure meeting you. I'll make myself available to you should you ever need to speak with me."

"The same here. Thank you again, Mr. Maxwell."

Leaning over the chair, Ken kissed his wife. "I'll wait for you to come by the office so we can have lunch, as planned. I love you."

Omunique stood up and fully embraced her husband, letting him know how much she appreciated him coming to the doctor with her. "I love you, too. See you shortly."

Once Ken left the room and Omunique had returned to her chair, Dr. Jackson leveled a concerned gaze on her new patient. "I heard all that you were saying, Mrs. Maxwell. More importantly, I heard what you didn't say. I got the distinct impression that you'd left a huge chunk out of your story. And I'm curious to hear your reasons why."

Omunique rubbed both of her arms, as if she was cold. Then she twisted her right hand around her left wrist. "I didn't think it was that obvious. But I guess a trained eye is able to zero right in on things like that. Patient-doctor confidentiality?" Dr. Jackson nodded. "There's something that happened that my husband doesn't know about. All these things seemed to happen at the same time. I don't know how to cope with any of them. I'm just not equipped."

The doctor appeared intent on every word spoken by her patient. Dr. Jackson recognized the anguish in her eyes, felt the tension radiating from her body, saw that she was nearly overcome with grief as she talked about the woman in the ER. Omunique was not only talking about the woman in the ER, she had become her. She had lived the experience of her giving birth and then she had died inside in the same moment of her death. She and this woman were now as one, as if their spirits had somehow collided into each other.

More than the difficulties with her feet, more than the death of her mother, more than the attempt on her life, this total stranger's death had pushed her far beyond her ability to reason or to cope with what she was now faced with. Fear had become the ruler of her soul and her spirit.

Omunique was now certain that she would die the same death, in the same exact way . . .

Twelve

While looking around for the California Central Hospital employee she'd come to see, and to hopefully talk with, Omunique spotted Melinda Sanchez; the nurse working in the ER the day she'd witnessed the death of the pregnant woman. She'd come there to try and make peace with the horrific memories of the death scene that plagued her day and night. But what seemed to gnaw at her insides even more than what she'd seen was what had become of the mother's baby.

She approached the nurse. "Ms. Sanchez, I'm Omunique Philyaw-Maxwell. Do you remember me? I've been here about my feet more than just a few times. But I met you when you came into the room while I was with the woman who'd lost her life while giving birth."

"Practically everyone in this hospital knows who you are, but I didn't realize who you were that day until later. You did the nation proud in the Olympics, especially us minorities. Are you having problems with your feet?" She looked down at Omunique's feet with concern.

"No, no." Omunique shook her head, looking around for a place to sit down. "That's not what I'm here for. Is it possible for you to take a break for a few minutes? I would like to talk to you in private."

"I'm on break now. I was just going to the cafeteria to

purchase something cool to drink. We can probably find a quiet spot in there if you'd care to join me."

"I'd love to. Just what I was hoping for . . . and please call me Omunique or Nique."

"Thank you. I'm just plain old Melinda."

A few minutes later Omunique and Melinda shared a table in a quiet corner, in the very back of the cafeteria, where they sipped ice cold pink lemonade.

Melinda looked at her watch. "I'm afraid I've only got twenty minutes to hear what you have to say. So we'd better get started."

Omunique licked her lips. "I'd like to know about the baby boy that was born that day, a few weeks back. I've been thinking of him constantly. Is he okay?"

"He's still here at the hospital. He's a Down syndrome baby. The little fellow's still fighting to survive. But he's a strong one. So I'd say the odds are in his favor."

"Down syndrome?" Melinda nodded. "How severe?"

"That's yet to be determined. More and more is learned as they go through each stage of development. How quickly or slowly they turn over, sit up, crawl, walk, and things like that, are the determining factors."

"I see. Has the baby become a ward of the state?"

"The county is responsible for the medical bills and all. Until he's strong enough to leave the hospital, placement will remain undecided. It's a tough situation. Without a mother or father to act in his behalf, his future will be determined by the system."

Omunique lowered her eyes as she rubbed her fingers across her chin. Tears glistened in her eyes when she looked up. "Is there a chance that I could visit with the baby boy? Has he been named yet?"

"No, not yet." Melinda smiled gently. "Because of who you are, I'm sure a visit can be arranged. I have to ask you something. I remember some of what you told me about your similar history, but why *are* you so interested in this particular baby?"

Omunique thought her question was fair enough. "To tell the truth, I really don't know. I just can't seem to get that whole sorrowful scenario out of my mind. My own history is definitely the common thread. My spirit's been so restless since the mother's death. It actually makes me very emotionally ill at times. My emotions have become so vulnerable since then."

Melinda's jet-black eyes checked out the wall clock. "I hate to end this but I have to report back to my duty station. Is there a number where I can reach you? I can only promise to look into a visit for you. I can guarantee nothing."

Omunique handed her a business card with her voicemail number on it. "Please, no press. By some miracle, should it happen, it has to be a private visit. I don't want this blown all out of proportion by the tabloids or other papers. Can you guarantee me at least that much."

Sanchez bobbed her head up and down as she got to her feet. "I'll inform the administrator of your request. I'm sure he'll honor it. And you don't have to worry a bit about me breaking your confidence. I'm just so thrilled to have met you. An Olympian, no less. Got to run. Oh, would you mind giving me your autograph?" She removed Omunique's business card from her uniform pocket. "Perhaps you could sign the back of your card."

"Of course." Omunique wrote a few endearing words before ending with her signature. Somewhat overwhelmed by the request, she still hadn't gotten used to being asked for her autograph even though it happened frequently, more so since her Olympic win. "Thanks for your help. I'll look forward to hearing from you."

"You're welcome," Melinda said as she rushed from the cafeteria.

While walking back toward the front of the hospital, Omunique realized that coming to the hospital wasn't helping her come to terms with her experiences. She felt more restless than ever before. Happy that she'd inquired of the baby boy, she would really like to see him and perhaps even hold him. Such a little person should have someone to care about him until he could find a good home. Should have someone other than relegated nurses obligated by duty. That's what she would've wanted for the child if he'd been hers.

As she looked down the hall and saw the same man she'd seen before, a scream nearly erupted from Omunique's throat. If it wasn't Officer Taylor, the man she saw in the wheelchair was a dead ringer for him. As if she had no control over them, her feet raced down the seemingly never ending corridor. The adrenaline rush she had now was nothing like the ones she experienced when skating. There wasn't anything pleasant or euphoric about this one.

Finally, she got to where she thought she'd seen the wheelchair turn the corner, only to have the elevator doors slam shut in her face. The closed doors denied her the opportunity to see if it was the face of the same man who'd stolen away from her more than just her peace of mind.

In a state of shock, her body trembling with the same unmitigated fear she'd felt when Taylor had held the knife at her throat, she watched the green lighted numbers to see which floor the elevator stopped on. When the car stopped on every single floor, she knew she didn't stand a chance of finding out that way. Determined to find out one way or another, she marched straight to the admitting office hoping they'd have an answer.

Thomasina wasn't at her desk so Omunique took the liberty of going on to Ken's office. But out of respect for her husband's business, she knocked first. She opened the door when his shout approving the entry reached her ears. Not wanting him to know what outright hell she'd been through in the last forty-five minutes, she promised herself not to allow this last episodic event to take over her life and interfere with the happy life she'd begun to build with her husband.

Despite it all her bright smile was genuine. "Hey, can you make time to take your favorite girl to lunch?"

Smiling, he got to his feet and crossed the room. "Perfect timing. I was about to go down the street to one of my favorite haunts. But what does your favorite guy get in return?" Bringing her into his arms, he kissed her passionately.

She looked up at him, laughing. His mouth was smeared with her lipstick, but she decided to be devilish and not tell him. "Here we go again. Why do I have to give you anything in return? It's not as if you've received a more attractive offer for lunch. Or have you?"

He thought about Thomasina's offer to pick him up something while she was out, but he thought that might be taking the bantering a little too far. While it appeared to him that Thomasina still had a slight personal interest in him in spite of the candid talk before and his marital status, he sure hoped he was dead wrong. If Omunique ever picked up on his secretary's cleverly veiled, but nonetheless flirtatious remarks, her excellent memory would refer back to this very moment. And there would be hell to pay.

"That was a simple enough question, Ken. Why is it taking you so long to respond?"

His tauntingly sexy smile made her insides quiver. Her breath had a way of quickening with a mere glance from him. "I was thinking of what I want for lunch?"

"What'd you come up with?"

"You! Should I lock the door?"

She blushed. "Not as vocal as we get. But it is an intriguing idea." She eyed his large desk with a bit of curiosity. "You really think we can get our sexual groove on atop your desk?"

In an unassuming manner, he shrugged his shoulders. "Why don't we lock the door and find out?" In his eyes, she read the bold challenge he presented. Perhaps meeting the challenge would take her mind off everything but her husband.

"What if someone knocks?" Walking back to his desk, he lifted the top of his briefcase. He removed a white card and held up the DO NOT DISTURB sign for her to see. It was another one written in both English and Japanese, just like the one at home. "Remember?"

"You stole two of those?" He nodded. "You *are* a thief. But why would you bring it to the office?"

"For when an opportunity presented itself. It seems that it has. Are you going to fulfill my fantasy, Mrs. Maxwell? That dress you're wearing will slide up over your deliciously curving hips very nicely." The challenge in his golden eyes grew more daring as he crossed his arms against his chest. But it was the sparkle in her eyes that told him she thoroughly enjoyed the deliciously taunting sex game he'd intentionally lured her into.

"What about the pantyhose?"

He leaned back against the desk, his every provocative move thrilling her senseless. "Not a problem for me. You know I got skills."

It was too tempting for her not to take him on, especially if he was bluffing. She really didn't think he was, but she had to find out for sure. She walked back to the door, opened it, and put out the sign. After shutting it, she turned the lock. Slowly, swaying her hips seductively, she walked behind his desk and closed the drapes. "Your move, Maxwell."

Joining her behind the desk, he took her purse off her shoulder and put it on the floor under the worktable. Lifting her off the floor, he sat her on the very edge of his desk and settled himself between her knees. "Your move, Mrs. Maxwell."

Running her tongue slowly across her lower lip, she kicked off her shoes. "Make your next move, Maxwell."

Eyeing her heatedly, he removed his suit jacket and unbuttoned his shirt. "The ball's back in your court, Mrs. Maxwell."

Returning his erotically burning gaze, she removed her earrings one at a time. "Well, Mr. Maxwell, I'm eagerly anticipating your next serve. Perhaps it'll be an ace."

Lifting her bottom for a brief moment, he slid her dress way up past her thighs with one very slick move. Hungrily, with near reckless abandon, his mouth took full possession of hers.

Intent on provoking him into being the first one to lose total control, she put her hands inside his shirt and pushed him away with flattened palms to his bare chest. "That was a couple of moves. Now I get two." She unbuckled his belt and unzipped his fly in one quick motion. "You're not the only one who's got skills." She raised her fists and thrust her elbows downward to show that she was also very capable with her hands.

Way too hot to continue the erotic game he'd started, he made quick work of her pantyhose, proving to her that he had *major* skills, expeditious ones at that. Seconds later, with his hips wedged firmly between her thighs, he entered her moistness in a most titillating way. In her opinion, he had surpassed his highest skill level—having increased it tenfold.

During the course of their highly erotic coupling, the paper cup dispenser went flying, neatly stacked papers sailed from the desktop like paper airplanes, and a cup filled with pencils bounced up and down on the blotter pad before landing all over the carpet. To keep the verbal foreplay under control, so as not to alert anyone in the building to their gloriously sinful desktop tryst, lips stayed locked together, only pausing to gulp in deep breaths as kisses grew so intense.

Slowing the pace just a bit, Ken took special care in bringing his wife the greatest pleasures. In return, Omunique gave all that she had inside of her. As their climax came simultaneously, in an amazing flurry of deep thrusts and feverish gyrations, Omunique bit down on her lower lip and dug her nails into his back to keep from screaming his name out loud.

Breathing hard and fast, Ken dropped down into the highback leather swivel chair and brought Omunique down onto his lap. "Baby," he breathed, "are you okay? Cause I feel like I'm about to die." He sucked in a few deep breaths. I thought about Max having a key to my office, but that only heightened the excitement of us taking each other right here on my desk. The thrill of possibly getting caught in the act is something to reckon with." He laughed. "But I really wouldn't want that to happen to us. You would be absolutely mortified."

"Mortified isn't a strong enough word. Oh, but I'm . . . feeling just . . . the opposite of . . . dying." With her chest heaving heavily, she took a moment to gain control. "You're right about how I'd feel if someone walked in on us, but didn't you remember that I put the sign out?"

"I had no thoughts after the one with Max and the key. From that point on, all I could do was feel. Feel the tantalizing rhythm of our bodies dancing so wildly but in perfect harmony." He gently squeezed her thigh. "Still want to go to lunch?"

"Wasn't I enough for you?"

"More than! But if we want to keep on making love like we just did, we got to get our eat on, girl." Before lifting her off his lap, he stroked the inside of her thigh with agile fingers.

"No more independent network shows for you, like the WB. You're starting to sound like you came straight from the Steve Harvey Show."

"Watching the WB is how I keep up with the for-real

brothers. Don't forget that every now and then I have an occasion to deal with an egotistical male athlete with lots of brawn but short on brain matter." He held out his hand. "Come with me, sweetheart."

After taking a key out of his top desk drawer, he picked up their discarded articles on the way as he directed her to the private executive washroom. "You see, you get one of these when you reach the major leagues." She'd never had an occasion to visit it before, but she sure knew that it existed. Wyman had told her about the Maxwell's executive washrooms long before Ken had become her husband, long before Ken had mentioned it to her himself.

"When you're finished washing up, I'm here to help you put those pantyhose back on should you need some assistance."

"You better stay away from me. Daddy would have a fit if he knew how you've been sexually corrupting his daughter. You were right when you said we were wicked."

He laughed. "I didn't say *we* were wicked. I was talking about our lovemaking."

"Same difference. There *is* no lovemaking without us being involved."

Fully dressed, Omunique sprayed her pulse points with one of her favorite scents, Casual, before following her husband out of the washroom and back to his office.

As he led her out into the reception room, she prayed that they wouldn't come in contact with anyone. She saw that her prayer had gone unanswered when she saw Thomasina seated at her workstation.

Thomasina's eyes went straight to Ken's office door, where the DO NOT DISTURB sign still hung from the shiny knob. Then she turned narrowed eyes on Omunique, causing her color to give rise. Omunique was the absolute worst at hiding her feelings, embarrassing ones, or otherwise. The most telltale sign of all was Omunique's lipstick smeared on his face and lips.

Having assessed the situation, Ken squeezed her fingers. "I'm taking my lunch out to wife." Damn it, he thought. He was the one who was supposed to take control here. Thomasina eyed him curiously. "Let me rephrase that. I'm taking my wife out to lunch, a long one."

Laughing inwardly at his smeared mouth and awkward blunders, Omunique decided to take over. "We both know what you mean, Ken." Shaking her head, she wrinkled her nose. "He's not feeling quite himself today, Thomasina. In fact, he's going to take the rest of the day off. He needs more than lunch. He needs rest. As you know, we've been really busy the past few months. Come on, darling, let's go home. We can have lunch there and then spend the rest of the day in bed." As if she were leading a blind person, Omunique steered Ken through the reception area and out the door that led to the hallway.

Inside the elevator, they both howled. Tears ran down Omunique's cheeks as she laughed as hard as Ken did. She felt bad for duping Thomasina, though she had a sneaky suspicion that she hadn't. But she would've felt much worse if she'd had to stand there a moment longer. Her color-infused skin was a dead giveaway every time. Oh, what were they going to get into next?

"I'm taking my *lunch* out to *wife*! What was that all about? Why didn't you just go ahead and tell her what we did in your office? By both of our actions and the lipstick on your face and mouth, I'm sure she guessed."

Pulling her to him, he muffled his laughter in her hair. "I know, I know. I screwed up royally back there. I was worried about you, but you handled things much better than I did.

"Do I really have lipstick all over me?"

She took out her compact and opened it. "Look in the mirror and see for yourself. I thought it was so funny, but I feel bad for not telling you it was there. I thought you'd see it, especially during our visit to the washroom."

He looked in the mirror and groaned, his expression making Omunique laugh. "Oh, my, I'm the one feeling mortified. You are so incorrigible at times. It'll be hard enough facing Thomasina tomorrow, but I can't go back there and face her today. Did you mean what you said about us having lunch at home and then spending the rest of the day in bed?"

"No, not until this very moment. But it sounds like I had a really wonderful idea. I'm starting to worry about us. Our sexual escapades are bordering on kinky."

"Just think, we've got a lifetime of fantastic lovemaking ahead of us. Nothing kinky about that. We just happen to be quite creative with our uncontrollable *love-jones*."

While Ken changed out of his dress clothes, Omunique was busy executing the idea she'd gotten from Wyman on her wedding day. The carpet picnics he talked about Patrice indulging them in sounded like a lot of fun. Glad that someone had given them a beautiful wicker picnic basket gift, she had pulled it out to fill it with all sorts of goodies.

Styrofoam bowls covered with Saran wrap held two fresh garden salads. After cutting a submarine-style roll in half, she filled it with turkey, chicken, roast beef, slices of cheese, black olives, and dill pickle slices. Ken loved mayonnaise and yellow mustard mixed together on his sandwiches so she'd lathered it on the bread before she'd added the other ingredients. She put in a one-serving size bag of Lay's potato chips for him and filled a plastic baggie with thin pretzel sticks and mixed nuts for her snack. For good measure, she threw in a couple of tangerines, two bananas, and a bowl filled with red seedless grapes.

Once she made sure the container of his special fruit juice had been put in the basket, she carried it upstairs to the bedroom. Glad that Ken was still in the bathroom, she spread out on the carpet the red-and-white checkered tablecloth that had come with the basket. Taking the food items out one by one, she arranged them on the cloth and set out the matching napkins.

Hoping she had enough time to slip into something comfortable, she stripped out of her dress and grabbed a pair of navy blue sweats. Quickly, she slipped them on. When Ken still hadn't come out of the bathroom, she loaded the CD changer with their favorite discs.

Omunique had already seated herself on the floor by the time Ken finally came out of the bathroom. It took him a minute to notice all her handiwork, but when he did he smiled broadly.

Dropping down on the floor beside his wife, he kissed her lightly on the lips. "This was a great idea. I told you we were creative." His gleaming eyes told her how much he appreciated what she'd gone through to make their lunch date so special.

She took his hand. "I didn't exactly create this idea. Dad told me about how my mother used to surprise him with carpet picnics. I liked the idea so much that when I thought about it on the way home, I decided to fix us one."

"Well, you created this one especially for us. Thank you. This is very nice. Ready for me to pass the blessing?"

In response she bowed her head. Ken prayed over the food. Something he never forgot to do, he thanked the Lord for bringing him and his wife together and for blessing them so abundantly, so richly.

He bit into his half of the sandwich like it was his last meal. That made her crack up. He put his sandwich up to her mouth for her to take a bite. He then waited for her to swallow it. "If you're trying to poison me, we're going out together."

"So, that's why you have me taste your food all the time. But you do that even when we eat out."

He shrugged. "If someone else is trying to poison me, we still go out together." He leaned over and licked the mayonnaise from the corner of her mouth. "The truth of the matter is, I like tasting you in my food. You have a habit of always sticking your tongue on everything before you eat it. Here, take a bite of my salad so I can taste your spicy self on that, too."

She gladly did as he asked. She didn't think there was too much that she wouldn't do for Ken, but she wished she could better communicate to him how she felt about him. He was much better at expressing himself than she was. In every way, verbally, emotionally, and most of all, by his actions. She loved him and she wanted to learn how to express that in every way possible.

He nudged her. "Why such a serious look? And you aren't eating. Is something wrong with you? I don't like it when you get too quiet."

She eyed him for several seconds. "Could we get serious for a minute?"

"Of course." Concerned with her mood change, he gave her his undivided attention.

"You do and say so many things that let me know exactly what you're feeling, especially about me. I was sitting here thinking about all the wonderful ways you show your feelings for me. I don't know why I can't convey through words all the beautiful things you are to me. You're the brightest star in my universe and I don't know why I can't tell you that. When I look into your eyes, I see my spirit looking back at me, yet I don't know how to express that. You're my unsung hero. Sometimes I lean on you too hard, but you never complain, you never get disgruntled. I know I'm still immature in a lot of ways, but I'm getting it, slowly but surely."

"There may be one exception to your immaturity."

"What's that?"

"You know how to express yourself like a real woman in the bedroom. There's nothing immature about the sexy ways you turn your husband on." He grinned, pulling her to him.

"You are my everything, Kenneth, and I'm going to learn how to tell you all of these things one day."

He laughed softly. "Baby, you just did . . . and so beautifully. You don't have a problem expressing yourself verbally, or otherwise. Your eyes tell me you love me, your body speaks to me so softly, it whispers to me your desires. The magic in your touch reveals to me a love story so tender, so compassionate. Your kisses and thrilling caresses have a way of getting the message across to me in spades. Omunique, I love the way you express yourself to me in so many delicious ways. There's not one thing I would change about the art of your expressions.

"Your expressions on the ice are by far the most vocal. Each time I watch you take to the ice, I listen to what your beautifully swaying hands are saying as they weave their magic over me. When your skates begin to sing, I know they're soulfully crooning a love song to me. Don't ever think you aren't expressing yourself to me. Because you are . . . and you do it so well."

"Thank you for that. On the occasions when I can't communicate things to you it's because I haven't worked them through for myself. I'm not good at telling people things that I haven't figured out yet. When I do confide it's because I have some idea of what's happening and usually why. That's the one thing I would change about me if I could. I want to continue to work on my communication skills. And I will. Now let's eat before I start crying." She took the Saran Wrap off her salad and poured a capful of red French dressing on it.

"You really took that sandwich out in a hurry." She handed him the bag of chips. "Care for these, Mr. I-know-I-can't-eat-just-one?" Keeping things from Ken was not her desire. In her own way, she'd just tried to explain why to him to the very best of her ability. But that would have to be enough until she found a way to conquer her fears, if they didn't conquer her first. They'd already made her see things that just couldn't possibly be real.

"That's right . . . and I'm not trying to lie about it. Anybody who says they've been able to eat just one of these delicious chips is a liar. What about a game of gin rummy after we finish eating? I feel really lucky today. Made love to my wife on top of my desk, took the rest of the afternoon off to spend it in bed with her, and I'm having a carpet picnic lunch with the sexiest woman alive. Now those are blessings. When I beat you at gin rummy, pure skill."

"It has nothing to do with skill, Ken. I just don't know how to play that well yet. I haven't won a single time in three months. But I'm going to. One day." She laughed. "You just said that you took the rest of the day off to spend it in bed with your wife. Was *that* a lie?"

"No, sweetheart. Are we going to bed to sleep?"

"If that's what we feel like doing. Let's not make any plans for our time together. We'll do whatever comes to mind at that time."

"We're striving for spontaneity. In that case, come over here to me. You've never worn sweats to bed before, so let me help you out of them." His sexy smile made her tremble inside. All she could do was smile back. Knowing how much he loved to help dress and undress her, especially the latter, she lifted her arms up and he pulled the shirt over her head. Without a bra to worry about, he took hold of the waistband of her sweats and worked them off her hips, down her smooth legs and over her feet. Leaving her black silk bikinis on, he got to his feet and strode over to her lingerie drawer.

After a few minutes of looking through her intimate apparel, he came up with fluid pants done in chocolate silk with a flat front and elasticized waist in back. The bustier top was fitted with sexy straps, underwire cups and decorative button front with hook-and-eye closures. "Now this is hot. For someone as innocent as you were when I first met you, you sure know how to pick out hot, sexy lingerie. The clerks in Victoria's Secret must love to see you coming."

She had to laugh since she hadn't purchased any of the brand-new items in her drawer. For sure, none of the sexy items. "They were all gifts."

His eyebrow shot up at least a quarter-inch. "Really. From whom?"

"The surprise shower Marion held for me."

"Yeah, but what's that got to do with the lingerie."

"Marion had what she called a personal-honeymoon shower. She even suggested that the items be chosen from the Victoria's Secret catalogue. It seemed like everyone took her suggestion to heart. Everyone gave me lingerie or provocative loungewear even if they didn't buy it from the catalogue or in one of their mall stores."

"Why didn't I know your shower featured sexy lingerie before now?"

She scowled with irritation. "I don't know. I guess it never came up. When we got together late that night, we were both so tired. We didn't go into great detail. You asked me did I enjoy the shower—and I said that I did. After I asked you the same question, nothing more was said about it. What lingerie I didn't leave out to pack for taking with me on our honeymoon, I just put in the drawer when we moved my things into the condo. Why the twenty questions?"

"I'm going to have to keep you and Marion apart. She's showing you how to be a sex kitten, not to mention her teaching you offensive words like 'quickie.' I'm beginning to wonder if she had a male stripper at this intimate apparel shindig."

"No she's not teaching me that, and no she didn't invite a male stripper. But it might've been nice to have some gorgeous man takes his clothes off for me. I thought you loved sexy silky and satiny things. You're the one who always rushes to pick out what I wear to bed."

"Are you serious about the stripper part? You'd sit still and watch a male strip down?"

She rolled her eyes. "You're starting to be a pain. This isn't the afternoon that I had in mind for us. Are you getting insecure all of a sudden? I already know what kind of bachelor party you had. Apparently Frank keeps nothing from his woman. X-rated lingerie and swimsuit videos, indeed. You didn't hear me questioning you about what went on at your party."

She had him there. But seeing that Omunique might be taking him too seriously, he couldn't help laughing. "I'm just messing with you. I love you dressed in sexy, softly feminine nightwear. I should be thanking the ladies. You're much too pretty to be looking as mean as you are right now. I'd rather see you smiling. Please smile for me."

"Well, Ken, I *am* sitting over here in nothing but my underwear, while you cross-examine me about my lingerie and male strippers. Don't you think I might be a little chilly by now? This is a girl who didn't mind sleeping in flannel and cotton before I met you. I've always wanted to buy sexy things like these, but I just never got all caught up in it. The ice was the only life I had before you. My butt gets cold when I'm on the ice . . . and it's getting that way with me sitting here practically naked. Clothe me please or let me do it myself."

He drew her to her feet and guided her to the bed. He pushed her back on to the bed and came down gently on top of her. "That's what I'm here for, Mrs. Maxwell. I'm always ready to heat you and your cold butt right up." He tossed the lingerie off to the side of them. "No use putting those on when I'm only going to take them right off again. Ah, I love spontaneity . . ."

* * *

Awakened in the middle of the night by Omunique's chilling screams, Ken reached for his wife and brought her into the safety of his arms. "What is it? Your feet?"

Sobbing uncontrollably, she managed to tell him she was sure she'd seen Officer Marcus Taylor again. It didn't take too much for her to convince her husband that she was sure of what she'd seen at the hospital, which put her terribly on edge. It put him on high alert.

Thirteen

Ken paced Ralph's Steele's office. "Uncle Ralph, how could this have happened? Why weren't we told a long time ago that Marcus Taylor was still alive? Omunique is being terrorized all over again."

Ralph looked terribly disturbed. "I'm sorry, son, but this was an administrative decision. When they realized he wasn't dead that night, which seems like not so long ago, they covered up his hospitalization. When it came to look as if he was going to live, they become more determined to keep it quiet. That's when the newspapers were contacted and phony stories about his death and his private, family-requested burial were given out. Once he began to recover, he was moved to a private mental hospital that specifically houses ex-cops who've lost it."

"By why keep it a secret from his intended target? In this case, my wife."

Ralph stroked his chin thoughtfully. "They wanted to study him, see what made him tick, learn what made him come unglued."

"Well, when we sue the pants off the city, we'll see what makes them tick, what makes them come to such irrational decisions. And to think that they may actually release him one day is ludicrous. How come he wasn't charged with something? Kidnapping, attempted murder, tampering with an official investigation, and withholding evidence are a number of the charges I can think of right off the top of my head. Some type of charges should have been brought against him. For God sakes, he held a knife to her throat. I thought he was actually going to kill her."

"He probably has been charged with something and he more than likely has an attorney."

"How can someone enter a plea for a client who's lost his mind?"

"I think you just answered your own question, Ken. With him being incapable of doing so, someone has to act on his behalf. In this instance, government lawyers would step in. The man may be found innocent by reason of insanity. If that happens, no one knows how much longer the system will be able to keep him locked down. This is our fine government at work."

Ken was outraged. "I swear, Uncle Ralph, if he comes near my wife, he's not going to survive this time. The man should never be let out into society again in the first place. And what in the hell do I tell my wife? She's been having numerous flashbacks. I'm glad she's seeing a doctor."

Ralph put a soothing hand on his godson's shoulder. "Take it easy, son. We can't figure this out if you get yourself all worked up. I can assure you that Taylor's not going anywhere for a long, long while. There will be plenty of hearings before they can even think of discharging him if he is found innocently insane. Son, I can't afford to put my job at risk. When I came back to active duty, I had to retake the oath of the office I hold. If anyone learns that I'm talking to you about this . . . Well, I don't want to think what would happen. For sure, I'd be in danger of losing my pension."

Tears welled in Ken's eyes, angry tears. At the same time, compassion for his wife filled his heart. "I understand. I won't go off half-cocked. I know you're taking a major risk in this. Nique doesn't deserve this. She may break under the pressure this time. She has a lot of stuff going on."

"Give me time to thoroughly investigate this matter. I don't know enough about this yet, but I'm going to find out all that I can, which calls for discretion. I promise you at least that much. I'll be contacting you as soon as I know more. There are a lot of strings that can be pulled but only in an extremely hush-hush way. Give Omunique a big hug for me. Amanda has asked why you two haven't been over. Stop by and see her when you find a minute to spare. She'd love to see you."

"I'll stop by on my way home. I'm picking Nique up at the arena so we won't be that far from your section of the city. With your house not all that far from ours, Omunique will more than likely want to go over to the house with me rather than have me take her home and go back. Aunt Amanda has grown to love her so much. Seeing her will also do my wife some good."

"Amanda does love you both, very much."

"Okay, Uncle Ralph, keep me posted. Please tell me they won't let that criminal bastard go without notifying us first?"

"It won't happen, son. I'll try to see to that personally. I didn't earn these silver bars without earning the respect and trust of my peers."

Thanks. I'll talk with you later."

No less anxiety-ridden than when he first entered his godfather's office, Ken took the elevator down to the parking level, where he got into his car and drove off. All he could think of was how Omunique was going to take the news. She'd been a nervous wreck since she first thought she'd seen Taylor at the hospital, constantly thinking he might be alive. He knew that finding out she wasn't losing her mind would come as a comfort to her, but the realization of him actually being alive might cause her to lose the very sanity she'd been so busy questioning in past weeks. This was a time-bomb situation. The real problems in this unfortunate situation were yet to come; direct results of not knowing how much time they had before it exploded in their faces.

Omunique was already outside waiting when he pulled up at the Palos Verdes ice arena. She slid into the passenger seat and leaned over to kiss him. "Baby, I missed you. I've been worried. How did things go today?" She looked anxious to hear about his visit down at the police department. She knew he'd specifically gone there to discuss her situation with his godfather.

He couldn't hide his troubled spirit. "Not a good day, Princess. We have to really talk this thing through. It's serious."

Trembling with fear, her eyes grew somber. "He's alive, isn't he? It *was* him that I saw both times at the hospital. I knew it. No one forgets the face of a man who attempted to murder them."

"Baby, I'm sorry. Uncle Ralph doesn't know a lot, but he's going to find out all that he can. Seems like someone made the decision to use an inhuman Taylor as a human guinea pig. My godfather seems to be working only on assumption in some areas, but we'll get it figured out. Is this a bad time for us to stop by Aunt Amanda's since we're already in the area? Uncle Ralph says she misses us. Seeing her might help out right now."

"I'd love to see her but I may not be sparkling company." She grew pensive. "Ken, you're not going to like this, but I want to see Taylor face-to-face. As soon as possible."

He looked at her like she had already lost her mind. "No way. No way in hell am I going to allow that to occur. Nique, it can't happen, shouldn't happen. This nut tried to kill you!"

"Yes, and I desperately need to understand why. I'm the one who has to know why he did all those horrible things to me. There are far too many questions unanswered for me to ever find any real peace of mind now that I know he's alive."

Ken pounded his fist on the steering wheel, causing the car to swerve a bit. "I can tell you why. Because the man is an obsessed lunatic, Nique—and you don't need to see him to find that out. You already know it."

"But he's the only one with the answers to many questions. He's alive and I want to talk with him. Please help me achieve that. Please talk to Uncle Ralph and see if he can arrange it?"

"Oh, Omunique, you don't know what you're asking of me, or how much it's going to cost me emotionally to either turn you down, or help you out in this. This isn't a wise decision, sweetheart. You're working on emotions instead of logic. You need more time to think this through. The man is deranged, not to mention his obsession with you. It could be a big mistake if you decide to push this. As for Uncle Ralph, he's already got a lot to lose if he's not careful."

"It could be an even bigger mistake if I decide not to push it. Can't you see that?"

"No, I can't. And it's obvious that you're not hearing or feeling me. Do you even remember the things you and Taylor talked about before the first shots were fired? Do you recall what he asked you before he shot himself? If so, you're not acting like it, not with the stuff you're talking about."

Shuddering at the thought, she gasped in horror. *"Do you love me, Omunique? Was Maxwell telling the truth when he said you cared about me?"*

"And you told him, yes, that you did love him, even before he shot himself. Nique, that statement alone is enough to make that deranged animal come after you again should they release him. Can't you see that? It's all so clear to me."

"In seeing him, I could clear that all up. I only said those things under duress and because I thought he might die.

But you're the one who told him I cared about him in the first place. What were *you* thinking?"

Growing exasperated, he blew out a ragged breath. "That it might possibly save your life. If he thought you cared, then he just might let you go. That it could distract him enough to allow the other officers to take him down but not completely out. That's what I was thinking. They should've killed him when they had the chance. I should've killed him!"

"Please don't say that, Ken. You don't mean it. You're not capable of killing. Let's not blame ourselves for something we had no control over. I know that you did what you thought was best for me at the time. It was an extremely stressful situation for both of us. I'm sorry if I sounded accusatory. That's not how I wanted to come across. I love you. We'll work this out, too."

"I'm sure we will, but you *are* in control this time. I have to go on record as being totally against you seeing him. I can't even begin to fathom you in his presence. I hope it doesn't occur."

"Duly noted. Two more blocks and we'll be at Aunt Amanda's. Let's try and relax so as not to make her anxious." She knew her request was unreasonable, but she had to get in to see Taylor.

"Relaxation at this moment is unachievable for me. I'm worried about you. Because I think you've truly lost your mind over this and you're trying to make me lose mine. Don't ask me to be okay with this. I'll never be. But I know you . . . and I know that you're not going to stop until you get your way. I'm beginning to think I was wrong about you not being spoiled rotten. I admit that I haven't helped matters any by letting you have your way so much. But that's going to have to stop. I won't be an instrument for you to use in bringing about your own self-destruction."

She took his hand. "I concede to giving this more thought, Ken. I promise."

"Why don't I believe you, Omunique?" He kissed her hard on the mouth, as if he thought she needed punishment for the crazy way in which she looked at this whole thing. "Let's go inside and get this over with. I can now see that it was a mistake to come here with this madness hanging over our heads. We'll stay just long enough to keep from being considered rude."

Amanda Steele was a tall, graceful woman. She wasn't a rare beauty, but her all-silver hair, cropped very short, made her a strikingly handsome-looking figure. Amanda was elated to see her godson and his lovely wife. She made a fuss over them as she led them into the big kitchen, modern, but warm and homey. Done in bright, spring colors, the room seemed to welcome its visitors.

"Sit down at the table while I serve the food. When Ralph called to say you two might be dropping by, I put the lasagna in the oven to bake. It was prepared earlier for Ralph and I to have for our dinner tonight. I just hadn't baked it yet."

Omunique remained standing as Ken took a seat. "Is there anything I can do to help?"

"Sure, Nique. You can get the tossed salad out the refrigerator. Also, the salad dressings need to be brought out. I have several different types already open. I've also mixed together with 7-Up a variety of juices for a delightful punch. Ken always did like my special juice punch."

"That's for sure. I keep trying to clone it, but it just doesn't come out the same as yours. You shouldn't have gone to all this trouble since we can only stay a short time. We've got a lot of things to take care of this evening. But both Nique and I are hungry . . . and we do have to eat. I can't think of a better place to have dinner or a nicer person to have it with."

Amanda beamed at Ken. "No trouble at all for my favorite godson."

"Your *only* godson," Ralph interjected from the doorway. "Smells good in here. I'm glad I decided to cut out early so that we can all have dinner together."

Ralph greeted his guests as he headed for his seat at the head of the table. Once the food was put in place, Amanda gave the blessing of thanks. The plates were then passed down to Ralph and he placed on each plate a generous serving of the already-sliced hot lasagna. Aware of her choice in dressings, Ken passed the bottle of low-calorie, fat-free Italian to his wife.

Amanda smiled at her guests. "So, kids, how are things going for you?"

"Everything is going great. We love our new home and Omunique's working at her pro figure skating career. Our company has had its best financial year yet. So it's been all good."

"That's so nice to hear." Amanda looked concerned. "You don't have to front for me, Ken. I know about the situation with the officer who stalked Nique. I just want you to know that I'm appalled at what the department has decided. Both Ralph and I are here for you and Nique should you ever need us. I know this has to be a difficult time for you both."

Ralph looked at his wife with a soft expression. "This might not be the best dinner conversation for them, Amanda." Smiling sympathetically, she nodded her understanding.

"Thanks, Aunt Amanda, Omunique and I know that you two are always here for us."

"Yes, we do," Omunique chimed in.

"Tell us about how it feels moving up from amateur to pro," Ralph requested of Nique.

Her smile didn't light in her eyes. "It was a wonderful feeling for a time. I like the idea of having a lot more freedom in choosing my choreographed routines. They do a lot of charity events and those that are just plain fun. I thought I was going to love being able to showcase my style of ice dancing and doing it to popular music. The thing I liked most about the training camp was being in the company of so many Olympic medal winners. Most of the people were so awesome."

Amanda momentarily gripped Omunique's shoulder. "They can't be any more awesome than you are, Nique. Ralph and I have seen you skate on numerous occasions, live, and on television . . . and we're left feeling breathless after every event."

"Thanks, Aunt Amanda. That means a lot to me coming from you."

Ralph looked questioningly at Omunique. "I was listening closely to what you were saying, Nique. But did I hear second thoughts in your comments on a pro career?"

Nique nodded in the affirmative. "Somewhat. But only because of the constant problem I'm having with my feet lately. I had to go to the ER not long after the housewarming. I'm feeling way more optimistic about the pros even though I'm taking some time off for now."

"Good to hear that you feel better about it! You had me worried there for a minute. For you not to skate in the pros would be a devastating blow to all your adoring fans, including Amanda and me. We'll pray for your medical situation." Ralph turned to Ken. "Did you get the gazebo put in?"

"That's been the hardest thing to get done, not to mention the outrageous cost of it. But when I told my friend, Brandon, what was happening, he couldn't believe that I hadn't approached him about it in the first place. The price he was able to get it erected for was less than half of what we were quoted. To answer your question, yes, we've had it installed on the west end of the property so we can watch the sunsets from there. It's beautiful."

Omunique smiled. "I knew I wanted a gazebo when we were having the plans drawn up, but I totally forgot to mention it to Ken and Brandon at the time. I knew something was missing just before the housewarming, but I couldn't pinpoint what. It's a wonderful addition to the grounds. We can see it from the balcony, from both of our offices, as well as from our bedroom."

"Amanda and I will have to come out soon and take a look-see. You guys have such a romantic theme going on up there on that secluded hill. Heart-shaped rosebushes, gazebo, swimming pool, Jacuzzi, and a host of other fanciful accents. Those are the kinds of things that make a *home* your castle."

Ken smiled at his wife. "It has become our castle. After our professional obligations are over at the end of the day, we can't wait to make it home. No matter what we're doing there, we always feel contented."

"Our favorite thing to do is to sit on the upper deck and watch the sunset," Omunique said. "We also can see the sun go down from several rooms in the house, but our special place is from the master bedroom."

Amanda stood up. "Freshly baked lemon meringue pie! Who's ready for a slice?" All hands went up at the same time. Omunique went into the kitchen to help her bring in the desserts.

"Uncle Ralph, this thing with Taylor is driving me nuts. It's causing Omunique to think and behave irrationally. We had a serious disagreement on the way over here. I hope this issue doesn't bring big trouble into our marriage . . ." The women entering the room caused Ken to stop talking.

Amanda handed Ralph the plate she carried and Omunique handed Ken one of the ones she had in her hands. Coffee was served before everyone began eating the delicious-looking dessert.

Ken waited for Omunique to join him in bed. Though he hated to bring it up again, they needed to talk about her wanting to visit with Taylor. He hoped it wouldn't turn into a major battle for them, but he knew how determined Omunique could get when she wanted something.

After sliding her feet out of the satin slippers she'd worn, Omunique climbed into their highly elevated, four-poster bed. Instead of cuddling up to her husband, she fluffed her pillow and turned her back to him as she slid down in the bed.

Though sure she'd gotten into one of her funky moods, he cuddled up behind her and placed his hand on the side of her face. "Are we going to sleep without kissing one another goodnight?"

"Why would you think that?"

"Well, your back *is* to me. And when you normally come to bed, you scoot right over here and settle down in my arms. I've never known us to go to sleep without kissing each other. That's what makes me think that."

She turned over and slid her body right up against his. "The look on your face told me that you had something to say to me and that it was serious. I know it's about Taylor, and I didn't think I wanted to hear it. So I thought if I turned my back to you, you'd leave it alone until tomorrow."

"You really think you know me, don't you?"

"How close was I to being right?"

"On target. But your little display didn't work. We're not going to wait until tomorrow. Neither one of us will get any sleep with this unsettled issue wedged in right between us. Will you at least listen to me even if you don't want to say anything?"

"Ken, I already know what you're going to say. You don't think I should see Taylor and I think I should. Talking about it is not going to make either of us change our position. We're going to end up on opposite sides of this issue no matter what. I don't even see a compromise in this."

"I guess you've got a point. If we don't talk about the issues, what this means for you, for us, we won't understand the positions we've taken. Is that what you want to see happen? Do you want us walking around impacted by things that we haven't brought to the forefront?"

"I understand that you don't want me to do this. You understand that I want to. What else is there for us to understand?"

"The reasons why we want or don't want it to happen, Nique."

"You're not going to understand if I tell you, which I've already tried to do. You can't get inside of me and feel all these things for me. I want this guy out of my life as much as you do, but the reality is he's back in it. It makes me crazy knowing this guy is not dead, as we were falsely led to believe. I feel like I could destroy something right now. I want these desperate feelings outside of me, behind me, completely away from us. The only way to do that is for me to see him. And I do want you to come with me."

"Nique, you can go see Taylor if you want. I'll drive you there, if arrangements are even possible. But I *will not* go into the room with you."

"But why not? You know how important this is to me."

"Because I *know* my limitations. It's obvious that you don't know yours. Besides that, you seem to think that this is just about *you*, about what *you* want. Do you ever stop to think of how I felt when I saw that lunatic with a knife to your throat? Does it ever cross your mind what Wyman went through that night after he learned that you'd been taken hostage? What he must have felt knowing that Taylor had actually made the decision to kill you, to murder you in cold blood?"

She visibly shuddered. "But, Ken . . ."

"But, Ken, hell! Listen for a change. If you think this is just about you, you're more selfish than I ever thought possible. If you can't listen to me, listen to yourself . . . and hear what you're saying, for God's sake. You're asking me to sit in a room with a man that terrorized you on numerous occasions, someone that nearly cost you the career you'd bravely fought so hard for, an obsessed man that ended up attempting to take your life. In asking me to sit in the same room with him, you're putting me in a position to commit a crime. Nique, I'm in love. I'm not stupid."

Tears fell from her eyes.

He held her close, resting his chin atop her head. "I'll be there to support you. Afterward, I'll take you in my arms. I'll continue to love you and be there for you. Princess, I *will not,* I repeat, *I will not* sit in the same room with the likes of Taylor . . . unless it's in a court of law, where criminal charges have been brought against him. Have I made myself clear?"

She didn't respond because she knew he'd never be able to understand.

Ken jumped out of bed, walked over to her side, and pulled her up on her feet. Without any explanation, he wrapped a terrycloth robe around her shoulders and led her downstairs. Omunique was too darn curious about where they were going to protest, but her eyes let him know she didn't like being pulled out of bed this way. It was late—and she wanted to go to sleep. Her curiosity further heightened when he led her down the hallway that led to the physical fitness room.

Inside the room, he flicked on the light. While she stood perfectly still, glaring at him with intolerance, he went into the equipment room and came out with two sets of boxing gloves. He tossed a pair to her. "Put those on."

"For what?"

"If we can't settle our issues by talking, we'll just slug them out of our systems."

Both her eyebrows shot up. "You're willing to spar with me over this? If so, are you actually planning on hitting me with these red-fisted leather weapons?"

"Of course I'm not going to hit you. We're both going to get our frustrations out on the punching bag. I'd never

hit you no matter how big of disagreement we got into."
Before lowering the punching bag into position, he brought
Omunique over to stand in front of it. "Give it a good
couple of whacks." She looked at him like he'd gone bananas. "Go ahead and hit it. Hit it hard, Nique. Knock the
hell out of what's come into your peaceful world and turned
it upside down."

She felt stupid, especially being dressed in silk nightclothes. At Ken's prompting, she stepped up to the red-
striped leather bag and took a wild swing at it. "Damn it.
I missed it by a mile." She hit it dead-center on her second
try. Within minutes, she was punching away with all her
might. Moaning and groaning, letting go with a few loudly
expressed expletives, sweating profusely, she took all her
frustrations out on the bag. As tears of frustration began to
fall, she hit the bag harder and harder. Frustration quickly
turned to anger, causing her to miss the bag more often
than she was connecting. The next few punches didn't come
close to the mark.

"You're now letting your enemy get the best of you,
Nique. Take control. Don't let anger become the instrument
by which your enemy takes you down. Not only can the
enemy see in you the signs of weakness; he can smell your
weakened condition. Pull it back together, Nique. Stay
focussed on your mission. Don't let anger win out."

Beginning to see the bag as an archenemy, as a real threat
to her existence, her next few punches were direct hits to
the target, making it swing back and forth with force. While
hitting it several more times, verbal abuse came spewing
out of her mouth, without her giving any thought to what
obscenities she was yelling. Hysteria soon began to win out
over determination. Her shots started going wide and wild
again. Her arms began to flail about like she had no control
over them.

"Nique, you're digressing. You were almost there. The
victory's so near. Don't give up."

She threw a few more hard jabs before her arms began to feel like lead weights. Too exhausted to take another jab, she fell to the thick matting situated beneath the bag. Her body shook as her hysterical screams filled the room.

A short time later, with the side of her face flat to the mat, she grew silent. Exhaustion had usurped every ounce of her energy. She was so extremely tired. Hoping that she'd gotten everything out of her system, praying that she would let go of the idea of confronting her real enemy, Marcus Taylor, Ken knelt down beside her. Before he could take her in his arms and hold her, to make sure she'd cried herself out, as was his intent, Omunique's gloved hand came up and landed a short, hard jab to his right eye.

Only when he yelped in pain did she realize what she'd done. "Oh, no, what have I done? Ken, are you okay? I'm really sorry for striking you like that. No, I didn't do that!"

With his right eye nearly swollen shut, he looked at her through the other. "If I didn't know better, I'd think you did this on purpose. You got a mean jab. You nearly knocked my eye out!"

She nodded. "I'm sorry. I don't know what came over me. I didn't even see you come over here. Maybe I sensed you, thought you were the enemy attacking me. You did tell me to hit hard."

"But that was some time ago, Nique, a long time ago. Since you're sorry, please get me some ice from out the freezer. I think I got one hell of a shiner coming on. How do I explain that? Husband abuse?"

After placing the cold cubes in an ice bag from the medical supply closet, Omunique came back to Ken and held it up to his eye.

"Ouch! Here, let me do that myself." He took the bag from her hand. "Think I should wrap the ice bag in a towel? I don't want to get ice burns."

Feeling sorry for him, even sorrier that she'd hit him like that, she ran her fingers through his hair. "Only if it's too cold for you. You won't get burned from that bag. It's made of cloth. How does your eye feel now?"

"Like a black eye, but I sure hope it's not. Max, Wyman, and Frank are going to have a field day with this. Please, Lord, please don't let it turn black." Deciding to milk his injury for all it was worth, he moaned and groaned. "I think I need help getting back to bed. I can barely see." As Nique bent down to take his arm, he pulled her back down to the mat. "On second thought, you can help me with something more important."

"Anything for you, love. Just tell me what you need me to do."

The sexy scent of her sweat mixed with her perfume, the way her perspiration-soaked attire clung to her body turned him on. Forgetting all about his injured eye, he pressed Omunique's back into the mat. His hands roved her body as if he had pent-up frustrations to release, as well.

Fourteen

Turning on his side, Ken looked at the clock and groaned. It was raining outside and he had no desire to leave his bed. His eye had healed pretty well and it hadn't turned black and blue the next day, which had been a couple of weeks back. It had simply gone straight to purple. The puffiness in his right eye had gone down completely, but not the swelling of his ego.

He had lost that battle on two counts. His wife had blackened his eye. A few days later, she'd announced her intent to find a way to confront Marcus Taylor, with or without Ken's help. He knew that the only way to ensure her protection was to solicit Ralph Steele's help.

It had rained all during Omunique and Ken's drive into downtown Los Angeles. The atmosphere in the car had been just as gloomy as the weather outside. The oppressive silence between her and Ken was tense and uneasy, but neither of them attempted to break it.

As Omunique waited inside the jail for the escort to take her to the special police-run hospital unit where Marcus had been temporarily housed for this visit, she surveyed the dreary surroundings in a stunned daze. Masses of people crowded into the waiting room like canned sardines. She was shocked to see that mothers and fathers alike brought their small children, and even babies, to such a cheerless place. She'd never been inside a jail, let alone paid a visit to an inmate. Omunique couldn't even entertain the thought of ever doing this again.

Poker-faced police officers stood behind bulletproof windows assisting those who were there for one reason or another. Babies screamed and toddlers ran from one place to another, without having a clue as to why they were there, or what type of place they were in. So many of the adults seemed to know the ropes, going about their business as if it was an everyday occurrence for them. Many laughed and joked as if on a special outing of some sort. But others looked sad, or just plain tired of waiting in long lines and sitting on hard, uncomfortable seating. Some of the babies just slept peacefully in their mothers' arms.

Steele had spent the better part of two weeks calling on everyone that he thought could help Omunique to get in to see Marcus, but only those that he knew he could trust explicitly. There wasn't a single person involved in this covert operation that would put Steele's lifelong career in jeopardy in any way, shape, or form. He'd called on officers that he'd once saved in the line of duty. He sought out officers seriously loyal to him because he'd gone to bat for them when their jobs or their personal lives had been on the line. Then there were several officers that he'd solicited because they were grateful that he'd helped them in some other extraordinary way.

The "code of silence" existed in more ways than one. Some for good, others for bad.

Just like Ken, Wyman had fiercely objected to the whole idea of his daughter visiting Taylor. Ken finally convinced him that it was necessary because he knew that Omunique wasn't going to let go of the idea until she had her way. It was then that Ken had put the "okay" call into his godfather. Immediately Ralph went to work, pulling as much together as he could, as fast as he could. Ralph worked hard to finish making all the arrangements for Omunique to gain access to Taylor. Before Wyman would agree to any of it, Steele had to assure him that no harm would come to his daughter, that Taylor wouldn't have a remote chance of doing anything to her.

Ralph Steele walked into the waiting area and searched the sea of faces for Omunique. Spotting her and Ken, he made his way to where they sat. Well over six-foot-four of muscled strength, Captain Steele caught the attention of many eyes as he passed through each section of connected seating. He saw Ken's injured eye right off but didn't comment. He'd promised not to do so.

As he neared, Omunique stood up, offering her husband's godfather a warm greeting. Smiling broadly, the captain hugged her affectionately and then lovingly embraced his godson.

"Nique and Ken, it's good to see both of you again, though I wish it were under more pleasant circumstances. I decided to personally handle this visit, so that's why I'm here. I also wanted to take this opportunity to see how you were doing. How *are* you doing, Nique?"

Wearing a slight frown, she bit down on her lower lip. Nervously, she pushed her hand through her loose, flowing hair. "To be honest, Uncle Ralph, I really don't know. This entire ordeal has me crazy. I just can't understand it. Basically, that's why I'm here." She sighed. "I hope Marcus can shine some light on things." Putting her hand behind her back, she stretched it out for Ken to take hold of it. She needed to feel the reassurance his touch would provide.

Though he didn't agree with this decision, either, Captain Steele smiled sympathetically, fully understanding of her tumultuous dilemma. But he was sure Taylor wasn't going to clear up a thing for her or anyone else. "If you're ready, Nique, I'll escort you to the hospital wing."

She took a deep breath. "I'm ready, Uncle Ralph." She looked back at Ken who was still seated. "Are you still determined not to come with me, Ken?"

His forehead wrinkled with worry, Ken got to his feet. His mind seemed a million miles away. "I'm coming to the ward, but you already know that I'm not going in to see Taylor. As I've already told you, I'm sure I can't practice that much self-control. I was sure I'd made myself clear on this issue. I know my limitations." He only wished that she knew hers. He looked to the captain. "Is there a waiting area where you're heading?"

Captain Steele put a calming hand on Ken's shoulder. "There is, and I understand what you must be feeling. Just remember that the guy is sick. I'm not sure he's capable of understanding what he's done. We haven't been able to get a thing out of him, but it's still felt that there's an excellent chance for a breakthrough. Try to be patient. Especially with your wife."

The trio began their long journey, which took them into another building. They walked through a small foyer and then approached the elevator. As they passed through a small corridor, metal bars clanged shut, startling Omunique. Looking back at the bars making them prisoners as well, she tensly clutched Ken's arm. The elevator was so tiny that there was barely enough room for the three of them. The cables creaked and moaned as the car ascended.

Coming to a quaking halt seconds later, the doors slid roughly open. Omunique rushed out, having felt the sharp pangs of claustrophobia inhabiting her nerve endings. She hated tight spaces, but she feared them even more. As a small child, she had been stuck in an elevator in Sears. Though she'd been rescued rather quickly, those few minutes had felt like years.

Captain Steele stopped at a small desk stationed in the hallway. Putting his hand under Omunique's elbow, he guided her toward a set of double doors. A minuscule seating area was situated to the right of the doors and he pointed it out to Ken. "You can wait right over there in that section of seating, son. We won't be too long."

Before entering the seating area, tenderly, Ken caught Omunique's face between his hands. "I'll be right out here waiting for you. Go do what you need to do, Princess. I still wish you didn't have to." Omunique hugged Ken to show that she understood his point of view.

Captain Steele inserted a key into a metal pad built into the wall. As the doors swung open, he led Omunique into a cold, empty hallway. Once again, the doors clanged shut behind them. A loud gasp rushed from her lips. As she surveyed the dimly lit areas around her, she grew more nervous with each step. Upon entering a locked ward, Captain Steele stepped aside, allowing her to proceed ahead of him.

Stopping cold, she turned to face him, apprehension flaming in her eyes. "I don't . . . know if I can do this . . . now that I'm here." Her voice trembled with fear. "I'm downright scared of what I'll find in there."

He placed a comforting arm around her shoulder. "If you're not up to this, we can abort this visit." He looked to her for the final decision, at the same time praying for her to come to her senses and run back to where her nervous husband waited. Back to the safety of the *unknowing*.

As nausea tumbled around in her stomach, she looked at the doors behind her and then the ones in front of her. "I guess I have to do this, Uncle Ralph. I'll never know the answers if I don't. I pray that I don't live to regret it. My doing this is costing my husband a lot."

"I hope you've considered the possibility that you may never know the answers. If what you're looking for doesn't come from Taylor, you may find yourself in a terribly disappointing state. Then what will you do to deal with the nightmares he brought to your life? I hope that you can go on with your life in the same way you did when you thought he was dead. I think we all would've been better off if you hadn't convinced yourself to come here and actually see him alive." Without further comment, Captain Steele entered the ward and waited for her to catch up to him. He saw that her steps had slowed more and more as they'd gotten closer.

All of the beds were empty except two. One man was asleep. Taylor stared blankly at the walls from a small cot. As he moved his hand, she saw the shackles around his wrist. Instantly, she slammed her eyes shut, trying to cast out the horrible reality sluicing though her mind. Uncle Ralph had known what he was talking about, so had her husband and father.

Captain Steele softly touched her hand, cutting into the preponderant racing of her mind. "Nique, remember everything I've said so far. I'll be right outside. If you should need anything, there's an officer right in there." He pointed to a man sitting behind a glass-enclosed partition. He really didn't expect her to need anything, just wanted to assure her that she wasn't alone. With a slight nod of his head, he urged her toward Taylor.

Grim faced, an opaque sadness in her eyes, Omunique edged her way over to the bed. Marcus never once looked her way. Gripping the back of a chair and pushing it closer to the bed, she sat down and took several deep breaths. "Marcus, its Omunique. I've come here to see you. How are you? I came here hoping we could talk about your reasons for wanting to hurt me."

Seemingly lost somewhere between disassociation and total madness, he barely blinked, never taking his eyes off the stark, white walls. His athletic form was much too large for the small bed, but he didn't seem aware of it.

"Why, Marcus? Why did you do those things to me?"

He looked directly at her. What she saw in his eyes nearly crucified her. His gaze, cold, unrelenting, appeared to look straight through her, yet a single tear rolled from the corner of one eye. The shackles rattled against the metal bed as he lifted his hands to wipe away the wetness. Still, he said nothing. He only stared at her and then turned back to the wall. His cuffed hands fell away from his face, landing heavily in his lap. The dried, cracked condition of his lips caused her to wonder if he was on medication.

She frowned, totally perplexed by his unresponsive behavior. "Help me to understand, Marcus. I didn't even know you, so how could I have possibly known that you were vying for my attentions. In fact, I don't ever remember seeing you until you gave me that ticket. Had you been watching me a long time before that unfortunate incident?" Her nerves felt raw and badly frayed. His failure to respond only served to heighten the tension fiercely gripping her insides.

Marcus suddenly diverted his cool blue eyes to her. Only a second had passed before he once again focused his gaze on the walls. Without so much as a single twitch of his eyes, he dragged his tongue across his dry, cracked lips.

She jumped up from her seat but stood well away from him. "I can't leave things like this! I want to know why you came after me with such a vengeance? I want to know now," she demanded, angry that she couldn't get through to him." Her anger had demanded answers from him, but now she wasn't sure that he was even capable of giving her what she so desperately needed from him. Uncle Ralph had been right. She felt terribly disappointed.

To her, he almost looked ashamed of himself. He seemed afraid of what he'd allowed fear to reduce him to. Then he closed his eyes. Inwardly, she fought hard to shut off her anger and disgust, hoping that somehow after this visit he'd simply go away from inside her head.

"Marcus, don't you think you at least owe me an explanation? I can't hope to move on with my life until I can understand what happened here. Please, Marcus, if there's an ounce of decency left in you, help me understand!" She was talking more to herself than him . . . and she knew it. She needed to get over the past incidents by any means necessary.

Her tearful plea appeared to cut him to the quick. A jagged cry, almost wounded animal–like in nature, ripped from his throat. Quickly, she cowered in fear, moving further back from the bed. Still, she wished she could somehow encourage him to speak. Tears rolled from his eyes, but the cold, blank stare in them hadn't changed one iota.

Omunique had always thought she was incapable of hating. She sometimes hated the things that people did, but never the people doing them. Now, faced with the man who had once seemed hell-bent on killing her, she was no longer sure that she wasn't capable of hating him.

Suddenly, he turned, facing her. She saw that his cool blue eyes were more lucid than before, as they made direct contact with her gray ones. Again, tears welled in his eyes, but his mouth never moved. In his eyes she saw the same fear that was often mirrored in her own. Then she saw it replaced with some other emotion; one that she couldn't recognize. She blinked back the hot, biting tears. Hate hadn't been born yet, but something very close to it was busy devouring what was left of her once very forgiving nature.

Her calm demeanor belied the stormy feelings brewing inside of her. She sighed heavily, wishing that he could come clean with her, hoping that an explanation would help her move on to the even greater things she was destined for. It had all begun with some silly teenager making prank telephone calls to her home; a teenager with nothing more than a schoolboy crush on her.

Then some demented adult, a police officer no less, took up the reign of terror; a sort of copycat routine, one could say. Only he'd taken it several steps further, following her every move, stalking her like a hunter tracking his prey, terrorizing her, putting her life in grave danger. Was it his desire that she would run to him for comfort? Had he gotten so caught up in the lethal game he'd been playing that it caused him to lose his mind? It certainly had nearly caused her to lose her own.

She closely examined his face for any signs that would let her know how he felt about her being there, but his expression carried a deadly blankness, causing her skin to pale. His own skin had turned paler than it had been when she first saw him. It had now taken on an ashy appearance.

In stunned horror, she sat back down, quietly watching him, intently so, as she continued to assess her feelings. Was it hate that she felt for him? Was it anger, or perhaps disbelief? Maybe it was just a disguised compassion? She rather suspected it of being all of them rolled into one, but much like Marcus, she couldn't recognize or name the emotions coursing through her. But whatever it was, she didn't like the way it made her feel; terribly unsettled. By clearing her throat, she thought she could chase away the butterflies dancing a mournful ritual in her stomach.

Marcus looked old and frazzled, nothing like the strong, athletic man she remembered. His disassociation scared her, one of the diagnoses that a psychiatrist might consider. She deeply pondered her many questions, impatient for some type of response from him.

When it appeared that he was struggling to bring her into focus, she moved the chair a little closer to the bed. "Help me, Marcus," she sadly pleaded. "Help me allay all these old fears, once and for all. Help me understand what I did to make you turn on me like you did."

As she looked at him through tear-blurred eyes, she realized that she really didn't want to understand what he'd been doing to her, didn't want to think about what it all meant. But somehow she did understand and she did know what it meant.

It all meant that Marcus was psychotic or schizophrenic, but she still didn't have a name for what she felt. Though, she now knew it wasn't hate. How could she hate someone who was so ill? How could she hate someone so out of touch with reality that it wasn't even funny?

Despite his attacks on her, she'd made the Olympic team. Not only had she skated in her biggest competition ever, she'd won the silver medal. Yes, she'd been fearless, Olympic material. She had showed off her talent and the ability to win, she silently asserted. She somehow felt that Marcus knew it, too; the fact that she'd come there to see him proved that she was indeed fearless . . . And it was these very things that had put her on the psychiatrist's couch. False valor had damn near wrecked her entire life.

It now looked to her as if Marcus had drifted off into a world somewhere between reality and insanity, which made it clear that it was impossible for her to communicate with him. Standing up, she bent over and brushed her hand against his smooth cheek in a show of sincere sympathy. That dangerous display of ridiculous nerve caused the on-duty officer to hurry from behind the glass partition. She'd simply gotten too close to someone deemed a madman.

The officer came and stood only inches from Marcus's bed, watching as she turned and walked away. The officer followed her across the room. He went back behind the partition as she reached the door. She then walked back to where Marcus was, but she only stayed for a second.

"I'll be getting out of here, you know. One way or the other. Then I'm coming for you."

Startled beyond reason, unable to believe her ears, she turned and looked back. Marcus still sat there quietly, staring up at the ceiling. Had he actually spoken or was she under way too much stress? She watched him a few more intense moments before determining that she'd only heard his voice inside her head, just as she'd done so many times before. More so since she found out that he was very much alive.

The officer came back to where she stood and unlocked the doors for her to exit.

Captain Steele was waiting for her and she took his offered hand. In complete silence, they made it back to where Ken paced the floor in nervous anticipation. To Ken, she looked fragile, more vulnerable than ever before. He gathered her into his arms, dropping kisses into her hair.

Omunique had a strong urge to tell them what she thought she'd heard Marcus say, but once again, she convinced herself that it was all inside her head. So many things were inside her head, images of the knife at her throat, images of the dying mother, images that she couldn't seem to erase no matter what she did; images that threatened her existence in so many ways.

They both thanked Ralph Steele for all that he'd done. Ken promised to call their home that evening as he steered his wife toward the parking garages.

As the car engine roared to life, Omunique began to feel dead inside. It felt as though her very life had passed before her eyes, while the memories of that night haunted her soul. No matter how desperately she tried to hold on to what her reality was, she wasn't able to stop it from floating far away from her. This trip hadn't done the trick anymore than her visit to the hospital had done in helping her erase the horrible memories of that event.

Ken's electrifying touch caused her to look up with a start. He saw something in her eyes that couldn't be explained, something that frightened him. "How did it go, Nique?"

She raised her hand up, gesturing for him not to begin questioning her. "I can't let anyone in right now. Not even you, as much as I love you."

His eyebrows shot up, his mouth flew open, but he said nothing. He knew that she didn't want to hear what he had to say, anyway. Feeling completely left out in the dark, par for the course, he turned on the radio and kept his eyes fastened on the road.

The rain still fell from the sky. To keep her mind off the unbelievable, uninformative conversation she'd had with Marcus, she attempted the impossible feat of counting rain-drops as they pinged against the windshield. Quickly tiring of the game, she glanced at Ken, feeling sorry for having been so short with him.

She slid a flat palm up and down his firm thigh. "I'm sorry if I hurt you, sweetheart. I didn't mean to. But if tell you that everything is eventually going to be okay, will you believe me? Will you have a little faith in me?"

Tenderly, he pushed a few strands of hair behind her ear. "I'm not so sure that it will ever be the same again for us, but I keep praying. It's not you that I need to put my faith in right now. Take as long as you need to work things through." Leaning toward him, she laid her head on his shoulder. At the same moment of contact, a feeling of sweet peace rippled through her.

For the remainder of the week all she could think of were the awful twists and turns that her happy life with Ken had taken so suddenly. She thought about the tiny baby. She needed to feel his little body against hers, needed to feel the warmth of his breath on her face. The way he looked at her had a way of lighting up her darkest moment. She couldn't wait to feel his little face against hers as she held him close. Twinges of eager anticipation swept her up in a torrent of emotion. Just the thought of scooping him up in her arms caused euphoria.

Ken was reading a book when she walked over to the sofa and dropped down beside him. "I . . . need to go . . . to the arena for a short time. I need some time. I need to start sorting out all my feelings so that I can move forward with my life. Do you mind?"

He laid the book aside, taking her hand in his. She closed her eyes as his tender warmth spread through her. "Do whatever it is you have to do, Princess, but don't forget that I'm here whenever you need me." He already hated the unbearable distance that seemed to be between them, though she was still beside him. Gently rubbing his finger across her lower lip, he lowered his head, bringing the sweet tenderness of her lips into direct contact with his. Moments later, he reluctantly released his hold on her, knowing she had to go, yet wanting desperately to urge her not to. If only they could turn back the hands of time, an impossible feat for a mere mortal.

Totally unprepared for her refusal to allow him to drive her there and wait, he scowled, fighting the urge to protest. Thinking better of it, tiredly, he walked her out to her car, which had been parked in the garage for days now. It had been a trying time for both of them and maybe they did need some time apart.

As Omunique drove off, he walked back toward the house, but a sickened feeling gnawed at his insides, making him grimace. Instead of going back to the house, he settled himself into his own car. Using the spare key, he took off in the same direction she'd gone. As he caught sight of her Jeep, he slowed down, allowing several cars to move in front of him to keep him at a distance and afford him the opportunity to follow her without being seen.

Something had told him she wasn't going to the arena. He knew he was right when she took a detour from the path that would've led her straight to the freeway. After a short drive, he was extremely surprised when she turned in to the parking lot of the local hospital.

Was she sick? Had her feet flared up on her? After giving her plenty of time to get inside, he got out of his car and slowly made his way to the entrance. As he entered the building, he noticed that only a couple of people were out in the waiting room but Omunique wasn't one of them. His autumn-gold eyes feverishly searched all the different areas on the lower level, including the ER, but she was nowhere to be found. She had disappeared without a trace.

He went back outside to sit in his car. He'd wait for her to come out, hoping to see her when she did. Emotionally spent, he closed his eyes for a few moments of rest.

Omunique paced the floor wondering where Ken could be at this hour. It was after eleven o'clock at night. He wasn't at all the type of man to run the streets. He always called and kept her informed of his whereabouts and most of his movements. Fearful that he was still upset over her seeing Taylor, she prayed that he'd come to understand. But Ken had been absolutely right. She shouldn't have gone there. Seeing Taylor alive only deepened her insecurities and made her more fearful of what might come. As a mental patient, they could only keep him locked up for so long. Even though he'd attempted, he hadn't killed anyone, which would make him innocent of a murder charge. Thank God, thank God he'd failed, she cried inwardly.

Hearing Ken's key in the front door lock sent her flying into the marble foyer. Even the click of her heels on the floor sounded anxious. As he stepped inside the door, she flew into his arms. "Where have you been? I've nearly gone crazy with worry."

He couldn't believe his ears. "You've been worried about me! I've been sitting out in the hospital parking lot for hours waiting for you to come out of the building. In fact, I was so exhausted that I fell asleep waiting. When I woke up it was ten-forty."

"The hospital parking lot?"

"Don't play coy with me, Nique. Don't start lying to me again. That's the worst thing you can do. You left here saying you were going to the arena, but that's not where you went. I followed you. I had a feeling you weren't being honest with me before you left. I played my hunch and found out that I was right. Why did you tell me one thing and do another?"

She looked defeated. "I had to get out of here. I needed some time alone. I went to the hospital cafeteria and had a cup of tea and watched the people come in and out." At least that was part of the truth. She had done exactly that. But she wasn't ready to tell him anything more than she already had. It wasn't time.

"But why did you lie about the arena?" He moved into the living room and she followed behind him. She sat down on the sofa and he remained standing.

"If I had said the hospital, you would've thought I was going there to see if I could learn anything else about Taylor since he'd been admitted there at one time. So I just said the arena."

He looked disgusted with the whole matter. "Whatever, Nique. You're really acting stranger and stranger with each day. I don't know what to make of your behavior anymore. We're two people who got married just a short time ago. And then we moved into our dream home . . . now one of us is beginning to tell lies to the other.

"Senseless lies, or so it seems. You could've told me that you were going to the hospital. Perhaps I would've questioned you, but only out of concern for your well-being. The hospital can't give out that sort of confidential information, which you found out from the admitting office. So I wouldn't have even thought of what you suggested as a motive. Nique, you really don't need to give me a reason for doing anything you decide to do. Nor do you ever have to lie to me. But you did. Let's end this little charade right now. If you're going to shut me out, as you've done a lot lately, why don't you just shut me out for good?"

She thought about what Dr. Jackson had told her: It would be the *lies* that would eventually push him away.

"Ken, could you just listen to me for a minute?"

Without comment, he walked into the family room and sat down in the reclining chair. "What is you want me to listen to now? If it's more lies, Nique, save it."

"Ken, there are a lot of things going on that you don't know about, a lot of things in my childhood that I haven't shared with you. I'm working them through, but I need time. Time that you promised to give me. Dr. Jackson is helping me to see myself as I really am, and to come to terms with the things I haven't been able to face, not until now. You suggested that I see someone to get psychological help, and now that I'm doing so, please give me time to learn what it is I need to know about myself. I've been running and hiding from my pain since I was a little girl. The girl you met and fell in love with is not the same person you've ended up with. I was an immature girl back then . . . who hasn't grown much beyond that today, at least, not emotionally. And I want so desperately to become a woman, but I have to learn what it really means to be one before I can achieve it. I can only get stronger if I continue to see Dr. Jackson. I don't like lying to you. There are just certain things I'm not ready to reveal . . . and when you ask me questions that I don't want to answer, I have a tendency to lie." *So many untruths exist already.*

"I just wish you didn't feel that you have to lie to me. I'm glad that you're seeing Dr. Jackson. I feel your pain, Nique, but you need to know I'm not the enemy. With Taylor still alive, I'm terribly anxious about your safety, especially when you're not right here in my eyesight. When you take off like that, and then lie about it, it worries me sick. I remember all too well how you confront dangerous situations. You cut two strange men off with your car that, by the grace of God, just happened to be police officers. But you didn't know that when you got out of the car and confronted them in the darkened parking lot of the arena. If you're out there finding ways to make sure Taylor pays for his crimes, please stop right now. You could get hurt.

"Officers Grayson and Hardin were so concerned for you after that incident that they not only wrote their deep concern for you into their report, they began using the same story when doing seminars on women's safety issues. Now that we know Taylor is alive, we have to let the system work this out. Until we see how they're going to handle this, we can't do anything foolish. Keep in mind that Uncle Ralph's job is also at stake. Even so, he's not going to allow them to let Taylor walk out of there without putting up one hell of a fight."

She came over to the chair and bent over. "I'm sorry. Please forgive me. Please help me get through all this madness. I need you . . ."

When Omunique looked at him in that way, the way that made him putty in her hands, he couldn't do anything but what she asked of him. Taking her in his arms, he kissed her in the same punishing way he'd found himself doing a lot lately. "I need you, too, Nique. I hope we never stop needing one another . . ."

Fifteen

Omunique's darn-near refusal to let him make love to her over the past couple of weeks had Ken totally baffled. Glad that she was downstairs making breakfast, he sat down on his side of the neatly made-up bed. She seemed so cold—and *that* he couldn't understand. Normally, when he touched her, she was always eager for it, always ready for them to create a bonfire.

He considered the strain she'd been under since learning that Taylor was alive, but somehow, he thought there was more to her strange behavior. She was withdrawn and sulky a good bit of the time. Conversations were short, and limited to casual topics. In fact, any meaningful communication between them had completely stopped, he realized with dismay.

Looking over at her side of the bed, he spotted something hanging out of the corner of her nightstand drawer. Curious as to what it was, he got up, walked around to the other side, and opened the drawer. It was only a pamphlet of some sort. As he laid it back inside the drawer, the word "contraceptive" leaped out at him. He retrieved it and read through it quickly. When he put it back in place for the second time, he saw the round blue container of birth control pills. Surprised to see it there, since they'd been trying to get pregnant, he opened it.

Much to his disbelief, it appeared that she was still taking the tiny pills. Sickened with grief, he counted the empty spots, counting back the days when they'd decided to just let nature take its course. He spotted a second container, picked it up and opened it, as well. It was empty, which suggested that she'd been taking them for some time now. As if the containers burned his fingers, he dropped them both to the floor. In the presence of the second container, he knew there was no way he'd miscounted the first one. The proof that she had stopped them was definitely there. The proof that she'd started them again was just as irrefutable.

Confused, angry, and downright shocked, he picked the containers off the floor and stuffed them both in his pants pocket. While trying to control his emotions, he started downstairs.

After entering the kitchen, he sat down at the table and watched her every move. Should he come right out with it? Or try and trap her in a lie? The latter didn't work for him, he quickly decided. He'd only be guilty of practicing the same kind of deceit she'd been exercising for a couple of months now. He was sure she'd lied to him a few times already.

Smiling, she walked over to the table and kissed him on the mouth. As usual, he melted under her probing sweetness. "The food's almost ready. Do you want a cup of coffee now?"

"I'll get it myself."

The gruffness in his tone caught her immediate attention. "Has something unpleasant happened since I came downstairs? You sound irritated."

Unable to control himself, he pulled the birth control containers out of his pocket and slammed them down hard on the table. "What's this all about? Why are you still taking these? At the same time you're supposed to be trying to conceive a child? Tell me that, Nique." The discomforting look on her face came like a sonic boom for him. The lies had been confirmed by that one look.

Not knowing what to say, she looked at Ken with an apology bright in her eyes. Like a heavy lead weight, she dropped down onto the chair across from him. "I don't know what to tell you, Ken. I really don't know."

"How about the truth? That's the only thing I'll accept from you."

"Nothing I can say will make you understand. Nothing at all." As much as she wanted to tell him the truth, she couldn't. The fear of it all kept her silent. She was more fearful of dying than of lying to her husband, the man she loved. That scared her even more.

He jumped up from his seat. "Secrets, Nique, should never be kept between a husband and wife. You've been keeping a huge dirty secret from me. I'm the fool here, the one who feels utterly stupid. I hope your secrets keep you happy because that's all you're going to have to keep you company. You're going to be all with alone with your stupid secrets. I'm moving out!"

"Moving? Ken, that's a giant step to take over this. Why would you want to move out?"

He gave her a sarcastic smirk. "Why would I want to stay? That should be your question. You've been cold and unresponsive to my love and affection for the past few weeks. We hardly talk and then I find out that you're still taking the pill. A man would have to be blind not to see all the danger signs you've been sending out. When you want to talk about why you're taking these pills while making me think you want to be the mother of my children, I'll listen. Otherwise we don't have a thing to discuss."

With her heart breaking, Omunique watched him walk out on her. How could she explain her fears? How could she get him to understand what she was feeling? All she knew is that she had to try. The situation she'd gotten herself into was costing her their marriage.

* * *

Upstairs in the bedroom they shared, Ken was busy tossing his belongings into a suitcase. Omunique nearly screamed out loud when she walked into the room and saw that he was really leaving her. When he unzipped the garment bag and put in several suits, she saw the inevitable, a separation that would probably lead to divorce. She had left him once, now he was leaving her.

Speechless, feeling stung and defeated, she watched as he continued to fill suitcases and garment bags. It looked as if he wanted to leave nothing of himself behind. He almost picked up the picture off his dresser, but he quickly withdrew his hand from the photo of them during one of their happier times. A picture of them so happy and in love was the last thing he needed as a reminder of what should've been. Besides, her beautiful face was branded into his memory.

It suddenly dawned on him that he wasn't in the room alone. That was unusual since he normally felt her presence even before she appeared. He looked over at her standing in the doorway. He wanted her even now, even after what he'd just learned. He wanted her so bad that it hurt. Only a brief moment had passed before he turned away. Looking at her beautiful face, still wanting her so much, wasn't going to help him do what he needed to do.

Out of desperation, Omunique tried to block his exit. "Don't do this, Ken. Please don't."

His anger at the situation kept him from responding. He pushed past her and kept going until he reached the front door. Once each item was stored in his car, he drove off.

After a two hour cooling-off period, he ended up at the guesthouse on their property. Why should he pay to stay in a hotel when they'd built wonderful guest accommodations?

Because he loved her so much he would call and tell her
where he was, but not until the next morning. His cell
phone had rung several times, but he'd been too upset to
answer. The guesthouse had a private line separate from the
main house. He needed time and space.

Ken just couldn't get over the fact that all the nights they
talked about getting pregnant, she was lying to him right
to his face. Omunique wasn't acting like the woman he fell
in love with. The softer side of him told him that there
could be valid reasons for her unusual behavior, that there
was more to her deviant actions than what met the eye. But
what the hell was it?

The two-bedroom guesthouse was lovely, featuring all the
comforts one could ask for. The linen wallpaper designed
in swirls of gold was warm and welcoming. A gold-and-
burgundy-striped sofa and wing chair looked splendid with
the gold wallpaper. A beautiful mahogany mantel majesti-
cally graced the marble fireplace.

Draped in fine linens, in colors of gold and burgundy,
the bed looked inviting but not enticing enough for sleeping
in it alone, Ken thought, as he hung his suits in the closet.
The shutters added a cottagelike look to the larger of the
two bedrooms. When open, they offered a panoramic view
of the wooded area at the back side of the house. Dark
cherry-wood furnishings, a queen rice bed, dresser, and ar-
moire, brought even more warmth into it. But it wasn't
home.

And Omunique wasn't there with him to keep him from
being lonely.

He couldn't help remembering them sleeping in the
guesthouse just to get a feel for it. They'd also made love
there, in both bedrooms. Those memories had come alive
the instant he'd looked over at where they'd slept the first
night. He recalled them trampling through each room, to
christen them, laughing together, constantly making new
plans for the future.

Overcome with anguish, he sat down on the side of the bed and picked up the phone. After dialing only three digits of their home number, he put the receiver back on the hook. Maybe he should've stayed and talked things through. At the very least, he should've heard her out. But his anger hadn't made allowances for that. Communication. Communication. How many times had the lack of it gotten them into trouble? It hadn't been that long ago that Omunique had talked of her desire to communicate more openly with him. Was it that difficult for her to express her feelings? Had he somehow made it hard for her to do so?

He knew that going in to work and managing to get things done was going to be next to impossible, but he had to keep himself busy. Otherwise he would go insane.

A shower and fresh clothes made Ken feel much better. Instead of the expensive suits he usually wore to the office, he chose to wear a black long-sleeved polo-style cashmere sweater, black slacks, along with a houndstooth sports coat. The casual, but elegant, clothing made him look striking, debonair. Omunique loved to see him in the polo-type sweaters. He already owned several of the same style, but she'd gone and purchased those in all the colors he didn't own. She was big on buying all the colors in the things she really loved.

His eyes clouded as he took off his wedding ring in order to lotion his hands. This solid gold band was a symbol of their undying love for each other, a continuous circle, symbolic of their eternal union. Yet he'd walked out on her at the first sign of trouble. Well, it wasn't exactly the first sign, but it was certainly the most challenging.

His marriage was not going to end like this, he vowed. However, for now, they both needed time and space. "Omunique, if you only knew what this separation is doing to me, to us. It hasn't been more than a couple of hours and I'm already half crazed."

* * *

Thomasina's eyes sparkled with giddiness as she looked up at Ken. "Other than your father, not a single person has called for you."

Looking thoughtful, Thomasina wondered what was up? This was only the tenth time he'd asked her that question, which seemed to come every half hour or so. She thought about the three times Omunique had called already, sounding desperate. She hadn't bothered to write the messages down. Omunique had Ken's private line. And he'd been in his office each time she'd called through reception. It seemed to her that he didn't want to talk to his wife.

"Thanks." He picked up the typed letters from her outbox and began to peruse them. When he didn't smile, as he usually did, Thomasina sensed that something serious was going on. Perhaps the honeymoon was over already. Maybe he was starting to see Omunique in a totally different light. Marriage often had a way of unveiling the true personalities once the honeymoon phase was over. Had the mask been ripped off the face of the Ice Princess? The *false face* that Thomasina had all along suspected the masquerading Omunique of hiding behind. If not, she promised herself that she'd be there to help him with the unveiling.

The phone rang just as Ken stepped away from Thomasina's desk. With hope emblazoned in his eyes, he stopped dead in his tracks and looked back at his secretary. Although Omunique rarely called for him through the reception area, he now had the attitude that anything was possible with her.

The deep disappointment setting in on him really shook him up. He could tell by Thomasina's conversation that it wasn't his wife on the line. With his chin practically down on his chest, he went back into his office and sat behind his desk. Opening the file folder he'd been working on, he had the appearance of reading it. But he could barely see the words for the tears that blurred his vision.

* * *

Unable to handle the silence another minute, Ken grabbed his sports coat and ran for the door. He stopped at the reception desk. "I'm out of here. I probably won't be back today. In fact, I'm almost sure of it. When Max comes in, please tell him to call me at home as soon as possible. I'll check in with you later. If something important comes up, you can page me. I won't have my cell phone turned on once I get home. If my wife should call, tell her I said to stay put, that I'm on my way home."

"Sure thing." Home in the middle of the day? What did that mean? She'd often been tempted to listen in on his private calls through the intercom, but she would've only heard his side of the conversation. Still, she'd already figured out his message-center password: his birth date. Ken looked desperate and upset to her. Some major trouble was going on in his life—and she'd bet her last dollar that it had everything to do with their marriage.

Ken searched the entire property for Omunique before he went back to the guesthouse. She must've gone out for the afternoon. It was strange not knowing where she was. No matter what, each of them had always known how to contact the other. Perhaps she was with Aunt Mamie. He dialed her number and let it rings several times, hanging up before the message center came on. Mamie wasn't in either.

Wyman came to mind, but he decided against making that call. Omunique may or may not have told him about their situation yet. He would just have to wait and see about that. If she hadn't done so, he would wait for them to do it together should that become necessary. Then it hit him. He hadn't called Omunique before he'd left for work and she had no way of knowing that he'd spent the night in the guesthouse. She couldn't have seen his car from any view in the house, not in the spot where he'd parked it. The garages completely obscured the area.

With nothing to do here but worry and wait, Ken decided it might be best to go back to the office where there was a lot for him to accomplish. First, he had to make a very important phone call—one that might save his life and his marriage.

Without Omunique, he wouldn't have either.

Omunique stood up until Marion was seated in the booth across from her. Immediately, the waiter was summoned. Once their order for Caesar chicken salads and cold drinks was taken, Omunique momentarily covered Marion's hand with her own.

"Thanks for coming to lunch with me. I hope we both have appetites after we talk."

Sensing that Omunique was nervous about something, Marion smiled sympathetically. "In that case, maybe we should eat lunch first. Neither one of us can stand to get sick with such busy schedules."

"That's okay with me. How's Frank?"

The mention of her fiancé's name brought a bright smile to her lips. "He's wonderful. When you get through talking to me about your situation, I'll tell you what we've decided for our wedding. We're going in a totally different direction with the plans."

"I can hardly wait. You sound excited about whatever it is you two have decided on."

The waiter served the salads and iced tea. Neither woman had ordered a meat entry, other than the grilled chicken on their salad greens. A loaf of freshly baked bread and whipped butter was also left for them to enjoy. Both women fell into an amicable silence as they prepared slices of the hot bread for consumption.

Well into the meal it began to trouble Marion to see Omunique so quiet. She was eating her salad, but it looked as if she didn't even taste it, as she carelessly put tiny piece after piece of lettuce into her mouth. Marion kept a watchful eye on her. She couldn't help wondering how deeply troubled she really was—and over what.

Unable to go on another second without releasing some tension, Omunique pushed her salad away. For the next few minutes she went from stretching her arms over her head, to drumming her fingernails onto the table in rapid succession.

Marion saw her friend's desperate need to hurry and get the things on her mind out in the open. "What is it, Nique? What's going on with you? You're awfully anxious."

"Our marriage is in deep trouble—and I don't have a clue how to begin to fix it."

Marion looked totally surprised, but more surprised that Ken hadn't come to his best friends with this bit of bad news. "In trouble? What kind of trouble?"

"The kind of trouble you can't really define, or even put a name to. But you know it's major when you and your man stop talking altogether. I'm sure you know that Ken and I are trying to get pregnant." Marion nodded. "Well, Ken found out that I'm still taking oral contraceptives. He confronted me this morning. I've never seen him so angry."

Marion wore a perplexed expression. "Why are you doing that if you two are trying have a baby, especially after having decided to do so? That makes no sense."

Omunique's eyes filled with water. "Fear, Marion, plain and simple fear. I saw something horrific a short time ago and I can't get the torturous images out of my head." She went on to explain to Marion what she'd seen in the ER and then on into what her mother had experienced.

"Oh, you poor baby. How awful for you to witness something as horrible as what you've just described. I never knew your mother died that way. Neither you nor Ken had ever spoken to us about it. I'm so sorry about all this. But have you told Ken this ER story?"

Omunique shook her head in the negative. "I haven't been able to. He was so angry with me when we had the showdown over the birth control pills. He feels that I betrayed him. He's right, too. You don't know how many nights I wanted to tell him about it, to ask him if we could wait a little longer for a child, wait for me to build up my courage. That was hard to do because I'm the one who got him worked up about having a family right away. Knowing how much he'd come to want us to have a baby kept me from coming clean with him. I honestly feared that he would leave me if I told him the truth."

Marion's eyes widened at that statement. "Even though you know how much he loves you? The man positively adores you."

"Even so. It seems that I've been living with so much fear since Ken first came into my life . . . and he seems to fear nothing. First, there was the fear of falling in love with him because he might not love me back. Then came the fears of managing a love affair and a career. And then the very first of my phobias arrived when I thought a heavy-breathing maniac, who turned out to be Officer Taylor, might kill one of us. While I never feared the competitiveness of the Olympic trials, that was still something huge to reckon with both mentally and physically."

"With your marriage so deeply troubled, what's keeping you from telling him now?"

Omunique wiped her eyes with the back of her hand. "I'm still lacking courage. I haven't found enough of it yet. Ken is so compassionate with me, but I know he feels terribly betrayed by me lying to him. We seem to have a knack for betraying one another. He didn't tell me about Dad hiring security way back then. And I can't seem to tell him about my fear of having a baby. It's easy for me to sit here and tell you, but I can't express myself to the man I love more than anything else."

"You're comparing apples and oranges here. Ken didn't exactly betray you. He was sworn to secrecy by your father . . . and it all had to do with trying to save your life."

"And you don't think that's what I'm doing here? Trying to save my life? I could die just like my mother did when she gave birth to me. But I am seeing a psychiatrist. Ken and Uncle Ralph thought that I should seek professional help for the flashbacks I'm having again."

"I see what you mean, sweetie. I'm sorry. Fear is such a big emotion for such a small world. It has a way of keeping you off balance. As intelligent beings, we know the things we should do and how to do them, but we let fear rule over our common sense and better judgment. Fear-driven is a lot of what we already are or what we eventually become when things in our lives become unmanageable. As for the flashbacks, when did they start up again?"

"During my Olympic performance." Omunique closed her eyes for a brief moment. "There's more. In the strictest of confidence, I'm going to tell you something unbelievable. But it could get Uncle Ralph fired if it ever got out. I know what I'm about to say will go no further than here. I can tell you so many personal things because I trust you implicitly. Officer Marcus Taylor is still alive. He didn't die from his gunshot wounds. He's in a police-run sanitarium."

Marion looked liked she'd been knocked down by a bulldozer. As though she felt Omunique's devastation down to the core of her being, Marion began to tremble, her head shaking from side to side in disbelief. "This . . . can't . . . be. How'd you . . . find . . . out about this?"

"I saw him in the hospital, twice. From what we've been told, he was having problems with his kidneys. The sanitarium wasn't equipped to meet his medical needs, so he was admitted into the hospital here. What I don't understand about that is why they chose to put him in a facility in the same area where Ken and I live. We still don't have the answer to that one, other than someone telling Uncle Ralph that it was the closest medical facility to the sanitarium."

"I'm too stunned to be of any help on that because I don't understand any of this. We see this kind of stuff on television all the time, but to learn that this madness really does exist in our society is mind-boggling." Marion covered Omunique's hand with her own. "You have every right to be fearful of this situation. Your love is indeed special. You two can survive these troublesome times. I believe this is just a temporary condition. I have faith that it will heal. But please don't let any more fear get in between you and Ken."

Sadness blanketed Omunique's eyes. "It seems I've already done that. Fear has induced so much insanity into my life—into our lives. I keep thinking that if I just tell him the truth everything will be okay. Then the insanity of fear itself returns and I find that I've let too much water settle under the bridge, enough to drown my entire life in it. Then fear takes over again. It's a vicious cycle that I can't seem to break. But that's enough about me. Tell me what direction your plans are now moving in."

"Vegas! Las Vegas, honey. Don't want to deal with flowers, gowns, invitations, and none of the rest of that complicated stuff. Frank and I decided on a quiet ceremony with just the four of us, with you and Ken standing up for us. We've decided on a European honeymoon cruise. We're leaving from Los Angeles so we'll come home first. Only a couple of months away."

"That's so wonderful. I'm excited for both of you. Hopefully Ken and I will have worked out our differences by then. If not, we're still going to help make your day perfect."

Suddenly, Marion's jaw dropped, causing Omunique to look in the direction her eyes had gone. An audible gasp burst from Omunique's lips.

Marion's hand instantly shot out to cover Omunique's with the intent to soothe. "Don't go jumping to conclusions, Nique. Ken is by no means stupid enough to be out in a public place so close to his job if he's involved with another woman."

"Then who the hell is she?"

Marion shrugged her shoulders. "Perhaps a colleague? I don't know and neither do you. That's my point. Shall we go over there and find out?"

Omunique looked horrified. "Not a chance in hell. Let's get out of here before he spots us. Though I doubt that he will. He seems pretty intent on her. I don't want him to think I'm spying on him or tailing him like some sort of fatal attraction. It was dumb of me to come to this café knowing that he eats here quite a bit."

Discreetly, quietly, the two women left the café, grateful that they'd had enough cash between them to take care of the check from the table. They were able to depart the restaurant with Ken none the wiser.

Well away from the restaurant Omunique dissolved into tears. "Please tell me he's not having a love affair with that woman. I couldn't bear it even if I am responsible for chasing him away. I pray that I haven't sent him fleeing into the arms of another woman."

Marion hugged Omunique, offering warm solace. "Don't take yourself there. He's not that kind of man . . . and you know that better than anyone else. Ask him when he gets home. Don't let this build into a major drama like in those silly soap operas. I'm sure he would've brought the woman over to the table to meet you had he spotted us."

"You're probably right, of course. But I'd still like to know for sure."

"Ask him, Nique."

"Maybe I will. Did you valet park?"

"No, I'm in the garage. Did you?"

Omunique shook her head. "I'm in the parking garage

next to the one you're in, the one in Ken's office building. I have a special parking sticker on my Jeep. Let's move on. We can talk on the way."

Sensing that Omunique could use a comforting hug, Marion brought her to her in a very gentle manner. "Your husband *is not* having an affair with that woman. I'm willing to stake my reputation on it."

"Thanks. I needed to hear that. But what do I do to bring us back closer to each other? We've grown so distant. In fact, he's moved out. I didn't have the heart to mention it earlier. I guess I was reluctant to bare all. So you see, I'm still guilty of keeping secrets."

Marion hid her shock very well. Things were worse than Omunique had led her to believe, which was already bad enough. Still, she didn't think Ken capable of running around on his wife. "All the things you did before you started harboring secrets. Ken is not one to push himself on you, especially if he's not sure what you might want or need from him. Nique, since it seems you may have been the one to erect the impenetrable wall between you, you may be the one to have to tear it down. Further deterioration of your relationship will happen if you don't do something quick and in a hurry."

Omunique nodded. "I see your point. I've got to take time to figure this all out. I'll be out of town next weekend. That should give me some time alone to come up with a positive course of action. I want my husband back in every way. I miss our closeness, the late-night conversations, not to mention the wonderful love life we once shared." She looked pensive. "Sex. I guess that's what this is all about."

Marion shook her head. "Not just sex, Nique. Your fears of having a baby are the heart of this matter. You should start tearing that wall down by coming clean with your man regarding your fears. He can't understand if he doesn't know what it is that he needs to understand. Talk to your husband, Nique. I know he'll want to talk back after he hears you out. Think about what happened after your ankle injury, how you sent him from your life because you couldn't tell him that you feared for his. I'm sure he's thinking about those difficult times, too."

"I'll give it my very best. We'll see what happens. Thank you for the great advice. Keep us high on your prayer list. We need all the prayers we can get."

Marion waved as she walked away. After only taking a couple of steps, she turned back. "Nique," she shouted, walking back to her friend. "One more thing. If I were you, I'd talk to Ken long before I left town. Time has a way of running out on us."

Sixteen

On shaky legs Omunique approached Wyman's hospital bed. For several seconds she watched his sleeping face. Fear crept in to shake her calm. A heart attack, no less. *Thank you, God, for sparing his precious life. Please don't take him away from me. I need him desperately, have always needed him. I don't ever want him to go away,* she cried in silence. *Mom and Grandma's spirits have already returned to you. Can you be content a bit longer with just having them? I know they might want Daddy there, too, but I still need him. He's all the immediate family I have left down here.*

Wyman's eyes fluttered open, causing Omunique to quell her pleading supplications. "Hi, beautiful one." He sounded so weak to her. His hand shook as he reached up and ran his thumb across her cheekbone. "Are those tear stains, my dear?"

Bending her head down until their eyes met, she kissed him softly on the mouth. "Just a little intermittent rain, but we're managing to get through a dry spell right now. You gave us quite a scare, big guy. But how are you feeling now, Daddy?"

"Remarkably well for someone who just had a heart attack. Seeing you is also very healing. But where's my son, Nique? Where's Ken?"

Omunique quivered inside. She couldn't tell Wyman they

were separated, not when he was so ill. That would kill him for sure. He dearly loved his son-in-law, thought of him more as a son than any in-law.

"He's right here."

Ken's sultry baritone voice reached her from behind, causing Omunique to turn with a start. Her heart immediately cried out to him, distressing over the tired, drawn look on his face.

"Ken," she said on a sigh. She walked over to the door to meet him. When he didn't open his arms to her, she flinched inwardly.

Briefly, he touched her hand as he moved over to Wyman's bedside. "Dad, it's good to see you awake and looking so alert. I can't tell you how happy that makes me. You sure put the fear of fire in us." Bending over the bed, he kissed his father-in-law on the forehead. Tears welled in both Omunique and Wyman's eyes.

"I'm going to be okay, son. But I got worried when I didn't see you with Nique."

"I was parking the car." He was sure that Omunique hadn't told Wyman that he'd walked out on her and that she didn't know where he was. It wasn't up to him to reveal what he clearly knew that Omunique hadn't. She was the only one who'd kept them being apart a secret, because he'd already confided in Max. When Omunique failed to come home all evening, he'd gone to bed out in the guesthouse without telling her that he was there. He didn't call around for her because he didn't want to arouse suspicion. He didn't get any sleep either, wondering where she was and what she might be doing.

At peace with seeing his two kids together, Wyman allowed sleep to capture him. Slowly, his eyes closed. Peace swept him upward toward an awaiting cloud.

Ken pulled the blanket up over Wyman before turning to his wife. "Have you talked with the doctor yet? What's the word?" She motioned toward the doorway. He followed after her as she left the room. Out in the waiting area they took seats facing one another.

Omunique pressed her lips together and then pushed them out. "Dr. Stanford says he's stable, but there's still cause for concern since he still doesn't understand why Dad had the heart attack in the first place. There were no symptoms leading up to this. But it's possible that Dad just hasn't spoken of any discomfort. At any rate, I'm the last one he would tell."

"Quite the contrary. I think you're the only person he'd tell."

Hurting for her, Ken took a moment to closely study his wife. Like him, she looked tired and her tearstained face broke his heart. What was standing between them? What made her turn away from their love, away from sharing with him? How could he have left her at one of the most vulnerable times in her life? She wouldn't be able to withstand any more of anything. Her fragile nerves couldn't hold any more weight than she carried now. He was surprised that Wyman's condition hadn't sent her over the edge. He hoped she didn't take the blame for that happening. Knowing that she needed him, he vowed to be there for her.

Unable to help himself, he touched her cheek with the inside of his forefinger. A longing for more intimacy with her shot straight through him, but he quelled that desire, too. "Have you eaten, Nique?"

She shook her head in the negative. "Not hungry. I'm afraid I haven't had an appetite since this happened. I didn't sleep all night either. I was afraid to."

He looked upset. "All night? When did this happen, Nique?"

"Around five-thirty last evening. At least, that's when they called me."

"Why didn't you call me on my cell phone? What if he had . . ."

"Don't," she screamed, cutting him off "Don't say that, please."

No force in the world was strong enough to keep his arms from closing around the woman he loved, adored . . . needed more than anything else in this world. In the circle of his strength she broke down and cried, weeping for everything that had gone wrong over the past few weeks. Her sobs came hard, distressful.

"Go ahead and release it, Princess. Let it go."

Princess! Gosh, when was the last time he'd called her that? It had been so long that she couldn't even remember. But it was all her fault. She'd once again hurt him deeply. Terms of endearment weren't normally used on someone who'd caused your heart to bleed . . .

He held her slightly away from him. "I'm going to take you home so you can get some rest. I'll come back here and sit with Dad once I get you settled down."

"You stay at home with your wife. I'll be here with Wyman." Ken and Omunique both looked up at the sound of Mamie's voice.

"Aunt Mamie," they said simultaneously, both getting to their feet.

Mamie hugged Omunique to her. "You look worn down, sweetie. We can't have you getting sick, too." Turning to Ken, Mamie also hugged the young man she'd come to love without conditions. "You don't look too hot, either. What's going on with you two? You both need to go home and get in bed. I'm taking over here for now."

Ken looked questioningly at his wife.

Not wanting her godmother to get even a hint that something was out of whack with them, Omunique leaned into Ken. "If nothing else, I need a bath and a change of clothes. Aunt Mamie, will you promise to call us immediately if something out of the ordinary comes up? I'll also keep my cell on till I get home."

"That goes without saying, child. Scoot, both of you . . .

and get some sleep, Nique. You'll have more bags under those pretty eyes than a grocery store if you don't rest them." For the first time in a long while, Omunique and Ken laughed, though, crying would've come easier.

Mamie didn't like seeing her goddaughter looking so distressful. She embraced Omunique again. "Baby girl, prayer works. I know. His *will* be done."

Stifling a sob, Omunique nodded. "I won't be gone too long. And, Aunt Mamie, I know what you're telling me. I haven't stopped praying for Dad . . . and I won't."

It was awkward for both of them. Ken hadn't slept in the main house for a short while now, but it felt like years. As if he were seeing the house for the first time, he looked around him to reacquaint himself with the layout. It felt strange. All the love that once abounded within these four walls had come to an abrupt end. Omunique stopped talking. He stopped waiting for her to do so. Impatience had replaced understanding. Anxiety now overshadowed serenity. The air that had once breathed the freshness of love had become stale with tension.

"I'm going up to lie down. I'll understand if you don't want to stay here. I'm sorry Aunt Mamie forced your hand, but she had no way of knowing. However, since my car is still at the hospital, I'll need you to come back for me." She looked uncertain about her comment. "Perhaps I could just call a cab. I imagine you're real busy these days."

Placing his hand over her mouth, he directed her toward the winding staircase. Without uttering a single word, they mounted the stairs. Upstairs, he led her into the master bedroom, the intimate space which they were supposed to have shared forever. Used to picking out her nightclothes, he did just that. Instead of the wispy silks and satins he loved to see her in, he chose something a little more modest, a pair of silk pajamas.

The silence between them continued as he withdrew from the bedroom and went into the bathroom where he turned on the shower. Remembering all the times they showered together made his heart ache. That was when they'd had it all. Now all they seemed to have was something he couldn't even explain if his life depended on it.

He turned around when he felt her behind him. Standing there with her lower lip trembling, her vulnerability reached out to him like a beacon in the black of night. What was she offering, if anything? Whatever it was, he couldn't accept it. He wanted her to come to him because of her love for him, not out of her obvious grief "Your water is ready." He turned and walked away. He had left her alone with nothing to look forward to. She had hoped; her hopes had been dashed. With tears in her eyes, she entered the shower and closed the door.

Surprising her, he was there with her bathrobe held open when she slipped out of the shower fifteen minutes later. Without touching her, though he longed to, he wrapped the robe around her, not daring to glance at her nudity. Missing what would normally come next, the application of lotion and massaging of one another's bodies, he sucked back his bitter disappointment of that which wouldn't come. But he couldn't stop himself from thinking of those times, times when they were the only two people who existed after the hustle and bustle of their occupations, a time when they relished getting home, appreciated being together.

Ken wasn't the only one missing all they'd once shared. It became apparent when, mindlessly, she handed him the body lotion while lowering the robe from her shoulders. Time seemed to stand still as she explored his eyes, searching for something that said this wasn't just a temporary thing, a single night of fulfilling their physical needs, with no possibility of a tomorrow on the horizon.

Misunderstanding him not taking any action, she pulled the robe around her and set the lotion back down on the nightstand. Exhausted, she slipped between the sheets, hoping to drown her misery in sleep. Omunique was asleep only minutes after her head hit the pillow.

His breath caught at the beauty of his Princess, remembering when he'd reigned as her hero, her Prince Charming, so to speak. Why had he been dethroned, abdicated, stripped of his princely crown, and then banished from their castle of dreams?

Positioning himself comfortably on the ivory love seat, he stared out at the beautiful grounds below. Recalling all the rose bushes he'd planted, just so she could have roses every day, he smiled. He'd planted roses in every color he could find. The look on Omunique's face had been priceless when he'd showed her what he'd done and told her his reasons for doing it. Just the thought of that event made him restless. No longer caring about the consequences, he removed his shirt and pants and left them on the sofa.

Sliding in alongside Omunique, he settled himself behind her, encircling her waist with his arm. Sure that he hadn't awakened her, he closed his eyes. But she had been awakened, unable to believe he was actually right next to her.

Fearful of him leaving should he discover that she wasn't asleep, she closed her eyes, welcoming the peace and comfort that lying next to him always brought to her. This scene reminded her of the first night she'd spend at his condo. She'd feigned sleep that night, too. For the first time in weeks she fell into a serene place, the same place she'd come to miss maniacally.

With very few words spoken between them, Omunique and Ken arrived back at the hospital. The silence was a strain on them, but neither one knew how to break it. The music on the radio kept the ride from being unbearable. Awake and sitting up when they came in the room, Wyman beamed when he saw them.

"There's my two wonderful children now." He sounded much stronger than he had earlier. Mamie smiled at the man who loved his daughter deeply. Mamie knew that if anyone could bring him to life it was Omunique. He loved her with everything in him, just as he'd loved his wife.

"Oh, Daddy, I'm glad to see you looking so much better." She turned to Mamie. "He *does* answer prayers."

"Yes, my dear, in His own sweet time."

Omunique hugged Wyman. "Promise never to scare me like that again? I can't imagine life without you."

Ken remembered when they couldn't imagine life without one another. How quickly things seemed to have changed. Still, he had no desire to live his life without his wife.

"I'm not going anywhere, Nique. I've got to be around to spoil that first grandchild you two are trying to present me with. You *are* still trying, aren't you?"

Omunique went pale. Wyman and Mamie didn't seem to notice, but Ken took special note of the terrified, ghastly expression on her face. Suddenly, something clicked inside his head as well as deep down in his heart. Maybe her strange behavior had nothing to do with not wanting his children. Perhaps she was still afraid of it even though she had convinced him that she wasn't. Was she still afraid of dying the same way her mother had? Giving birth.

Helplessly, Omunique looked to Ken for him to intercede on their behalf.

"That's not something you need to worry about, Dad. Getting you well is the first order of the day. You can't enjoy those grandkids if you're not feeling up to it."

Omunique's expression was one of gratitude. He'd rescued her yet again.

"Everything's going to be fine. The doctor said I'll be home in no time at all."

"Yes," Mamie chimed in, "but you can't be home alone. Nique, perhaps you can talk some sense into your Dad's head. Maybe he'll come to stay with you and Ken since he refused to come and stay with me. Says he doesn't want to be a burden on anyone."

Omunique once again looked to Ken. Her expression showed her discomfort. If Wyman came home to live with them, he'd soon find out they weren't living in the same space. But their home was the only place she wanted him to be.

Sensing that Omunique needed him to bail her out again Ken wasted no time in taking charge of the situation. "We'll have the downstairs guest room spot-cleaned immediately. Can't have you climbing our complicated staircase. We'd be delighted to have you stay with us. Won't we, Omunique?"

Though shaking on the inside, Omunique managed a bright smile. "We wouldn't have it any other way." *Thank you, Ken,* she whispered inwardly. The thought that he'd be coming home, even if it was only temporarily, calmed her instantly. Maybe she'd be able to tell him the truth of why she'd become so withdrawn from him. It certainly hadn't been because she didn't love him. She loved him as much as life itself.

Ken allowed a discreet amount of time to pass before he excused himself and Omunique, telling Wyman and Mamie that he thirsted for something cold to drink. Again, he led her out to the visitor's waiting area.

He sat down across from her. "I hope I did what you wanted."

She nodded. "Thank you, Ken. Dad can't know we're separated. He's still very fragile. I hope I haven't made things too inconvenient for you. I can only imagine what this must be costing you."

"We do what we have to do when family trouble brews. But we're going to have to tell him and Aunt Mamie at some point. As you know, I've already told Max, but he's been sworn to secrecy. Are you going to be okay with me moving back into the house and us sharing the bedroom again? If we do otherwise, he'll catch on quickly. I don't like deception in any form, but these circumstances seem to somewhat justify it." He looked into her eyes. "I can pull it off, but can you?"

"Pulling it off? Is that what you'll be doing?"

Quickly, to keep his frustration in check, he disconnected emotionally from her. "We're not getting into a war of words right now. We've made our bed . . . and now we're going to sleep in it, together. What I'll be doing is of no consequence at this point, not when this has to be done. Let's go back to Dad before he starts to worry."

"I hope you didn't have this heart attack just to get those two back together again, Wyman Philyaw. Knowing how much you love them, I wouldn't put it past you."

"I didn't, Mamie, but I would've considered it had I thought it might work. They're going to be so busy trying to put up a front for me when I go there to stay. I hope it makes them see how much they still mean to each other. I don't know what's happened between them, but I'll be damned if I'm going to sit by and let them throw their love away. I know those two are still madly in love. They may think they'll be acting for me, but I'll know better."

"You're right, as usual, Wyman. We're just going to have to find out what's pulled them apart so suddenly. I certainly thought Nique would've talked to me by now . . ."

"Talked to you about what?" Omunique interjected from the doorway. She'd only heard the last sentence, enough to make her curious.

Mamie grew slightly flushed. "About Marion and Frank's wedding."

Wyman snickered inwardly at Mamie's white lie, glad that she was a fast thinker.

"Aunt Mamie, I'm sorry. I forgot to tell you that they're

just going to go to Vegas. They're frustrated with this whole idea of having a big wedding."

"Frank and Marion are pretty private people, not to mention very frugal," Ken added. "Marion is especially not one for a lot of hoopla. Frank usually wants whatever Marion desires. That's the kind of love they share." *The same kind of love we once shared,* his eyes seemed to say to his wife.

Ken saw a look of empathy on both Wyman and Mamie's faces, making him wonder if they somehow knew the truth about their relationship. For sure, he wouldn't be that surprised. Wyman and Mamie hadn't made it to their golden years by being gullible.

Dressed in a short, white-cotton gown-and-robe set trimmed in blue satin, Omunique paced the bedroom floor. It was after midnight and Ken hadn't shown up. Icy fingers of fear raced up and down her spine. Maybe she'd misunderstood him. She thought he'd said it would be better for him to move back into the main house now, so they'd get used to it by the time Wyman came there to stay. She tensed up when the phone rang, sure that it was her husband.

"What's happened?"

"I've just been sitting here thinking. Lost track of time. I just realized that I'm the one who made all the decisions about moving back into the house with you. You didn't offer any input . . . and that's why I'm calling. What do you want, Omunique?"

I want you. I want us, the way we were, she cried inside. "I don't know what I want anymore, but I know I don't want Dad upset right now. He has a lot of recovery time ahead of him. I went along with your suggestions because I'd look to you to make the decision. But I didn't want you to feel pressured. We've always been the best of friends, Ken. Is it okay for me to need my best friend? Because I do."

A lump arose in his throat. She needed him, but not as

her husband and lover. She needed her best friend. Well, he needed his, too, and she was that to him . . . and so much more. "Be up to the house in twenty." He started to tell her to count to a hundred, but it wasn't like that anymore. For whatever reason, they were just friends. Just like when she'd damaged her ankle. Though it seemed like eons ago, he'd never forgotten the pain of that lengthy separation.

Omunique cradled the phone and sat down on the bed. Would he sleep with her tonight or take one of the guestrooms? Neither of them had spoken of him having been in bed with her earlier. She wasn't sure he even realized that she knew he'd been there. When she'd awakened several hours later, he was already up and dressed. For people who talked so much, it was hard to believe that they now seemed to have nothing to say.

The doorbell rang and she leaped from the bed. He hadn't used his key because he no longer had any. He'd left them on the dining room table, even his two sets of spares, a couple of days after he moved into the guesthouse.

Omunique had reached the top of the staircase when she turned around and went back into the bedroom. Inside the cavernous walk-in closet, she took a caftan from the hanger and put it on. After what had happened earlier, she didn't want Ken to think she was trying to seduce him. The caftan completely covered her body. Nervous as she could be, she descended the stairs. After taking a few deep breaths, she opened the door.

With two suitcases in hand, he followed her into the foyer. When he started upstairs, she felt hopeful, since they had a guestroom on the first floor. But when he turned left instead of right, the direction of the master bedroom, her hopes were once again dashed. There were four bedrooms in that direction, two of which were used for offices.

Unable to move, she just stood there looking up at him as he made his way down the long hallway. She wiped her eyes with the sleeve of her caftan. *Was this how it is going to be for the next several weeks? How unbearable.*

He came to the top of the stairs. "Nique, how about making your best friend a cup of coffee?"

She looked up and smiled. "Do you want me to bring it up to you?"

"I'll just come down and drink it in the kitchen. Be there in a jiffy."

With optimism growing, Omunique went into the kitchen to fulfill her estranged husband's simple request. *Maybe it wasn't going to be so unbearable, after all.*

Once the coffee began to brew, Omunique cut a huge slice of pound cake, one of Ken's favorites. Aunt Mamie had brought it by the day before Wyman had suddenly taken ill. Knowing that he'd probably want coffee, she'd stopped by the grocery store and picked up the half-and-half, which had been a regularly stocked item in their refrigerator up until he'd left. Deep in thought, she poured the cold liquid into a small cream server. He didn't use sugar, but he did use natural honey when he drank tea, though that was a rarity.

Suddenly noticing her in the electric-blue caftan brought his forward motion to an abrupt halt; it was the same caftan she'd worn the first night they'd ever kissed. That had also occurred in the kitchen. Watching her from the doorway, he wondered what messages she was sending. All of them had been mixed over the past month or so. Her sending messages wasn't going to be enough for him this time. She was going to have to tell him, in no uncertain terms, what she wanted from him, needed for him to do, and what she expected of him.

As usual, she felt his presence. "Hi. Ready for that nightly fix? I just happen to have your favorite." She showed him the thick wedge of moist cake.

He was ready for his nightly fix, all right. Though just as sweet, it certainly wasn't cake. He grinned. "Aunt Mamie, right?"

She narrowed her eyes at him. "The way you said that makes it sound like you knew I hadn't baked it."

He raised an eyebrow. "Why would I sound like that? Perhaps because you've never baked a cake from scratch in your life. For sure, not since we've been married, although you've gotten pretty good with the boxed mixes."

"That you know of!" She set the coffee down in front of him.

"What do you mean by that?"

After pouring a glass of milk for herself, Omunique joined him at the table. She gave him a warm smile. "It was your birthday." He looked nonplussed. "I tried to bake a cake from scratch for you for your birthday. I was sure I'd followed all the directions Aunt Mamie had given me, but I forgot one important ingredient, the cake flour . . ." He couldn't stop himself from howling. "Oh, mister, I'm not going to tell you the rest of the story after that boisterous display. It wasn't funny then, and it's not funny now." Feigning displeasure, she poked her lip out. It was all she could do to keep from laughing herself.

Still laughing inwardly, he took a sip of coffee. "Please don't deprive me of the rest of what has to be a very interesting story. I promise not to laugh again."

"Cross your heart." He did as she requested. "Well," she continued, "when you try to bake eggs, sugar, vanilla, salt, and baking soda without flour, you come up with one chunky mess. When you burn it, to boot, you've got one horrible, smelly mess. Now go ahead and laugh because I can't hold mine back any more than you can." They both burst into a gale of laughter at the same time. Ken was so glad that he didn't have anything in his mouth since he probably would've choked to death.

The laughter seemed to somehow ease the awkwardness and dispel the tension. A few more minutes of laughter and a bit of unimportant chitchat allowed them to relax in one another's company. It suddenly seemed like old times again, but it wasn't. A chasm existed between them and each was counting on the other to figure out how to get to the other side, so they'd once again be on the same side, back on the same identical mountain cliff. Without a single word of protest, Omunique accepted Ken's help in putting the kitchen back in order, a duty they'd almost always shared.

Ken walked Omunique to the door of the master suite. Much to her displeasure, he pecked her on the cheek and headed down the hallway to the guest room. Since he'd left her and their bed on his own, she thought he should come back the same way. On the other hand, he thought that she'd forced the separation and that she should be the one to end it. They'd just have to wait to see what would happen once Wyman was well enough to go back into his own home.

Inside her bedroom, Omunique sat down on the bed and let go of her tears. Although he was only down the hall, much closer than the guest house, he may as well have been in Russia for all the good it did her. How would she sleep knowing he was only a few yards away, yet unobtainable, unreachable, and completely out of her grasp. Physically, he was there. Emotionally, she just didn't know anymore.

At two in the morning Omunique awakened from a horrible nightmare. Wyman had left her all alone to join his beloved Patrice. So shaken was she, that she called the hospital to make sure he was okay. Everything was fine with Wyman she learned from the on-duty nurse.

Unable to sleep because the nightmare haunted her still, she slipped out of bed and went down the hall toward the guest room. Outside the door, she paused and then knocked. When there was no response, she quietly slipped into the room. Much to her horror, Ken wasn't in the bed. Thinking he'd changed his mind about being there, she slid into the bed, right in the spot where he'd obviously lain earlier. The indentations of his body were still there.

Minutes later, when Ken came out of the adjoining bathroom, he slid back into bed and came into direct contact with his wife's warm, tender body. As he'd done on so many nights, for a long time now, he simply curled up behind her. Trying hard, desperately hard, to block out the aching of his desire, he closed his eyes and prayed for sleep. Unlike earlier, having now lost a major battle to fatigue, Omunique was dead to the world and all that was in it.

At predawn, Omunique turned over and felt her husband's warm breath on her face. Smiling with content, she turned back over. *How did I let us fall from heaven right into the blackened pits of hell? Why doesn't he understand my fears?*

Because you haven't shared them with him, the voice of reason responded. Turning back to him, she lodged her body full against his.

It was only natural for him to bring her into his embrace. He did so without the slightest pause. Pressing his trembling lips into her forehead, as he'd done many times before, he entwined his legs with hers. "Are you here because you're frightened, Nique?"

"Do I need a reason to be here? You *are* my husband, unless there's been a change that I don't know about. Has there been?"

Sorry he'd started any type of dialogue with her, his arms tightened around her. "In that case, let's just lie here in peace, with no analyzing. There's been no change. I *am* your husband."

She wanted to do more than just lie there, but his tone of voice made her refrain from starting something he might not be interested in finishing. Being next to him like this was a big step in closing the gap between them. And she was willing to settle for that, for right now. With him holding her within his strength, they fell back to sleep.

* * *

Reaching over to the nightstand, he picked up the book he'd been reading before going to sleep. The same little purple book they'd read together every single morning. Along with a passage or two from the Bible, reading *Acts of Faith* was a part of their morning ritual. Both believed that prayer followed by the reading of other inspirational materials was a great way to start their day: on the right foot, the good foot.

He opened it to the right day and began reading. Interestingly enough, the daily reading was about relationships. Omunique listened intently as his sultry voice fed her desire for spiritual inspiration. After joining hands, spoken aloud, individual prayers followed the morning reading.

Ken had always been able to inspire her. But having him away from her wasn't the least bit inspiring and she now realized just how much she missed his awe-inspiring presence.

With Omunique's culinary skills much improved from when they'd initially met, she fixed breakfast while Ken showered. Scrambled eggs and turkey-ham was one of the many things he'd taught her to cook. Unburned toast was also an accomplishment, especially since she liked to make it under the broiler portion of the oven. She couldn't leave out all the wonderful goodies she'd fixed for their first dinner party. Cooking steaks and hamburgers under the broiler, or on the George Foreman grill, and even on the outdoor gas grill, without burning them, was a major triumph for her.

Ken's cell phone rang just as he buckled his belt. He picked it up and sat down on the side of the bed. "Good morning."

"It's Uncle Ralph. Are you where you can you talk privately? It's urgent. That's why I called your cell."

Tension grabbed ahold of Ken's stomach. "Omunique's

downstairs. What has you all worked up? I hear the strain in your voice. Uncle Ralph, what's going on?"

"It's Taylor. I received word that he's committed suicide. We're not sure how long he's been dead. I thought you should know. And word of this will never come out since the department had officially buried him. In reality, they'd only laid him to rest on paper. He was one sick puppy. I guess now the department knows just how sick he was."

Ken sucked in a deep breath and blew it out. "Well, I can't say that I'm sorry, even though I know I shouldn't feel that way." Ken grew silent. Then he moaned. "Oh, God, my wife is going to think she's responsible for this, too, especially since it hasn't been that long since she confronted him with what he'd done to her. This is only going to add to the mountain of problems that she's already faced with. She somehow thinks she's responsible for what Taylor did to her, thinks she may somehow have led him on unknowingly."

"How is she justifying her thinking?"

"Nique often makes reference to her dancing with him at the after-party of the Christmas skating event last year. That's why it was so important for her to see him. She needed to make sure that it wasn't something she did, unwittingly or not, to cause him to think she had a personal interest in him. That made no sense to me because she'd never laid eyes on him before he stopped her for the traffic violation. How did he die? Are we sure he's really dead this time?"

Ken hated sounding so callous and unconcerned. How was he supposed to feel about someone that tried to kill the woman he loved? How should he react? He didn't know how to feel any differently.

"I don't know the facts of how he killed himself. But there's talk that he saved up his medication and took it all at once. From what I'm told, he was on some heavy-hitting drugs. I guess he had to be. Personally, I haven't seen the body. But I will see it for myself. I'm going to make sure that it's really over this time. I've got a connection in the morgue, but I have to act on this right away. It's my guess that the department will cremate or bury him as soon as possible."

"Thanks. I may have an even bigger dilemma than the department. I don't want to tell Omunique this with Wyman coming home in a few days, but I know I have to. This is going to burst the bubble on her homecoming for her dad, but it can't be helped. I'll tell her about this over breakfast this morning."

"That's what I would do if she were my wife. Talk at you later, son. Keep your spirits up. Don't forget to fall on your knees and pray. It works. Give Omunique our love. She's going to need you more now than ever. Nique is having a real time of it. This whole thing with Taylor being alive and all has hit her hard. I've seen some things in her that worry me. It seems like she's having a delayed reaction to the nightmares Taylor created for her."

"I think you're right. She had to stay focused to get through the Olympics. Now that she's completed her mission, she's beginning to fall apart. Uncle Ralph, it *has* hit her very hard. I've always been there for my wife. Nothing has changed."

He hadn't mentioned the difficulties in their marriage because he was still hoping that he wouldn't have to. There was no point in getting the family all upset. Max was the only one who had any knowledge that something was wrong in their marriage. His dad would never utter a word about anything that his son had told him in confidence.

Ken began to get a flicker of understanding as to why Omunique so desperately needed to see Taylor, to understand why he tried to bring harm to her. Out of the same desperation as hers, he wanted to be there for his wife, to learn what made her do the things she was doing, to understand what was really behind the recent rash of deceit, behind her every struggle.

Ken gently steered Omunique away from the stove and over to the table where they both sat down. While taking her hand, he kissed her forehead. "Listen to what I have to say before you make any comments." Her eyes widened as she nodded. "I just got word from Uncle Ralph that Taylor committed suicide." She fell apart in his arms, screaming at the top of her lungs.

When it took him the better part of a half hour to get her calmed down, his concern for her mental health had grown tenfold. If Omunique wasn't having a nervous breakdown before, she was now much closer to it than at any other time.

Swiping at the falling tears with trembling hands, she looked up at him "I need . . . to see the . . . remains. I have to know . . . that he's really dead. I've got to . . . know for sure this time. Please . . . talk to . . . Uncle Ralph and see if he . . . can arrange it."

He brought her head to his chest. "Uncle Ralph is going to make sure of that."

She pulled away. "No, I need to see this for myself."

Stern was his gaze when it met with hers. "If anyone other than Ralph is going to confirm his death, *I'll* be the one to do it. I'm not allowing you to put yourself through another trauma, not if I can help it. If seeing his remains is doable, you can consider it done." Her out-of-control trembling made his heart quiver with anxiety. Tenderly, he brought her back into his warm embrace. "We have to hold it together. Wyman is coming home in a few days."

The stable ground that his wife had once stood on was slowly caving in. But he didn't know how to keep her from being buried alive beneath all the debris . . .

* * *

Omunique watched from the doorway as Ken wheeled Wyman up the walkway. Mamie followed close behind the wheelchair. Omunique was so glad that he was out of the hospital, although he wasn't quite out of the woods. His heart attack had put the fear of God in all those who loved him.

She moved aside to let Ken push the chair into the house. "Welcome home, Daddy!" She bent over and kissed the top of his head. "Right off to bed with you—doctor's orders. We have the downstairs guest room all ready for you. Ken even brought over your own bedding from home. We're going to do everything we can to make your stay a comfortable one."

Wyman smiled at the little group rallied around him. "Thank you both for having me here with you. You're all a comfort to me. Now we'd better put this old boy to bed. Just the trip from the hospital to here has me worn out. Nique, if you don't mind, I'd like some juice."

Mamie patted her goddaughter's hand. "I'll get it while you two settle him in. Do you want anything else, Wyman?"

He grinned. "Oh, a glass of sherry would be nice even if my doctor wouldn't agree." Everyone laughed.

Omunique turned to Ken. "Go ahead and take him down to the room. I'll be right behind you. I need to speak with Aunt Mamie for a moment."

Omunique went through the kitchen and straight into the laundry room to retrieve the bunch of colorful WELCOME HOME helium balloons she'd stored there.

Mamie got excited when she saw the bouquet of balloons. "You know how your father loves happy surprises. I bet you can't wait to see his face. I can't wait either."

Giggling, Omunique kissed Mamie's cheek. "Let's not wait any longer!" Looping her arm through Mamie's, the two women proceeded toward the guest room.

Seventeen

Wringing her hands together in anguish, Omunique paced the floor. "I have a wonderful man who loves me so much. So much so, that he went to a hospital morgue to confirm for me that Taylor is actually deceased. I've been lying to him, outright, but I can't seem to stop it. I didn't ever want him to be disappointed in me, but he is. I've continued to pop birth control pills while letting him think that we're trying to start a family. What could be any crueler than that? I lie to him, I lie to me, and then I hate myself for doing so." Feeling worn out from the maniacal pacing, also from thoughts of Taylor's suicide, Omunique dropped down onto the leather sofa.

"But I'm afraid if he knows the truth about my fears that he'll hate me even more than I detest myself. What strong, virile man wants a woman that fears the most natural thing in the world for a woman to do: give birth? I feel so inadequate in that area. My husband will probably leave me when he finds out the truth."

"Maybe you're selling your husband more than just a little short. He doesn't seem like that type of man to me. I've only just met him, but I observed him very carefully. His love and concern for you were in his every movement, in every soothing stroke to your arms, in every word he breathed. Since we've had a few sessions now, I'm ready to speak on several assessments. The first and most glaring problem I see is that you're not ready to become the type of woman he needs."

Omunique raised an eyebrow at that. "I'm sorry, but could you explain that?"

"Omunique, for all that you've accomplished, for all the strengths you've shown, even in how much independence you display, you're very immature. I noticed that right off. You're still stuck. Stuck back in your childhood, stuck in the traumas of your youth, stuck in the death of your mother. You haven't gotten past her death, even though you never knew her. You blame yourself for it. *Had she not been pregnant with you, she would've lived."*

Omunique looked astonished.

"How many times have you told yourself that very thing over the years? You're telling yourself and your husband the same kinds of lies that you said the kids told you about your mother leaving your father. You lie to yourself every day about not being woman enough to face birth. It has nothing to do with being woman enough. It has everything to do with your fear of ending up just like your mother. I say that you're not ready to become the type of woman that your husband needs because you can't be a woman, period, until you get unstuck."

Omunique sighed heavily. "Unstuck? That's an interesting term. Would you explain to me exactly what you mean? I know that I'm immature, but stuck?"

"Maturation follows growth. You have yet to grow into the great woman that I expect you will one day become. First, we have to slay the dragons and exorcise the demons of the past. I want to help you come to understand that the burdens you carry are not yours to bear. Therefore, I want to teach you how to unload the weight of guilt, to remove the heavy anchor of the *past* from around your ankles. It's causing you to drown. I want you to unpack the suitcase filled with uncertainty, fear, and pain. These things are weighing you and your marriage down."

"I'm beginning to see what you're saying. But what I really don't understand is why I initiated with my husband the idea of starting a family right away when it's one of my biggest fears? That seems to be my worst mistake yet."

"In that moment of honeymoon euphoria you believed you could do it, that you wanted nothing more than to have your husband's baby. Those are very natural feelings for a woman in love. Also, because that's what you thought he expected of you. You were trying to keep him happy so that he wouldn't leave you. Deep down inside you probably knew it was a lie when you told him that you wanted to start a family right away. You got all tangled up in the lie after he expressed the joy he felt over it. Then you got caught up in the fear of disappointing your husband when you realized you couldn't do it. Telling him the truth at that point was a big risk; a risk you aren't mature enough to take."

Omunique frowned, amazed at what was said. "You hit the nail right on the head with that one. One fear seems to trigger another; another is triggered off that. It seems to go on and on."

"Like you said earlier, you couldn't stop yourself from lying. You can't be honest with your husband because you haven't learned how to be honest with yourself. You're not the typical liar. Someone who just lies to be lying, knows they're lying from the moment they open their mouth, and who lies with the intention of inflicting pain. You lie to protect others from the truth of your pain. To protect yourself from becoming a victim of that same truth you lie to yourself, which has made you a victim of the pain instead of saving others from experiencing it. Your husband is not the real casualty here, you are. No, he hasn't left you because you fear having a child. It's the lies."

"That's certainly a nasty plateful to digest, too much to swallow it all down at once."

"The real bombshell is this. Not only do you blame yourself for your mother's death, you blame yourself for what your attacker did. You somehow think you provoked him into it."

"I've thought of that. All I really know is that I have worked my natural-born behind off to become a world-class figure skater. Since I was a small child, I trained, and trained, and trained some more. There were times when I trained until my feet swelled to near bursting. I was driven by my desire to win it all. More than that, I was driven by the need to show something to the cruel people that I grew up with. People that laughed at me because I couldn't participate in certain sports activities at school and those that made fun of my corrective shoes and told vicious jokes about them. I had a need to show them that I could accomplish my goals despite my physical handicap. To spite their desire to make me feel less than human, I became a champion."

"An unhappy champion."

Yes, very much unhappy. I'd set out to prove something to a bunch of people who could care less about me, people who taunted me daily, people who made me cry. That was absolutely the wrong reason." Omunique fought back her tears. Remembering still hurt her deeply.

"Are you saying that you only worked hard at becoming a champion to prove something to all the people who'd hurt you?"

"In a way, yes. Because that was my intention, when I got a little older. Initially I wanted to skate because my mother loved skating. Then, later, I thought if I could realize her dream for her, it would take away the guilt I felt for her death. As I grew even older and began to understand my father's grief, I wanted to be a champion for both my mother and father, to make it up to them for ripping them and their lives apart . . . for taking my mother's life. My reasons for why I was skating kept changing with age. Then the minority children became my focus, which is probably my one true reason for wanting to be the real champion of champions. This is something that Omunique Philyaw-Maxwell actually wants even though it's not for herself. It's her strong desire to make a difference in the lives of minority children, in the lives of her people. I believe that by the time all my other reasons for skating get sorted out, that my own ice arena and the children are the only desires that will remain. Outside of the love I feel for my husband, my family, the ice is the only other thing I've ever truly loved. I live for the day when the ice arena is actually complete. But even that won't be a joyous occasion without my marriage."

"In that case, it's up to you to put your marriage back together. I get the feeling that your husband is waiting for you to make the first move. While taking time off from skating, take time off from being your own worst enemy. Give Omunique the emotional break she deserves."

After finding out from Thomasina that Ken was having lunch in the nearby café he frequented, Omunique took off running. Eager to try and talk to her husband about the things she'd discussed with Dr. Jackson, eager to talk to him about her pain and fears, anxious to get everything out in the open, she sprinted out of the elevator. Once she got outside, she ran all the way down the street despite the tenderness rising up in her feet.

Slowing down to a snail's pace, she peered into the cafe window as she passed by. Her heart practically stopped. There her husband sat across from the same woman she and Marion had seen him with before in the same café. Backing away from the restaurant entrance, she turned and ran back the way she'd come. Her courage had also left in that very second.

Halfway down the block she stopped dead in her tracks. In this instance she couldn't help remembering Marion reminding her of how she'd jumped to all the wrong conclusions back when she'd seen her and Ken together in the Sports Connection. But she didn't know all the people in his life back then, back when they'd first started dating. For sure, she now knew just about everyone connected to him on a personal level, even most casual acquaintances. This strange woman wasn't fitting into any one of those categories.

Chewing on her lower lip, she contemplated her next move. What was the mature way to handle this? How would a *real* woman deal with this delicate situation? Should she go inside or walk away? "That's still *my* husband, separated or not."

Inside the restaurant she headed straight for the table where Ken was seated. With a slight nod of her head, she acknowledged the other woman. Ken was definitely surprised to see his wife, but he quickly slid over when it appeared that she intended to sit down next to him.

As if nothing unusual was happening, Omunique smiled at him. "I went by your office. Thomasina told me you were here. Hope you don't mind my barging in like this, but I really need to talk with you. It's important." Omunique recalled the look of triumph on Thomasina's face when she told her where Ken was, but only after showing much reluctance to do so.

Thomasina had known that Ken was here with a woman. And she wanted her to see Ken with this woman. Omunique strongly suspected the secretary of having a crush on her husband; suspected her of intercepting her phone messages to him. She wouldn't be a bit surprised if Thomasina knew Ken's message-center passcode.

Shrugging his shoulders, Ken looked to the other woman. "Sorry about this. I know your time is valuable. Can we get back to our business at a later time?"

Omunique thought the black woman was very attractive, but she couldn't guess at her age. For sure, she was older and certainly more mature than her own twenty-two years.

While her shiny sable-brown hair framed her slender face, she had large, yet unexpressive, brown eyes.

Without any expression to show how she felt about the untimely interruption, the woman nodded. "Sure, Ken. We can resume this another time. Anytime. Give me a call."

Without further comment, the woman gathered up her things and left. When she stood, Omunique saw that she had a gorgeous figure, one that would easily bring about envy. Politely, she nodded to both Ken and Omunique as she left the table.

Omunique got up and slid into the side of the booth the woman had vacated so she could face her husband. "Why didn't you introduce me to your friend?" Her calling him by his first name had further heightened Omunique's curiosity. That somehow made it more personal.

"I didn't think about it. You appeared out of the blue demanding to talk with me. I was more concerned with what you had to say than I was on introductions. You said it was important that you talk with me. At any rate, I didn't see much point in introductions, anyway."

She rolled her eyes. "That's so damn weak. Are you seeing her on a personal level?"

"No, I'm not."

"Then why were you here with her?"

"Having lunch."

Her eyes narrowed at his smart-aleck remark. "Business or personal?"

"Business."

"So, how is she affiliated with the goings on at Maxwell Corporation?"

"She's not."

"Then it couldn't have been business. What are you hiding?"

"Hiding! You've got to be kidding. You're the one who's been playing hide-and-seek for the past few weeks. You seem to skip out every evening at the same hour. You do more disappearing acts than David Copperfield. I'm not hiding anything. Are you?" It nearly drove him mad, when around six-thirty practically every evening Omunique announced that she had to go out. As things stood, he didn't feel that he had the right to ask her where she was off to.

Looking him straight in the eye, she sucked in a deep breath. "I can see that you're not going to come clean with me, but I think I deserve to know if you're moving on with your life, if you've given up on our marriage?"

Not wanting to add to her burdens, his expression softened at the anguish in her eyes. "It was strictly business— and that's that. As for moving on, I'm moving at the pace *you've* set. I don't want to give up on our marriage, but it doesn't seem like we have one anymore. I'm one place and you're another even though we're back to sharing the house, back in the same bed. What's going to happen with us when Wyman is well enough to move back to his home?"

She looked weary. "I know this is ridiculously complicated. I've been nothing less than an evil bitch to you. I wouldn't blame you if you were seeing someone else. In fact, you have my blessing if you desire to do so." She got up and walked out. *Great job, Nique, real mature.*

It took everything in him not to chase after her. He'd been too understanding where she was concerned, too giving. That had to change if he was going to save his marriage. Taking a hard line with Omunique was a must. Otherwise she was going to think she could walk over him in any situation. He'd never before seen Omunique as a woman he needed to play hardball with. In his heart, he still didn't think he had to. But he wasn't going to have her thinking of him as weak. Loving her was one thing, but being a fool for her wasn't about to happen.

It didn't go unnoticed by her that he didn't follow her outside. She stopped and looked back at the café entrance.

No Ken anywhere in sight. Though she had no intention of catching city transportation, she sat down on the bus stop bench. She put her face in her hands and cried.

A few moments later, when she felt someone sit down beside her she looked up. It wasn't her husband, much to her dismay. Embarrassed by her tears, she got up and walked back to Ken's office building.

Instead of going to the parking garage where she'd parked the Jeep, she took the elevator up to the suite of offices. She'd even slowed her pace on the way hoping he'd catch up to her. Without even looking in Thomasina's direction, she went straight into Ken's office and closed the door behind her.

Seated behind his desk, she wrote him a note apologizing for her bad behavior and asking if they could really try to talk things through later, at home, over a nice dinner. She propped the note on the phone where he was sure to see it. It was time for her to confess everything. Time for them to talk, time to have a real heart-to-heart. In fact, it was way past the time.

As she left the office, Thomasina called out to her.

Omunique turned to face her. "What is it?"

"Can I do something for you? You seem so unhappy."

Omunique glared at her. "I think you've done quite enough. Don't you?"

Thomasina attempted a puzzled expression but had a difficult time at it. She knew exactly what Omunique was talking about. What she didn't know is that Omunique had come to know the truth about her feelings for Ken a long time ago. "I don't know what you mean by that."

"I somehow doubt that." Omunique wrinkled her nose. "At any rate, you're a smart girl, or so you think. I'm sure you'll figure it out. But I'm not going to waste my breath on you, or explain something to you that I'm sure you already know about."

Thomasina jumped out of her seat, but not before she

saw Ken coming through the door. "I don't know what's wrong with you. Don't know why you've suddenly turned so rude to me. But I'm not responsible for your unhappiness. I feel really bad that you think that. You can't keep attacking me this way. I'm just an employee here. No matter what you say, I don't know why he was having lunch with another woman. I'm not hired here to keep up with his personal comings and goings."

Omunique's eyes narrowed to dangerous slits. She hadn't said one thing to Thomasina about the other woman. Then she began to laugh. Seeing Ken made her realize what his secretary was doing. Laughing harder now, Omunique clapped her hands. "Command performance! You're really a cunning piece of work. If I wasn't such a respectable lady, I'd call you a *bitch* and tear your hair out, strand by strand . . ."

"Omunique," Ken shouted to get his wife's attention. "What is really going on with you? I've never seen you like this before."

"It's not me you should be talking to or asking questions of. You'd better talk to your secretary about it. I'm leaving here right now because I *will* hurt her."

Ken was positively stunned at Omunique's strange behavior. Hearing the slamming of the front door is what brought him out of his state of near shock. Before he could go after Omunique and demand an explanation, he heard loud sobbing. He turned around and saw Thomasina standing behind her desk crying her heart out.

"What was going on in here?" He came and stood in front of Thomasina, which only made her cry harder. Hating to see her so distressed, he put his arm around her shoulder for comfort. Before he could blink an eye, she had thrown her arms around his neck and her head against his chest. Then her face came to meet his. With her mouth only inches from his, he genuinely feared what might come next. Her lips were now only a breath away from his.

Untangling her arms from around his neck, he stepped a safe distance back from her. "Can you tell me what's going on with you and my wife? Why is she talking about doing you bodily harm? Did you do something to anger her?"

Thomasina sniffled, wiping her eyes with the handkerchief he'd handed to her. "I don't know what's going on with her. Your wife has been acting a little crazy with me for a while now. I didn't come to you with what I've observed in her because I didn't think it my place. Earlier, she came storming in here looking for you. When she sensed that I was reluctant to tell her where you were, she started going off on me. That's when I told her where you were. Looking angry as hell, she stomped out of here. I tried to get you on your cell phone but it was turned off." He knew that was an outright lie. The only time he turned his cell off was at home.

Frowning, Ken sat on the corner of the reception desk. "Why would you be reluctant in telling her where I was? She's my wife." He decided to let the phone remark go unchallenged.

"I didn't know the nature of your business with the woman with whom you went to lunch. Since she's visited you here a few times, staying close to an hour each time, I didn't know what to think. You've never said who she was."

"First off, it's none of your business who comes into my office or how long they stay, unless I make it so."

She gulped hard. "I see."

He saw way more than what Thomasina realized. He didn't like any of it. "There's no reason in this world that my wife can't be told of my whereabouts. As my wife, she has a *right* to know where I am every moment of the day. Do you understand what I am saying to you?"

Max had heard the loud voices before he'd come through

the door. He'd also seen his daughter-in-law in the parking garage—and he didn't like seeing her in tears.

Immediately making his presence known, Max came forward. "Son, I'd like to see you in my office." It looked like Ken might put him off. "Now." Though he'd spoken softly it had come across to Ken in no uncertain terms.

The minute the two men went behind closed doors, Thomasina went into Ken's office to see what destruction Omunique may have visited on his desk. A woman scorned was known to turn to vandalism to get her point across.

Inside the office, she saw a note propped upon his telephone. Hurriedly, she read it. A smug smile played around her mouth. *"Bitch,* indeed! Let me show you how much of a *bitch* I can really be, Mrs. soon-to-be-divorced Maxwell."

"Have a seat, son."

Ken didn't obey. He was too riled up to sit down. "What is it, Dad? This isn't a good time for me. I'm not in the best mood. In fact, I'm nothing less than pissed off."

Max's white brows knitted together with concern. "I saw my daughter-in-law, your wife, in the parking garage. She fell into my arms and dissolved into tears. I can't tell you how much that distresses me. I couldn't make sense of most of what she was saying, but I did pick up something about you having lunch with another woman. It sounded to me like she thinks you might be involved with this woman in a romantic way. Are you emotionally or even physically involved with someone else?"

Ken looked angry enough to bite a bullet in two. "Dad, I'm just going to pretend that you didn't ask me that. What's going on between Omunique and me has nothing to do with anyone else but us. Are you feeling me, Dad?"

"Deeply, son. Sorry I felt I had to ask. Seeing Omunique all broken up is what compelled me toward this conversation. Is there anything I can do to help?"

Ken ran trembling fingers through his hair. "My wife and me are the only ones who can change our messy state of affairs. I'm not going to let this go on any longer. The silence of what we need to say, or what we're not saying, is savagely masticating our marriage to pieces. We started putting up a front before Wyman came there and we continued on with it afterward. All of it's coming to an immediate halt. We're going to live as man and wife because we love one another, because we want it to work. Or we're going to get apart. Permanently."

Max looked abashed. "I have to tell you something, son. You're not going to be too happy with me."

"Why's that, Dad?"

"Wyman already knows that you two are fronting. I told him that you were having problems. I felt compelled to tell him. He only agreed to come and stay at your place until he recovered because he hoped it would make you two see the grave errors you were making. He had an idea that you two would move back in together to protect him from the truth, which he hoped would make you learn the truth of how your love still runs so deep for each other."

"I'm not shocked by this. I felt all along that he knew, but I am surprised that he learned it from you. You've never before betrayed my trust." Ken walked over and embraced his father. "In this case, I understand it. I know that both of you love your children. I believe I probably would've done the same given the nature of the circumstances. There's a part of me that wishes you hadn't done so, but only because I now feel compelled to explain myself to Wyman. He deserves to know the truth about all the troubles that are visiting our marriage."

"No, you don't have to explain yourself to him. He understands what's going on more than you think. He also understands his daughter better than anyone—because he's had her around twenty years longer than you have. Now this is my advice to you. Go to your wife as soon as possible. Like you've already said, it's decision time. I will pray that you two make the right one. Good luck, son."

Ken embraced his father again. "Sorry if I've shut you out of this critical time in my life. I felt that I needed to handle this one on my own. It's high time I show my wife the ironclad strength of the man she's married to. It's been her way for too long now. Now it's going to be my way. Even if it means that I'll be the one hitting the highway. Talk to you later, Dad."

"Don't be too hard on her, son. She's still very young. You need to find out as much as you can about what's happening with her before you go getting too high-handed. She's very delicate right now. Lots of drama has occurred in her life—and in such a short amount of time since your wedding day. Try to cut her as much slack as possible."

"Thanks for the advice. I'll keep in mind everything you've said."

Time inched off the clock as Ken sat quietly at his desk thinking about all the things that he needed to say to his wife. Now that Wyman had been strong enough to move into the guest house, privacy wouldn't be an issue. They could talk and talk and talk, until everything was cleared up, one way or the other.

Deep in thought, he didn't hear Thomasina come into the office. He only looked up when he saw a figure standing in front of his desk. Hoping she wasn't there in hopes of getting his personal attention, he steeled himself just in case she had sinful thoughts on her mind.

"I'm leaving for the evening. Do you need anything before I go?"

He shook his head. "It's all under control. Have a nice evening, Thom."

"Ken, are you sure there isn't anything I can do for you? Anything at all? I can only imagine the things you've been deprived of. And I do sense that you're suffering from deep, deep deprivation."

He knew he shouldn't go there, but it was too tempting not to. "What is it that you think I'm being deprived of?" If she was going where he thought she was, this would be the last time she'd ever go there again.

She felt giddy inside. He had at last taken the bait. It was up to her to reel him in. She put her foot up on the chair in front of his desk, pretending to tie her shoe. As she did so, she made sure her skirt raised up high enough for him to get a great glimpse of her thigh. His male imagination would do the rest.

"I'm not exactly sure. Maybe you should tell me. As your secretary, I'm here to meet your office needs on a daily basis. As I woman, I'm prepared to meet the needs of what I suspect you're being deprived of."

"Care to expound?"

"Your physical needs. Anyway you like it, I can deliver. If it's just release you're after, without involving yourself in the actual act, I can deliver that, too."

His thoughts went straight to Bill. He couldn't help wondering that if this was the same sort of conversation Monica might've presented to him. Only difference was that he wasn't Bill, Thomasina wasn't Monica, nor were they in the oval office. Furthermore, he would never cheat on his wife—under any circumstances.

Watching the heaving of her voluminous breasts, which told him she'd excited herself with her very own provocative come on, he folded his hands and placed them on his desk. "Thomasina, you came in here to tell me you were leaving for the evening. Perhaps it's time for you to do that. I hope you have a great one. Drive carefully." Knowing that he'd provoked her, in order to see just how far she was willing to go, he decided he'd seriously set her straight at a later time. Getting her out of his office was foremost.

Feeling totally degraded, the look on Thomasina's face

was one of great unhappiness. Not only had she immorally exploited herself in a demoralizing way, she'd caused utter embarrassment to herself. Wishing she had wings that would take her straight through the ceiling, she hurried from his office.

It was practically eleven o'clock when a crumpled piece of paper on the floor under his desk caught Ken's eye. Curious about the balled up wad of paper, since he always used the paper shredder for security purposes, he picked it up. He scowled when he recognized Omunique's beautiful handwriting.

He looked at the wall clock. "Damn blast it! She had asked him to meet her at home for a quiet dinner, for them to have a heart-to heart talk afterward. He didn't even want to think about what she must've felt when he didn't show up.

Taking a piece of paper from his desk, he scribbled a note on it in haste.

Dear Ms. Bridges—
  In deciding to practice sabotage, one should never leave behind the evidence. You're fired!

After signing his name, he put the note in a place where he knew she couldn't miss it. If he'd known the irony of deciding to prop it up on her telephone, he would've laughed.

Eighteen

A crystal bowl of freshly cut, slightly opened rosebuds floated atop the water in a beautiful hand-cut crystal bowl. In colors of orange, yellow, and red, the wonderful perfumed scents were nearly intoxicating. Tea-light candles bathed the room with a glowing softness while their subtle fragrances mingled with the scents from the roses.

Seated across from one another around the Asian-style table inside the Oriental room, Ken and Omunique sat on the floor on large black, red, and gold pillows designed with Asian symbols. While looking into each other's eyes, they tried to make sense of their broken lives.

She was cute tonight rather than beautiful. She wore childlike thermal pajamas with padded feet and yellow ducks waddling all over the blue ribbed fabric. On each side of her head her unbraided pigtails were wrapped in yellow ribbons. Night creme was generously dotted on her nose, both cheeks, forehead, and in the center of her chin.

His fingers itched to smooth out the creamy lotion and deeply massage it into her skin, something she did just before getting into bed. Her face only looked like this after she'd given herself an herbal facial mask. Ken had already apologized for not showing up for the special dinner she'd prepared for them. She had gone to great lengths to prepare his favorites.

Ken smiled gently. "Do you want to go first?"

More nervous about this heart-to-heart than she'd imagined, Omunique licked her lips. "I think I'll do much better bouncing off you. You're always able to articulate so well."

Grateful for the compliment, he smiled, giving her a resigned look. "I'm going to start out by saying I love you, that I've never stopped, not for a second. We've had some difficult times this year. I'm not a man who normally gives way to fear, but I have to admit that I've been really scared, fearful of what's been happening to us. I'm not really sure of how it all got started, but I know I want it to stop. I miss you, miss you and me together. Baby, please, we have to find a way to rekindle the fire beneath the ice. I'm freezing and I need the heat of our passion to warm me up. Otherwise, I'm going to die from the bitter winter cold that has invaded our lives."

Deeply touched by his comments, she brushed a single tear from the corner of her eye. She wanted so badly to go into his arms but they needed to talk, needed to rediscover the fire beneath the ice, the type of fire that had always existed between them. "I love you, too, more than I did when we first married, even more than I did just yesterday, more than this morning."

He looked relieved because he was no longer sure how she felt about him. "Thank you for that, Nique. Knowing that you still love me will make this somewhat easier to get through."

Doubtless about her love for him, she smiled warmly. "You said you didn't know how it got started, but I do. It all started during a trip to the emergency room when my feet were badly swollen—"

To clarify her statement, he cut her off with a halting hand gesture. "Are you talking about the day you first saw Marcus Taylor?"

"That, too, but what I'm really talking about is a woman dying before my very eyes. A woman dying while giving birth."

Both eyebrows raised in response to her staggering remarks. Reaching across the table, he took her hand. "I'm sorry, Nique. I had no idea. But I have to say that I'm feeling angry with you and your revelation. Instant anger."

She now looked puzzled. "Angry?"

"In fact, I'm damn angry." He didn't want to do this, hadn't intended to get angry.

"Anger isn't something I would've expected from you, particularly on this matter."

"Why not? You've only shut me out of what sounds like the most horrendous day of your life and our married life. Have you forgotten that I'm the man you call your hero? I'm the one you're supposed to come to with everything. I'm the one you should trust when you can't trust anyone else. I own the *only* shoulders that you should've needed that day."

"Even if my womanhood felt threatened? Even when I thought you'd look at me differently than before. Perhaps as only half a woman, one afraid of dying giving birth? The most natural thing in the world for most women to desire to go through."

"Especially then." He also wanted to take her in his arms, comfort her, but they'd never get this conversation out in the open if he did so. This talk between them was imperative. "You've done a damn good job of shutting me out of every important aspect of your life. What makes you think I'd look at you any differently when I can only see you through the eyes of my love?" He quickly held up his hand. "Don't answer that. It could hurt too much."

Feeling ashamed, she momentarily lowered her eyes to the intricate inlaid design of the glass tabletop. "You don't know how it was for me."

"You're right. I didn't know because you didn't tell me. I couldn't possibly have known. I imagined a lot of things, crazy, insane things. I felt that you got me all worked up about having a baby only to dash away the hopes of ever having a family. I felt as if you'd set me up. Big time, I might add. Nique, you're the one who decided you wanted children right away."

"I'm sorry, Ken . . ."

"You should be. I found myself totally fed up with you and your B.S. excuses when it came to making love. More than just my pride was hurt, Nique. My soul was damaged. So much so that I thought it was irreparable. How do you explain that away?"

She saw that his mood was near volatile, but his obvious pain ran even deeper. "It can't be explained away. But if you'll listen, I'll tell you what happened that horrific day."

"I *am* listening. I'm eager to know, eager to understand."

She closed her eyes briefly. When she opened them, the pain there was bloody, raw, raging, darn near touchable. "From the cubicle where I lay waiting for the doctor, I heard bloodcurdling screams. Through the opening of the curtain between treatment rooms, I saw a snowy-white blanket and white sheets turn crimson right before my eyes. I actually watched a woman hemorrhaging to death, a pregnant woman." She had to stop and take a few deep breaths. Agony was etched all over her face. Ken didn't look any less agonized. He could clearly see on her face the high cost she'd paid that day . . . and was obviously still paying.

"Just like my mother, she died, leaving behind a tiny infant. Only this baby didn't have a loving daddy to turn to. In fact, the mother had already decided to give him up for adoption, I learned later. But I think that if she'd lived, she would've changed her mind. I heard her screaming to the staff that she was bleeding to death and that her baby was drowning in it. That mother wanted to save her baby at all costs, even knowing the detriment to her own life. When the cubicle grew deathly quiet, after the mother had died and the baby was taken away, right after the staff had cleared the treatment room, I got up from the bed. Then I went over to see the woman who was now covered from head to toe with a clean sheet. As I turned the sheet back, that's when one of the nurses came in and told me that I couldn't be there. I was there because this woman had been left all alone, because she didn't have a Wyman Philyaw waiting out there demented with fear over the fate of his wife and unborn child."

The need to hold and comfort her was much stronger now, but he sensed that she wouldn't be able to get through the rest of it if he distracted her for even a fraction of a second.

"By the time I left the ER I was numb with trepidation. Then came the double shock to my system. I thought I saw Marcus Taylor. On crippled, sore feet, I followed that wheelchair only to have it disappear without a trace. The second time I thought I saw him, the elevator doors slammed in my face denying me the opportunity to see if I was right. After all I'd witnessed with the mother and baby, I left that hospital a broken woman, with my courage depleted beyond revival, with my hopes dashed beyond belief. I wanted to tell you the moment you came home from work that day, but my fears were stronger than any emotion I'd ever known."

"Even our love, Omunique?"

"Even our love. Every time I closed my eyes, I saw *myself* lying on that table. It was *me* who was bleeding to death. It was you that I saw crying, mourning over my dead body, telling me that you'd never love again. You were the one left with a child to raise on your own. As you held our tiny baby, his cries sounded like that of someone grieving. He was, because he somehow knew he'd lost his mommy, the woman he'd lived inside of for nine months. Imagine how sad that was. I relived that scene so many times I lost count. You don't know how many nights I lay awake, afraid to close my eyes, afraid of what I knew I'd see again. I didn't mean to shut you out, but I saw myself doing it, day in and day out, over and over again."

The time was wrong for what he was about to do, the questions he was about to ask, but there would never be a right time for something like this. He stood up and paced the floor. "Then why didn't you stop yourself, Nique?" His voice was high from the restraint of his emotions.

"I don't know, but I did try. If you can't forgive me for what I've done to you, to us, where do we go from here?"

"God, Nique, I have no clue where to go from here. Forgiving you is the easiest part of it. Trusting you with the care of my heart again will be the hardest for me. This isn't the first time I've been shut out and it's not the first time I've had my heart broken in this relationship."

Hearing his pain, she stood up, too. "I'm truly sorry for that, but I know my saying that is not enough. Could you please hold me, Ken."

He backed away from her as she came to him. "Not this time, Nique. It's more complicated than that. I'm terrified of you, terrified of what you're capable of doing to me. I won't let you destroy me with your blatant disregard for my feelings. There's so much more that has to be said, needs to be said, none of it pleasant." Far too many meltdowns had already occurred. Briefly, he turned away. Determined to finish what he needed to say, he then faced her.

More emotional than he'd ever been with her, he threw his hands up in the air. "Do you think you're the only woman who fears pregnancy? Are you going to go through the rest of your life thinking you might die in childbirth? Dying from childbirth is not hereditary. Because your mother died that way doesn't mean you will die that way, too."

"For your information, my fears are very, very real. How can you discount them like this?"

He sighed with discontent. "Death can occur in a number of ways, Nique. You fly all over the world without fear of dying in a plane crash. You drive way too fast at times without fear of dying in a car accident. You skate like the wind but you don't fear falling and breaking your skull open, which you could easily die from. You swim practically every day, but you don't fear dying from drowning. When it's your time, you're gone. It won't matter where you are or what you're doing."

"That's not the same thing, Ken, and you know it."

He felt his anger beginning to subside. "Death is no respecter of persons or circumstances, Nique. If you die in childbirth, then that's your fate. If you die by drowning or in a car accident, that's your fate, and so on and so forth. If you die and our child lives, I'll do the same as Wyman did. I'll raise our child to the best of my ability. Do you ever think about what Wyman would've been left with had you died along with your mom? If you haven't, you need to. I'm sure he was glad to have a part of Patrice with him rather than to have been left with nothing of her at all."

She began to cry and he was glad that his anger had subsided substantially. He didn't want to intentionally inflict pain upon her, but he had to make her see what she was doing to herself, to him . . . and to their marriage. He was glad that he hadn't said these things to her when he'd been so angry.

Kneeling down before her, he laid his head in her lap. Taking her hands, he placed them atop his head. "I don't mean to hurt you. I don't like feelings of anger, but I feel that I have to get through to you somehow. I think I'm more flustered than angry right now."

"You're just being plain cruel," she sobbed. "You're not taking my feelings or my fears into consideration when you go on the attack like that."

He lifted his head and looked into her eyes. "That's not true, but you're not the only one who has feelings. I'm going to ask you something because I feel it's necessary. Do you ever think about the fact that I lost my mother, too, after having her up until my teenage years?"

Shocked by his question, she placed her hand over her heart to ease the ache.

"No malice intended, Nique, but you never knew your mother, never felt her arms around you, never had her kiss you goodnight, and for her to be the first person to kiss you in the morning. My mother and I were so close that it defies description. It wasn't easy for me to go on living after her death, but I had to. Especially after my father seemed to die right along with her."

"I *do* think about you and your mom, a lot. You had some of the same fears I had, Ken. So why are you refusing to understand mine? They're aren't too different from your own."

"True, I feared loving someone so deeply lest I should lose them the same way my father lost the love of his life, the same way Wyman lost your mother. Then I met you. I couldn't, wouldn't let fear cause me to back away from the one person I wanted more than anything in this world. So I addressed my fears. Then I conquered them. You know why?"

"Yes, but only because you've told me."

"I told you it was because you were worth it. To have your love was worth fighting fire-breathing dragons for. Damn it, Nique, I want to be your hero. I want you as my princess and I desire to be your prince, for always. Mushy stuff, huh? Damn right, mushy, but oh, so true."

She looked and felt injured, but she didn't blame him. She threaded her fingers in his hair. "I deserve everything you've said. You've never deserved my callous treatment of your heart, Ken. I didn't realize until now, until after hearing your pain, how much I've hurt you. I convinced myself that I was fearless, just like I did when Marcus was terrorizing me. Will I ever conquer my fears? Ken, don't you think I would conquer them if I knew how?"

"No, I don't. I think you're comfortable with your fears. If you hold on to them, then you won't be held accountable for an outcome that might be less than desirable. We've had some really rough times together, and I do try to understand what you're feeling. But, sweetheart, I'm not God. It's time for you to fall on your knees and give your fears to Him. Divine intervention is the only thing that's going to bring you peace, peace that you deserve to have. Give up the ghosts of the past, Nique. Get your foot out of the grave before you find the other one in there, too. The next thing you know, you'll be buried alive. Start living again. We have it all right here in each other. We had a fairy-tale wedding, but we're now living in the real world. I'd like to see you rejoin that world, Nique."

"What should I have done when I felt so overwhelmed with fear?"

"All you had to do was come to me and tell me your fears. How could you think that I'd leave you because you had fears, legitimate ones? I would've helped you through it. We would've worked it all out. I had my doubts about you being ready to have a baby, but you were the one pushing it. I wanted you to really experience life before you had to change your lifestyle altogether. I'm not selfish. I went along with it because I thought that's what you wanted."

She looked stunned. "Are you saying that you didn't want a child?"

"I'm not saying that. Sweetheart, I want you to be the mother of my children. But I wasn't in any real hurry. We could've waited five or six years. That would've been okay. Our marriage would've had time to grow solid by then. A lot of couples have kids in the first year or two, and then they divorce before the child's a year old."

"So you weren't exactly forthright with me, either. Why didn't you put it on the table when the subject of us getting pregnant first came up?"

"For one, I wanted to please you. I now know that that wasn't the right approach. Then I truly got caught up in the wonderful idea of being a father. We both have been negligent in being forthcoming. Now that it's all out in the open what do we do with this forthrightness?"

She smiled at him for the first time in a long while. He was glad to see it and he smiled back. "Take it issue by issue, Ken. Discuss it and work on finding the solutions, diligently."

"That sounds like a mature suggestion. I'm willing to work on myself, our issues, and on our marriage. Do you think we're up to such a big challenge?"

"I'm sure of it. One of my biggest problems is that I really didn't have anyone to teach me how to become a woman. My grandmother died before I hit puberty. Aunt Mamie was there for me, but we never got into talking about the things young women need to know. She may have been waiting for me to ask her about those delicate types of things since she wasn't my real mother. I realize now that Dad couldn't teach me to be a woman simply because he isn't one. Women's issues are what I had to deal with on my wedding day. I wanted my mother in the worst way. I needed her to sit me down and tell me all about loving relationships between males and females. I'm not using that as an excuse.

"That was just the way it was. It hurts me to know that you perceive me in a much different manner than I thought you did. I guess I had blinders on. I thought I could never do anything wrong in your eyes. I was naive and I'm still very immature for twenty-two." No truer statement had come from her mouth, but he'd be loath to say it.

"Can you tell me where you went all those times you just up and disappeared?" *The times when no one knew where you were.*

She lowered her lashes for a brief moment. "I'll do one better than that. I'll show you. Will you agree to let me take you somewhere tomorrow? I need you to see something." *Something truly wonderful.* "It's one of my biggest secrets yet."

He nodded. "Sure, why not, if it's going to help clear up the mystery disappearances." He couldn't help thinking that he was allowing her to set him up again. As many times as she'd kept secrets from him, he should at least know by now to be wary.

Omunique took a chance of putting her arms around him. She loved him. She'd hurt him, but not intentionally. She was just a scaredy-cat, afraid that he'd leave her because she wouldn't have his baby. She now realized that she'd sabotaged their happiness, though, unwittingly. If he was going to eventually leave her, anyway, then why not help him out the door.

When his arms suddenly tightened around her, she started crying. "Don't, sweetheart. We're going to get through this somehow. I don't know how, but we will. Don't cry any more. Let's go to bed. Come on."

She didn't know if he intended to sleep in the same bed with her, but now was not the time to question his intentions. With his arm around her waist, they climbed the stairs. At the door of their bedroom, he kissed her on the forehead. "Get some sleep, Princess. We'll resume our talk in the morning. We still have a lot to settle between us. We're not out of the woods yet."

She watched as he went down the hall and into the guest room. It was apparent that he wasn't going to join her in their bed. That broke off another little piece of her heart. Two people who loved each other so much had suffered greatly. He had suffered more at her hands than she had at his. How had she come to hurt him so terribly? Not once, but on many occasions.

Without knocking on the door, Ken came into their bedroom. She turned with a start. Not uttering a word, he came and stood in front of her. He then walked to the dresser and took out a nightgown for her. One of his favorites, a leopard-printed chemise with a crisscross back.

Walking back to his wife, he stopped right in front of

her and began unbuttoning her blouse. That rendered her speechless. Next he removed the thin T-shirt she wore. He looked into her eyes as he unbuttoned her jeans and pulled down the zipper. Lifting her off her feet, he carried her over to the bed. Before setting her down, he stood her on her feet and slid the jeans down over her hips. After seating her on the edge of the bed, he pulled the jeans the rest of the way down and over her shoes: the next item targeted for removal.

Once he'd stripped her bare, he put the chemise over her head and smoothed it down over her body. Pulling the comforter and top sheet back, he helped her into bed. It took him much less time to rid himself of his clothes. In a matter of seconds he was in bed next to his wife.

He reached for her. "Come here, sweetheart. Let me hold you until you fall asleep. We both have had an emotionally exhausting day."

Without hesitation, Omunique curled up in the safety of Ken's arms. Still speechless, she kissed him on the mouth to convey her deep appreciation of him being there with her. After kissing her back, he turned off the light and brought her in closer to his body.

As much as he wanted to make love to her, to lose himself deep inside of her sweet, engulfing heat, the timing was, once again, all wrong. They first had to find a way to regain their trust for one another before they could come together in any sort of passionate coupling. With promises of more secrets to come from her, he vowed to take things slowly and to proceed in their relationship with extreme caution.

Both of their lives were at stake.

All through breakfast Ken had been in a pensive mood. He'd barely said three words since he'd told Omunique good morning. Thinking about this secret had kept him wide-awake most of the night, while, throughout the night, she'd slept in his arms like a newborn baby.

She refilled his coffee cup and set it down on the table. "All talked out from last night?"

He looked up at her as she sat back down. "I've got a feeling the talking has just begun. Therefore, I need to know what your secret is before I go running out of here with you—and possibly run into something that will catch me totally unprepared."

"Don't you trust me?"

He raised an eyebrow. "I'm not going there. That's just another street that dead-ends every time we go down it. I've made up my mind not to walk unaware into this secret. If you want me to go with you, wherever it is you're going, I need to know the facts."

"You said you would go last night. Are you going back on your word?"

He gave her a matter-of-fact look. "Nique, I've already said what my intentions are. It's all up to you now."

She bit down on her lower lip. "You wanted to know where I go every evening. I want you to see where I've been spending my time. I've been volunteering time in the newborn nursery so that I can be near the baby whose mother I saw die. He's been sick, but he's coming along nicely, yet not quite well enough to be placed in foster care."

The look on Ken's face was more than just a bit surprised. "I don't understand. Why do you want to be near this child so much?"

"I want us to consider adopting him."

Unable to believe what he'd just heard, he put his face in the palm of his hands. When he took them down, tears were visible in his eyes. "This isn't a secret, Omunique Philyaw-Maxwell. This is a damn nuclear explosion! What *is* really going on with you?"

"There's more, Ken."

As though he couldn't imagine there could be anymore than that, he looked totally bewildered. "Why didn't I already know that, huh? I think what I better do is just sit back in this chair and let you talk. I'm not going to ask a single question, but I do want it straight—all of it. No holding back this time. There's been too much of that already."

"He's the cutest little African-American baby boy that I secretly call Scott Brian, and he has Down syndrome."

He lowered the boom onto the table with a closed fist. "Woman, are you losing your mind? Let me rephrase that. You *have* already lost your mind!" He stared at her like a perfect stranger was sitting at his kitchen table . . . and that he had no clue as to why she was there.

"I thought you weren't going to ask a single question?"

His emotions frazzled to the very endings, he threw up his hands in a show of concession. "Sorry. Forge ahead." He wasn't sure his heart could take another nuclear blowout like the last one, but he was sure there was more hazardous fallout yet to come. At the very least, the look on Omunique's face told him there was much more than this to come.

"Ken, he's so adorable and he's alone in the world. When I pick him up, he curls up next to me as if I were his mother. He's spunky as hell, too. They keep a hat on him in the nursery, but he rubs the back of his head against the blankets until he gets it off. I don't think he likes anything on his head. He coos and does so many other positively adorable things."

He was amazed at how she'd blossomed while talking about the baby. Her gray eyes were soft and moist. He could see through them, right into the heart of her compassion for the orphaned infant.

"How severe is his condition, Nique?"

"That will be discovered through the developmental stages, like when he crawls, walks, talks, that sort of thing. But he's getting all the necessary therapies now. Getting help early is very important to the child's development. Ken, everyone at the hospital refers to him as the Down baby, but I call Scott Brian my 'ups' baby. He keeps me so upbeat, so high. When he smiles at me, I can't help but pick him up and squeeze him tight. You're going to love him, too. I just know it."

Ken frowned slightly. "I don't want to burst your euphoric bubble, Nique, but this is a major task you're considering taking on. Are you doing this to keep from having a baby of our own, or do you genuinely care that much for this baby."

She wrinkled her nose in dismay. "Please refer to him as Scott Brian. This baby, that baby, the Down baby all sound so insensitive. This little bundle of angelic smiles and soft flesh is very real to me. I know there may be medical or even mental complications down the road, but I'm up to this. Scott Brian has changed my life. I genuinely love him."

"Love?"

"Yes, love. If only for a few minutes, I've seen him practically every day for the past couple of months, except for when I'm out of town . . . and then I call the hospital and talk to Melinda Sanchez, the ER nurse. She checks on him for me and reports back. She's the nurse that found me with Scott Brian's mother after she died. I learned about the adoption from her and that he'd be placed in foster care when he was well enough to leave the hospital."

"Do you have any idea when he'll be ready to leave?"

"Possibly another month or so. That's why I want you to meet him. I want you two to bond like he and I have already done. Please don't deny yourself the opportunity to see him, Ken. I promise that you won't regret it."

He was really worried now. This wasn't just a passing fancy on her part. He could see that clearly. She seriously saw herself in the role of Scott Brian's mother. That scared him, only because he wasn't sure she knew what she might be getting herself in to. "Nique, what about your career? Are you ready to give that up? Scott Brian is a special child with special needs. Do you really think you can handle all the challenges that lay ahead of you if you take this on?"

"If *we* take this on, Ken. I can't do it without you. I know that for sure. As for my career, I don't have to give it up entirely. I can pick and choose the events I want to participate in, which is what I'm doing now. There are several major events during the course of the season, but they're spread far enough apart for me to manage. And then I have my off-season time."

"What about the ice arena, Nique? Brandon should start building within the next month or two."

"With all the other in-house facilities that we've considered, I've also been thinking of having a daycare center there. A lot of figure skaters have babies and a professional career. I think they'd be thrilled to have a nursery at the training center they'd choose to workout in. I think to add a daycare to the facility would be an extra added benefit." He couldn't deny that her idea was another great one.

"You've really given this a lot of thought. I'm just so amazed at how much of this you've already figured out and how much you've chosen to keep from me. That hurts so much. You've practically planned a whole new life. And I have to ask you if you ever intended to include me?"

"I've played out telling you in my head so many times. Every time I went to the hospital, I wanted to ask you to go with me. Fear of what you might say kept me from asking. I've gone about this the wrong way. I'm sorry that I didn't trust in you, trust in our love, or put enough trust in us. I never thought we'd be anything less than awesome together. But look at what's happened to us. The lack of communication is at the core. I failed to communicate my feelings to you, not the other way around. Even though you let me know every day how much you loved me, I didn't trust that you loved me enough to help me through my fears. I'm afraid I haven't yet reached the level of maturity that would've allowed me to deal with this much differently. I'm getting there, slowly but surely. With Dr. Jackson's help, I should come out of this okay."

"I have another dozen or so questions, but I think I'll wait until after we go to the hospital. Give me about fifteen minutes. I have to call into the office and talk to Max about an important matter. Yell upstairs at me if I take too long."

She bit down on her lower lip. "We've talked about a lot of things, but the woman in the restaurant hasn't been mentioned. So since we're getting everything out in the open, were you sleeping with her? I've seen you with her twice now. Thomasina seemed to think that something might be going on between the two of you. At least that's what she wanted me to think."

"This was going pretty good up until now. I'm not going to dignify that with an answer." He got up from the sofa to walk out of the room. Getting into it with her over this didn't work for him. In the frame of mind she was in now it was a lose-lose situation for him.

"Why can't you give me a simple yes or no, Ken?"

Eyes blazing like two firing six-shooters, he turned around. "This is the last straw, the last insult to my integrity, the last of any abuse that I'm going to take from you. It's time for you to grow up and learn how real women deal with troubling things. I realize you're just twenty-two, but you're in an adult game, sweetheart. Marriage is not for kids."

Her defiant stare cut him to the quick. "All this because I asked you who that woman was?"

Grabbing the top of his head with his hands, he blew out a ragged breath. "You didn't ask me who she was. You *specifically* asked me if I was sleeping with her. If you can ask me a question like that, I'm afraid that you don't know me at all. I'm a man of integrity, Nique. Screwing around on my wife is not listed in my personal resume. My morals are never compromised for the sake of getting a woman into bed. When you jumped to all the wrong conclusions about Marion, I told you that I wouldn't ever see anyone else as long as I was seeing you. That same principle applies to my marriage. Only one woman at a time for this man." He put a forefinger to his temple in a thoughtful gesture. "But perhaps I've mistakenly picked the wrong woman."

His comment caused her to shrink inside. "Why are you getting vulgar. What's up with this sudden bad-boy image?"

"Vulgar? Girl, you don't know what vulgar is. There are men out there who treat women like dirt and make them love it. It's how you're acting right now that turns men into bad-boys, that turns women into nasty-girls. They get a bad rap, but it's their partners that give them permission to do what they do and to be what they are. Is a bad-boy the kind of man you want, Nique? If so, I'm not the one!"

Totally offended by the conversation, her disgust raised up in her eyes. "What are you trying to tell me? What is happening to you? I've never seen you act like this." She fought back the tears born from her injured feelings. Ken had said things that stung her hard.

Disgusted himself, wearily, he dropped back down on the sofa. He wanted to take her hand but decided against it. Anyway, she looked like she'd slug him hard if he dared to touch her. "This is all I'm trying to say here. When a man is as good as gold to a woman . . . and vice versa, they're often considered as soft, too easily dominated, and a wimpy man or a weak woman. I'm none of those. I just happen to love my wife very much. And I love myself, too, first. I wouldn't think of abusing myself, therefore, I can't imagine abusing the woman I love. But, Nique, I'm starting to see that I'm not showing myself too much love here recently. Because of it, I'm afraid that you're starting to think that you can just say or do anything to me and I'll be okay with it. That may be the role that your daddy takes on, but I won't slip into that role as your husband."

"Are you playing the dozens with me?"

He almost laughed. She *was* still very immature. Of all the things she'd told him that Dr. Jackson had said to her that was the most accurate observation. "Maybe you better learn what that really means. Then you'll have your answer. I've had enough of this. I'm out of here."

"Walking away is not going to solve this, Kenneth Maxwell Jr."

He loved the way she said his name when she was angry. It had a way of melting him. But not this time. "No, but it will keep me from knocking some sense into your pretty little head, the bad-boy kind of way. I will divorce you before I'd ever reduce myself to laying a hand on you. Even though you could use a good shaking every now and then, young lady. But that's not a role I want to play either. All I'm interested in being is your husband. Now you need to decide what *you* want to be to me. My wife, or a spoiled brat who has to have everything her way. Word of advice. Don't make me wait too long. I think we both know that time waits for no man. The clock is fast ticking on our relationship, Nique. I pray to God that we haven't come close to running out of time." With nothing else to say, he left the room.

"Ken . . . !" When he didn't look back, or even answer her shout, she dissolved into tears.

He'd heard her cry out and desperately wanted to turn back, could've easily done so, but not this time. She'd never grow up if he kept giving in to her. A good cry might do her good, especially in the absence of his comforting shoulders. The time had now come for *her* to pick up the pieces and try to put them back together again.

He was simply tired of putting the pieces back in place only to have her shatter them into millions of fragments every time things didn't go her way . . .

Omunique watched him walk out into the foyer and then out the front door. With his car parked in the driveway, she waited for the sound of the engine roaring to life. When seconds had passed and she didn't hear the car start up, she went to the window. Her heart broke at the sight of him walking the grounds with his hands stuffed deeply into his pants pockets. His shoulders appeared to slump with the weight of unhappiness . . . and she felt totally responsible for taking away his joy in loving her unconditionally.

It was never her intention to bring her man's integrity or his manhood into question, but it seemed that she'd done just that. She wanted to go to him, to beg his forgiveness, but she first needed to deal with herself before she could ever hope to reconcile their relationship.

Seated back on the couch, she put her feet up and stared at the wall ahead of her. The things he'd said hurt too much and she needed to go over every single utterance so that she might try and understand what made him feel that way. The glaring light he now saw her in was totally different than that which she'd seen herself in. She didn't like what he'd seen in her, but she knew she needed to try and see herself from his prospective.

Spoiled? Somewhat, but not unreasonably so. Wanting everything to go her way? Perhaps some of the time, but not always. Insensitive to his feelings? She cringed at just the thought of how many times she could've possibly been that way with him.

Her wanting her way about seeing Marcus Taylor had been the worst of all . . .

She'd done something that Ken had been totally against. Then she'd had the nerve to ask him at the jail if he had changed his mind about seeing Taylor with her after he'd made his feelings clear on the subject, on more than just a few occasions. He was right about her acting like a spoiled brat when she wanted to effect a certain outcome. But she wasn't sure she'd have seen it so clearly had he not pointed it out so blatantly. Something he'd been doing a lot lately.

He seemed so fed up with her and that was frightening. To lose her husband was the last thing she wanted. *Then you better get to work on yourself and remember Dr. Jackson's advice to you,* said a voice inside her head. *Only you can change things by working on the things that Ken has mentioned if you want to save your marriage.*

No one had to tell her that her life would never be the same without him in it; she'd already experienced that.

Once was enough for her . . .

Nineteen

The tears wouldn't stop coming, but she had to pull herself together unless she wanted the nurses to think she had gone insane since her last visit. A shiny thatch of curly hair magnetically drew her fingers in. While crushing each curl between the pads of her thumb and forefinger, Omunique called the tiny baby Scott Brian, but only in her mind. The slight slants at the corners of his coal-black eyes were hardly noticeable. Round cheeks, blushing-pink in color, looked soft as clouds and so "kissable"—and she did just that.

Her tears came again. Such an outward sign of vulnerability annoyed her. This baby needed signs of strength, not weakness; her compassionate strength; Ken's unyielding strength. "I'm so sorry, little one, so sorry you lost your mommy. I lost mine, too, a long time ago. But it feels like only yesterday." She brought the baby close to her breast. He curled up against her as if she were his natural mother. "You are so sweet." Omunique cooed and awed at the wondrous gift of God's love that she held so tenderly in her hands.

"He *is* that, isn't he?" Nurse Sanchez responded. "In fact, he's adorable. He seems to love you and you him. You two get along famously. I'm so glad he has someone to care for him."

"It would seem so and I have to come to love him. Oddly

enough, I have found so much comfort in being with this little child." Omunique lifted the tiny baby up high. As she brought him back down, she kissed his forehead. "Has anyone inquired about him in regards to adoption? He's special and he needs an extraordinary home."

"Not a living soul. It's hard to adopt out physically and mentally challenged children." Watching how tenderly Omunique held the baby caused Sanchez's heart to cry out. Quietly, she slipped out of the nursery. When the baby had curled up against Omunique like it was the most natural thing for him to do, Sanchez thought they made a perfect pair: a caring mother, a precious son.

So engrossed was she in the sweetness of the little boy that minutes had passed before she realized that Sanchez had left the room. After placing the tiny bundle of joy back into his crib, she covered him up. When Omunique was told that Sanchez was on supper break, she left the nursery and walked to the elevator, taking it down to the lobby level.

Rushing into the cafeteria, Omunique saw that Sanchez was with a group of nurses. Deciding not to interrupt her dinner break, she walked away. She would call her later, at home. Sanchez had made her private number available to Omunique some time ago, telling her to use it when she needed to talk with her about the baby, or for just a friendly chat.

Before she could reach the front entrance, Ken came through the revolving door. Just the mere sight of him caused her pulse to quicken. So handsome, tall, virile, and wickedly sexy. Omunique wanted so desperately for her husband to let her back into his heart. She wanted him back in their bedroom, back in their bed, period, back where he belonged. Her hunger for him clenched in her stomach like liquid fire. The soft flesh between her thighs pulsated with need, the need to have him touch her with his hands, his mouth, his tongue, and the heat of his desire.

Things had gone sour for them again right after she'd asked the question about the other woman. It would've been better not to ask him it all, because she still didn't know the answer. He hadn't said too much to her since then. With Wyman still in the guest house, he'd gone back to sleeping in the upstairs guest room. How many nights had she ventured down that hallway only to turn back out of fear of his rejection? Every night since he moved back into that room.

The moment he came upon her she could smell the libido-teasing, manly scent of the soap he showered with. The fresh, lemony fragrance of the cologne that he wore had a way of physically arousing her. It was late afternoon, but he smelled as though he'd just finished showering. That wasn't unusual at all for him since he usually worked out right after lunch at the health spa near his job.

"Hi, Nique. How are you? I didn't get to see you before I left for work. I came home to talk with you, but you weren't there. I thought you might be here so I took a chance and came by. I didn't know exactly where I was going to find you, but I intended to start by questioning the nurses in the nursery. Have you already seen Scott Brian?"

She couldn't keep from smiling at the tender way in which he'd said the baby's name. "Yes, I've seen him. Would you like to meet him?"

"That's one of the reasons why I came here. How's he doing?"

"Come on. I'll let you see for yourself. We'll have to scrub our hands and arms with a special liquid soap and then put on sterile gowns before we go into the nursery. It doesn't take up much time. They don't want us to bring the outside germs around the babies, which makes perfect sense."

He held back the elevator door to make sure that it didn't close on her as she stepped inside. "That's interesting stuff to know. I've never been to a hospital nursery before. I'm sure it'll be an experience that I won't soon forget. When my former secretary had her baby, I didn't see the child, Max's godchild, until she was already at home."

"I'm sure you won't forget it."

Dressed in a yellow paper gown, and scared to touch such a fragile little fellow, Ken stared down at the baby his wife had come to love. He could see the physical characteristics of Down syndrome, but to him it appeared very slight. Beautiful black hair, lots of it, capped his tiny head. His little fingers were long, slender, and rosy-pink.

Ken could imagine those tiny little digits curled around his wife's own delicate fingers. When he looked at Omunique, he wanted to cry. Immature or not, genuine compassion filled her. The expression on her face was angelic. The halo around her heart shone outwardly bringing loving warmth to the baby and to him. It looked to Ken as if her entire being had turned into a soft, radiant light. An angel couldn't have glowed with any more love and beauty than that which he saw coming from his wife. His aching desire for her nearly brought him down to his knees.

Omunique could see that her husband was nervous. "Go ahead and pick him up, Ken. He won't bite you."

"I don't know about this, Omunique." He backed away from the crib. "I've never picked up a baby that small before. He looks so fragile. I know it's silly, but I'm afraid he might break if I don't handle him with extreme care."

Omunique laughed softly. "He won't break. Scott Brian is a pretty tough little man. He's been fighting with the likes of the devil just to stay alive. Do you want me to pick him up and hand him to you?"

Ken backed further away. "I don't think I'm ready for this, Nique. It wouldn't be fair of me to hold him when I'm not sure of how he fits into our lives, if at all. We have yet to settle our own future. There is still so much stuff that we have to get through."

"Afraid of getting attached?"

"That, too. What I'm really afraid of is that we don't know enough about his challenges to make a decision as serious as the one you're considering."

"What are you saying? That we shouldn't get so close to him in case he should happen to face serious physical or mental challenges, or both?"

He gave her a hard look. "I didn't say that. I'm speaking of being educated in whatever his challenges may be. He's a very special child. Do we have what it takes to adopt him, to see that all his emotional needs are met, and to raise him properly? How fair is it to bring a child into our home with the crazy schedules we live with from day to day?"

"We would've had the same schedules had we gotten pregnant. Why don't you just spell it out for me?"

Rapidly, he crossed the room. Stopping right in front of her, he put both his hands on her shoulders. "This is not the place for us to have this discussion," he whispered softly. "I don't want our little friend to feel any negative vibes from us. This isn't something that can be decided overnight, but I agree that we can and should talk about it. Can you accept that for now? It's all I'm prepared to give."

"Okay, I'm feeling you. When can you find time for us to talk?"

"Omunique, I will always make time to talk to you. It's just that some of the things you want to talk about are what I don't have time for. I made a covenant to you and you to me. Those vows still hold true for me. We've got some serious problems, but another woman is not one of them."

She looked slightly abashed. "I'm sorry that I brought that up." She looked at her watch. "Are you going back to the office?"

"Not if you have something better in mind for me."

"What about a nice walk on the beach? We haven't done that in a long while."

"You're dressed for the part, but I don't think I am." He looked over her tight jeans-and-sweater clad body. She looked refreshingly vital. It was hard to imagine that Omunique would ever lose her looks to age. She was a natural beauty and he could only see her becoming more so with age. Her heart was beautiful, too. That's what he'd fallen in love with first.

"I remember a time when what you wore wouldn't have mattered. We've walked on the beach with you dressed just like you are now, in a suit. I admit that sand got all in your dress shoes, but you didn't seem to care back then. Are we so far removed from that place that we can't go back and recapture what we've left behind? As husband and wife, as best friends, and lovers, have we fallen completely off the charts?"

"As I said to you before, we need to rekindle the fire beneath the ice. How we go about doing that seems to be the problem for both of us. What about us taking a brisk walk around our property? I can change clothes first. Later, perhaps we could watch the sunset from the gazebo? We can talk as long as you want to. I want very much to hear your concerns, your needs."

"Then it's settled. We walk and talk. Are you ready to go?"

He looked down at the baby. "Maybe I could hold him for just a second. But I'll need you to hand him to me. I won't be comfortable picking him up."

Omunique brushed away her tears before Ken could see them. Whether he knew it or not, he was about to get hooked. And just like it had happened for her, he was going to need a massive daily dose of Scott Brian. He was about to become addicted to the love that flowed from within that tiny little heart, the little heart that she could almost feel beating inside her own chest.

Carefully, Omunique lifted the sleeping baby from the crib. She couldn't help snuggling him against her one more time. She felt his warmth the instant she brought him to her breast.

Before she handed him to Ken, she saw that he was looking for somewhere to sit down. Spotting the rocking chair next to another crib, he pulled it over to where Omunique stood with the baby. "I think I'll feel more secure with holding him if I'm sitting down." He stretched his arms out after situating himself in the chair. "I'm ready now."

Slowly, gently, she placed the baby in Ken's arms, instructing him on how to support his little head. "That's it. See it's not so difficult. Oh, look. His eyes just popped open. I think he knows that someone that's never held him before is holding him, someone new. Look at the way he's looking up at you. He likes you."

Puzzled by her comment, Ken looked up at Omunique. "How do you know that?"

"Because he's not yelling his head off. Babies know who their friends are. They're smarter than some adults when it comes to knowing who has their best interest at heart."

Ken placed a tissue-soft kiss in the center of the baby's forehead. His finger lazed down one soft cheek and then the other. His finger then gently traced the little pink bow mouth. Omunique knew firsthand the magic in Ken's stroke. His magical touch had a way of bringing her so much pleasure amidst the storms of their passion, so much calm in the choppy seas of her turmoil, so much comfort when things became too emotional, too much for her to bear.

While rocking the baby back and forth in the chair, Ken couldn't keep his eyes off of his wife's love child. The baby curled into him just like he'd done with Omunique. His little fingers suddenly wrapped around Ken's baby finger. It was all he could do to keep from crying. With tears in his eyes, he brought the baby up close to him and kissed each of his rosy cheeks. Omunique looked on. It was a precious sight. Such a strong man holding a tiny, fragile baby in his arms with such tenderness was indeed a most beautiful sight to behold.

"Omunique, you'd better put him back in his crib. He's so sleepy that he can hardly keep his pretty eyes open. Here you go." Ken handed her the baby and watched as she bundled him up in the blanket to put him back into the crib. She couldn't resist hugging him before laying him down. Ken saw the halo surrounding her heart every time she looked at the baby.

Quietly, they tiptoed out of the room. The fact that Ken had reached for her hand without giving it a moment's thought gave her reason to entertain optimism. Outside in the corridor, he led her to the elevator. As they waited for the car to come, he looked at her. In fact, he stared at her but said nothing. The elevator came to a stop and the doors eased open, allowing them entry.

"I've got a couple of stops to make on the way home, but I'll get there not long after you. I'll need to change clothes, as well. Maybe you could check on Wyman in the meantime."

"Sounds okay to me. If Aunt Mamie isn't out at the guest house visiting, I'll sit with him until you're all set. See you later."

Looking deeply into her gray eyes, he took both of her hands in his and rubbed the back of each with the pad of his thumbs. "Count to a thousand." With that said, he walked away.

Count to a thousand, she reiterated in her mind. Depending on how far away he was, or how close, he'd always given her a number to count up to until he made it to where she was. Reviving wonderful memories was a great start on the road back . . .

A great start in resurrecting the fire beneath the ice . . .

* * *

Quietly entering the guest house bedroom, Omunique carried a tray of food in to Wyman. He was resting comfortably in bed while reading the daily newspaper.

His smile was bright for her as he patted the side of the bed. "This daddy needs to talk with his little girl. But not like I used to do. I need to say to you what I'm sure your mother would've said. In other words, I'm going to talk to you like the woman you've become."

She sucked in a ragged breath. "Eating first is what's coming for you. I didn't prepare this hot meal for you to let it get cold."

"You have a couple of microwave ovens." He needed to say nothing more. The determined look on his face, much like the ones she'd had an occasion to wear, caused her to put the tray down and prop herself on the side of his bed.

"I knew this was coming sooner or later. I'm ready to listen."

"Good." Wyman took her hand and kissed the back of it. "I don't want you to take these things as personal criticisms, but if you decide to take that attitude that's all right with me. There's been a lot of serious things going on with you over the past few months. I understand all that. I've tried to let you work this through in your own way. But when I see you going in the wrong direction, as your parent, it's my duty to steer you back toward the right path. I'm just sorry that I let you get so far off the right path before I stepped in. Nique, I'm the one who can and should tell you when you're wrong. You've been wrong, daughter, dead wrong . . ."

"But, Dad . . ."

To quiet her, he held up his hand. "This is my time to talk, your time to listen. Okay?" Knowing she had no choice but to hear him out, she nodded. Either today, next week, or a month from now, Wyman Philyaw was going to have his say.

"You and Ken have been putting up a valiant front for

me, but I know your marriage is in trouble. The tension that exists between you is thick and unpalatable. I've known for a while that there were serious issues for you both to conquer." He took a moment to study his daughter's expression. "I know that look on your face, the one that says, 'I've been betrayed.' No, Ken didn't betray you. No one has betrayed you . . . but you. It really doesn't matter how I know what I know. What matters is what you're going to do about it."

"Dad, if you could just let me say a few things, you'll see that things are changing."

"That's all well and good, Nique. And you can say those things, but not until I finish. It would be so kind of you not to interrupt me again. You've always had a problem listening. When you're so busy thinking about what you want to say, you can't hear what I'm trying to convey."

Even though she didn't like his scolding, though it had been done with assertiveness, she gave a resigned look but an impatient sigh.

"When you returned from your honeymoon and told me that you and Ken were going to start a family right away, I got very concerned. I didn't think you could've possibly thought this through, not with the depth in which it should've been probed. You were just married, just beginning a new phase in your career, lots of new people to acquaint yourself with, and numerous new routines to tackle and then try and master. Starting a family should've been the last thing on your agenda, especially with an already full slate of new things."

Wyman sipped on a glass of water through a straw. "That's when I should've had this talk with you. Shortly after the housewarming, I noticed that you were brooding over something a good deal of the time. I saw rapid changes in you—and they weren't very positive ones. Then this situation with Taylor came up. That horrendous news tossed you right into the center of the hurricane. Even with all that, which was more than enough for any one person to deal with, I suspected there were other critical things going on with you, going on inside of you. I'm not a woman . . . and God knows that I wish Patrice were here to share her womanly wisdom with you, but she's not. I've got to do the very best I can at playing the role of both parents. When I see my daughter in the kind of emotional and mental trouble that I believe you're in, I've got to try and throw you a life raft. Now, I'm prepared to let you speak. I'm hoping that you will tell me what's *really* been going on with you . . . and then we can take it from there."

Before launching into her story, she gulped hard. Telling him about what she witnessed at the hospital would be the most difficult—because there was no doubt in her mind that her story would bring back excruciatingly painful, soul-stirring memories of the day his wife died, the same exact way. Mustering up as much courage as she was capable of, she began to tell him about one of the two most horrific experiences of her twenty-two years. In her opinion, this nightmarish episode in her life was just as harrowing as what Taylor had done to her.

Once she'd finished with that story, she talked to him about Dr. Beverly Jackson's assessment of her and of the things she'd allowed to take over her life.

As Wyman listened to every single word, he fought back his strong need to break down and cry. More than ever before, his daughter needed his unwavering strength right now. It hurt him so deeply to know what she'd been through, that she'd gone through it alone because she couldn't share her fears—for fear of hurting others.

Taking tissues from the bedside nightstand, he wiped his daughter's tears. "I know that was extremely hard for you, but I'm thrilled that you were able to share your story with me. I can better advise you when armed with all the details. The first thing I need to say is that I'm sorry for your pain and sorrow, deeply sorry. However, I still have a serious parental duty to perform. Secondly, I'd like to see you find another way to adjust to your fears, a more constructive way. You're now seeing a psychiatrist. In making that wise decision, you placed the right path directly beneath your feet. Thirdly, I think that you've abandoned yourself. By deserting your own needs and desires you ended up alienating your husband and forsaking your marriage. Ken is the one person you should've been able to confide in, no matter how black your darkest hours became."

She blew her nose into the tissue. "I know that now, Daddy. I've hurt him so much. I can't help but wonder is the damage undoable."

"The damage that has occurred already can never be undone, but what you do from this day on can keep further destruction from devouring what's left of your marriage. It's rescue time, Nique. As I'm attempting to throw you a life raft, you have to get inside of it and save yourself first. You can't save your marriage until you begin rescuing Omunique Philyaw-Maxwell. I happen to know she's worth saving."

Smiling at his astute words of wisdom, she stroked the back of Wyman's hand. "I've come a long way in the past couple of weeks, but I still keep making silly mistakes. I've seen Ken with a woman twice and I confronted the situation by asking him if he was sleeping with her. Real mature approach, huh? He hasn't answered me and I don't expect that he ever will. However he did say that he had remained true to his vows, so I guess he did answer. He just hasn't told me who she is."

"He's probably so injured by your thinking him capable of cheating on you, that he may never tell you who she is. That's something you just might have to live with. If you believe what he has already told you, then move on. If you don't, you'd better have solid proof of his wrongdoing before you should even dare to bring it up again. Are we clear on that issue?"

"Very clear. Dr. Jackson blames a lot of my problems on immaturity. I know she's right about that. I'm still not equipped with all the tools that I need to move forward into womanhood."

"Don't use your immaturity as a crutch, Nique. You're old enough to know the difference between right and wrong. When you know in your heart that something is wrong, it's wrong no matter how you try to justify it. Your conscience will tell you exactly what you need to do in that moment of indecision. Listen to those small voices inside your heart and head. It's the Holy Spirit guiding and lighting your path. We, as humans, have learned to shut out the very voices that were given to us by the Creator. These are His instructions to us in what to do in every single situation. If we don't listen to our inner voices, we completely miss the message."

"But what about the guilt?"

"Oh, the *guilt*, my dear child. The things I can tell you about that nasty word. That destructive illness is called by many names: culpability, liability, fault, error, blame, condemnation, criticism, reproach; just to name a mere few. I have a pretty good idea of why you suffer with guilt, but I want to hear from you on that in case I'm mistaken."

While ordering up another heaping helping of courage, Omunique drew in a shaky breath. "Mother's death, for one. Then there's the guilt of causing you to lose your precious love, the guilt of you possibly never finding happiness again, the guilt of me not dying so that my mother could live. I've tried so hard to make things up to you for taking her life. I wanted to be a champion for her so that her dream of being a champion figure skater would be fulfilled, so that she might forgive me for separating you two. I desperately needed to make you both so proud, so much so that you would hopefully be able to overlook the injustice I'd done to you by being born. But I've done a miserable job at all of it because those were nonrealistic goals for me to try to attain. In fact, they're impossible for anyone to try and achieve. My constant guilt has weighed me down for most of my life. It's responsible for the emotional trouble I'm in now."

Wyman shuddered at the thought of what she'd put herself through all these years. "My beautiful child, there has never been anything for you to feel guilty about. Patrice died because it was her time. It was nothing more than that and nothing less. As you will find the Bible says to everything there is a season. It was simply the season of her death. I've also been plagued with guilt. Like you've done, I abandoned myself. I could only love as a father should love his offspring. I had deserted the ability to love any other woman as a flesh-and-blood man. And now that I believe I can love unconditionally again, I find that the woman I could fall in love with is romantically interested in someone else. But we'll talk about that later.

"You see, Nique, that's the very thing that I don't want to happen to you. I don't want you to lose the ability to love and appreciate those that are still among the living. Ken is alive, Nique. And it's my guess that he needs his wife to recognize that fact. The only love that you will find among the living that's greater than his love for you is that of self."

"I remember you telling me something like this when I got injured. You said that you buried your love with your wife." Tears sprang to her eyes. "I know how you feel. I've been burying myself with guilt in the same way. *Had I not been born my mother would've lived* is the chorus that I've written to the saddest song. I've been singing that chorus to myself for as long as I can recall. With the help of Dr. Jackson, I'm ready to confront and annihilate the guilt and the fears that I've literally drowned myself in. Dad, I *will* cling to the loving life raft that you've thrown out to me. I *will* hold on to it for dear life—and with all my might. I *will* only let it go when I'm strong enough to make it back up to the top of the water, up to where the still waters, though deep, will once again embrace me. I *will* no longer abandon my husband and my duties as his wife during my period of self-rescue. I *will* no longer use my immaturity as an excuse to lean on and to have my own way. Together, Ken and I will both rescue our marriage. That is, should it not be too late for us."

"Those, my dearest daughter, are very achievable goals. Take what you've said as seriously as if you were retaking your wedding vows. It's never too late to try and make things right. The outcome may not be that which you desire, but at least you'll know that you gave it everything that you had to give while desperately trying to make it right."

By the time Omunique and Ken reached the gazebo, the sun hung low in the sky. The evening air was cool and the combined heady scents of the flowers and trees floated like a cloud on the breeze. With the property situated high up on the hill, the ascending rays of the sun bounced off the dome roof of the white gazebo adding a brilliant yellow glow to the majestic edifice. Ken took a seat in the white domed structure while prompting his wife to sit next to him on the built-in bench seating.

In silence, they watched as the sun, now orange in color, dropped lower and lower from the sky. Until it had completely disappeared, their focus remained steadfast on the near-blinding orange fireball. A deep sigh of contentment from Ken followed Omunique's gasp of reverence.

The same as he'd done earlier, he took both of her hands. "This type of serenity is what I'm after." His autumn-gold eyes connected with the essence of her. "Is it possible for us to have this kind of serenity in our lives again? I'm going to be honest with you. I can't see it happening for me without you by my side. Serenity and you have always been as one for me. I've always made the best of the hand that's been dealt to me. In the cards passed out to me over a year ago, I found the queen of spades among them. To me, you are representative of the black queen that gave me the winning hand. I still see you as my black queen, the queen of my heart. The question is: Am I still the reigning king of your heart? Is the crown still mine to wear?"

Omunique's heart was so full she couldn't speak. Her eyes were too full of tears for them to become her voice. But when her moist, hungry lips met his in an explosion of passion, her emotionally positive answer came through to him loud and clear. With their arms entangled around each other's necks, the kiss went on and on, as if their primitive cravings for one another could never be satisfied.

Ken tasted her again and again before he held her away from him. "There are many things we have yet to work out. I want us to take it slow. I don't want to see us get all caught up in our physical desires too soon. When the wild, uncontrollable passion that exists between us begins to taper off, though I don't think it ever will, I don't want us to wake up one day and discover that that was all we ever had. Let's work on our issues of trust first. At the same time, we can work together on conquering our fears. We have quite a ways to go before we get back to where we were before all this madness started. Are you with me on this?"

Once again, her lips responded for her.

Twenty

After being in his office for a couple of hours, Ken picked up the phone and dialed Sandy Wilson's number. Sandy had been with them for so many years and her sweet babylike voice hadn't changed a bit. "Sandy, it's Ken, returning your call. I want to know what's on your mind, but I first want to find out how you, Rob, and little Cassidy are doing?"

"Hey, Ken. Our little angel is doing just fine. Congratulations on your marriage! I tried so hard to make it to the wedding, but Cassidy came down with the sniffles the day before. I hadn't arranged for a baby-sitter because we intended to bring her with us. I gave Max your wedding present when he came by to see his godchild. I know you have it because we received the thank-you note. I hope to meet your beautiful bride one day soon. Max simply raves over her. I watched her Olympic performance. It was riveting! I kept thinking how well my once confirmed bachelor boss has done for himself."

"Omunique is terrific. And you will meet her as soon as things calm down around our house. Her father has been staying with us after a mild heart attack. We love having him there, but he's about ready to make the move back home."

"I'm hoping to meet her sooner than that. Max called a couple of days ago and said that you might be looking for a new secretary. He wanted to know if I was interested. I'm calling to let you know that I'd love to come in and help you guys out for as long as you need me. My mother-in-law has agreed to keep the baby. She is only one of a couple of people that I'd even consider leaving Cassidy with. So tell me, is there a need for my services at Maxwell Corporation?"

It was just like Sandy to be so thoughtful. She'd been the Maxwell men's private secretary for over five years. She was always thoughtful, considerate, and extremely conscientious in her duties.

"Wow, Sandy, this is great news for me! Of course we need you back here. We hated it when you decided not to come back after having the baby. You know this operation inside and out. Can you come into the office so we can talk about it? We will definitely hire you back at a higher rate of pay." Feeling eyes on him, Ken looked up. Thomasina stood in the doorway.

"Uh, Sandy, I'm going to have to call you back in a few minutes. Is that okay?"

"Sure. I'll be anticipating your call."

Ken looked back at Thomasina. "Is there something I can do for you, Thomasina?"

She waved a piece of paper in the air. "Is this your idea of a joke? How can you fire someone by just leaving them a note?"

"The very same way that you can crumple up a note written to me and then toss it."

"Is it the note or our little late-evening tryst that has you so worked up? Or perhaps your wife is behind it all? She never did like me."

Ken saw where this was going. It wasn't a good place. He picked up the phone and buzzed Max on the intercom. "Dad, could you come into my office for a minute? Thomasina is here and I need you to be present as we discuss the conditions of her dismissal."

The look on Thomasina's face said that she hadn't expected him to involve his father. It made her nervous. But if Ken thought he could just rid himself of her without serious repercussions he was sadly mistaken. She was going to have a piece of Ken Maxwell Jr. one way or the other.

Max came in and closed the door behind him. It only took one look at Thomasina's face for him to know that she wasn't going to go away quietly. "Good morning, Thomasina. Why don't the three of us go over and sit at the conference table so we can discuss your grievances."

Once seated, Ken laid a yellow notepad on the table. "I've already given you my reason for firing you. After giving it even more thought, I find that my decision is the only conclusion that I could've come to. When you took it upon yourself to try and sabotage my personal life, you made a grave mistake. Whether Mrs. Maxwell likes you or not has nothing to do with my decision. In fact, I haven't even discussed this incident with her. Though, I doubt it will change things, Max and I are prepared to at least listen to your defense."

Thomasina gave a sneering smile. "We'll get to my defense, though, I don't think I'll need one after your father learns the truth about his son."

Ken knew what was coming next, but he was even more aware that he couldn't stop it.

"Why don't you tell your father the real reason that you fired me? I'm sure you haven't told him about your little sexual exploitations of me when we work late into the evenings. The truth of the matter is you fired me because I told you I wouldn't feel right sleeping with you since you were married. You've been coming on to me since this trouble with your wife first began. The sexual innuendoes were constant. I admit that I seriously considered getting into bed with you, but you fired me when I decided that it was wrong for us to do that."

Ken jumped up. "Dad, these are malicious fabri—"

"Son, say no more. Sit back down. I'll take it from here." Max looked over at Thomasina. "Young lady, this is the last thing I would've expected from you. But now that you've played your hand, I intend to play mine. I'm afraid this discussion has to come to an end. We will only speak to you again on this subject in the presence of our lawyers. Thank you and good day."

Thomasina's eyes raged with contempt. "You might not want to talk with me, but the press will certainly hear what I have to say. One Jack Prescott would like nothing better than to take this company down, especially after that huge settlement you received from the *Sun*. Not to mention your attempt to get him fired and have his press credentials revoked."

Max stood up. "Good day, Thomasina. Don't force us to call security."

Throwing down on the table the note Ken had written firing her, the only piece of evidence she had, she stormed toward the office door. Turning, looking ferocious with anger, she pointed her finger at Ken. "You haven't heard the last of me. We'll see what your precious little wife thinks of you after the press cuts you into teeny pieces and feeds your sweet black behind to the world. You and your *Olympic champion* will be featured on every rag sheet from here to Africa. Count on it!"

The office door slammed so hard behind her that the books on the shelves shifted.

Ken tilted his chair back, placing his feet on the desk. Thomasina had devastated him. He wasn't so much worried about himself. His concern for his wife was another matter. As if they didn't already have enough to overcome in their marriage, now they had a pack of lies to add to the already strained situation. "Dad, I'm sor—"

"You have nothing to be sorry about, son. I don't believe a word of what she's saying."

Ken frowned. "Dad, you'd better hear me out first." He

went on to tell Max what had happened in the office that night, before she'd left for the evening. "So, you see, I do feel somewhat responsible for what's happening. I provoked her so that I could see just where she was going. I had an idea of what she was up to, but I had to make damn sure before I could build a case for firing her. The note she'd tossed from Nique was the straw that broke the camel's back. Apparently she and Omunique had words on a few occasions, according to Thomasina, but I'm now beginning to believe that she's lying about that, as well. I think they only had words that one time. I clearly remember Omunique threatening to hurt her that day. That tells me she had good reason to believe that Thomasina had been up to no good, yet she never mentioned a word to me about her suspicions. I guess she didn't have enough proof, either."

"Your intentions should be easy enough to prove, but I must say that that's not the kind of risk you ever need to take with someone that you suspect of having a personal interest in you. However we have documentation regarding the incident with the type of dress she wore when she first started to work here. I'll set up an appointment with the lawyers and have them advise us on what our next move should be. I've got an idea they're going to suggest that we do a monetary settlement with her to keep a scandal from occurring. Given Omunique's silver medal win it's something we might have to consider. This could affect your wife's career more than it could ever hurt this company. How *are* you going to handle this with Omunique?"

Ken pounded the table with a closed fist. "Damn it! How could this happen now? We had a great talk and a serene walk around the grounds last night. After an in-depth discussion of a lot of things, we decided to work out our differences and try to get our marriage back on the right track. There hasn't been an ounce of love lost between us through all these trials. But we have a lot of challenges ahead of us. Now there's even a baby to consider in all this."

Max's eyes widened with excitement. "Omunique is pregnant?"

"Oh, I'm sorry for misleading you on that. No, she's not pregnant. She wants to adopt an orphaned baby that she's fallen completely in love with. Sit down and I'll tell you all about it."

Omunique sat quietly as she listened to the social worker. While talking with the MSW, Rita Johnson, at the hospital, and learning all the first steps they'd need to take should they decide to adopt the baby, Omunique paid close attention to every detail.

"Here are the names of a couple of therapists that are employed by the hospital. This is a list of the many different types of therapists employed by outside agencies. Please carefully look over all the information I've given you. These pamphlets will help you and your husband better understand the genetic disorder of Down syndrome. There are hosts of medical complications that can come with this disease ranging from mild to severe.

"Down syndrome is the most common chromosomal disorder. Let me know if you have any questions about anything. That's what I'm here for. It was such a pleasure meeting you. Everyone gets so excited when you come here to see the baby. The majority of us have never had the opportunity to meet and share so much time with a celebrity."

Omunique laughed. "A celebrity I'm not." She got to her feet. "Thanks for all the valuable information you've given me. My husband was supposed to meet me here but something extremely important must've come up. It's not like him to miss an appointment. I apologize for him not being here. I'm sure we'll be contacting you within the next few weeks."

Omunique left the social service office smiling, but her heart felt like a brick of cement inside her chest. Had something happened to Ken? Or had he just gotten cold feet at the last minute? She checked her cell phone for messages, pages, or missed calls, but there weren't any. After punching in the memory code for Ken's private line, she put the phone up to her ear and waited. Her heart fluttered with anguish when the message center picked up. "Ken, I'm leaving the hospital now. I have to see the therapist and then I'm heading for home. I hope everything's all right. When you didn't show up for our appointment with the social worker, I didn't know what to think. Call me as soon as you get this message. My cell will be on until I get home."

Omunique was still worried over Ken's no-show as she sat in Dr. Jackson's office waiting for her to come back in. She'd stepped out for a moment to take a confidential emergency call from another patient. Omunique had totally dismissed the idea of him having cold feet. Ken simply would never allow himself to operate in such a cowardly manner. She looked at her watch before once again checking her cell phone for messages. With still no word from her husband, she grew apprehensive.

Using her cell, she checked their home message center. Intently, she listened to each of the messages, but when the recorder had played back all the calls, none were from Ken. Dr. Jackson's return kept her from making any further telephone inquiries into Ken's whereabouts.

"I'm sorry about that, Omunique." Omunique smiled at the use of her first name since the doctor had only recently started calling her by such. "Emergencies happen around here all the time. Let's get back to where we were." She looked down at her notes. "Okay, I was asking you what your first thought was when your husband first told you that Officer Taylor had committed suicide."

Omunique swallowed hard. "That is was my fault, that if I hadn't gone to see him he might still be alive. As you've already pointed out to me, I have a tendency to shoulder the blame for everything bad that happens around me. I believe I adopted this habit as a small child, when I first began hearing stories about how my mother had died. It wasn't me that Dad was telling the story to. I'd overhear him talking to my grandmother, my godmother, and other relatives and friends about that day. He didn't tell me the story personally until I was sixteen. By then the guilt had been solidly erected, to a point where it couldn't be penetrated. I felt guilty about everything. I remember when another skater got hurt, Sara Davies, I felt that had I been on the ice with her I somehow could've prevented that disaster. Why I ever thought that, I don't know. I know now that there's nothing I could've done about her fall, especially since I wasn't even there—and nothing I could've done about all the other bad stuff."

"Why did you believe you'd done something to make Taylor come after you?"

"When he gave me that ticket, I fought it in court and won. That embarrassed him something terrible. The judges words for him weren't too kind when he learned about the nonexistence of the stop sign that the officer had given me the ticket for running. He tried to talk to me after court that day, but I wasn't trying to hear what he had to say. The next time I saw him was at a skating event after-party. I danced with him when he asked me to. He told me that he'd heard my people were looking for a bodyguard—that he was the best man for the job. Little did I know that he was the reason my father thought I needed security in the first place. He started coming after me with a vengeance when I first started dating Ken."

"How do you feel about his death now?"

"Relieved. If Ken hadn't gone to the morgue to view the body, I probably still wouldn't believe it. I even thought that I'd heard him threaten me the day I visited. If the department covered it up once, they could do it again. We decided not to file a lawsuit against the city because it would put Uncle Ralph's career in jeopardy. I'm at peace with all that has happened."

"Okay, now we can move forward and talk about the baby you've mentioned."

Omunique suddenly looked very apprehensive. "There's something else I want to talk about before we move on. I've seen my husband with a woman twice and he refuses to tell me who she is. I even asked him if he was sleeping with her. He only said that he's not seeing her in a romantic way, but I'm still curious as to who she is. My father told me to leave it alone unless I had concrete evidence of wrongdoing. I'd just like to know why he won't tell me who she is if there's nothing personal between them. Should I just let this go?"

"Do you doubt that your husband is telling the truth?"

"I believe him wholeheartedly. But I still want to know who she is. She's very attractive." Omunique went on to describe in great detail the woman in question.

As if she'd had a light-bulb moment, Dr. Jackson snapped her fingers. "Omunique, I'm going to tell you something that's strictly between you and me. I'm exercising my right to the confidentiality clause. The woman you're talking about is my dearest friend, my colleague."

Omunique raised an eyebrow. "Why would Ken be having lunch with her?"

"Your husband called and asked to come in to see me to discuss the problems in the marriage, which was a definite conflict of interest. He wanted desperately to save your marriage. I referred him to my friend, Dr. Michelle Laron-Bryant, a marriage counselor. That's your other woman!"

Omunique had a sinking feeling in the pit of her stomach.

"But why wouldn't he just tell me that? That's not something he would need to hide from me since he's the one that convinced me to seek out a therapist."

"Eventually, he probably would have, if you hadn't asked him if he was sleeping with her. As an innocent man would, he took it very personal. His integrity had come into question by the woman he loved. Men take it much harder than women when the people they love challenge their trustworthiness. Especially when they're not guilty of the charge. Let me say this to you so we can wrap this topic up. Don't bring this up to him again. If he's going to tell you, he'll do it in his own time. If not, you know the truth now, so move on with your life. Make a commitment to completely close this chapter of your life. Today, before you leave my office."

"Chapter closed. Now, about Scott Brian . . ."

With a deep scowl on his face, Ken leaped out of his seat. "Oh, my goodness, Dad. I got so caught up in this Thomasina Bridges drama that I forgot all about meeting Omunique at the hospital. Then we got into talking about the baby. She's probably been beside herself with worry for the last hour. I'm going to go to my office and check my messages. I'm sure there's one or two from her. After tying up some loose ends, I'm going to cut out of here. I'm certainly not behind in any of my projects, but I plan to do some work at home over the weekend, stuff that pertains to our arena. I'll call the temporary secretarial service and get someone in for Monday."

"I'll do that, son. I'll also make the arrangements for Sandy to come in and talk to us about hiring back on with the company. You go take care of your wife. I'm behind you and Omunique in whatever you decide about the little boy. It would be nice to have a baby to run around after. By the way, Mamie and her friend, Teresa, are taking me to see the gospel play that you and Omunique saw last year. It has returned to the west coast for six weeks."

"Have a great time. Call me over the weekend." If Ken hadn't been in such a hurry, he would've asked Max point blank what was going on with him and Mamie. But that would have to wait for another time. Getting home to his wife was his most important mission.

Having changed out of her dress clothes and into black denim jeans and a black-and-gold Los Angeles Lakers sweatshirt, Omunique went out to check on Wyman. Finding him fast asleep, she turned off the television and started back to the main house. As she walked along the colorful flower-bordered pathway, she turned over in her mind all the reasons why Ken wouldn't have made the meeting. The one thing that she didn't doubt was that he'd have a good reason for not showing up. Still, his safety was a question left unanswered.

Once inside the house, she went straight to the family room. Before relaxing in Ken's recliner, she glanced at the wall clock. Her sigh came hard and deep. Then she thought about his cell phone. The reason why she hadn't tried to reach him on his cell completely eluded her. Without giving it another thought, she picked up the phone and dialed his cell number.

His phone rang just as he inserted the house key into the lock. When he saw their home number come up on the lighted screen, he smiled. Instead of answering, he checked the rooms where he thought she might be. The minute he spotted her in the family room, he answered the phone. To keep her from hearing an echo he stepped a good distance back. "Hi, beautiful . . ."

"Where are you? Are you okay? I was worried when you missed our meeting. When will you be home?"

He chuckled. "Slow down, baby. Do I get a chance to answer at least one of your questions?"

"Okay, okay. I guess if I'm talking to you, you're not lying in a ditch somewhere bleeding to death. But when are you coming home?"

"Count to five."

"Five?"

"One, two, three, four, five," he counted out to her. "Baby, turn around and look behind you now that we've reached five."

He came up behind her just as she turned around. Grabbing her by the waist, he brought her to him. "I thought for sure you'd catch on when I told you to only count to five."

She grinned. "I knew where you were all the time.

He nodded his head up down. "I just bet you did! Girl, you didn't have a clue."

She was so happy and relieved to see him that she forgot the rules they'd decided to play by until their trust issues were settled. While pushing both her hands through his hair, she completely covered his mouth with hers, kissing him long, hard, and deep. One hand immediately went to her buttocks, pulling her closer into him. The other hand crept up under her sweatshirt to feel the soft, firm flesh of her back. Moving his hand around to the front of her body, as his hips ground deeply into hers, he cupped her naked breast. His breathing was completely out of control when he suddenly thought about Thomasina and her false accusations.

Immediately, he pulled back from his wife. His manhood was so stiff, ached so badly, that he wanted to sweep Omunique up into his arms and take her straight to bed. That was the only way he'd ever find relief for the agonizing pain of his swelling desire. But he had to tell her about the drama queen's accusations before he could even think about making love to her. Besides, he was the one who said they needed to quell their uncontrollable passion for the time being. He must've been out of his mind when he suggested something as ludicrous as that. He and Omunique had a way of setting each other on fire with just an innocent hug or kiss.

"I'm sorry. I shouldn't have done that. I didn't forget what you said about us controlling the passion, I just wasn't thinking about it at the moment." Her lower lip quivered. "Damn it, Ken, all I was thinking about is that you were home safe. I had some anxious moments when you didn't show up for the meeting. But I knew if you were okay, you had a darn good reason for it."

He drew her back into his arms. "Please forgive me for that. Something very serious came up at the office and I lost complete track of time. I didn't forget you, I just forgot to monitor the time. Can we get another appointment to see her?"

She nodded. "It's okay. I have enough information pamphlets for us to go through together when we find the time. What happened at the office that was so serious?"

Fighting his ever-rising desire, he kissed her forehead. "Let's go in here and sit down. This explanation might take me a minute or two."

Once he saw that Omunique was settled in the reclining chair, he took a seat on the sofa. He started out by telling her how Thomasina had tossed the note she'd left for him asking if they could have dinner and talk. Then he told her what had transpired, and then all those things that had led up to the confrontation that happened earlier at the office.

Omunique slapped her palms on each side of her face. "My God, has she gone crazy? How could she accuse you of something as horrible as sexual exploitation? Like I told her, she's a cunning piece of work. If you hadn't come into the office when you did the other day, you would've had to peel me off of her. I've never before felt like striking another human being, but I wanted to slap her until she would need a Seeing Eye dog to get around for the next six months."

Her remarks completely shocked Ken, but he had to laugh. "You may've operated in a white world all of your life, but you're definitely a sister-girl. What made you so mad at her?"

"She wanted me to believe you and the woman at the restaurant were somehow involved in something other than business. The triumphant look on her face when I walked out of there is the first thing that came to mind. She thought she was setting me up for a painful experience. I also suspect her of not giving you my messages. Sometimes I call through reception when I can't get you on the private line. Furthermore, I think she knows the pass-code to your message center." The *other woman*, she mused, the *other woman* who just happened to be a marriage counselor.

"What makes you say that?" He thought about telling her who the other woman was, but quickly decided against it. The question she'd asked about him sleeping with her still rankled deep within him. Given their history together as husband and wife, no matter how brief, it was a question she should've never had to ask him.

"Because you don't return my calls, which is not like you. You always call back as soon as you get the message. But if you don't get it, you don't know to call back."

"When did you start suspecting her of doing that?"

"When I first realized that she was hot for you. I've felt those vibes from her to you for a very long time. I never said anything because I didn't have anything to prove my suspicions. I'm a woman before I'm anything else. And I know when a woman is interested in a man . . . even when he belongs to someone else. My trust was in you, not her."

"Well, I certainly need your trust in this. Thank you. We've got our hands full with this one. She is ready to go to the tabloids and anyone else willing to listen to her pack of malicious lies, including Jack Prescott. She had the nerve to tell me that he'd like nothing more than to bring the company down because of the large settlement. Little did either of them know that we donated every single dime of that money to several African-American causes. The lawyers will handle Thomasina Bridges in the same expert and expedient way they handled Prescott.

"But Max is afraid that we're going to have to settle this out of court. He thinks that if those blatant lies find their way into the print media that it will hurt your career. The last thing you need is to see your name smeared all over those disgusting papers. We can recover the money, but we may not be able to save your career and our good name. The great reputation we've worked so hard to achieve could just simply go up in smoke."

"Over my dead body! Maxwell Corporation is not going to pay out a dime to that conniving hussy. We will not let her destroy the reputations we've all worked so hard to build for ourselves. We've all got to work together to figure this thing out."

Taking her hands in his, he kissed the back of each. "You're a real warrior, aren't you? You sound ready to charge right into the middle of this battle. But this is something we have to let the lawyers handle. We'd be way out of our league in trying to tackle this one ourselves. We'll get through this, too. Now I want to hear how your meeting at the hospital went."

"Don't you first want to go and change into something more comfortable."

"I'm good to go. Where are the brochures you mentioned?"

She reached over and picked them up off the table next to the recliner. "I'm going to go over the highlights of the social worker's comments. First off, Down syndrome is caused by three 21 chromosomes instead of the normal two. Congenital heart defects are frequently present, but Scott Brian's heart is just fine according to Sanchez. That's a plus in his favor. We already know the physical characteristic. But one thing I found interesting is something called a 'simian crease.' It's found in the palm of the hand. Apparently this is one of the things doctors look for in making the diagnosis. Special education and training is offered in most communities. There are all sorts of resources that would be available to us should we make the decision to adopt." She then went on to tell him the very serious things that could happen.

Ken twisted his lips as he thought about all she'd said. "I'm still not convinced that this is something *you* can handle, or that *we* can handle, or otherwise. It's a lot of responsibility for two people who lead extremely busy lives. I don't think it would be fair to the child. He needs someone that can be there all the time. I'm not sure that we're the ones to take on this serious of a task. I know that I can only speak for me. And I have to tell you, I don't think I'm up to this big of a challenge. That's as honest of an answer as I can give you right now. It's the only answer I can give."

"I still maintain that it would've been the same challenges with a child of our own."

"Come on, Nique, get serious. We don't know that we would've had a child with special needs like this one has. Sweetheart, I'm not trying to be cruel here. But we need to get real about this. It's one thing holding him and loving him for a few hours a day, but it will be totally different when it comes down to every single minute of the day. That's the kind of commitment he needs, the kind that he deserves to have from the people who decide to adopt him. Realistically, considering all things, can we really and truly offer him that?"

He walked over and wiped the tears from her eyes. "Look at you," he said, kneeling down in front of her. "You're so emotional over this already. You've always been extremely sensitive and that's only going to increase. Do you think you crying every day is what that beautiful little boy needs to see from a mother? To be real honest with you, I don't think you're mature enough to handle this kind of responsibility. You're only twenty-two years old. You've just come off the biggest win of your skating career. You've given up so much of your life already while training to become a champion. As young as you are, do you really want your career to come to such an abrupt halt? It will if you insist on taking up this type of responsibility."

She sniffled. "Damn you, Ken. Why do you always have to play the devil's advocate?"

"Because somebody has to! I'd really like to try this if it wasn't so unfair to the baby. I think you need to know about everything serious that could occur in this situation. Nique, this is not a baby doll we're talking about, and we're not children playing house. First of all, though I do think you genuinely love the baby, I believe this is nothing more than your unmanageable guilt at work again. Because you were there when the mother died, I wouldn't be surprised if you feel that there was something you could've done to prevent the outcome. Nique, it was God that made the decision to take the mother. There's nothing that you could've done about it. Please hear what I'm saying to you.

"With our lives still in so much turmoil, we'd be doing a disservice to ourselves to try and take on one more thing. It is imperative that we get our marriage right first. Then there's still the mess with Thomasina to get through. Lastly, we're already just about up to our necks in getting the ice arena project off the ground."

This was the second person in one day that had told her the same exact thing Ken had just said. Dr. Jackson had also told her that she'd taken on the guilt of the mother's death when they'd earlier discussed her wanting to adopt the baby. She could now see that she wasn't as far along in conquering her guilt as she'd earlier believed. The road to total recovery was looking as if it might be a long distance away.

Bringing her forward in the seat, he wrapped his arms around her. "Don't say anything more on this subject for the moment. Just think about what I've said. Think long and hard. If you still want to look into adoption after you've seriously thought this entire matter through, I'll do everything within my power to try and support your decision. I promise to give you the best of all that I can."

She lifted her head and looked into his eyes. "And I promise to give this a lot more thought. Thanks for being as patient with me as you've always been. I love you."

"I love you, too."

Twenty-one

Thomasina tried to shut her apartment door in Omunique's face, but that wasn't about to happen as Omunique practically forced her way inside. "We need to talk. Woman to woman."

"All the talking that's going to be done will be done through my lawyers."

Without any invitation to do so, Omunique moved over to the sofa and threw a folder down on the coffee table. "I'm not moving until you take a look at what's inside this file. Furthermore, I don't believe you have any lawyers. If so, why haven't they contacted ours? These false accusations of yours are almost three weeks old." Omunique picked up the file and shoved it in Thomasina's hand. "If I were you, I would read this before I'd even consider hiring a lawyer, which is probably the reason you haven't done so yet."

Thomasina frowned heavily as she perused the file folder. It appeared that her entire life story had been written down—and she was only on page one of four. The first page addressed the two previous jobs she'd been fired from and that she'd filed sexual harassment charges in both instances. Then there was the story about the professional basketball player that she'd claimed had sex with her when she was far too intoxicated to make a rational decision one way or the other. When pregnancy resulted from the so-called nonconsensual sex act, she threatened to bring rape charges against the popular sports figure. The last page showed in detail the outcome of all three incidents. All were settled out of court with monetary awards. All were settled to protect the person's career and personal life against scandal. The one that Omunique found most interesting was the one with the basketball player. Where was the child? Omunique hoped that the absence of a child would be her ace in the hole. Thomasina had never mentioned having a child, a good indicator that none existed.

Apparently Thomasina had gone unchallenged on all three counts. The fact that she'd practically settled for peanuts told Omunique that these stories were all probably bogus. It looked as if Thomasina had used the threat of scandal to gain the edge for extortion purposes.

Settlement was the easiest way to avoid bad publicity, even though lawyers probably could've proved otherwise. A single hint of a scandal involving prominent and extremely popular world figures would bring out the tabloids' bloodsuckers in droves. Even the most innocent of people could be totally destroyed by bad press. There was just no way to combat tabloid lies when there was such an avarice smut-reading audience. The one thing that Brent Masters had feared most for his champion figure skater was bad publicity.

In this instance, Ken had only been used as the bait. Omunique felt that her Olympic medal win had made her husband the prime candidate for Thomasina's present extortion scam.

"How did you get these sealed documents? The terms of these settlements were never to be disclosed. Don't answer that. I just want you to leave my apartment. I won't hesitate to call the police and have you arrested for trespassing. You *did* force your way in here."

Ready to defend herself if necessary, Omunique raised up. "And I won't hesitate to have our lawyers take this proof to the district attorney's office and have you brought up on extortion charges. You're nothing more than a two-bit scam artist. Let me give you a word of advice. Maxwell Corporation is not going for it. As for my career accomplishments, I won't allow you to use them as a weapon to threaten my family with. If you insist on going forward with this bogus claim against my husband, you won't succeed. I'm prepared to sacrifice everything I've accomplished to stop you cold. By the way, where *is* your child by the basketball player?"

"You don't stop, do you? For your information, Mrs. Maxwell, I had a miscarriage."

"That's the exact answer that I thought you would give. At any rate, I have a onetime offer to make to you. One that only you and I will ever know about. Prepared to listen?"

Thomasina narrowed her eyes. "I'm listening."

"I'm prepared to write you a severance check that will equal six months of your current gross pay. The offer is nonnegotiable and you'll be responsible for paying the taxes on it. Also, this offer will not extend beyond the next few minutes. If you don't accept, it's anyone's guess what will happen next. But for sure, you're not going to win this without Maxwell Corporation putting up one hell of a fight. I'm sure the DA would love to take this case on. As a fearless Olympian, I'm not the least bit intimidated by your threat to take your lies public. Intimidation and fear of total destruction of one's career and personal life is usually what allows people like you to win bogus cases like these. This could backfire on you. Public sympathy for me could actually help my career!"

"The severance pay in exchange for . . . ?"

"You're the extortionist. You tell me what your terms are."

Thomasina eyed Omunique with a mixture of curiosity and a hint of admiration. Ken's wife had way more savvy than Thomasina had given her credit for. And she didn't get the feeling that Omunique was doing this for any other reason than to protect her husband's stellar reputation. "I'll sign whatever you like."

Omunique pulled a blank sheet of paper and a pen out of her bag. "You write what you think I should have in return for the severance pay."

Omunique looked on as Thomasina wrote a letter of resignation with no coercion whatsoever from her. In her letter Thomasina stated that she considered the generous six-month severance package as a gift from her employer—and that no other monies were due her from Maxwell Corporation. After writing about her responsibility where the taxes were concerned, she signed it and handed it to Omunique. Thomasina accepted the written check and Omunique walked away without so much as a nod of her head in Thomasina's direction.

Settled behind the steering wheel of the Jeep, Omunique felt very satisfied with her clandestine meeting with one Miss Thomasina Bridges. She had come away certain that the extortion charges she'd made against Thomasina were true. Ken had said that since they'd hired her on through a temporary agency, they hadn't done any type of employment check of their own. Maxwell Corporation couldn't have known about Thomasina's checkered background because of the deals that she made to keep it quiet. But enough money had a way of rendering deals null and void. Tossing a few dollars here and there, in the right places, could create miracles out of hopeless situations. Both the Maxwell and Philyaw families had major contacts in high places.

There was no other explanation but extortion for Thomasina's record of threatened lawsuits, none of which had actually been filed. She'd simply won all her cases by default, based on the threat of what she would do. What had already happened to a few big-name stars and numerous professional sports figures when they refused to pay, had set the precedence for other high-profile people to be very wary of. A lot of high-profilers ended up paying, anyway. Why put yourself and the family through the endless smear-campaign when you could go ahead and shell out the megabucks up front instead of after the scandal had been made public? That seemed to be the general consensus as of late.

Omunique turned on her cell phone and saw that several messages had come in. After connecting with the voice mail number, she listened to each message but paid closest attention to the one from Melinda Sanchez. As soon as the recording was over, she put a call in to Ken.

She was so nervous over Sanchez's call that her hands began to shake. "Ken, can you meet me at the hospital right away? Sanchez left a message for me that said to come to the hospital and see her as soon as possible. She gets off at three-thirty and it's already after two."

"Omunique, I'm getting ready to go into an important meeting, but I'll be there as soon as I can. She didn't give any indication as to what this was about?"

"None at all. I told you everything that she said on my voice mail. I'm going to hurry over there now. I don't want to miss her. Call my cell when you're on your way."

Ken found Omunique up in their bedroom crying like there'd be no tomorrow. His first thought was that something had happened to the baby. He stretched out on the bed next to her and brought her into his arms. "Does your emotional state have something to do with Scott Brian? Is he okay?" While praying that the baby was fine, he held his breath.

Hard sobs racked her body. "He's . . . leaving . . . the hospital . . . tomorrow. He . . . won't be . . . there anymore. We . . . missed out . . . because we . . . didn't make . . . a decision soon . . . enough."

"Where's he going, Nique?"

As hard as it was for her to get through she managed to tell him that a family wanted to adopt him, but they were first going to take him in as their foster child. Adoption proceedings would soon follow. Sanchez had informed Omunique that this family had recently lost one of their own biological children. The three-year-old also had Down syndrome. They were not only very well educated in how to care for a child with special needs, they also had the experience in meeting the child's many different needs.

"Oh, Nique, I'm sorry. I know you may not think so right now, but maybe this is what's best for Scott Brian. We have to be unselfish in our thinking of him. These people sound like they're very experienced in what he's going to need from a family."

"It also tells me that they had a wonderful experience with their child. If it was so bad, why would they want to put themselves through it a second time? I think our experience with Scott Brian would've been just wonderful. But it looks like we'll never know for sure. I love that baby and now I have to live without him." She fought her desire to dissolve into tears again.

He lifted her head by putting two of his fingers under her chin. "Are you blaming me for the outcome of this?"

Having pulled herself together a little more, she shook her head. "I'm not blaming anyone, especially not you. For the first time in my life, I'm actually not trying to shoulder the blame myself. I'm just feeling terribly crushed. I've thought a lot about the things that you've said to me as it pertains to the needs of the baby—and I think you've made some very accurate assessments. For the last couple of days I've been really itching to get on the ice again, but so much has been going on for us and around us. It's like we're back on that roller-coaster ride which started well over a year ago. I've always used the ice as a way to grind out my frustrations and release my tensions."

She smiled up at him. "But then I learned much later that there are some types of tension releases that the ice just can't help me with—"

"Such as?" he interjected.

Leaning into him, she connected her lips with his, kissing him deeply. "Kissing." She stuck her hand under his shirt and caressed his bare stomach and then his chest. "Caressing." Her hands found their way to his crotch where they massaged his manhood through his slacks. "Massaging." Unzipping his fly, she reached inside and stroked his erection. "Stroking."

He moaned as her touch seared into his pulsating flesh. "Omu—"

Her eyes twinkled with mischief as she pulled her hand away. "Oh, I forgot, Ken. We're not supposed to do passionate stuff like this. Please forgive me."

Narrowing his eyes at her, he moaned and groaned. The phone rang, causing him to groan even louder. "This had better not be some freaking solicitor!" Rolling over on his side, he picked up the receiver. "Hello."

"Is this Mr. Kenneth Maxwell?" a soft, female voice asked.

"It is. How can I help you?"

"You don't know me, but my name is Melinda Sanchez. I'm one of the nurses at the hospital. The one that's mostly been conversing with your wife about the baby boy she visits on a regular basis. Is it possible for us to get together without your wife's knowledge? I have some information that you may or may not be interested in hearing. I don't want to get her all worked up until I know where you're coming from. She has spoken to me of your reluctance where the baby is concerned." Melinda was glad Ken had answered the phone. If Omunique had done so, she had prepared herself to hold another conversation entirely.

"When?"

"As soon as possible. I get off in an hour and I won't be back to work for three days. I can meet you in the cafeteria. How about in a half hour."

"Okay. I can manage that." Looking thoughtful, Ken disconnected the line.

Omunique's eyes bulged with curiosity. "What was that all about?" He stood up and zipped his pants. "Talk about bad timing. Just when I thought you might've been able to coerce me into breaking my own rules, something extremely important comes up. What do you think? Think you could've made me break the rules?"

Every single one of them, boy! "We'll have to see about that later, now won't we? Where are you off to in such a big hurry?"

"A meeting. I won't be gone long. Why don't you call up one of the restaurants that delivers and have them whip us up a delicious meal? We haven't had a romantic dinner together in a good while. I think it's time that we should renegotiate the terms of the rules I'd set."

A meeting? Omunique's thoughts went straight to the other *woman* the minute the bedroom door closed. She wondered if he was still seeing the therapist. It looked as if they were finally getting their marriage back on track, but she could see how they both should continue with the counseling—and should at some point receive it as a couple. It no longer bothered her that Ken hadn't told her about seeing a therapist. Just knowing that he wasn't involved in an extramarital affair helped her kill the curious cat.

She went over in her mind all the things that had happened since their marriage, the things that had sent both of them scrambling for professional help. It was unbelievable that so many tragic things had happened in such a short span of time: the death of a woman, learning that Taylor was still alive, lying to her husband and keeping secrets from him, Wyman's heart attack, and then Thomasina's false accusations. What else could happen?

The one thing that she hoped would happen was that she would learn the lessons each tragedy was supposed to teach her. There was no doubt in her mind that there were important lessons for her to learn from each of these unfortunate occurrences.

Her thoughts drifted to Scott Brian and she smiled. As much as she would've loved for him to be a part of their family, she now saw that Ken had been right to play the devil's advocate. She'd had to admit to herself that he had pointed out so many things that she hadn't even thought about. In thinking about them, she realized that she wasn't ready to be a mother, especially when she hadn't yet learned how to be a real woman and a good wife. As she'd done with everything else in her life, she would've given it her best shot. The only problem there was that her best shot may not have been good enough when it came to meeting the needs of a special child. Still, she couldn't stop thinking of how it could've been for the three of them.

Loosening his tie as he stepped into the foyer, Ken wondered why there were no lights on in the house. As he moved further into the hall, he caught the subtle glow of candlelight. As he made his way through the house, he saw that candles softly lit all the rooms. Mellow music could be heard throughout the house as it played soft and low.

Instead of calling out for her, he went around the house briefly poking his head in the doorways of all places he thought she might be. With the kitchen and dining room in total darkness, he didn't bother looking for her there. When he didn't find her in any of the other downstairs rooms, he made his way up the winding staircase. As he stepped inside the master bedroom, the soft glow of candlelight reached out to warm him.

His breath caught at the sight of her.

Romantic rendezvous was the first thought that came to his mind.

Sitting on the edge of the bed, she wore the most seductive gown he'd ever seen her in. The black satin gown had high side slits fashioned with lattice ties laced all the way up the sides until they met the top of the bodice. A Victoria Secret gown labeled "pure seduction."

Ken blinked hard at the sexy image in front of him. Her physical communication skills came across to him like a screaming siren. Without uttering a single word, she came across the room, took him by the hand—and led him back to the bed. Looking up into his golden eyes, she unbuttoned his shirt and loosened his tie before slowly removing the rest of his clothes.

Once he was completely disrobed, she helped him into the burgundy and gray silk lounging pajamas and matching robe she'd purchased exclusively for the magical evening she'd carefully planned. She'd only come up with her plans after he'd indicated to her that he might be ready to break all the rules.

Taking his hands in hers, she led him over to the beautifully set table, where she had him sit down. "I'll be right back. Don't go anywhere." Before leaving, she lit the candles in the middle of the flower centerpiece. On her way out the room, she turned on the gas fireplace.

He was too eager to see what was coming next to think about going anywhere. Besides, where would he go? He was home and apparently his wife had planned for all their activities to occur indoors. Ken couldn't wait to see exactly what those activities included.

Omunique came back into the bedroom carrying a tray with two silver domed covers and two Saran Wrapped fresh garden salads. She set the tray down on the table and removed the silver lids off the dishes beneath. The rack of lamb she often talked about was featured on each plate.

Asparagus spears, steamed carrot coins, and baked potatoes were the fresh vegetable entrees.

"No, I didn't cook it," she said in response to the question in his eyes. "I took your suggestion and called one of our favorite restaurants. I expected you back a lot sooner, but since they delivered the meal just before you got here, I'd say the timing was perfect. The food is still warm. Shall we eat?"

He got up and pulled her chair out. "I'll get us something to drink from the wet bar. What would you like, Nique?"

"I think I might try a glass of red wine. I'm not driving tonight and I'm currently taking time off from my profession." He liked seeing her this relaxed and this flirtatious. He hadn't seen either in a long time. The old Omunique was starting to surface and he wasn't about to let her get buried alive again.

Since Omunique rarely imbibed, he raised both eyebrows. "Red wine for the lovely lady coming right up."

Ken came right back carrying two crystal wine glasses filled with cabernet sauvignon. He set one glass in front of his wife before seating himself. Eager to eat their meal and get on with the rest of the evening, he immediately passed the blessing.

"This is a very special surprise, Nique. Thank you. I love sitting here with you in the candlelight. I've missed these very romantic evenings. I hope we'll do it more often."

"I've missed them, too. How's the lamb?"

"Delicious!" He gave her a seductive smile. "I have something to ask you. Where were you last night? I missed you."

"I thought I was right here with you." She looked puzzled. "Am I missing something?"

"No, I'm the one who missed something, something that normally occurs every single night. You didn't appear in my dreams last night."

She blushed. "Oh, that was so charming. But I can understand how it happened. You were dead tired last night. You were actually snoring. I don't think anything could've penetrated your sleep."

"I'm not so sure about that, but we'll get into that later. Would you like to hear some good news? As far as I'm concerned, really good news."

"Thomasina dropped the lawsuit?"

"How I wish." Before giving her the details of his meeting, he told her that the call he'd received earlier was from Melinda Sanchez and that he'd met her at the hospital and that she told him something extremely interesting about the adoptive parents.

"What did she tell you that you found so interesting?" Omunique could barely breathe as her hands trembled in anticipation of what he might say.

"Well, Sanchez told me that Arlana Smith and her husband, Scott, were interested in meeting us and talking with us in the near future. With him having the same name as you gave the baby—is that a coincidence or what? I was so eager to hear what they had to say that I had Sanchez get them on the phone while I was in the social worker's office with her. After talking with them for just a few minutes, they asked me if I wanted to stop by and visit with them face-to-face. I leapt at the opportunity to do so. That's why it took me much longer than I expected. They asked me to bring you along, but I wanted to hear what they had to say, first."

Omunique had a hard time keeping herself calm. "Please tell me the bottom line! I'm going crazy over here."

"The bottom line is that we can see Scott Brian as often as we like! Apparently the nurses have raved to them over how good you were with the baby. These two people are wonderful and they are educationally, financially—and most importantly, emotionally equipped to give the baby everything he needs. Scott Brian is blessed to have these two people to love him and vice versa. We are very blessed that they want us to be a part of his life. Is that good news, or what?"

Her tears ran a race down her cheeks as she practically skipped over to her husband. She was trembling so hard that she had to take a few deep breaths to keep from fainting dead away at his feet. The excitement tumbled around in her breast as sensations of euphoria took her over.

"This is probably the best thing that could've happened for all of us. I just couldn't imagine not ever seeing my 'ups baby' again. Oh, Ken, this is God's work. No human could've ever effected this outcome. Thank you, Jesus," she cried. "Thank you!"

She kissed Ken until they almost got lost in it, lost in each other.

He lifted her chin until their eyes met. "Let's move into the other room, where we can relax in comfort. We'll leave the dishes for later, probably until tomorrow, or even the next day," Ken joked, kissing her on each ear. He then nuzzled her neck for several seconds.

Ken picked up the two glasses of wine and carried them into the recessed alcove off their bedroom. Omunique held on to his hand as she walked beside him. The fireplace greeted them with delicious warmth and a lighted torch in flaming colors of blue, red, orange, and yellow.

Once the glasses were set atop the wet bar, Omunique engaged her husband in a seductive slow dance as their newfound friend Hillary Houston began to croon her platinum single 'Destiny.' It was the perfect song for what, thus far, had all the ear markings of a perfect evening. Holding one another intimately close, they danced wrapped up in each other's arms.

Moving slowly to the music, they teased one another with soft kisses and tender caresses. As his hands threaded through her hair, she filled hers with the firmness of his silk-clad buttocks. Ken's fingers moved down to caress the bare flesh exposed between the lattice ties on her gown.

While continuing to sway to the soft music, Ken and Omunique's lips came together in a passion-filled kiss. Tongues probed one another's mouths, hungry for the taste of each other. As he lifted her straight up off the floor, she wrapped her legs high up around his waist, causing her gown to raise above the top of her thighs. They continued to slow dance as his fingers gently probed the inside of her firm thighs.

Her silver gaze penetrated deeply into his golden eyes. "Mr. Maxwell, I've quelled the heat of my passion for as long as I can. Before this gets any hotter, I need to know if the restrictions have been lifted? All of them?"

His lips grazed her temples. "Mrs. Maxwell, what we're going to give and receive from each other will be incomparable to any other late-night rendezvous. Consider the passion ban lifted. Are you feeling me, sweetheart?"

"Everywhere on my anatomy."

Lifting his hand, she briefly stuck his finger in her mouth and sucked hard on it. With one arm around his neck, the flattened palm of her other hand tenderly massaged his chest. Omunique nearly exploded on the spot when she suddenly felt his thickened, granite-hard organ penetrate the moist, soft flesh between her thighs. Her low moans drew a few groans from him.

Mindlessly, she clenched her muscles around his fullness as he tenderly thrust upward, pressing himself deeper inside of her. The friction from the silk around his pajama fly made her eternal flames burn even hotter for him. As if keeping in tune with the rhythm of the music, he danced around inside of her molten heat. With Ken locked tightly up inside of her, Omunique lost herself atop the heady waves of their indescribable ecstasy.

Slowly, he moved forward, one step at a time, until her back was flat against the wall. His heavy breathing mingled with her shallow gasps as he pressed into her with one deep thrust after another. Responding with a wild urgency, nearly causing him to prematurely erupt into a climax, she clenched and unclenched her muscles around the marble structure imprisoned so deep inside of her; so deep inside that he completely filled her up.

Moving away from the wall, he carried her over to the fur-covered body contour chair. Releasing himself from inside of her, he sat down and straddled the chair. Kissing her neck and throat, he slid her downward onto his maleness until he felt her moistness completely wrapped around his erection. Omunique cried out from the sheer bliss of sliding down his hardness.

Tenderly, but with minimal restraint, Ken continuously filled Omunique with the fiery desires of his overheated, naked flesh. While the wall had been cool to her bare back and buttocks, the furry material on the chair, as well as the inferno detonating between her legs had her body temperature soaring off the scale.

His kisses came wet and wild as he felt himself beginning to lose the grip on his control. Omunique's moist, flaming flesh seared his manhood inside and out. She moaned with pleasure as his tongue probed one of her ears and then the other. As his mouth moved down and laved each nipple hungrily, she began to come unglued on the inside. As teeth nipped, tongues entwined, fingernails scraped, and bodies meshed into one another, multiple eruptions came, shaking them with such force that Omunique bit down on her lower lip hard enough to draw blood.

With barely enough strength to breathe, he lifted her off of him and somehow managed to get to his feet. Encircling her waist with both hands, positioning her out in front of him, he nudged her from behind while making their way over to the fireplace where they dropped down to the soft white rug.

"So," he said between kisses, "we've finally reclaimed the fire beneath the ice."

"Yes, we have," she cooed breathlessly.

Epilogue

Skating to Santana's "Maria, Maria," Omunique had the audience on their feet from the moment she began this latest routine in the first performance ever inside her very own ice arena. Breaking new ground, she had choreographed the routine herself with a wee bit of help from her choreographer, Jake Neilson. Next, in keeping with the Latin routine, she skated to a popular song by Whitney Houston and Enrique Iglesias: "Can I Have This Kiss Forever."

Just as she'd told Ken that she would do a while back, she had Jake choreograph her third number to music by the popular rap artist, Justified. The upbeat number "I Want To Rock With You" gave her the opportunity to execute on ice some of the hip-hop dances she'd recently learned especially for this performance. Her favorite was the "bounce."

The next number she skated to had special meaning for her in many ways. "Because You Loved Me" by Celine Dion perfectly defined the kind of love Ken had always exhibited toward her. As he was seated in the front row holding six-month-old Scott Brian on his lap, Omunique skated over to him and gently plucked the baby from his arms.

While showing off her loving godson to the audience, she held her beautiful "ups" baby close to her heart as she skated around the perimeter of the arena. In a private christening ceremony, Omunique and Ken had become godparents to Scott Brian. Just as if he'd been their very own, the couple had turned one of the guest rooms into a delightful nursery for when he stayed over with them during their once-a-month weekends.

Once several other very popular skaters joined her on the ice, she returned the baby to Ken. While the lively, colorfully costumed group formed several lines the "Harlem Shuffle" stormed into the arena and the capricious performance of the "Electric Slide" on ice began. Omunique hadn't forgotten how much fun she'd had while dancing at her wedding shower.

As if they couldn't get enough of this dance, they stayed in the line formation while the same song played twice. In the next performance of the evening, Omunique, Sara, and Ian skated together to Whitney Houston's "One Moment in Time." This was Sara's first appearance in front of an audience, her *one moment in time,* since her injury. Omunique was so happy that Sara had finally gotten another chance to shine. And shine she did, brilliantly so.

There was a brief intermission before Omunique came back out on the ice outfitted in a stunning, hot black-lace costume designed to show off discreet patches of bare skin via the see-through lace. The top of the lacy costume was soft and sensual with an off-the-shoulder shape done in scalloped trim. In a special tribute to her husband, she skated to Whitney Houston's remake of the Four Tops' "I Believe in You and Me."

The ribbon-cutting ceremony had taken place before the ice show. Refreshments were now being served in the large arena's reception room. Mamie had prepared all the foods so that everyone could sample what delights they would find in Café Gordon. Along with many of her delicious recipes, she knew that her special teriyaki chicken wings and sweet potato tarts would definitely go over big. They'd already been replenished three times in less than ninety minutes.

Besides the numerous refreshment tables, there were two large display counters. One of them held brochures for Wyman's insurance agency and the other counter held catalogues of the great-looking sports apparel available for purchase in the boutique. A sign-up sheet was also made available for those who wanted to make use of the in-house nursery when completed.

Mamie, beaming from head to toe, held on to the arms of both Wyman and Max as they walked over to Ken and Omunique who were talking with Arlana and Scott, Scott Brian's new parents. Her friend, Teresa, was right along with them. Omunique felt a little sorry for Teresa Banks since Mamie had had both men sewed up tight for the past several months, but there was no evidence of a heavy romance blooming between her and Max or her and Wyman.

Wyman hugged his daughter and his son-in-law. "Kids, you've made one hell of a major impression on this inner-city community. So many parents are excited about the prospect of having their kids come to the arena for lessons." He kissed his daughter. "You have raised quite a bit of delightful fuss around here, young lady. These residents feel blessed to have you operating a business here in the area where they live. I've heard a lot of talk about government grants for this facility. You may have gotten more than you bargained for, but I'm sure that you see it as a definite plus."

"Yes, Ken and I both do."

Max walked up to the small group. Ken thought his dad had an odd expression on his face. He actually looked as if he'd just stolen something. "Hi, kids. I just want to take a moment to congratulate you. This is an awesome structure! This place is going to have more business than we

could ever imagine." He grinned. "Now that I've congratulated you, I think you might want to congratulate me after
you hear what I have to say." Max beamed at Mamie.
"Mamie and I have some great news to share with you all.
We've been keeping this little secret to ourselves until we
knew how things were going to go."

Omunique swallowed so hard it felt like she was choking
on her tongue. Her eyes went right to her father. The fact
that he wasn't smiling made her even more nervous. While
he'd never come right out and admitted to her that he loved
Mamie, he surely had hinted at the fact that he could. Ken
was also concerned with what was going on. Aunt Mamie
and his father as a couple wasn't distasteful to him at all,
but like his wife, he was worried about how Wyman was
taking this news. Wyman and Mamie seemed to fit together
like a hand to a glove.

Max then walked over to Teresa Banks and put his arm
around her. That move seemed to surprise everyone.
"Kids, this is the new romantic interest in my life. We've
kept things on the quiet side until we decided where or
how far we wanted to go in building a relationship." He
hugged Mamie to him. "This wonderful lady has been our
go-between and our chaperone, so to speak. She was gracious enough to hang out with me for a while and answer
the million-and-one questions I had about Teresa. She's
been going out with us until we felt comfortable with one
another to venture out on our own. We've been solo dating
for about a month now."

Weak with relief, Omunique couldn't stop giggling. Ken
hadn't been able to shut his mouth from the moment it had
dropped open in disbelief. Wyman was also learning about
this for the first time. The look on his face spoke to nothing
short of utter relief.

Wyman wasted no time in stepping forward to embrace
Mamie. "I thought for sure Max was going to announce
that he'd asked you to marry him. Since that's not the case,

young lady, does that mean you're still an eligible bachelorette?"

Mamie smiled brightly. "That depends on if you're asking that question as an eligible bachelor?" Her eyes flirted boldly with him.

Gripping Ken's arm, Omunique held her breath in anticipation of her father's answer.

"Very eligible." Much to the delight of everyone present, Wyman kissed Mamie in a way that a man kisses a woman that he has a romantic interest in: passionately. Then a celebration of a totally different kind began to take place.

Omunique and Ken were the only ones left in the arena. The lights had been turned down until they appeared as a soft yellow glow in the darkness. Soft, romantic music floated throughout the room. Happy with all the wonderful surprises and joy that the day had brought, now dressed in street clothes, Omunique pulled a letter out of her purse and handed it to her husband. "This is my surprise to you. But the real surprise will come after you read it." He took the letter and read it.

He whistled softly. "Thomasina wrote this? How, when, what?" Omunique told him the story of her visit to Thomasina's apartment.

"This is unreal. You really are something else! We never could figure out why we were never contacted by her lawyers. How did you get her to write this letter?"

"As for the content of the letter, no coercion on my part at all. Let's just say we came to an understanding."

He grinned. "But, Nique, I thought you said we should never pay extortion money. What changed your mind?"

"I haven't changed my way of thinking on that. We'd just been through enough. We needed to begin the healing process. We couldn't do that with her threat hanging over our heads. I decided to pay her off just so we could get on with our lives."

"You said the real surprise will come at the end."

She kissed him on the mouth. "The check was never cashed. How about that one for a big surprise? If I'd really wanted to be mean, I would've put a stop payment on it since she'd already written the letter of resignation. But like you, I have integrity. Apparently she must have a little integrity of her own left. We should wish her nothing but the best."

Misty-eyed, he looked around the arena. "No one left in here but us chickens. What do you say about us christening this place? We've made love in every room in our house. So I can think of many spots in this big place that we can claim as our love nests."

Tears filled her eyes. "I've got the visuals going."

Taking her in his arms, he kissed her under the soft lighting of their very own ice castle, the castle where the accomplishments of their love would forever abide . . .

Dear Readers:

I sincerely hope that you enjoyed reading FIRE BENEATH THE ICE from cover to cover, the continuing story of figure skater Omunique Philyaw and her love interest Kenneth Maxwel, Jr. I'm interested in hearing your comments. I'd love to know your thoughts on the much-requsted sequel to ICE UNDER FIRE. Without the reader, there is no me, as an author.

Please enclose a self-addressed, stamped envelope (SASE) with all your correspondence and mail to:

Linda Hudson-Smith
2026C North Riverside Avenue
Box 109
Rialto, CA 92377

You can also e-mail your comments to:
LHS4romance @yahoo.com.

Please visit my Web site at:
http://romantictales.com/linda/index.html.

ABOUT THE AUTHOR

Born in Canonsburg, Pennsylvania, and raised in the town of Washington, Pennsylvania, Linda Hudson-Smith has traveled the world as an enthusiastic witness of other cultures and lifestyles. Her husband's military career gave her the oppurtunity to live in Japan, Germany, and many cities across the United States. Linda's extensive travel experience helps her craft stories set in a variety of beautiful and romantic locations. It was after illness forced her to leave her marketing and public relations administration career, that she turned to writing.

Romance in Color chose her as Rising Star for the month of January 2000. ICE UNDER FIRE, her debut Arabesque novel, has received rave reviews. Voted as Best New Author, African-American Online Writers Guild presented Linda with the 2000 Gold Pen Award. Linda has also won two Shades of Romance awards in the category of Multicultural New Romance Author of the Year and Multicultural New Fiction Author of the Year. SOULFUL SERENADE, released in August 2000, was selected by *Romance in Color* readers as the Best Cover for August 2000.

Linda Hudson-Smith is a member of Romance Writers of America and the Black Writers Alliance. Though novel writing remains her first love, she is currently cultivating her screenwriting skills. She has also been contracted to write other novels for BET.

Dedicated to inspiring readers to overcome adversity against all odds, Linda is a member of and national spokesperson for the Lupus Foundation of America. She is also a supporter of the NAACP and the American Cancer Society. She enjoys poetry, entertaining, traveling, and attending sports events. The mother of two sons, Linda and her husband share residences in both California and Texas.